From the reviews of *The Voices*:

'An outstanding novel, among the be[st] gives the lie to literary doom-monge[r] and to those who regularly complai[n] when compared to America's. Her wri[ting] v[i]brant, innovative, and amazingly assured . . . [Elderkin's] description of the inhabitants of a far-flung town in the outback is very persuasive, her ear for dialogue remarkable. Elderkin takes giant risks . . . It works brilliantly well.'
Spectator

'From the very first page of *The Voices* you can see why Susan Elderkin was one of the twenty young writers chosen by Granta as the best in Britain. Only her second novel, [*The Voices*] is ambitious, unsettling, muscular. Elderkin is clearly unafraid to be difficult and she is to be congratulated on her boldness, as well as her skill . . . Her feel for land-scape and her ear for dialogue are perfectly realised, mature and confi-dent. The confused, uncommunicative Billy is a wonderful creation and the depiction of Aboriginal life at the beginning of the twenty-first century is heartbreaking and very funny. This is a peculiar book: beau-tifully written, melancholy, fey, angry and utterly absorbing. It may not be comfortable, but it is certainly brilliant.' *Daily Telegraph*

'Elderkin's novel is laced with proof of talent in abundance . . . [her] writing has unstoppable momentum . . . Hugely enjoyable.' *Scotsman*

'A tour de force . . . beguilingly readable . . . [her] characteristically dazzling techniques are on display in all their virtuosity and freakish inventiveness. Voice and perspective rove indeterminately from the very believable, rough-spoken and tenderly observed Outback community to the spirit world . . . You've never read an apocalypse as poignantly comic as this . . . For sheer narrative invention and wanton brio [Elderkin] is without an equal.'
Independent

'What is remarkable is Elderkin's ability to conjure up the Australian outback with such confidence. Her use of the flattened vernacular of its unreconstructed male culture, her knowledge of its peculiar landscape, her dismantling of all solemn notions about ancient spirits and her

assured handling of Aboriginal politics betray nothing of the breathless visitor in awe of sacred territory. Elderkin reads, to English ears at least, like a true Oz.'
Guardian

'Susan Elderkin richly deserves her place [on the Granta list], given the range, strength, gustiness and sheer verve of her second novel . . *The Voices* asks no less a question than: How can we survive in a de-spiritualised and godless world? And the answer, of course, is we can't, and we won't . . . Elderkin is fascinated with the world of male work and bonding, in a way that immediately puts one in mind of Annie Proulx. She understands how these men talk, and what makes them laugh, and is able to orchestrate passages of ribald social comedy . . . [She] introduces a whole range of spiritual and ecological concerns that meld perfectly with plot and landscape. Elderkin has imagination to burn.'
Literary Review

'I resent being told what to read – literary prizes, bestseller lists, lists of authors to watch for, all leave me cold . . . [but] now I admit I may be wrong. Elderkin is a remarkable writer. This is an original and captivating work that transports while being read and haunts for long after. *The Voices* is an absolute pleasure. Do what you're told and read it.'
Big Issue in the North

'When novelists write about countries and cultures other than their own, often what is missing is an authentic atmosphere. This accusation cannot be levelled at Susan Elderkin. She immerses herself entirely in the harsh and beautiful terrain of Western Australia and the idiom and culture of its people. *The Voices* is a strange, elegiac story . . . a novel of great strengths . . . vivid and ambitious in its scope.'
Times Literary Supplement

'Fascinating and complex . . . [with] themes that resonate far beyond its setting.'
BookSense

'[*The Voices*] leaves a mighty wake. Elderkin's descriptions of the outback are haunting. Feel the human characters being ripped from the earth . . . the children being ripped from their parents . . . the screams of spirits as they are taken from all living things and banished into the dusty future.'
Los Angeles Times

Sunset Over Chocolate Mountains

the voices

Susan Elderkin

HARPER PERENNIAL

Harper Perennial
An imprint of HarperCollins*Publishers*
77–85 Fulham Palace Road
London W6 8JB

www.harpercollins.co.uk/harperperennial

This edition published by Harper Perennial 2004

1

First published in Great Britain by Fourth Estate 2003

A catalogue record for this book is available from the British Library

This novel is a work of fiction. Any references to historical events; to real people,
living or dead; or to real locales are intended only to give the fiction a sense of reality
and authenticity. Other names, characters, places and incidents either are the product
of the author's imagination or are used fictitiously, and their resemblance, if any, to
real-life counterparts is entirely coincidental.

ISBN 1-84115-202-1

'Waterloo' used by permission of Bocu Music Ltd, 1 Wyndham Yard, London W1H
2QF. Excerpt from 'Casablanca' granted courtesy of Warner Bros. 'Pub With No Beer'
BMG Music Publishing Ltd. 'Boys from the Bush' words and music by Lee Kernaghan
and Garth Porter © 1992 Warner/Chappell Music Australia Pty Ltd, Australia,
Warner/Chappell Music Ltd, London W6 8BS. Reproduced by permission of
International Music Publications Ltd. All rights reserved.

Set in Stone Print by Palimpsest Book Production Limited,
Polmont, Stirlingshire

Printed in Great Britain by
Clays Ltd, St Ives plc

To Mark and Mary

Have you not heard of that madman who lit a lantern in the bright morning hours, ran to the market place, and cried incessantly, 'I seek God! I seek God!' As many of those who do not believe in God were standing around just then, he provoked much laughter. Why, did he get lost? said one. Did he lose his way like a child? said another. Or is he hiding? Is he afraid of us? Has he gone on a voyage? or emigrated? Thus they yelled and laughed.

Nietzsche, *The Gay Science*
translated by Walter Kaufmann

contents

PROLOGUE 1
it comes from the inland desert 3

PART I
the largest pair of knees 9
here is a town 13
something torn 18
we've been thinking 22
the clangers 25
look who's here 33

PART II
a gap in her orderly heart 41
early man versus kylie minogue 47
the coffee shop pings 53
a nice fat bundle 55
every crushed beer can 56
beneath the belly 58
the wowser 63
a fist flies out 68
full moon rains 72

PART III
he shivers and sweats 75
a vast, ancient heart 81
the pink cockatoos 86
lace-trimmed bra and matching knickers 90
little brother to ayers 93
stretching his shadow 95
the chasm 99

PART IV
the longest serving inmate 105

tonight's main headline   109
the learned professor   116
a real dunny   122
the air is spiked   130
the existence of frogs   132
the perfect arc   135
a filthy puddle   136
the whole bloody axle   137

PART V
quite some yarning   145
a feed like that   148
west of sydney   160
your little tin heart   164
it is dark and dank   168
the signal to jump   170
the oxley moron   174
a new skin   181
who stole my batteries?   182
noises   184

PART VI
nowhere in the landscape   189
thirty kays south   203
go, cathy, go!   204
from deep down rossco's gullet   211
more noises   214
grog   217
the language of the underworld   221
how to eat a cow   225
who's a pretty boy, then?   228
not unless dogs can fly   233
put yourselves in our shoes   235

PART VII
the outbreak of intergalactic war   245
any picaninnies here?   255
a load of bloody savages   260
the creaking of insects   264

as if a ghost has passed through   269
the last *laaa*   272

PART VIII
a large fire stoked   283
the bush tucker tour   292
a secret from the world   297
i hope this finds you   305
this is my band   307
the only one who steps out into the rain   309
it moves on   317

EPILOGUE
the voices   321

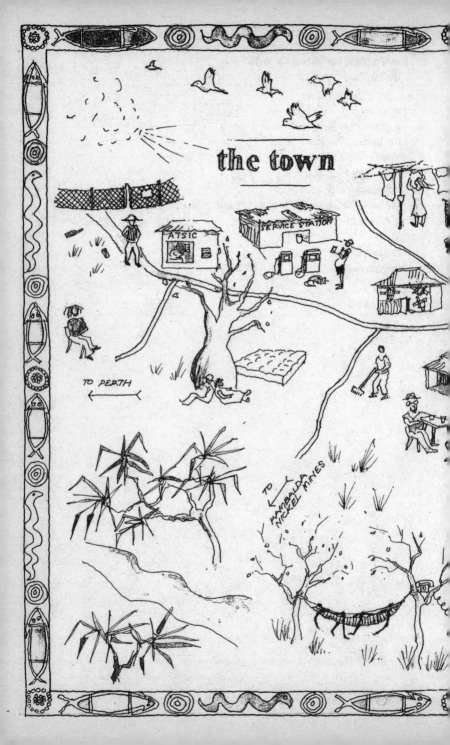

prologue

it comes from the inland desert

A warm wind is blowing tonight.

It comes from the inland desert and it's heavy with red dust, handfuls scooped up and cradled tight against its chest. So far the plain has been as seemingly endless and without modulation as an ocean at sleep: crowns of spinifex hug the flat; the occasional sun-bitten gum tree, stripped of its leaves, reaches out of the earth like a claw. But now a sandstone escarpment rises from nowhere like a submarine emerging from the deep, and the wind pulls up short, whirls around in an eddy of indecision, sprinkling a little of its precious cargo on the land.

Which way will it go? First it gusts to the right, then to the left, and here, sheltering within a patch of grey box and scraggy cabbage gums it finds a crooked tin roof rusted to a pink and orange patchwork. It circles the house in a double lasso, finds an open window at the back, plays at bellying the curtain in and out. Then slips inside.

It's a small, square room. Rectangles of white-bordered posters glimmer through the mealy grey air. Their edges snake where they haven't been fully stuck down. Along a shelf is a row of stones, small enough to fit in the palm of a child's hand. Near the far wall a spray of blond hair crouches on a pillow like a spider. There's the sound of shallow, fretful breath.

Suddenly the hair flies into the air, hangs suspended for a moment like a ball at the top of its toss, then drops back down again – a fresh corner of pillow this time, a little cooler than before. Maybe now he'll be able to get to sleep. But no: a second later the hair flies up again, an elbow jabbing angrily at the sheet.

This is Billy, we say.

Ah, says the wind, so *this* is him. What's all the tossing and turning about? Is it the heat?

No, no, he's used to that.

Was I making too much noise in the cabbage gums?

No more than usual. Look, just there, on the bridge of his nose. See that dent?

Like a drawstring tugged tight?

Yes.

A gathering up of his confusion?

That's right. All the unanswered questions.

I see, says the wind. No wonder he can't sleep.

Quite.

Still don't know what you lot are bothering with him for.

Though curious enough at first, the wind doesn't really care about this boy – and why should it? It has no need of people; it doesn't depend on them like we do. Instead it curls around the room looking for something to disturb, a loose sheet of paper to flutter to the floor, a pencil to roll off a chair. But the contents of this room are disappointingly static. On the floor by the bed is a thin, hardback book called *The Universe*, face down, its pages buckled and trapped beneath it. On its cover is a picture of the planet: swirls of white and blue and green like blobs of ink twirled round with a nib, and all around it is the perfect blackness that sets the scenes for this boy's nightmares – more like sensations than nightmares, when gravity has lost its hold and he's falling through space, arms lashing out for something to hold onto, all the time falling faster and faster and still the blackness goes on, plenty more where that came from – ah yes, an infinite supply. Will it ever come to an end?

We've all had dreams like that, sneers the wind. They aren't anything special.

But this boy beneath the sheet, this boy that we are starting to love, has more than his fair share of solitary fears. He is small for his age, skinny. The wind ruffles the edge of the sheet so that we can get a peek – yes, there it lies, meek and pale as a cracked brazil nut just out of its shell. Any day now he will turn the corner, sprout hair, an Adam's apple budding in his throat, those arms and legs shooting out and down until they're long and gangly with heavy hands and feet on the ends – just like his father's, too big and clumsy to be much use. But he's not quite ready yet.

A thin arm whips up as he flings himself onto his back, exposing a slight, honey-brown torso, ribs showing through like the roots of a tree. Fingers curled on the pillow, as if he wants to ask a question.

Excuse me, Mrs Tucker, I don't understand.

What don't you understand, Billy?

Any of it.

What do you mean, any of it?

Her irritation curbs his confidence but doesn't shut him up completely.

What we're doing here. What it's all about. Who we're supposed to go to for the answers.

See the anxious eyeball flickering beneath the lid? It is as if he refuses to make the transition into adolescence until he gets some answers. And who can blame him? Not us. Certainly not us.

Such ridiculous questions, mutters Mrs Tucker.

It doesn't make sense, that's all. How am I supposed to know what's right and what's wrong? I don't know who to ask.

Even as we watch he begins to slip, the muscles in his cheeks sliding into softness, the delicate mouth crushed against the pillow where a little pool of dribble will collect before morning. In a snap of a finger, he's gone.

Ah, what a shame, Billy, we appear to have run out of time. Jiss have to wait until tomorrow, won't we?

Rebutted by Mrs Tucker, the useless cow.

Before our eyes, the unconscious body draws its extremities in towards the warmer core: the knees pulling up, the elbows folding in, the freckled nose burrowing down. And so the questions draw in too, their curious searchlights aimed now at his steadily thumping heart. If there are no answers out there, they will just have to make do with whatever they can find inside him: instincts, primeval knowledge – whatever they call them these days. Perhaps they will be found stencilled into the walls of his gut, secreted down blood-red tunnels, tucked inside folds of tissue like fossils. A tightly twisted spiral of a snail shell preserved in all its wondrous detail. Palaeozoic, Mesozoic, Cenozoic. All these epochs hidden inside the body of little Billy Saint.

The bridge of his nose is smooth now, perfect as the bowl of a spoon.

And the wind is bored. There's nothing to play with here and it wants to move on – it's what winds do, after all – and we'll go with it, although we'll be back to see this boy again. Once we've made up our minds, we never back down – and anyway, who are we to be choosy these days? The wind takes one last spin around the room and then, childishly, when we're not looking, darts behind one of the slouching posters so that it flops right off the wall, doubling over in a little thunderclap of stiff paper, and the boy sits bolt upright in his bed, blinking in surprise, sees nothing but a disembodied square of pale curtain floating at the window, hears a quick rustling of the gum trees outside.

And then everything goes quiet.

part I

the largest pair of knees

– How long you gunna take to fill that bedpan?

He opens his eyes to find himself confronted by the largest pair of knees he has ever seen. They are bold and black, the skin paler where it's stretched over the humps, darker in the dips and hollows. They are not a perfect pair: the left is more bulbous than the right. It is as if they had been crafted by hand.

His eyes travel upwards. Thick, folded arms struggle to extricate themselves from beneath a heavy wedge of breast. When he reaches her face he sees that she is a full-blood. Her solid, protruding brow reaches right over the black eyes like the overhang of a cliff.

The nurse squints up at a bag of saline hanging from a metal stand. A plastic tube dangles down and disappears beneath a bandage on the back of his hand. Her lips move, counting drips. Four, five, six. Nine, ten, eleven. Then she flicks up the edge of his sheet with a finger and gives a small, breathy cry of exasperation.

– Get a move on, wontcha.

She is sharp with her high-pitched words, as if they are prickles in her mouth she has to spit out.

He turns away from her, mortified.

– It's the position.

– Want me to get it moving?

Out of the corner of his eye, he can see that she is wriggling her forefinger: a child's imitation of a mouse. Instinctively, he jerks his buttocks away and almost slips off the pan.

– Ya kiddin.

She waits just long enough for him to realise his mistake.

– You bet I am. You'd hev to be prettier for that.

She relishes the look on his face, practically licks her lips at it. Eyelids lowered to contain her satisfaction, she turns her body in the way that heavy people do, moving the chair to one side to save herself the job of stepping around it, and saunters off, her high-boned arse swilling from side to side like brandy in a glass.

She's smiling to herself, he can tell. At the door of the ward she looks around and sniggers again.

Cecily thinks the whole business is hilariously funny. Billy can't remember the last time he gave someone so much cause for amusement. He knows her name is Cecily because she has a badge pinned to her uniform. It hitches up the thin cotton fabric so that one breast looks higher than the other. The uniform is made of pale-blue graph-paper hatches.

He has an urge to use her name – both out of a desire to feel those Cs on his tongue, and to show that he likes her, that he might soften for her – but he hasn't had a chance yet, and he's not one to force these things. She reminds him of the women from back home, with her harsh voice and her air of absolute disinterest in what's going on around her. She has a way of standing still amid the scurrying, her gaze skimming the tops of people's heads.

Cecily.

It doesn't suit her one bit, he decides, the hard rim of the bedpan digging into his coccyx. Far too delicate, ethereal a name for someone so solid, so real.

A woman in a flapping white doctor's coat, her hair scraped back in a severe bun, sits on the edge of his bed and looks at him with unconcealed impatience. She has introduced herself simply as Ann, as if everyone should know who Ann is, what Ann does. Only by scrutinising her badge does he discover that she's a psychiatric consultant, and that her full name is Ann Gould. Billy responds with contempt: she, after all, is the one who talks to the freaks.

– Can you tell me what you remember? she asks, rearranging the pink and green forms on her clipboard.

Billy's not in the mood. He suspects that any probing will push his already sketchy memories even further into the shadows. But she presses him, says there's a cop coming along shortly who will bully him into giving a story, any story, so he might as well get one worked out. She prompts him, as if he were a child.

– This incident on the train. There was a fight, yes?

– Surely the other bloke's filled you in already.

– I need to hear your side of the story. The hows and whys of it.

– I'm not a fucken philosopher.

She raises the narrow arcs of her plucked eyebrows, lets the disdain spill freely from her eyes. Bullies come in many disguises, he thinks. He sighs.

– Yeh, we had a fight, he says.

– We?

– That man, the American tourist, and me.

– Describe him, please. For the record.

– Big and fat. Video camera slung over 'is shoulder. White knee-high socks, freckled thighs. About as much subtlety in him as a fork-lift.

He tails off, fragments of memory beginning to surface now. He lets them go, a separate strand from the story he is going to tell her.

– Go on.

– He wouldn't get out of me way. He was sittin in me seat.

– Sitting in your seat? But you didn't *have* a seat –

– And so you had to hit the bugger, interjects Cecily. Unseen by either of them, the black nurse has crept into the curtained-off cubicle and is rearranging the glass of water and box of tissues on his bedside table, even though neither has been touched. Evidently she hadn't wanted to miss Billy's account.

– He was that shocked you'd have thought he didn't know what fists were for! She is holding back a snigger but it escapes, a little gumpf of a snort, and she decides to give in to it. She stands up straight and wipes a tear from her eye. – Oh, you shoulda seen his face when they brought im in! It was like 'e was saying, This wasn't in the tourist brochure!

Billy can sense a stiffening in Ann's body at the foot of his bed, forcing herself to sit out this interruption in good humour. Her pointed features are pinched shut like the clasp on a purse.

– Cecily –

– Seemed to think Billy had bin planted out in the bush for their entertainment, part of the tourist show. *Out to your left is a wild bushman, a very lucky sighting, you don't see em often.*

– Cecily, I want to hear Mr Saint's version of events. She nods at Billy. – Go on.

Billy shrugs. He was enjoying Cecily's jokes. – I don't remember any more, he says. Everyone was staring at me. I don't know why.

Ann cocks her head. – I can tell you why, Mr Saint. You were blistered from the sun and rank as a five-day-old carcass. The driver of the Ghan Express saw you lying between the steel sleepers, as though you were waiting either to be hit by the train or to be carried back towards civilisation. Towards life. If he hadn't been going so slowly it would certainly have been the former. I don't think you appreciate how lucky you are.

Cecily is blowing her nose now with a cotton hanky and Billy smiles as he watches her blocking one nostril and then the other. She doesn't look like the women back west any more. She is just a nurse, at home enough here to disrupt the doctor's interrogation and not care. Billy is impressed by her, how she has found a niche for herself in this white institution, hoisting herself firmly out of no-man's-land and dumping her bulky frame down here as if she had never doubted her right to it all along.

– I was thirsty, Billy says quietly. I didn't want to die. I was looking for a drink of water.

– And so you thought you'd hitch a ride.

She bores in with her determined eyes. Billy turns away, scrutinises the cream and tan geometric pattern on the curtains by his bed.

– Do you remember anything else at all, Mr Saint?

– Yeh, I do. They were playing *Casablanca* on TV.

Afterwards, Cecily wheels him to the bathroom and positions him squarely in front of a full-length mirror. She says she wants to get him neatened up before the cop arrives. The bathroom is a large, rectangular room, fitted out for the elderly and infirm – metal rails either side of the toilet, a raised plastic seat. Billy hadn't thought he'd find himself using a bathroom like this just yet.

He slouches in silence while she opens a cabinet and takes out a pressurised can. She squirts a ball of foam on to her palm and offers it to him as if he were a horse, a white cloud cupped beneath his mouth. He sits there sullenly, intent on his humiliation. She waits a full half minute then she picks up his chin and slaps the foam against his jaw. Specks of it spray out like the froth of a wave hitting rock. Billy looks up with the shock of it, catches her eyes in the mirror. They direct him to his own. And there he is, not yet twenty-four years old but going on ninety – the face of a man who has travelled to the limits of his existence and witnessed something horrible lying beyond. The blue-ringed eyes are sunk deep in his skull, the skin falling away beneath with all the sagging hopelessness of a bloodhound. Billy notices with what little curiosity he has left for such things how bony his nose has become, how it's topped with a raised black scab. How the skin on his cheeks is blistered and raw in some places and peeling off in others. Straws of pale hair stick out in odd directions and clots of old blood are trapped in the straggles of beard around his mouth. Jesus, it was an ugly beard – not a thick, curly, ruddy one like Rossco's, but a scrawny, willowy thing, like the greasy tufts you see curling over the collar of a bagman.

– Fucken 'ansome fella, ay.

Cecily's face is composed. She can be the consummate professional when she chooses to be.

– It's all looking a bit crook now, but it'll soon come right.

He's touched by the tenderness in her voice. She holds up a disposable razor, her pink tongue pushing through the gap in her front teeth.

– Go on then, Billy says softly.

She spreads the foam to the edge of his jaw. Then she holds the skin taut with the span of two fingers and bends close. Concentration ruckles her brow. Billy keeps his eyes open, daring himself to stare at the black skin close up, the individual pricks of the pores, the few stray hairs encroaching onto the temple; daring himself not to look away.

In the quiet of the bathroom, they listen to the sound of the stubble being shorn. For Billy, it is something to cling to, the first unequivocal sound in weeks. Cecily makes no mention of the tiny white scars that appear on the surface of his face like flotsam in the razor's wake.

---

here is a town

Here is a town, if you can call it a town: a dusty bitumen strip cutting a swathe through a sprawl of buildings with flat tin roofs. There's a disused roadhouse at the near end, its upper-floor windows boarded up with crisscrossed planks, its door jammed shut with a brick. Beyond it, a servo with one petrol and one diesel pump. A coffee shop diagonally opposite. Beyond that, half a dozen shops and as many side streets feeling their tentative way out into the bush. None of the houses are more than one storey. Empty oil drums lounge on corners, while street lamps spot the town irregularly with circles of yellow light. Overhead, thrown into shadow, the sky has turned milky and shed itself of stars.

The wind digs us in the ribs.

Look. There's that man, the new one.

A man with a lively mop of curly black hair has stepped into one of the circles of light. His name is Jimmi Rangi and he's pitched up in the last few days from who knows where, a drifter who doesn't seem to know where he belongs or where he's heading. Perhaps he's just out of jail; perhaps he was sent here by the government because there's a house to spare in the Aboriginal community tagged onto the edge of the town.

It's hard to tell his age: silver bristles stud the dark skin around his firm mouth, but he is lean and agile and holds himself with a youthful grace in his brown, flared polyester trousers and sun-bleached singlet. His eyes move lazily across their dark, shadowy pits but his sinewy neck and arms are well defined – tough little knots of muscle that suggest an athlete's quick reactions. Veins wrap his forearms as if they had been loosely bound with string.

As we watch, Jimmi Rangi peers inside the cage of his fingers. It looks as if he has something precious in there, something he likes to steal a look at from time to time. There's the snatch of a lighter, a clamour of pale flame. As he draws himself up, he sucks in his gaunt cheeks and nicks the cigarette between finger and thumb, exhales a smoky blue plume and walks on, leaving the plume to unwreathe itself slowly in the circle of light.

> – How many roads must a man walk down
> Before you can call him a man?

This is unexpected. He doesn't look the sort that likes to sing. He has a high, thin voice and once it leaves his mouth it climbs up and away with ease into the starless sky. The wind pricks up its ears.

> – The answer, my friend, is blowing in the wind
> The answer is blowing in the wind.

It doesn't take much to enchant the wind. It looks at us excitedly, then swoops down on an empty wine bottle, spins it in a circle, and rolls it along the road – *clink-clink! clink-clink!* it goes as it hits the pavement, spins by Jimmi's feet, rolls on. And so Jimmi Rangi sings and the bottle clinks, accompanying one another down the street.

Having nothing better to do, we amble along behind.

Halfway down, Jimmi's attention is caught by an office building in which the light's still on. There's a poster in the window. On the poster are the chunky, black figures of a paperchain family – a man and a woman and a child, holding hands. OFFICE OF THE DEPARTMENT OF ABORIGINAL AFFAIRS it says in chipped black letters on the door, beneath which someone has made a correction on a cardboard sign: THE ABORIGINAL AND TORRES STRAIT ISLANDERS COMMISSION (ATSIC), KIMBERLEY AND PILBARA OFFICE. Inside, a woman is typing.

Jimmi sends another blue plume into the sulphurous light. He steps up for a closer look.

Children should be seen and heard and loved and cherished and hugged, he reads, *and played with and talked to and teased,* and so on and so on it goes, cradled and sung to and kissed on the tops of their eyelids and the tips of their snot-encrusted noses; raspberries should be blown on their chubby bellies, *you're the best* whispered into their wax-bunged ears . . . It lists all the things that children need, none of them hard to give – and yet, thinks Jimmi as he looks again at the accusing paperchain figures, if someone felt the need to put this poster up, and to print it in the first place –

He backs away from the window, a heaviness welling up in his stomach like undigested damper, and casts his black eyes down the street with its sickly lights, all the way down the road until it tapers into the darkness of the surrounding bush, wishing he could see something to give him hope – a pair of headlights would do, driving off into the distance – just some sign that there are other places to go, other people to be, other ways to live than those he has stumbled on here.

– Who's forgotten how to love a child? he whispers to himself, although he suspects we might be here. Easiest thing in the world, no?

Oh yes, we tell him, it is. We should know, we've loved enough.

Jimmi shakes his head in bewilderment.

– Then why . . .?

He stands still, listening out for our answer, waiting so long that the hot ash of his cigarette pricks at his fingers, and all this time we look the other way, too ashamed to meet his gaze, raking our eyes instead over the closed-up shop-fronts on the other side of the street, grateful to them for their inanimate faces, for not possessing the wherewithal to pass judgement on us, until eventually he tosses the stub of his cigarette into the gutter, gives a disappointed tut of his tongue. He moves on. The typing woman catches the movement and looks up, briefly.

Hang on, we say. You have to put it in context . . .

But he doesn't respond. He has shut himself down to us; he doesn't want to listen any more. He walks from one circle of light to the next.

Oblivious as ever, the wind bashes the empty wine bottle against the pavement: *clink-clink*. Come on, join in, what's wrong, it was just getting good. *The answer, my friend, is blowing . . .*

Can't you see? we snap. He's had enough of your stupid duet.

At the far end of the street is a wire mesh fence, some ten feet high, a necklace of broken green bottles, crushed Emu beer cans and torn cardboard cartons at its base. Finding the gates locked, Jimmi jumps onto the fence with fingers and toes wedged into the hexagons, firm as a cat, one two three and he's over, his shin brushing the sign that says No Alcohol Beyond This Point, a light-footed drop down the other side, and within a few strides he's disappeared into the darkness of the Aboriginal community. There are no street lights in there, not many headlights either, although at least he'll be able to see the stars.

Maybe he'll sing with me another night, after he's had a bit of grog, says the wind, forlornly.

We laugh at the wind, our mockery fuelled by the pain of Jimmi's rebuff.

He doesn't drink, you galah. How else d'you suppose he knew we were here?

The wind doesn't come here often, but we know this town well. Just last week the local council rounded up four hundred stray dogs and carted them off to the paddock behind the roadhouse, shepherding them into a corner. The dogs knew something was up; they cowered together, eyes bulging, hind legs quivering. The council men took turns with the gun. Stevo from the servo heard the yelps and the shots from his forecourt. Each one sent a ripple through the quiet, still ponds of his tobacco-brown eyes. He hooked a finger under the collar of his collie cross, Yakka, and pressed her tight to his knee. They'd never hear the end of it if they shot his precious Yakka. She earned her keep in this town, alerting him with a bark whenever a customer pulled in at the pumps.

Stevo's eyes are still churned up when he arrives at the Spini tonight. He hoists his sizeable belly onto a high stool at the bar, a nipple in a nest of wiry, black hair peeping out from the gaping armhole of his singlet. He tells Rossco and Gerry and Clay and anyone else who'll listen that the whites in this town are a bunch of fucken wankers, it sets the blackfellas a bad example, the way they sit around drinking piss all day, nothing else to do but shoot them godforsaken mutts.

Rossco and Gerry, their shoulders hunched over their beers, say nothing. Stevo has a tendency to sound off every few weeks about some black–white issue, but he'll revert to his usual lethargic self soon enough. Gerry tucks his pack of Winfield Reds up the sleeve of his T-shirt. Rossco pushes his metal-rimmed glasses back up his nose. Only the barman, Clay – always happy to adopt an opposing view – folds his thick arms across his chest and scratches around in his stubble for something to spur Stevo on.

– It's a bloody mess, Stevo continues, before Clay has had a chance. The way the government pours dollars into the blackfellas' laps, as if money will solve everything, some stuffed shirt from Perth or Sydney flown in to give a lecture on sustainable development and the blackfellas stand up when it's time for questions and ask are they gunna get a green ute or a blue ute? And when they get their nice new ute they run it dry and roll it over in the dirt and go back and say, c'n I have another one, sport, jiss like a kid, no idea where it comes from, how to look after it, what it could be used for except the grog run, ay.

By now he's worked himself into a sweat. He takes his baseball cap off, runs his hand over the crease it has made in the back of his concertinaed neck – a crease that is practically a part of his anatomy now – and stares around with those stirred-up brown eyes. He pats his pockets, looking for the raw materials for a rollup.

Rossco peers down his nose through thick, smeared lenses and wipes a layer of beer scum off the red bristles studding his lip. Gerry hangs his buzzcut and repeatedly bounces the end of an unlit cigarette on the bar. Neither will meet Stevo's eye. It's them he's talking about – them and himself as well. Surely he can't be exempting himself from this barrage? He's at least fifty per cent white after all. Only Clay, rocking on his heels, unearths a dirty chuckle.

But Stevo is distracted now. The pockets of his stubbies were empty. He rehitches his rubber thongs over the rung of the stool, puts his cap back on, then picks up his glass and gulps. Fat drips spot the front of his singlet as he drains the glass down to the end.

He'll have to change the subject, he thinks, if he wants to cadge a smoke.

something torn

Even before the sun is up, he's standing at the back door and peering into the smoky-blue haze of pre-dawn. A slight, small figure, with something torn about him, shivering, his shoulders pulled up to his ears and his palms flattened into his pockets. His green T-shirt is still twisted where he's pulled it roughly on and half-heartedly tucked a fistful into his jeans.

The yard is engulfed in an absolute stillness, as if everything had been swallowed – wind, flies, noise, the lot. Billy scans for movement – the darkened land, the broad slate of paler sky – but even the gum trees are still. Their fistfuls of leaves droop sulkily down. He eyes them with contempt. *Rustle-rustle-rustle* – all night they were at it, keeping him awake.

Another shiver runs through his thin body. The air is night air still, cold-chipped. The harboured chill of the concrete step seeps into his bare soles as if by a deathly osmosis. He shivers again, and this time he allows the shiver to become a larger movement and propel him into the yard.

Billy's used to navigating the obstacle course created by his father's tools and car paraphernalia, even though nothing is more than a looming black shape in the dimness. A teetering Pisa of stacked tyres, a clutch of fishing rods, a rickety camping table piled high with metal tool boxes, sprouting coils of number eight wire, whittled fish hooks, open trays of nuts and bolts which Stan pushes around with an oily, black-rimmed finger, looking for the exact right size. Billy steps over a Cornflakes packet and a plastic bowl with a ring of old milk in the bottom, ducks beneath a pair of underpants turned stiff as cardboard on the line.

At the edge of the yard are two strands of barbed wire a foot and a half apart, forming what has always seemed to Billy a pointless quibble between land that looks the same on one side as it does the other. The only point of it, as far as he's concerned, is to keep his father's mess from spilling any further into the bush. He slips his small body cleanly between the wires. Ahead, the massive hulk of the escarpment blocks out a chunk of sky.

On this side of the fence, something in his chest expands. It is as if he is now untrammelled: a boy and a landscape with nothing between them. He runs into this space, heading towards the escarpment, surefooted in his bare feet on the spiky, uneven ground. A path glimmers palely and he takes it. The gradient steepens at once, the grass thinning out and giving way to grit with not much poking through. Soon he's leaping from one rock to another with loud slaps of his bare feet. Sometimes he uses his hands to help him balance as he follows a natural staircase, a left turn here, a dead-end there, a hoist onto the next level provided by the branch of a gnarled little box tree, its twisted arm as familiar beneath his grip as the backs of the kitchen chairs. He moves easily, the height of each step programmed into his muscles.

By the time he reaches the top the sky has lightened to a hazy purple. He rubs an itch on the side of his face, marking himself with red dust. Up here the air is sweet, almost astringent: the taint of eucalyptus. He crosses to the far edge of the escarpment, looks sheerly down at the muffled plain lapping at its base. It is still swamped in shadow down there, a murky primeval soup. Billy can make out the pale, bald skull of the abandoned Inter truck, the snaking form of the red dirt road, the swollen forms of boab trees.

Without warning, the horizon brightens behind him: a white rim rubbed clean. It is a signal to Billy. He licks a finger to check the direction of the wind, feels only the merest of traces. Ahead is a cluster of trees. When he's a stone's throw away, he brings his hands to the ground and sticks his bony arse in the air and creeps forward on all fours, one slow, careful step at a time.

Behind him, the horizon slits open. A steely, yellow eye peers through.

All the time he keeps his gaze locked on the shadowy spaces between the trees. He knows they're there. A sharp stone digs into his palm but he ignores it and carries on. The whole escarpment is lightening now. The rocks are no longer black but a soft, grey monotone – although he never quite knows how much is the sun rising and how much is his eyes getting used to the dark. When he's close enough, he squats back on his haunches, elbows tucked in as he searches for an unbitten corner of fingernail with his teeth. Any second now the sun will prise open the shadows like thick-skinned fruit.

Suddenly there's a movement. His eyes dart to meet it. The flick of a white-streaked head. Or was it a wavering branch? No, it was a head, he's sure. And there it is again – perhaps even the hasty pawing of an ear. For a few seconds there's nothing except the shallow excitement of his breath. And then a watery sneeze from under an umbrella bush that makes him jump. Now he doesn't know where to look – at the bush or the trees – and his eyes jump between the two, not wanting to miss anything.

Eventually he gets his reward: a tired limb stretching out clearly from beneath the trees. A lovely off-white inner flank. Almost immediately, there's a clean snap of a twig to his left and he whisks his neck around to be startled by a young roo venturing right out into the open, stiff-limbed and cautious, heading in his direction. It takes each jump in two parts – front paws out, a good sniff, then hind legs hopping in. It's barely ten feet away and he can see it perfectly: the little hovering forefeet, the twitching nose. Billy's heart is pulsing in his throat. The joey hops again, sniffs, finds a place it likes and begins to dig with scrabbling paws, a scatter of grit, then turns around and angles its rear end into the newly softened patch. It looks over its shoulder, directly at Billy, blinks. Apparently sees nothing but a faint grey form that could be a rock, or a bush.

There are near a dozen of them this morning: two or three large bucks, twice as many females. The rest are young. They lounge in various states of nonchalance or out-and-out boredom, draped around the furniture of the trees and rocks like a family in their living room. Some are flat on their bellies, their paws comfortably crossed, others are propped on one elbow as if to read a book. All have their noses twitching, ears flicking. There is something old-mannish about the large ones with their square jaws, the huge matted carpets of their bellies, long limbs splayed wide to air dangling balls. The way they look morosely down their noses with heavy-lidded eyes, or hunch a shoulder to reach an itch on their back.

Everything is monotone still, the roos and the rocks hatched from the same soft grey. No shadows to complicate matters just yet. Sometimes what Billy thinks is a rock shifts the hump of its back, flicks up ears. Then, without warning, the first ray of sun spears the pelt of an upright male, releasing a wash of stunning, coppery red, and soon the rocks turn too, as if in league, as if the blood of the kangaroo had spilled and was now running freely, staining the rocks and the termite mounds and the trunks of the gum trees and seeping down into the earth itself.

Billy's near enough that he could shoot half of them, point blank. He'd say all of them, but he knows the other half 'd be away by the time he got to them, triggering the springs in those mighty back legs which slam the earth so hard you'd think they were responsible for making it spin. In one big commotion they'd scatter, big ones and little ones wildly out of sync, the muscles of their tails thumping down in fury, sending them flying over rocks and around trees, raising the dust up to cover their flight. There'd be a smell of flayed grass, of terrorised earth. In less than ten seconds these beautiful, graceful creatures would be gone.

But he'd never shoot a roo. Never ever. Billy loves these kangaroos more than anything else in the world – more than himself, he reckons. He wouldn't kill a roo even if he was dying of hunger and thirst, he'd swear to it, never in a million years. What he wants is to watch them. To be with them. He observes every movement they make – how they sniff, how they chew, how they fight. Every day he narrows the gap between himself and the kangaroos.

The sun is beating on the back of his head now. It must be seven o'clock. The shadows of the rocks and the trees and the roos have leapt behind them, a more precise black than anything the night could muster. Some of the joeys seem taken aback by this dark shape that follows them. Billy takes his T-shirt off and drapes it over his hair, stretching the sleeves and tying them at his neck to create an odd little bonnet. In ultra-slow motion he scrapes a patch of earth clean with the side of one hand and leans on an elbow. With the other hand he arranges a flap of T-shirt along the back of his neck. As long as he keeps these movements slow and contin-uous, the roos don't seem to notice him. An ant runs across his shoulders and he steels his mind against it. Some of the roos are munching grass, or swiping at the lower branches of the trees for a fistful of leaves, but it's not the first time they've looked for breakfast here and there are no leaves low enough any more.

When it gets too hot, he drags his sticky body over the grit and into a small circle of shade behind a bush, holds up a corner of T-shirt like a tent awning and looks out from beneath it. Sometimes what he thinks is an ant, or worse, is just a trickle of sweat. He strains his tongue to catch one of these dribbles, but it's not in the place where it feels as if it is. A fly lands on his tongue. He spits it off.

There's no wind to speak of today, but he knows the roos must pick up his scent some mornings. Sometimes he wonders if they have already smelt him for what he is – a young male on the cusp of manhood, too young to be considered a threat. He likes to think they've got used to him being here; even that they consider him one of the mob. When at last he levers himself up, his chest will be stained red, just like theirs, just like the trees and the rocks and the earth, so that he is a part of the chain that joins one life form to another, an inseparable part of the whole.

---

we've been thinking

Straddling the upward-slanting branch of a sturdy bloodwood tree, one behind the other, we watch him.

See? we say.

Mm, murmurs the wind.

And that?

Uh-huh.

And the way he jerked when the spider –

Yeah, yeah, I saw it.

The wind raises its eyebrows and lets out a long-suffering groan. It has coiled itself around an opposite branch.

For heaven's sake, it cries. Even Billy must be bored by now.

Billy never gets bored.

Out here by himself all the time with no one to play with? *I* would get bored.

We shrug. He's got his kangaroos.

Lonely little bugger, I reckon.

If he is, he doesn't know it. There's no one to put the idea in his head.

I certainly know how *that* feels, says the wind with a dejected sniff. Not getting enough attention.

We throw the wind a look that could split a piece of wood in two.

Not everyone needs others to notice them all the time, you know.

Huh! As if you lot can talk.

We glare at the wind and the wind glares back, but after a while it gives up, because there are many of us and only one wind, and a miserable one at that. It loosens its grip on the tree, unravels and slouches off, muttering with pique.

We turn our attention back to where Billy lies sleeping in the mottled shade of the bloodwood. Every so often we fire a little pellet made of rolled-up, masticated leaves on his home-made bonnet. It isn't good for him to sleep too long in the sun; he'll give himself a headache.

Gottim!

He clamps his neck with his hand, peers around with bleary eyes.

Morning, Billy Can!

He hauls himself onto an elbow, wipes a dusty hand across one cheek. One by one we jump down, wincing as our knee joints take the brunt of the impact. We tug at our yellowing beards, pull at the twisted crotches of our trousers. Wipe our sap-sticky hands on sun-bleached shirts.

Hey, Billy. We've been thinking. You don't have to be alone, you know. People around here may refuse to let you see the full story going on behind their eyes, they may swallow what they mean to say and say something else instead. But we're always close handy, if you want a bit of a chat. You call and we listen – and vice versa, of course. That's the deal. What do you reckon? You won't ever be alone again.

Billy sits for a while on his backside, arms resting on his knees. The early morning sun tries to lever itself between his squinting eyes. On the edge of the escarpment, nodding spikes of rat's tail grass glint like scratches in glass.

Time to be heading home, Billy Can. The roos cleared off ages ago and Crystal will be wondering. Look at you, coming up here in your bare feet! Anyone'd think you'd never heard of the phenomenon of stubbed toes. Not to mention scorpions.

Suddenly he's up – up and running over to the edge of the escarpment and down the path, jumping from one rock to another, skidding and slipping on the grit. The twigs of the red box scratch his bare arms.

For Chrissakes, Billy, slow down! It's the weekend and we're not going to exhaust ourselves chasing after a thirteen-year-old boy. Look, why don't you take a seat on that old ghost gum over there, the one that the wind blew down last week, and we'll get to know each other? That's the ticket. The termites have found it already but we won't let them bother you. Imagine someone's handed you a carton of chocolate moo juice, a little bit warm, just like it is at the tuck shop at school, but if you poke the straw in deep, that's the trick, past the bit that's too rich for drinking neat, you'll find it's like the water at the bottom of a billabong, cooler and thinner than on the surface. Ah, doesn't that taste good! You're almost making us want some ourselves.

We take the chance to rest, hands on thighs. We're not as young as we used to be: our hearts and lungs are ragged, our sinews are sore, our joints are seizing up . . . We could go on.

This tree, we tell Billy as soon as we've got our breath back, will be gone forever before long – such quick work the termites make of things around here. Although there's a great deal of reluctance to die, of course, and some things take longer than others. Take people, for instance. We've lost count how many there are getting up in the morning and walking around, eating, drinking, copulating – acting for all the world as if they were still alive when in fact they died a long time ago: their spirits got so bored they left their bodies and came to join our mob. All that's left behind is a bunch of skin and chattering bones. You know the ones we're talking about, Billy, the ones who've shut themselves down, who can't hear us any more. They're as good as dead, and they know it – or at least they would if they'd only stop to think about it for a moment. Which is exactly the problem, of course, because they don't. Chrissakes, Billy Can, do you have to make such a noise with that straw? Well, we can't accuse you of not playing along with our game.

Billy chucks the imaginary carton over his shoulder and makes as if to get up. We put out a restraining hand.

Hang on a minute, Billy Can. There's something you'll need to learn to do. Stay sitting where you are. Sit very still. Nice and quiet. Listen to the drone of the flies, to the distant rumble of the road trains driving through town. To the alien squeaks and whines of the radio in your front yard as Stan tries to pick up the test match. Listen to these noises, Billy. And then listen *through* them, as if – how can we describe it? – as if putting your head under water.

Yes. That's it.

Underneath the surface there's a silence. Can you hear it, Billy? It's as rich and complete as anything you will ever have known. You might not find it straight away, but with a bit of practice it'll come, easy-peasy, and you'll be able to tune in whenever you want. Plunge into this silence, Billy Can. Plunge in deep! Let yourself sink right down to the bottom. Because deep down here in this soft, private world, you'll be able to hear the voices. There are reams of them, Billy Can – a complete encyclopaedia, from all over Australia. You might not believe it from what you've encountered so far within the four walls of your house with its lopsided, patchwork roof, blessed as you are with a mother who does not know how to be a mother, a father who is too unsure of this world himself to guide you safely through it, but there are spirits out here, Billy – some gentle, some wise, some pretty bog standard, it has to be said, but all of them with a lifetime's worth of living behind them, who know what it means to be alive, and what it means to be dead.

Billy gnaws on the blood-speckled skin around his thumb.

We know what you're thinking, Billy Can. You're thinking, why believe in these voices when no one seems to believe in anything any more? Don't give us that *who, me?* look. We are offering you guidance, Billy Can. The chance to live by our rules. In return we'll hold your hand.

Billy looks into the distance. Puffs at a fly on his lip. And then he stands up, balances on the fallen trunk and leaps off, continuing to bound with both feet together – hard work without a tail. Soon he loses momentum and breaks into a proper run.

Our hands make tunnels for our voices:

If it makes you feel better, Billy, in safer hands, then some of us have been kangaroos too!

At which we catch one another's eye and collapse into howls of laughter.

---

the clangers

Crystal slams the fryer onto the gas ring and lets out a joyless sigh. She must make Stan an egg. Stan's world would fall apart if she weren't around to make him a bloody egg. She takes out a wooden-handled spatula from a drawer and drops that on the benchtop as well, making as much of a racket as she can. Then she bangs down the salt and pepper. Stan's hopeless in the kitchen – no surprises there. A few days after they were married she caught him trying to cook a meat pie in a saucepan with the lid on, the gas searing full blast underneath.

Another clanging starts up outside: this one the high-pitched *ping-ping-ping* of a small hammer against metal. Listen to the pair of us, she thinks. The clangers. *Clang clang clang* all day long, as if this was the only way they communicated these days. Crystal looks out of the window, sees a bright red panel locked in a vice, Stan's long back bending over it. The panel catches a fistful of sunlight and throws out a long-spined star.

Crystal winces. She already has a headache brimming behind her eyes and it isn't even half-past seven yet. The bottom of the pan looms blackly before her. All I have to do is crack an egg into it, she thinks. It can't be that bloody hard. Nick it on the edge of the pan. Follow it with another, and another, and another, the whole bloody box of them if I get really in the swing of it, and then I'll whizzy them up into some sort of cross between an omelette and a scrambled-up mess, a few shakes of salt and pepper, maybe a dribble of milk. She goes through the motions, trying not to think too hard. Plops a couple of pieces of sliced white into the toaster. Lays out strips of streaky bacon on the grill. She even makes tea in a pot. When the bacon starts to wriggle and spit she levers open the window and calls out in a billow of smoke.

   – Staaaaan!

   – Coming!

She closes her eyes and counts to ten. That's how long it generally takes before she hears the sound of him snagging his Blunnies off on the step. By the time she's got to thirteen, his large frame is blocking out the light. She turns around and sees once again how everything seems to droop downwards from his shoulders. You'd think he was carrying the weight of the world in two buckets, one in each hand.

Stan gets to eating without a word, scraping his knife on the plate. Every so often he looks wistfully out at the car in the yard. When the last bit of yolk's mopped up he coughs a muddied thank-you into an oil-smeared fist, dumps his plate on a teetering pile by the sink and goes back out, stooping to clear the door frame.

Crystal leans back in her chair with another sigh and helps herself to a cigarette from a pack of Horizon 50s. Then she gets up and wanders down the hall.

It's not that she worries about him being outside, it's more that she can't quite settle to anything when she doesn't know where Billy is. Behind her half a dozen jobs cry out for her attention: laundry pulled from the basket and left unsorted on the bedroom floor, dishes to wash, shopping that needs to be done. She tugs irritably at her black and white polka-dot dress. It never feels right, this dress – the waistline is high of her own waist, and the hem is just high of her knees. And it's got spots on, for God's sake. She doesn't know why she wears it. As for her hair, which is sticking damply to the back of her neck, she's washed it, but the last thing you want to do at this time of year is generate more heat so she's left it to dry naturally and now it's got itself into a right old tangle. Propping the fly screen open at the back door, she steps over to the Hill's Hoist, helps herself to a couple of plastic clothes pegs and uses them to fix a fistful of loose orange curls to the top of her head.

She's always been a slap-dash sort of woman, but it's not through lack of caring. She likes the look it gives her – the frayed, leggy, sleepy-eyed look, as if she's only just got out of bed. Men adore her for it. She's been the sexiest white woman in the Kimberley for fifteen years and she'd rather die than lose her claim to the title. She'd certainly rather die than turn into one of those capable, muscular station women who chop up beef joints for the freezer with a butcher's cleaver, bake half a dozen loaves on a Monday and keep a tally of the number of bags of flour left to last them through the wet. Put a bullet in me head, she told Stan, if I ever show a flair for all that crap. Righto, he had said, in full confidence he'd never see the day, and she'd felt his eyes on her arse in her tight jeans, still perched tight and high on her long slim legs: a sure sign of a woman who has her priorities right.

When Billy appears, it is as a little brown speck leaping out from behind a tree. He runs towards the house on invisible paths of his own creation, lifting his face once in a while to check he's on collision course with the house. He's taken his T-shirt off and tied it in complicated knots around his head, sleeves flapping over his ears like a pair of ineffective wings.

Crystal shakes her head in disbelief. This strange creature, her son.

Leaning against the door jamb, her right arm swinging the cigarette to her mouth and away and back to her mouth again, she wonders how she will greet him. Perhaps she'll smile – a big, welcoming smile that invites him to tell her everything, to empty his pockets, show her the stones he has found, because he always comes back with stones. She rehearses the scene in her head, sees them knocking easily against one another as they go down the hall to the kitchen. She'll pour him a glass of milk and he'll eat the toast and Vegemite she's made for him, hungrily, like little boys eat, running out of steam just before he's finished, then getting up from the table and asking to do something else, the skin around his mouth still speckled with crumbs.

Or perhaps she'll tell him off. For stretching his T-shirt out of shape, for not brushing his teeth, for leaving his bed unmade.

Oh, for goodness sake, Crystal, she thinks. Give the bloody boy a bloody break.

She doesn't need anyone to tell her that this is all wrong: this thin veil of uneasiness that has always hung between her and her only child. They don't touch in the way that a mother and son should touch. Even when he was a toddler and beginning to attract admiring glances from people in the town – the freckles stuck in the shape of a Bandaid across his nose, one or two stray ones tumbling down and catching on the crag of a narrow, red lip – she was already refusing to believe, in some deep place, that he was anything to do with her. She was still so young herself; she couldn't be expected to step out of the spotlight just yet. By the time he was seven or eight, he seemed to have worked this out for himself, and he'd wrapped himself up in a blanket of wariness that had kept him apart ever since.

It was all there for anyone to see, stored up behind his eyes – penetrating, grey-green eyes, the colour of a stormy sea. Everyone noticed his eyes. Mrs Tucker, his teacher at school, said he'd be a preacher one day, that they burned with an evangelical zeal. Stan said they were a wanderer's eyes – that he'd always be looking for something just over the horizon. Probably never find it, ay. He'd said this cheerfully one Saturday morning as he and Crystal watched their son water the petunias in the front yard – cheerfully and blandly, the way Stan said most things, even when what he was saying was dealing some devastating blow.

Crystal had, of course, dismissed both notions outright.

– They's more like the eyes of the blokes in the Spini on a Friday night, she'd said loudly – too loudly, wanting somehow to ridicule Billy, to make her son more ordinary than her. Pissed as farts and sizing up for a blue. Thassall it is. I'll hev to watch im when he gits older – everyone'll think he's got it in for em. They'll git im into all sorts of trouble, them eyes.

And then she'd laughed, because it was so absurd, so hilarious, this idea that he could ever be a threatening man, her Billy, little skinny Billy, who loved his roos and talked to his stones when he was upset. She'd laughed noisily, nasally, grateful for the release of it, allowing herself to get almost hysterical, and Stan had looked on, big-boned and uncomfortable, his large hands hanging down.

At moments like this Crystal is grateful to Stan, though she'd never admit it, of course. She knows that Stan is kinder, more honest than she has it in her to be. God knows, Billy deserved more from her than mockery. But given the opportunity, she's got to laugh. There is safety in laughter, a rope to catch onto, and she can't bring herself to let go.

Even before he's cleared the fence, she can hear the words tumbling out of her, an edge sharp as wire to her voice.

– What on god's earth dja find to amuse yerself out there, three hours and not a squeak out of ya, could be lying dead in a gully for all I know, and ya niver take any water with ya, although it doesn't seem to matter, yer like a cow fillin up at a waterhole, drinkin a heap before ya goes out, more than ya think a boy of your size could hold without leakin, and then ya go for eight hours at a stretch –

She shifts her body a little to give him space to pass, then follows him down the hall.

– One of these days you'll jiss not come back. I c'n see it. You'll jiss not come back, and we'll niver know if you ran away or got taken out by a king brown, or jiss crawled under a rock and forgot to wake up –

She's halfway down the hallway before she realises that the draught at her back must mean she hasn't done up the zip of her dress. She sticks the cigarette between tight lips and reaches awkwardly behind her, trying not to catch loose strands of hair in the teeth of the zip. *Jesus*. Is everyone so slack when they spend all day at home? Then she realises that she's left her rubber thongs on the step, and she stomps back, gathers them up with an impatient sweep of her arm, slaps the soles together to get rid of any ants, puts them on, slaps back down the hall.

– Billy, are you listenin ter me?

He's at the sink getting a glass of water, his hair a medley of white, blond and gold in the light from the window, luminous against his sun-browned skin. Crystal sits down behind him. She crosses her long legs and accidentally bangs her shin bone against the table.

– Aw, Jesus.

She rubs the skin where the shadow of a bruise is already threatening to surface. She's got his attention, at least. His eyes are magnified through the distorted, upturned glass. She splays her toes, scrutinises the orange enamel she painted on them last week.

– Look at them nails. All chipped and jagged. I'll wake up one morning and find I've crossed that line between young 'n carefree and old 'n ruined, and there'll be no goin back after that, ay. She gives a little laugh. Whatja reckon, Billy?

She picks a fleck of tobacco from her bottom lip, tucks one arm into her waist, the palm a pivot for the smoking elbow, and tries to get another last drag out of her cigarette, though it's burnt right down to the filter. Everything returns to this, her smoking pose, the reassuring to and fro swing giving the moment its purpose.

Gasping for air, Billy fills up again, staring out of the window. Crystal studies him as she smokes. He's hardly ever inside the house, and when he is, he's looking out. Unlike her, he looks as if he expects to see something interesting on the horizon. *There's nothing there*, she feels like telling him, to grip his shoulders and shake him with that fact. *There's nothing bloody there*. Just a big boring desert with nobody in it. Hev ya got something wrong with yer eyes?

He fills up a third time and now he takes his glass and leaves the room. She hears the click of his bedroom door.

– Billy?

She grinds the cigarette into the ashtray. Then she looks in the pack to check how many she has left.

This is what she'd tell Billy, if he'd ask her – what she tells herself from time to time, whenever she needs reminding. She met Stan in a bar. She was young, naive and pretty. His hair was thicker then, although already mousy, and he was a bit too lanky in the body to carry off the macho look with conviction; but he had this smile that curled up more one side than the other. A touch of Elvis, you could say. Hard to spot it now, quite frankly, but it was there, just like it's there on you. And he had these long, long arms that looked like they could wrap all the way around you twice. She even liked the big nose with its extra bulge on the end – like you were getting twenty per cent extra free.

Fact is, she'd been pretty smitten by Stan.

The whole package was all the more alluring, of course, for being seated on a bar stool in the middle of Western Australia. You noticed men there that you wouldn't have missed a blink for back in Sydney. This was fifteen years ago, remember, when most men in the outback referred to you as a sheila, and when you came across one that didn't you reckoned you'd got yourself a pretty good lurk.

Now, sitting at the kitchen table, she almost manages a smile. Perhaps it's a good job Billy isn't here, after all. She shouldn't take the piss out of the outback fellas when he's one of them himself, after all. She catches a glimpse of her smiling face reflected in the kettle, and closes her mouth abruptly. She gets self-conscious about her crooked incisors, way too prominent for her small mouth. Beginning to stain at the edges too.

She and her friend Elise had been travelling around Australia for two months by then – four weeks as jilleroos on a station in New South Wales, fencing, tagging, drenching – then over to Fremantle to stay with Uncle Jack and Auntie Pam, and now they were on their way to Darwin, not intending to stop in the godforsaken stretch after Broome, but all anyone could talk about on the bus was the rodeo at Fitzroy Crossing – the highlight of the Kimberley year, they said. Some year they have out in the woop woop, she muttered to Elise, but they decided to give it a go, got tizzed up in their moleskin shirts and hitched a lift on the back of some station-hand's ute.

The place was swathed in dust. It coated your tongue and settled in the corners of your eyes. Here and there a blade of sunlight sliced through, showing up a swirl of motes, golden splinters of hay. Cattle with hot, runny noses brayed and butted each other's hind quarters, keeping a shifty eye on the commotion outside their pens. There was a smell of beer soaking into the earth. Bandy-legged men in chaps and Akubras knocked a finger against the worn rims of their hats as they swayed past. Crystal prickled with excitement. She narrowed her eyes against the sun, ripped the pull-ring off her can of Emu and tossed it on the ground. She was a match for these men. She knew it. She hitched a foot on the rung of the fence, mimicking their stance. Beside her stood a row of horses, steaming, placid, their eyes covered with back cloths. Crystal laid her cheek against a flank, sucked in the warm smell of horse hair and horse manure, until someone wrested her back roughly by the shoulder.

– Mind yer face, mate.

A brown leather boot presented itself an inch from her eye. A gun went off. The cloth on the horse's eyes was whipped away and immediately the creature reared up, transformed into a maddened brumby. Its nostrils flared and eye whites rolled as it leapt into the circle and within seconds had flung the rider over its shoulders, kicking its back legs higher than its head. Crystal was thrilled at the dangerousness of it all. Only as the thrown rider scrambled quickly to her feet and leapt out of the ring did Crystal realise she was a girl of about her own age, two long plaits uncoiling when she flung her hard hat off. The men yooped and wolf-whistled and clapped and Crystal swigged her beer and fought for their eyes. Yes, she had met her match.

At the end of the day she and Elise jumped on the back of another ute and sung their way into a hotel bar, arms looped over the sweat-sodden shoulders of men and women they didn't know. Everyone was outrageously drunk by then. Dirt-smeared faces reeled on undecided legs, swinging around on the sawdust. There were flailing imitations of a dance. Every few minutes came the crash of a glass on the floor. Plenty of men turned to look at her, but he was the only one who lifted his Akubra, the action implying she'd come here expressly for him. She smiled and took the bar stool next to him. Only then did Crystal realise that his eyes, the same faded blue as his jeans, were barely able to focus, and he'd probably mistaken her for someone else.

Still, she was here for the ride, and she wasn't going to cop out now. Besides, she had something to prove. She raised her voice, shouted orders at the barman, flung her hair around. She cast off her old reserve so easily she wondered why on earth she'd been hauling it around for so long. Conversation with her new blue-eyed friend was fairly monosyllabic. He was clearly a man more used to the elements for company than other human beings. He had a desiccated face, everything dried and dusted, scabbed over and peeling off. His sun-blasted lips were more brown than red. Freckles cropped up in unusual places – on the lobe of an ear, in the crease of an eyelid. His eyes were patient and soft with something hopeful about them. He reminded Crystal of a dog tied up outside a shop. He offered her an Extra Strong Mint and when she said no he shrugged and helped himself, then looked around, sucking noisily to make her laugh. The mint made him sneeze and his hat fell off. He ran a hand through his hair and found a stray cigarette lodged inside a curl. He turned it over in his fingers.

– That's a worry. I don't smoke. Do you?

Crystal said yes. He put it in her mouth and lit it. Then he gave her his hitched-up smile.

She had presumed he was a stockman taking part in the rodeo, and it wasn't till later he told her he was a panel-beater – see, look at the oil on me hands, it never comes off – holding up ten black-rimmed nails for her inspection. But by this time it was half a dozen beers later and she didn't give a toss what he did. When he offered to escort them both to their room, Crystal, high on this unexpected chivalry, whispered to Elise to take a run around the block. Stan propped Crystal against an outside wall, slipped his hand inside her jeans and cradled her wet crotch with his fingers.

– So he had this lopsided Elvis smile, you see – a flicker of borrowed sexiness stuck on him like a badge, she says out loud. But he had no idea that he had it. At the time I thought that was endearing, but now I'd prefer him to *know* what he has. The awareness would be more attractive. He isn't very clued up, your dad. Probably niver heard of Graceland in his life, as a matter of fact.

She sits up straight, embarrassed to catch herself speaking to an empty room, and looks out the window again. The shiny red bonnet gapes open like a jaw. She can't see him from here but he'll no doubt have his head stuck inside it, the radio in there with him, his big, cavernous nostrils investigating all those dirty pipes. Stan Saint, the man that she'd married.

She flicks her ash in the sink.

And so they'd fucked against the wall – or at least they'd tried to fuck, neither of them managing to get the angle quite right. He was much taller than her, and he had to either bend his knees or stick his bum out. At one point a bit of him got caught in her zip, and he'd yowled and yowled in pain. She'd put her hand over his mouth.

– You've got beautiful hair, he'd said afterwards as he tucked himself in, leaving her to disentangle herself from jeans that shackled her knees. – Pretty. The colour of five o'clock wheat.

That was what did it. So simple, so childlike, a snatch of poetry from the heart of this sun-roughened man with big, bungling hands. There was more to him than the others. He seemed to know how lucky he was to have done what he'd just done.

I'd never met a man who treated me with respect before, she'd tell Billy, if she could. You should've met me dad. Then you'd see how it all makes sense.

She wished he'd hang around long enough to listen. Surely he was old enough to hear these things by now.

———

look who's here

A red sandstone plain, dotted with broken circles of spinifex, spreads as far as the eye can see in all directions. Only a solitary, naked gum tree interrupts the arched horizon. Overhead, in an otherwise seamless, midday blue, a small cloud hangs breathlessly. A dark twin stalks it on the ground.

Across this sunbaked plain strides the lean-limbed spirit child, her cotton skirt dancing around her knees, her hair one thick, black tangle.

We nudge one another in the ribs.

Uh-oh. Look who's here again.

We stare at the spirit child and then turn to look at one another. Nervously, we take a fortifying breath.

She looks just the same as ever.

The wind lets out a yelp of delight and flurries across the plain to greet her, frothing up the dust in its wake. The spirit child laughs and hops about, dodging out of its way. Then she breaks into a run. The thuds of her feet travel along the ground and we feel them in our ribs. When she gets to the shadow of the cloud, she hurdles it as if it were solid.

Eventually, she looks up and sees our stand of snappy gums with their straggly, grey-green leaves waving a mirage of welcome in the distance. She gives a brief wave back.

Here we go again, we say. Prepare to love and lose once more.

We nestle back down in our hammocks and wait.

Within the stand of snappy gums, a shadow mosaic falls over her face. Used to the brightness of the sun, she cannot make us out very well.

What on earth are you doing? she asks, peering over the edge of a hammock.

What does it look like?

But it's the middle of the afternoon!

Ah, just the same as ever. Always watching, questioning. Already, our hearts begin to soften at the edges, despite ourselves. Something catches her eye on the ground and she picks it up.

This for me?

Without waiting for an answer, she grips the shiny pink ribbon between her front teeth, pulls her untamed hair back roughly and ties the ribbon in a bow, tugging the ends hard to make it stay. Then she sees a pair of drawstring pyjama bottoms hanging over a hammock rope.

These too?

She slips off her skirt and hops around in her off-white undies while she struggles to put the pyjama bottoms on.

I've just been in the town, she says, as if she's only been gone a few hours. She hops on one foot, struggling to find the leg hole. Want to hear the latest? There's a new bloke who thinks it's all our fault. He blames us for the mob sitting in the long grass drinking grog all day. He thinks we don't understand them any more. That we haven't kept up-to-date.

Slowly, we manoeuvre ourselves upright in our hammocks. We stretch sleep-deadened arms.

That's what he says, eh?

No, but I know that's what he's thinking.

We yawn and scratch our scalps, easing the mid-afternoon tension from our heads and necks.

What do you think? she asks.

We shrug. We've met him. He gave us the cold shoulder.

No, about *these*!

Hand on hip, she strikes a fashion-model pose, lips pouting to perfection. The pyjama bottoms are made of brushed cotton and decorated with a recurring motif of a sheep jumping over a fence.

They're an inch or two short in the leg.

She looks down at where her bony ankles stick out, disappointed. Then she goes back to surveying the hammocks with her long-lashed eyes.

So what *were* you doing sleeping in the middle of the afternoon? Are you ill?

We murmur something suitably non-committal, shaking out our blankets and folding them into squares.

It won't help, you know, she says, archly. Sleeping is just a way of escaping your emotions. You should get over them, otherwise they'll just get passed down to me.

Is that so? We eye the spirit child sceptically, tossing our blankets over a bough. Next you're going to recommend we have therapy.

Well, that's not such a bad –

Don't even think about it.

The spirit child shrugs, diplomatically. Well, anyway. Time is the only healer, as they say.

All time has ever done for us is give us crow's feet and shrivelled-up balls.

That shuts her up. The spirit child looks at the ground. She squats and draws a wobbly circle in the dirt with a finger.

This is exactly what's happening to the people in the town, she says.

What, wrinkled balls?

She shakes her head, concentrates on drawing eyes and nose and mouth within her circle.

Fear.

You think we're *frightened*?

She pretends to be lost in her drawing.

And something else as well.

Well, come on, spit it out. It can't exactly get any worse.

Farting, she blurts. She looks up, wincing.

We beg your pardon?

They've all got wind! It's gross!

She jumps to her feet, relieved to have said it at last.

It's cooking up a hideous stink!

She waves her arms up and down, as if in an effort to dissipate the stench.

It'll deplete the ozone layer, just you wait. Suffocate new-born babies. Put everyone off sex –

She spins around and around, caught up in her own maelstrom of foul-smelling catastrophes.

Is it some newfangled virus?

She looks at us as if we're stupid.

No! It's because they're frightened, don't you see? There's an aromatherapist in Darwin who says that if you keep your fear and anger inside it turns its talons inward and damages your internal organs, particularly messing up your digestion, which leads to flatulence and an incessant desire to burp.

We catch one another's eyes, unsure whether to laugh or cry.

Are they writing about it in the papers?

No. It's practically an epidemic but no one wants to admit they've got it. Every time there's a bad smell, they all pretend that someone else did it. They tell themselves the world's always been full of gas, but it's not true – it's never been this bad before.

We shake our heads.

Well, well. Who'd have thought it.

You have to do something quick. If I were a magician I would pull a rabbit out of a hat, or shake my fist and produce a handful of glitter that would make them go ooh and ahhh. Anything to make them sit up and take notice.

If only it were that easy.

Well, we've got to think of *something*. What are the others doing?

The ones in the cities have all but given up and moved out, we tell her. They're holding strong in Arnhem Land, but they don't have the problems to contend with that we do.

Well, you'd better think fast, or we'll all have to start wearing gas masks.

We sigh.

Don't you worry your pretty head about it, we say, knowing it will annoy her. You leave it all to us.

A few days later we stand in a circle with our backs to the wind, busy with the finishing touches. We shush and whisper excitedly. Occasionally a white feather escapes, fluttering between our legs.

The wind, hating to be left out of anything, paces up and down behind us, grumbling.

I can't think what's taking you so long.

It picks up speed, trying to rouse a bit of dust.

If you don't let me see something soon –

Shut up! We're trying to concentrate.

Half an hour later we're ready. We tighten our circle, pressing shoulder to shoulder, heads bowed. A pleased little smile hops from one pair of lips to another like a pollinating bee. There's even an off-kilter snigger. And then, on a count of three, we throw our arms into the air and release a flurry of black and white and apricot-pink feathers – up, up they go, hundreds of cockatoos, flying from the tips of our outstretched fingers. A magnificent, wondrous sight! They swoop into the blue with raucous cries, twist to the left, then turn with one mind like a shoal of fish, tilting as they round an invisible corner so that their breasts flash silver in the sun.

Wowee! gasps the wind. That's quite something.

They are natural show-offs, these birds, especially the sulphur-crested cockatoos, and there's nothing they love more than an audience. They ride the air like surfers cresting an invisible wave, the tips of their wings a-flutter. Just as the wave is about to break they dive straight through it, plummeting towards the earth. We stand with our mouths agog, shielding our faces, giggling to hide our mounting panic. Surely any second now there will be a terrible crash! But, of course, at the very last moment they sheer the pinnacles of the termite mounds and effortlessly soar into the blue again.

We babble with relief, clap in admiration of their dare-devil, flamboyant natures, their instinctive confidence.

Lovely manoeuvre! Very good!

The cockatoos draw a few more patterns in the sky – beautiful, graceful curves that make us want to weep – before they divide, black with black and white with white, some going one way, some another, and we fold our arms across our chests, swapping words of reassurance, not really wanting to let them out of our sight.

Oh, these beautiful cockatoos, we tell one another as they get smaller and smaller in the sky. They cannot fail to be noticed. They simply cannot fail.

Squatting up high in a snappy gum tree, the spirit child clasps her arms around her knees and watches as a small black feather zig-zags down through the air. When it draws level she grabs it.

Cockatoos, she scoffs, scrutinising the flimsy feather. As if *they're* going to do any good.

With a puff she sends it packing.

part II

a gap in her orderly heart

At the end of the first week there is another visit from Ann, the psych consultant. Cecily stands sentry beside her.

– The canula in the back of his hand is tissued, Ann says. Change it. And tidy up this drip.

Billy suspects that it is not Ann's place to give orders about such things, but Cecily doesn't argue. She unhooks the drip impassively, winds the plastic tubing under the crook of her elbow and over the bridge of her hand, the way his father used to store tow-rope. Meanwhile, Ann peels back the bandage on his hand and takes out the plastic tube.

The two women get on with their work in silence. You could call it a mark of their efficiency, but the air is too heavy for that. Once a new canula is in place, the doctor motions for Cecily to clear up.

– They won't press charges if we insist that it's a case of diminished responsibility, she is saying to Billy. If *I* insist, that is. Severe dehydration, fatigue, a hallucinatory state brought on by the osteomyelitis. I presume you'll go along with this?

Billy is busy noticing how dishevelled Cecily looks this morning. She is full of creases and fissures. One eye is livid with a tangle of red veins. And she has bed hair: the coarse black waves flattened completely on one corner of her large skull.

– Will you go along with this?

He looks at Ann in confusion, then gives a slight nod of his head. She gives him a brisk nod back, decisive, as if to show him how it's done, then moves on, not a hair of her tight little bun out of place, not a gap in her orderly heart.

He turns his attention back to Cecily.

– So, what'll it be, Cecily says, evidently embarrassed that Billy is staring at her red eye and wanting to distract him. The lunch boy needs to know. Macaroni cheese and carrots, or lamb stew and mashed potato.

She gathers up the discarded piece of bandage and adds it to the blood-stained tube in the kidney tray.

– Ey? Ent you hungry or what?

Billy shrugs. It's a long time since he's paid any attention to the calls of his stomach. Turning round, Cecily knocks the loop of tubing from its hook on the metal drip frame. It falls to the floor and she has to wind it up again.

– Sup to you. You'll just have to stay hooked up to this else.

All this time she never looks at him directly – just lets her gaze wash over his face as it travels from one side of the bed to the other. He relishes this lack of scrutiny – even feels a stab of love towards her for it. He feels ashamed now of having stared at her infected eye.

– Oi, are you listenin to me or what?

– What?

– Don't eat, and you'll be on your back for another week. Start eating now, we'll hev you walking by the weekend.

He pulls his lips down at the corners. – Don't make any difference.

– Home in six weeks, no worries.

Billy gives a derisive snort, which Cecily understands instantly. She as good as knew it already. What is harder to tell is whether or not he cares that he has nowhere to go. Most of them do, under all the bravado. The tougher the exterior, the greater the subterranean pool of need, as a rule. This one is not as tough as some, but still she has glimpsed it – that remnant of the boy he used to be. After she's returned the drip apparatus to its moorings she takes the lift down to the kitchens, helps herself to a white ceramic bowl from a stack and loads it up from the chip pan, splashes of grease falling onto the rim and hardening like dripped wax. She adds salt and tomato sauce sachets and brings it back up. She tucks her graph-patterned dress in around her as she perches on the edge of the bed.

If he's interested, he doesn't show it. With great deliberation, Cecily feeds the chips one by one between her own full brown lips. She's over-done the salt, but she won't let it stop her. Unlike most of the doctors and nurses here, she relishes this sort of patient: they're her favourites, the bums. She bites down on a chip, the soggy insides still hot enough to scald, the salt adding to the sting. She knows she can get a rise out of him. She licks the grease off her fingertips. In her peripheral vision she can tell he's watching. At one point she gets up and draws the curtains across to stop the blatant goggling of the other men in the ward.

Eventually she spots a flicker at the corner of his mouth. Oh, she can hardly wait to see it. When it comes, it is even better than she'd expected. A beautiful, lopsided cracking: the smile of her patient, Mr William Saint.

*   *   *

The night they brought him in they bound his wrists to the arms of a wheelchair with lengths of crepe bandage. Some of this he remembers, some he hears about later from Cecily. They passed a little huddle of white-coated doctors in the corridor, stethoscopes around their necks, rows of blue pen lids hitched to their breast pockets. One of these doctors turned and fell automatically into the wake of Billy's entourage; another veered off with the American tourist and his howling wife. The doctors raised their palms in silent acknowledgement at the breaking up of the group.

They hauled him onto a bed and two male nurses quickly snapped the metal sides up, while the others began examining him, feeling for his pulse, brusquely wiping away the worst of the blood on his face with a wad of damp cotton wool so that they could find the source of it. When he tried to get up, the nurses pressed him back, one gently holding his shoulders, the other his shins. Only Billy seemed to be aware of the absurdity of this. Here he was, Billy Saint, never hit a man before in his life and now look at him, causing a scare in the hard old town of Alice Springs. I mean, the *Alice*! He tried to hold up an arm, show them how little strength there was left in it, but they pushed him back. It was like the paralysis that comes in sleep. He just had time to think how his mother would've laughed at the sight when he felt a sharp stab in his thigh and moments later the darkness caved in.

For the next twenty-four hours he felt like a fish at the bottom of the ocean, trying to swim to the surface, towards the light, but lacking the strength in his tail to propel himself. At one point he was visited by a doctor with a sun-tanned face and a quiff of yellowy-white hair swept back from his face like a cockatoo, two younger lads in attendance. You've been in theatre, this doctor said. The voice was muffled by the thickness of water. Billy could detect a musky, sweet aftershave on his freshly scrubbed skin. We've cut out the dead tissue in your wounds and drained them, the doctor said. There has been considerable muscle damage, and the infection has spread to the bone on both sides. He paused, then embarked on a stream of questions, his yellow crest bobbing up and down as he talked. Where was Billy from? How long had he been out bush? How long ago were the wounds inflicted? Why on earth had he taken so long to get treatment?

Billy had no idea how to formulate answers. Did he want them to contact anyone – a family member, a friend? Billy shook his head: that much at least he could do. He noticed the two younger lads catching one another's eye, a shared moment. Ah, they had his number in a flash.

Unlovable, uncommunicative, taking up precious bed space. They'd seen it all before. One after the other they checked the readings on the charts at the foot of his bed in a perfunctory way, feigning an air of authority. Billy turned his face before they could turn from him first, sank back down to the bottom of his nameless sea.

The next time he woke, a slab of sunlight had fallen across his face. He saw a line of hospital beds, glinting metal frames, white sheets stretched taut. A sense of efficiency and activity up and down the ward. He recognised the shush of the air-conditioner that had punctuated his sleep. On a table by his bed was a glass of water with bubbles suspended in it, as if it had been there for days. An image of himself as a fish flashed through his mind.

– Mr Saint?

The voice was clear, youthful. A boy who didn't look more than twenty was peering down at him, clipboard clasped to his chest. It was one of the lads that had come round earlier with the doctor. Billy could see the backs of the other two behind him, further down the ward. They were doing their rounds again. Twenty-four hours must have passed.

– I hope you don't mind, mate. I don't mean to stick my beak in.

The boy had a fresh, fine-boned face with two bright spots of pink daubed on his cheeks. He stared straight at Billy with wide, blue eyes. Eyes in which you could see right down to the bottom.

– I'm James, one of the junior docs. I was here when they brought you in the first night, don't spose you remember?

Billy said nothing. His head felt groggy.

– That's alright, mate. They gave you a hefty dose of sedative to quieten you down. Reckon the heat was playing tricks on you.

The young doctor allowed himself a small grin before glancing anxiously over at his colleagues, checking on their progress. Billy realised his throat was dry. He reached for a slug of water.

– It was only when we got your trousers off that we saw the state of your thighs, and your –

He balked at deciding on a word for this part of Billy's anatomy.

– It looks like someone slit it open like a hot dog, mate!

The spots of pink in his cheeks intensified. Billy stared back, daring him to keep the contact up.

– I've never seen anything like it.

He gave another small smile, still meeting Billy's blazing gaze full on.

– Later on, in a moment of consciousness, you called out to me as I was passing. You gripped hold of my hand.

Billy could hardly believe the boy's nerve. No one had looked him in the eye like this for years. Not even Harri, his shift boss down the mine, had been able to hold Billy's gaze for more than a couple of seconds. The boy was blushing frantically, but he wouldn't let go.

Billy rolled his head away.

– No amorous intentions, doc, swear to God.

The boy laughed loudly, relieved to have a vent for his tension. Out of the corner of his eye, Billy saw the colour spread down his throat.

– Actually, mate, you asked me to help you. I could tell from your eyes that you were lucid. You were very clear about what you wanted. Any of this ring a bell?

Billy hesitated, then let out a dry cough.

– Jesus, doc. You don't want ter take the ramblings of some doped-up bloke too seriously. You should know better than that.

– You might have been on the delirious side but you were speaking from the heart. I know it. You told me the name of a girl you wanted me to help you find. Look, I wrote it down.

He fumbled in the breast pocket of his white coat.

– I promised I'd help you find her. I gave you my word.

He unfolded a scrap of paper.

– Maisie, said the young doctor, his face lighting up. That was it. Maisie.

Billy averted his eyes. – Listen, Mr –

He reached again for his glass.

– My name's James.

– Listen. I don't know what planet I was on last night, but it's a load of bull, whatever I said. Forget it.

He was no longer thirsty, but he lifted the glass and drank.

The young man folded the paper and returned it to his pocket. – You talked about redemption. You made a lot of sense, actually. I'm not the religious sort, but –

Billy looked up sharply, the glass knocking against the edge of the table. A splash of water hit the floor.

– What the fuck would you know about redemption, doctor?

He had expected the boy to stiffen, but he didn't. He didn't even back off. He stood there so brightly, his back so upright, that Billy even felt a little ashamed.

– Not much, Mr Saint.

For a while they stared at one another without blinking.

At last, the junior doctor bowed his head. At least he knew to let Billy win out in the end. He knew better than to touch him, too. Instead, he gave the bed a single, considered pat before moving on.

He sleeps so much during the day that he spends half the night awake, listening to the noises of the ward. There are two dozen patients in here, each one with their own repertoire of nasal percussion: snorts and grunts, strange, owl-like hoots and high-pitched whistles, the occasional sneeze. All night there is something going on – bed frames rattling, the squeak of wheels as the nurse brings her trolley round with its blood-pressure testing equipment, sometimes pockets of whispering as two nurses pass one another in the dimness.

Tonight he hears the tap of plastic soles on the lino floor – three or four pairs at once – and curtains being pulled roughly along their rails at the far end of the ward. Urgent, low voices, not bothering to keep to a whisper. A single, alarmed shout.

– *Sister!*

There's a scurry of footsteps, then silence. A deep, rich silence that unleashes in him an unexpected appetite, as if he has been unwittingly harbouring a yearning for silence of this quality for years. While it lasts, his body sinks into the hard mattress beneath him, as if finally discovering a capacity for absolute rest. Of course, over the last few weeks – was it weeks? – he had barely uttered a word, opening his mouth only to accept a swill of Coke or a soft, bitter piece of fruit, offered to him with fingers as if he were a baby. But there had been the rumble of the engine, the creaks and groans of the vehicle as it rocked and swayed over rough ground. The murmur of strange, unfathomable voices. And then there had been the clamour of pain.

For a long time, he realises, he hasn't dared go near silence. These years spent hiding underground have been a sentence. He always accepted his own guilt; he hadn't needed to be told. No punishment is greater than the one you inflict on yourself. He sees this now; how a guilty man denies himself the thing that he loves most.

Perhaps, now, he can afford to acquit himself, to let the silence back in.

The tap of feet starts up again, accompanied this time by the squeaking of wheels. Emerging from the gloom at the far end of the ward are four figures, nuns on their way to vespers with pale foreheads dipped demurely towards the floor. They are wheeling a bed between them. The tap of their plastic shoes gets louder, all the feet out of sync: *pat, pat-pat, pat-pat-pat*. As they pass his bed, the light from the street lamps illuminates a sheet snagged high over the peak of a nose.

Ha!

He has to stop himself from laughing out loud. Of course! He should have recognised it. That special absence of sound that accompanies a death, even out in the bush – the air sucking in, gulping noise, suspending time.

He'll know it next time, that's for sure.

---

early man versus kylie minogue

On weekdays in the dry Billy takes the school bus into town, along with the kids from the stations and the communities out towards the Great Sandy Desert. He's been driving since he was ten, and he doesn't see why he can't take the ute when Stan doesn't need it – it's not as if he hasn't got enough cars to spare – but Stan gets huffy and runs his hands through his hair and says, wait another year, why not. Sometimes when Stan's on a trip, Crystal slips him the keys to the old Ford Fairlaine with a wink and a finger on her lips. Stevo lets him borrow his Triple J tapes: June 7th, March 19th, random dates when Stevo's cousin Bylinda in Perth remembered to stick a tape in her radio-cassette player and press record. Billy listens to the same songs from one day three months ago over and over, perched in the low leather seat with the windows wound down and the hot air rushing in.

Sometimes he parks on the corner where the hull of the road train cabin lies on its side with its windows punched out, wires hanging like entrails out the back, the International lettering still advertising itself to the birds. It was Jon-Jon's big brother Ted Frost from Watery River who crashed it, a hundred head of cattle on board, two trailers with four decks each, twenty-five on each deck. He took the bend too fast and hit a corrugation that sent him into a zig-zag, and the rear trailer bucked and twisted like a bull with its front legs in a noose, rocking the whole contraption out of balance. Not as if it was his first truck drive, either – he'd been up and down that road a hundred times. They say he knocked the front wind-screen out with his jack and hoisted himself clear without a scratch, but the two-way was broken and no one passed for four or five hours and by the time they did he was sitting on the side of the road singing to himself in an effort to drown out the bellows of the dying cows. They'd had to shoot most of them in the head because their legs had broken where they were sticking through the bars before it rolled.

In the wet when the river is high he doesn't go to school but listens through the crackles and whines to the School of the Air around the kitchen table with Jon-Jon, fingers on the console between them. Usually it takes so long for Jon-Jon to get his stutter around the answers that the teacher gives up on them and goes somewhere else instead.

– How dja calculate the length of the longer side? Daphne?

– Something to do with Pythagoras, Miss? Over.

– Yeh, but what. Jon?

The right light's on, but he's only got as far as making an O with his mouth.

– Come on, you guys! Henry?

Crystal, unable to bear the agony, gets out a packet of white bread mix, empties it into a bowl, makes a depression in the middle and sloshes in water from the kettle.

– Every other one will do, jiss wait for the next one, Billy, she says.

She throws the lump of dough onto a board with a thump and starts kneading it. After a while she speeds up, rushing it, and soon after that she loses heart and there she is with a lump of white dough sitting like a bloodless, aborted creature on the wooden board and no urge to do anything with it.

– Give it here, Mum.

Billy clears away the books and the console and tears the lump of dough in two, strands stretching like elastic. Soon the two boys are too deep in dough to pay any more attention to the radio. They make round rolls in irregular sizes with knobs on top and put them on a baking tray, and then they start sculpting armies, Jon-Jon's facing Billy's over a floury no-man's-land. Nobody mentions the fact that Billy's soldiers have tails and long, pointed ears. Crystal lights up and rests her feet on the next chair and swings the smoking arm back and forth and lets the up-and-down voice of the School of the Air teacher rock her, even amuse her with an occasional boom-boom joke. The oven's on and belting out heat but the tray with the uncooked rolls sits forgotten on the draining board. By the time

Stan comes in and washes the oil off his hands and shakes them over the floor, they're all three of them lulled into a smoky stupor and Billy catches the dubious look on his face as he takes it all in, the little dough figures on the table, their bottom halves pressed firmly down but their tops drooping over, the open exercise books collecting a line of flour in their gutters.

Crystal snaps at him before he has a chance to make a comment.

– Can't you do that over the sink. Jesus. You're worse than a bloody dog.

She jumps up and gets to work at wiping the splashes away as if she's been slaving at making the kitchen spick and span all morning, while Billy catches Jon-Jon's eye and they gather up their dough armies and roll them back into a ball.

Sometimes, during the school months, Billy brings home projects to show her. He waits till they've had their tea and for Stan to go back outside. They do the dishes, her washing, him drying. Then he takes a large cellophane-covered scrapbook out of his school bag and places it on the table, shyly.

– What's this?

– My project on Early Man.

He opens it at the drawing of the migratory movements across the continents, the red lines emanating from Africa, the green ones crisscrossing Australasia. Crystal looks from the rough, green pages of his scrapbook to his freckled face and back again.

For the first time, this curious bipedal ape known as homo sapiens began to cultivate the land, she reads.

She tells him she likes the way he's drawn lines with a pencil and ruler. His handwriting is very neat, she says. The backward sloping letters are packed in right to the end of each line.

– It's much better writin than either me or your dad does. Whose bloody idea was it to do it on Early Man, though?

Billy wraps his feet around the legs of the chair.

– Mine, he whispers.

– No one told you?

– No. You c'n do them on whatever ya want.

– What're all the others doin?

He bends over the scrapbook, peeling off a little red sticker marking an area in southern France and repositioning it slightly to the left. The end of one nostril glistens where he needs to wipe it.

– Different stuff. Peter Matera and the West Coast Eagles, mainly.

Billy gets out a fluffy black pencil case from his bag. He unzips it and rummages around until he finds a red crayon. The pencil case exhales the friendly mustiness of pencil sharpenings and dried ink cartridges. On the map are four arrows pointing out from beneath the words *Homo Erectus*, and he uses the crayon to thicken them. One arrow leads to *Caucasians*, one to *Asians*, one to *Africans*, and one to *Aborigines*. He works backwards and forwards with the crayon, spoiling the fine lines. Crystal watches in silence, allowing her tired eyes to slip in and out of focus. Billy gets out a pencil and ruler and draws another line joining *Africa* to a sentence floating at the bottom of the page: *But remember that man was not just a predator, he was also prey!* Lining up the ruler, he creates an additional line linking *Aborigines* to a sentence running down the side of the page: *Ninety-nine per cent of all the species which have lived on Earth since the world began are now extinct!!* After a moment's hesitation, he adds another exclamation mark.

Crystal forces her eyes to snap to.

– What about the girls?

– What about em?

– What are they doin their projects on? I don't imagine they're doin the Eagles as well. And don't tell me they're doin Early Man.

Billy shrugs. He doesn't look up. – Telly stuff. Kylie Minogue.

– Hmm. Early Man versus Kylie Minogue. I don't know who I'd choose.

He turns the page, protectively. He doesn't want her looking at his project if she doesn't understand it. On the next page there's a picture of a big red, cut from the *Sunday Times* magazine, a joey in its pouch, nose turned sideways. He is going to link it in to the evolution story, though he's not sure how yet – something to do with Australia being the only land mass with kangaroos on, how that means they must've evolved after it separated from South America and Antarctica. This is one of his favourite kangaroo pictures. The caption tells you how they look at you from the side because their eyes see two different pictures at once.

He would have liked to have explained this to her, but she's reaching to the sink to stick her cigarette butt under the tap. It gives a little sizzle and she opens the cupboard door underneath and pitches it into the bin. Billy doesn't want her to see the big red anymore, either. He has a sense of having shown too much already. He flips the scrapbook shut, piles the fluffy pencil case and the ruler and the loose red crayon on top and presses the bundle to his chest, trying not to let any of it drop before he gets to the door.

Crystal looks up. There is a moment in which it is all there for her to see: the tears just beginning to prickle, a dimpling of the chin. She flounders around for something to say, quickly, a comment about what she has just seen – what was it – a photograph of some animal or other, a kangaroo most likely, it always is – but by the time she's collected her thoughts it's too late, he's turned his charged-up little face away and is heading off to his room.

Somehow she always lets this happen. Him going one way, her going another. Him to his stones, and her left here, nothing but ten Horizon 50s left and the telly. The long, slow hours til nine o'clock, when there'll be the familiar scrape of Stan taking off his Blundstones on the step. Do you want a cuppa tea or somethin stronger, he'll say – always the same line. She could set her watch by it. Might as well; it already sets the tempo of her heart.

Oh, keep it coming, Stan, she thinks. Predictability is what you do best.

Billy shuts his bedroom door, a quiet determination settling over him as he swallows the catch in his throat. He lowers the pile of pencils and scrapbook on the bed. Only the red crayon escapes. Then he feels in his pockets. Already he's forgotten what he has in there exactly.

They make a satisfying clunk as he puts them on the shelf, adding them to the collection. Eennie, meanie, minie, mo. They are small and grey, these unsnappable, perfect pieces of the earth. They fit snugly in his hand. Some of them are cut through with streaks of white like threads of cotton. Tomorrow after school he'll take them to Stevo's and they'll look them up in *The Geology of the Kimberley* and decide when each one was created and where it came from. He likes going over to Stevo's, the two of them sitting quietly together until Stevo looks at his watch and says he's got to report for duty at the Spini.

But for now he wants the stones to himself. He wants to fully admire them, the patterns made by the white strands that look like they're spelling a message – a letter A in that one, almost a K in another.

– They're nice, Stevo had said, the first time Billy took some round. I like stones too. Nice and still. They don't talk to ya.

Sitting on a car tyre in the galvanised iron shed that serves as his house, Stevo had laid the stones out on the concrete floor.

– Compared to stones, we're not really very important, are we? Billy had ventured. I mean, we don't last very long.

The doleful brown eyes had blinked at Billy solemnly.

– They were always part of the plan, weren't they? Billy went on. They were here from the beginning, and they'll be here right to the end. Not like us. They've got more right to be here than we have, if you think about it.

Stevo had sat back and taken a long, slow draft of his beer. Curled up in a dog basket, Yakka moaned in her sleep.

– I reckon you might be onto something there, mate, collecting them stones, said Stevo at last.

Crystal never mentions the stones, even though she comes in his room every couple of weeks and runs a damp cloth over the surfaces. She picks them up in a noisy clump, runs the cloth underneath, and dumps them back down again, as if they had no life in them at all. Afterwards he has to return them to their proper places.

Stevo bought a tumbling machine and some of Billy's stones have been smoothed and polished in it. Between them, they've got stones from all around Australia – agates from Queensland and the red Centre, Zebra rock from Kununurra with perfect, even stripes. The tumbler vibrates like a washing machine in its final phase. First they throw in a handful of grit and a beaker of water, and the machine bangs and clatters so loudly that Yakka runs out on to the forecourt, barking back at them.

– Go fetch her, will ya? Stevo had said. I don't want her runnin away with those trigger-happy baastids on the loose.

Billy had found her cowering behind the petrol pumps. He'd dragged her back by the collar, her head hunkered down, reluctant claws scraping and skittering on the concrete. Stevo nodded toward the crates of Coke stacked up in a corner.

– Ta, mate. Go on, help yerself. Enough to last through the wet.

They had had to shout to be heard above the din of the tumbling machine. Stevo had read to him from *The Geology of the Kimberley*. Billy listened to descriptions of the ancient pre-Cambrian sandstones and shales of the central Hann Plateau, with their soaring escarpments and plunging gorges; the Archeozoic quartzites and schists of the Carr Boyd ranges; the cracking clay plains; the exposed granites between Fitzroy Crossing and Halls Creek; the Jurassic sandstone that lay beneath Cockatoo Sands. He heard about the different vegetation that grows on each: sorghum grasses, wattles, acacias. He heard about how the spacing of vegetation works, about how some seeds lie dormant on the ground until they're broken open by fire. Stevo left the tumbling machine on day and night and by the end of three weeks, when Yakka was a quivering wreck and no longer touching her food, he invited Billy over again and opened the tumbler up.

– Plunge yer hand in, Billy, go on.

The stones were still warm and gave off a faint dusting of powder. Billy stirred his hand around in the clutch of them, pulled one out, held it against his cheek. It was smooth and warm as a newly laid egg.

Since then Billy has always kept one in his pocket. He never goes anywhere without one to wrap his fingers around, borrowing the stone's solidity, its quiet confidence, its absolute right to exist.

Zebra rock is a banded quartzose rock from the Lower Cambrian age found near Argyle Station, Billy reads out loud from *The Geology of the Kimberley*, which Stevo lets him take home. He reads it in a grown-up voice, testing out the words, the sound of them coming from his mouth.

the coffee shop pings

The door of the coffee shop pings and Estha looks up, frowns in confusion when she sees that no one's come in, then goes back to emptying the dishwasher of its steaming mugs and plates.

We saunter up to the counter and peer through the angled Perspex windows. There are rows of deep-fried chiko rolls, hot chooks and dingo pups, grease spots steadily seeping through the grease-proof paper wrappings. Blowing onto our necks, the air-conditioning competes with the billowing steam from the dishwasher, and the smells of warm grease, over-brewed coffee and cigarette smoke churn amicably around the room.

G'day, Estha. How's business?

Estha draws herself upright and looks round, wipes the back of her hand across her nose, over the tiny black hole on the crease of one nostril where she used to wear a stud, and then bends over again, sticking her pert backside in our faces.

Just as well we know the answer already. Business is terrible, and has been since the cappo machine broke down last year, when Estha – nineteen years old, always dressed in runners and training daks beneath her apron, part full-blood, part Stevo from the servo (a fact which everyone suspects but Stevo has never acknowledged out loud) – told her customers that if the coffee tasted tinny to let her know, she'd make youse another.

Of course they told her the coffee tasted tinny for days, weeks, months after that – I won't know till I get to the bottom, Estha, jiss one more sip and I'll tell ya, darlin, *aggh*, yeh right, it tastes like it came out the back end of a camel – then free refills all round. The ritual went on till it bored everyone to tears – none more than us. But the free refills have been part of the deal ever since, and profits have steadily declined.

A barking starts up across the road. Estha dumps the mugs she had hooped over her fingers and rushes to the window. Yakka is running back and forth across the servo forecourt, blocking the path of a triple-rigged road train with sixty-odd wheels that's trying to pull in.

– Idiot, mutters Estha, either to the dog or the driver or perhaps Stevo himself, who's failed as yet to come out and settle the commotion.

She turns her back and almost immediately the door pings behind her.

– Mornin, Estha.

Estha grunts a greeting and gets back to emptying the dishwasher. Rossco and Gerry take their usual seats by the window, spreading the *Kimberley Echo* out between them. They don't bother to place an order: she knows what they want, and she'll make it when it suits her. Rossco, his dense red beard encroaching from all sides like an uncontrollable creeper swamping the front of a house, seems unbothered by the fact that the paper's upside down from where he's sitting; his eyes move from side to side anyway behind their metal-rimmed glasses. Estha lays out two cups and saucers on the benchtop, two teaspoons, the chocolate shaker. Gerry, his densely tattooed neck jammed between squat, muscled body and squared-off buzzcut, leans forward and occasionally reads a few halting lines out loud.

– Aw, Christ fucken almighty, he says. I don't fucken believe it.

Rossco pushes his glasses up his nose.

– Whatizzit, Gerry?

– It's that bloody wowser, the one who's always tryin to tell everyone what to do.

– Not Coldiver? The one who tried to fix us a job last year?

– That's the one. He's only gone and bought up the bloody roadhouse.

– You gotta be joking, Gerry.

– Listen ter this. *When concluding the sale last week, Sydney Coldiver told our reporter:* 'This town needs a kick up the arse and I intend to provide the boot.'

– Well, we don't need to take no notice of him, Gerry.

– That's right, Rossco, we don't.

Looking up, Estha notices their rounded shoulders shifting uncomfortably, a new uneasiness in the air. They'll be in here for most of the morning now, three cappos each – that's six altogether, all for the price of two. Absent-mindedly, she tugs too hard on a packet of coffee and it erupts, fine brown grains spraying over her damp hands.

---

a nice fat bundle

Oi, *Billy*!

The wind grips the trunk of a tall, stately gum tree just beyond the boundary of the yard and shakes it violently. There's a frenzied jostling of leaves. One or two twigs break off.

Oi, Billy, *wake up*!

We march over to the base of the tree.

Ssshhhh! Stop that racket, will you? He's asleep!

The wind stares at us in disbelief.

I know he's asleep! That's the point.

We don't want him woken up.

Why not? You're always trying to spoil my fun.

Oh, stop whingeing. And stop following us everywhere. You'll only mess things up.

The wind huffs in exasperation but we pay it no attention and after a while it gives up and slouches away. We clamber over the window sill and take our places around the edge of the bed. Everything's a shambles in here: the poster is still hanging half off the wall and there's a pile of dirty clothes on the floor, the jeans yanked inside out. *The Geology of the Kimberley* lies on top of *The Universe* on the floor by the bed. His face is pressed into the pillow so that we can't see much more than his ears and the golden hair spiralling out from the crown.

Billy, we've been thinking. Perhaps you should just come out with it. Tomorrow morning, first thing. Shake them from their sluggishness and ask: can I have it now please, the portion that's allotted to me. It should have my name on it. Ah, there it is, a nice fat bundle of love tied up with string, that's the one. Thank you very much indeed.

He breathes shallowly, like a baby, a fist curled up by his cheek.

We heard of a family recently where it took an asthma attack and a couple of broken legs before the parents kicked in with the hugs and kisses. We don't want you to have to go to that extreme.

Billy grinds his pelvis into the mattress.

Go on, Billy Can, why don't you give it a try? You'd be surprised how people come up with the goods when you make a straightforward request. Sometimes all it takes is to ask. We'll be right behind you.

Without warning, Billy snatches the pillow out from beneath him and slams it over his head.

We glance at one another.

Was that a no?

The pillow rises and falls with his querulous breath.

Well, *be* like that, then. We're only trying to help. Go and listen to Mrs Tucker instead. She'll stuff you full of facts. She'll give you mathematical formulas for calculating the circumferences of circles. She'll give you chemical equations for the air. She drum into you grammatical rules that forbid you to split infinitives or omit the definite article. She'll tell you Captain Cook discovered Australia in 1770. She'll give you all this Billy, all this and more besides, but she won't tell you anything that'll even remotely help.

---

every crushed beer can

Outside the community fence, the sun deals out a morning shadow to every crushed beer can and broken bottle, every ripped cardboard carton, every stem of tough grass. Although he doesn't look at his feet, Jimmi Rangi somehow dodges the debris. He clutches the seat of a wooden chair to his chest.

He hasn't changed since we saw him the other night: he's still dressed in the same flared brown trousers and sun-bleached singlet. The trousers look as if they were part of somebody's business suit once, a 1970s cut: tight around his thighs, flapping at the shin. According to the spirit child this bell-bottomed style is enjoying a renaissance in Sydney and Melbourne these days, and our Jimmi wouldn't look so out of place in the trendy bars and restaurants of Paddington Street. By all accounts he wears the style well, with that slightly concave stomach and long, thin legs.

He looks up and sniffs the air. It's heating up nicely already. He places the chair down, firmly, right in the middle of the grass and sits down.

Morning! we call out, but he either doesn't hear, or chooses not to.

It has a woven string seat, this chair, bits of which are coming unravelled, and one leg is a fraction shorter than the others. He tips back onto the shorter leg, closes his eyes and angles his face in such a way as to catch the sun where it's just bristling over the tops of the red river gums down by the water's edge. As it rises, it laps his forehead, then his eyes, then his nose, finally lighting up the silver stubble on his chin. Before long a blistering, red orb has imprinted itself on the insides of his eyelids.

What on earth is he up to? asks the wind.

We are sitting in a row along the top of the community fence, our heels wedged into the chickenwire.

No bloody idea.

Doesn't he have anything better to do? Doesn't he have a job? A family to look after?

We say nothing, tangle our fingers in the wire.

I thought you were supposed to know everything around here, the wind mutters, spitefully.

For the entire morning, the only part of Jimmi Rangi that moves is his face, following the progress of the sun: his chin tilting further and further up until his neck is stretched horizontal and he is receiving the full pelt of the overhead rays. Soon we are leaning our elbows on our knees, too tired to sit upright. Round about midday there is a moment of excitement – relatively speaking – when for a while it looks as if the chair will tip over backwards. But to the wind's bitter disappointment, Jimmi keeps his balance, and after midday he gets up, picks up the chair and turns it round to face west. As the afternoon wears on, he follows the sun as it sinks – oh, so slowly, so achingly slowly – behind the town, eventually snuffing itself out behind Deacon DIY Supplies and the roof of the bottleshop. At which point he picks up his chair and carries it back inside the community gates.

Thank heavens that's over! wails the wind in an agony of restlessness. Can we go home now? I can't believe we waited all that time and absolutely *nothing* happened.

One by one we drop down to the ground, bending over and clutching our ankles so that others can step on our backs.

No one said you had to stay and watch, we mumble as we wander back down the street. You could've gone and entertained yourself elsewhere, just for once.

The wind retreats into a sulk. On either side of us, the streets fan out, lined with houses and scruffy front yards. A dog growls as we pass. A tyre on a rope dangles from a tree. From inside we hear calls to come in for tea.

---

beneath the belly

Beneath the belly of the Humber Snipe, Stan registers the sound as he might register the call of a bird: a sharp snap of a cry, far-away, familiar, but nothing to do with him. He has his finger up a rusted exhaust pipe, feeling around in its congested interior for what might be causing a blockage, a lump of dried mud, perhaps, or a loose bolt just out of reach.

– *Stan*!

This time he knows it's for him. With a sigh, he bends his knees as much as he's able and pushes his body backwards, caterpillar-style, inching himself into the light.

– What is it?

Crystal is standing in the doorway peeling the wrapper off a fresh pack of Horizon 50s.

– That was Stevo on the phone. He's got something for ya.

– What sort?

– A beaut, he reckons. Says you should pick 'er up from Derby before lunch.

– Before lunch?

He looks back at the Humber Snipe, the beautiful red paintwork glistening like some rare and poisonous beetle. He's only got the exhaust to fix and then he's done, a lovely stealthy machine to line up with the others.

– Can't it wait till tomorra? I'm right in the middle of things.

– 'E said it'd 'ave gone by then. Anyway, you should ring im straight back, 'e says.

Stan sighs. He doesn't want to leave this cool, dark space beneath the car. Of all the spaces in the world he can think of nowhere better. It is rich with all the smells he loves most – the complicated odour of an engine that has been heated and cooled more times than you've eaten roast chook, of chrome polish on the fenders, of the sweet, gluey perfume of petrol.

It doesn't matter too much what the car is, although he has his soft spots. There's the baby-blue Kingswood he found in Darwin last year, a delicate, difficult car that didn't look like it would survive longer than a week in the bush, yet here it is, safely stowed beneath the corrugated iron lean-to, its round headlights shining out at him girlishly. Then there's the metallic green Cadillac with chrome edging and soft vinyl top, in almost mint condition bar the engine. When he first found the Cadillac its suspension was busted, and the resultant lopsided gait had endeared him to it as if to a wounded bird. He has a fondness for panel vans too, robust old friends that they are, redolent with a family's history – stains on the carpet, dog hairs everywhere. He's kept one of those, and also a classic station wagon the colour of thick cream, a beige tarp pinned across the back. You'd be pushed to find a more handsome wagon than that.

– Whatcha waiting for, Stan?

– Jiss give me half an hour, then I'll call im.

He hears the fly door slam with more force than if it had dropped back of its own accord, raises an eyebrow briefly, then thinks no more about it. Back in the world of the Snipe's underbelly he lies still, waiting for his eyes to get reaccustomed to the dimness. The sense of anticipation is just as great as, if not greater than, a roomful of people at the opera before the curtain goes up – or so he likes to think, never having been to the opera personally. As soon as he can make out what's what, he unscrews an oily nut and tucks it into the pocket of his cheek for safe-keeping, then pulls a cloth from up the sleeve of his overalls and cleans the grooves on the bolt. Something's wrong, although he can't think what it is. A nagging anxiety tugging at his stomach. He delves into his pockets for an Extra Strong Mint, but changes his mind once he's found them – they always make him sneeze and it's a job doing that beneath a car. Ah, yes! Blindly, he flails into the daylight, hits the wooden edge of the Roberts radio and drags it under there with him. It's so old the tuning knob has come off, but he has a trick of twiddling the stick with his teeth, and after the usual whines and crackles and spits there comes the cosy up-and-down drawl that he longs for, the soothing male voices that make up the cornerstone to his world.

– *So now they break for tea, and they're coming off with their heads down, looking a little pensive . . .*

– *Didja know, Gary, whilst we're on the subject of tea, that they eat bananas and jellybabies during these breaks. Strange but true. I was told by a veteran tea lady of the Gabba grounds.*

– *I didn't know that, Reg, no. Whatever it takes to get them taking a few more wickets by stumps today, eh?*

But still the unease is tugging. No doubt it's the usual thing. She has a way of making him feel ashamed of his passion for cars, just as his parents used to do. Growing up on the farm in the south of WA, he had spent weekends and summer evenings in the old car graveyard. This is where he was first seduced. Abandoned vehicles with their doors ripped off, stuffing oozing like fungi from the seats, engines scabbing over with rust. He crawled over and under every inch of them until he knew them better than he knew his own body. These cars taught him about axles and stick shifts and what engines needed to run. They had a haunting beauty; shambolic, ruined, yet gravely persisting in their stationary afterlife. In summer, when hot, dirty winds blew through the farm, and the men would cuss it for gritting their cold lamb sandwiches, and his mother would cuss it for soiling the damp clothes on the line, Stan was happy as a dog with two tails. He loved that wind, loved the way it rattled the trunks and made the hinges sing so that it was as if the cars were chattering, and beyond the cars, in the paddocks, the wheat was brought to surging, carousing life. Even the trees would sing, if you listened – each tree with its own silvery voice, as if it were a shell on a beach. Sometimes, when he passed a whole stand of trees, the racket could be deafening, cacophonous – a full-tilt orchestra of crashing branches – and he'd stand there, riveted, awed, open-mouthed, unable to speak.

His parents had owned a Humber Snipe like this in the 1960s. They didn't use it to go anywhere, just to drive in grand, proud circles around Geraldton, making sure everyone got a peek, his mother waving affectedly, like the queen. They christened it the Living Room. He can see them now: all five kids sitting on the back seat trying not to let their thighs touch.

– Staaan!

The image withers like a popped balloon. Stan sighs. Not much hope of getting any peace this morning. He hauls himself out into the glaring light, clutching the radio to his chest. The second he emerges, something sloppy and warm lands with a splat on his forehead. Out of the corner of his eye he catches sight of a black cockatoo tipping to the side and veering round the house.

– *STAN!*

He wipes at the offending mess with his sleeve.

– Com*ing*!

She's holding the receiver out for him in the hall, glowering accusingly. He dabs at his eye as he takes it, starts to say hello, then realises that something's stopping him from speaking properly. He slips a finger and thumb in his mouth and unearths the bolt from his cheek.

Crystal makes no attempt to hide her disgust.

– Yeh? Hey, Stevo.

Looking at her, then, Stan has a sudden vision: Crystal, transplanted back into that soft, swaying land down south, the oceans of wheat cresting up the inclines and down again. All three of them are there. Crystal is gentle and smiling, a neat, lemon cardigan draped over her shoulders. Billy is running helter-skelter through a paddock, just as Stan used to do as a boy, arms spanned into aeroplane wings, crushing the splintery sticks beneath his feet and marvelling at the patterns of destruction he can make. A terrible thought comes to him: would it all have been different if he'd never come north, if they'd settled in that more hospitable country?

Lord knows, Crystal moans about the Kimberley enough. She says it's a savage land, barely fit for the scraggy cows with their sorry humps and bony ribs and sawn-off horns. She hates the oppressive humidity of the wet, the parched heat of the dry. Stan agrees – it *is* a savage land, no two ways about it – but there's a heightened beauty to the savageness, more passionate and ecstatic than anything he's come across before. It takes longer to love, but once the love is there it lasts longer, goes deeper. He won't give up the struggle to convince her, now that he's started. Even the southern wheatbelt, he reminds her when he finds her staring in despair at the cracked red earth of their front yard and the unforgiving outback beyond, even *that* wasn't always a soft, inhabited place. Just a generation back it was still raggle-taggle bush much like here, beautiful to those that knew it, wild and unwelcoming to those that didn't. His father and the fathers of the other men farming there now had taken their axes to acre after acre of salmon gums, York gums, acacias, stripping the land down to a brittle nakedness. In a few months they'd raze an area the size of a farm – two men, half an acre a day between them. You could always tell the ones that cleared the land in the old family photographs, he would tell her: they were the ones whose axe arms wouldn't straighten out.

Stan's father once told him you seek out the landscape that fits your spirit. Stan reckons there's truth in that. The wheatbelt was all light, space and air, and the people that lived there were easy-going types, generous with a laugh and a slap on the back. The Kimberley was altogether more difficult, with its dusty immensity, its strong, unapologetic colours, its violent storms and sapping heat. It was a harsh, complicated place, and those that lived there were harsh and complicated with it.

– Yeh, he says into the phone, not really listening to Stevo. Crystal is hovering, picking at a thread on her dress. Why she cares so much that he gets this particular car, God knows. She's never given him a word of encouragement about buying old bangers before. It's always been gripes: how he'd get bitten by a snake curled up in a cool footwell one day, how she's sick of cleaning the red earth stains from his clothes, how he works too bloody slowly. Like when he did up the Kingswood last year. True, he had no intention of parting with that little corker, and Crystal soon got wind, listening in on the conversation with Fred Frost from Watery River:

– Well, Stan, does it go?

A noncommittal shrug from Stan. – It depends on where you want it to go, Fred.

– For the food and mail run, down to Samson's once every coupla months.

– Samson's in Perth?

– Yeh.

A dubious face from Stan. – She'll make it to Halls Creek.

– That's less than eighty kay away, Stan.

– Aw, yeh, well, she's a beaut, ain't she? Stan's face bright with love.

– Looks may be enough in a woman, Stan, but you need a bit of *umph* in a car.

And that had been it, another sale averted, another one to line up with the F J Holden, the panel van, the Oldsmobile, the Buick, the biscuits and cream Ford Falcon. Relief pumped in the vein on his temple until it'd met with a slap from Crystal. A slap! It was the first time she'd ever hit him. No words passed between them for a week.

What she failed to appreciate was that he'd made a niche for himself here that outsiders rarely succeeded in doing. He was always busy and they knew him in all the towns – Fitzroy Crossing, Halls Creek, Kununurra, even folks in Derby knew of Stan Saint, panel-beater. He could even afford to advertise. One of his happiest moments had been seeing his own ad on GWN, between an ad for a haulage company in Perth and the Toyota ad with the rooster getting blasted crossing the road – and there he was, a brightly lit still of him in his blue overalls, his hair combed back and one hand resting on the bonnet of a smart red Buick, Stan Saint, Your Friendly Kimberley Panel-Beater, will knock just about anything into shape. Sitting in his armchair, he'd folded his arms high on his chest and swapped the cross of his feet over and over, wishing Billy or Crystal had been there to witness it too.

Now, standing in the hall with Stevo barking into his ear, Stan suddenly feels his gut contort.

– I'll be there in an hour, he interrupts.

Crystal glances up at him briefly.

– Yeh. That's what I said. Good job, he says, then puts the phone down and knocks against Crystal's shoulder as he hurries down the hall to the loo.

——————

the wowser

A bottom-heavy man in a striped, garrulous shirt lumbers past the poster of the paperchain family without a glance, and pushes open the ATSIC office door.

Who the hell . . .? demands the wind.

The wowser.

The *who*?

Sydney Coldiver, the fella who's bought the roadhouse. Now *there*'s a man who battles with wind. He tries to cover it up by launching into a messy, spittle-projecting cough and that overly loud, bombastic voice which is always being heard in adjacent rooms.

What does he do?

We haul ourselves up from the edge of the pavement and wander across the street.

That depends on your politics and point of view. He's known variously as an entrepreneur, a financial advisor, an overblown accountant, a parasite, a good man, a rightie, a leftie, a rightie in disguise as a leftie, a fat-arse, a wowser, and a two-timing bastard.

And what do *you* lot think of him? insists the wind.

Oh, he's always good for a laugh.

We slip though the door behind him.

The woman at the desk looks up, her helpful, expectant expression quickly disintegrating into one of unconcealed dislike. She knows this man all too well. No doubt he's just lobbed in from the next town, thirty kays down the bitumen road, where for the last five years he's been investing the money the government sends the local Aborigines in the Australian stock market and now they are doing rather nicely, or so he'll tell you: a profitable concern. They have pension plans and bush fire insurance and various left-wing lawyers fresh out of law school cooking up land rights actions for them. Why dontcha charge for the white man's pylons stalking like giants in their seven-league boots right across your land? he'll ask them. Why are you selling that beautiful painting when you could rent it out by the week, or even by the day? That way you could live off it for years, you'd niver have to paint another dot, and I would be able to play golf on Fridays. Just think about it, mate. Ya need to think canny like the whitefellas do.

No doubt he's come to sniff the air for the scent of new blood to suck. She furrows her brow and goes straight back to her work. Her name is Tama, and she won't let any of her mob get netted into one of his schemes. They're mostly too dark for him anyway: it's the half-bloods he goes for, and most of those have moved out of this town and gone to live in Broome or Perth, or even Sydney, where they work in social services, welfare, primary schools, shops. There are plenty of folks who want to give an Aborigine a fair whack at the ball, after all – as long as they're not too black. She and Coldiver see eye to eye on that one, at least. The half-bloods milk the system for what they can get, education grants, CDEP, scholarships – you name it they get it, and good for them, he'll say, they'd admit they're on to a rollickin good deal themselves, it's the only way to stay on top. Meanwhile you stubborn full-bloods dig yerselves down in shit-hole towns like this, yer sons getting wrapped up in humbug and your daughters knocked up before they're even sixteen. And who can blame em? All they got to see is everyone on the grog from midday till midnight. We all like a bit of a piss-up, he'll say, I'm not any different, but you lily-livered blacks can't take it. If you want to talk to Arthur out there on the long grass, or his fat missus Emmeline, you gotta catch em before the grog has pulled the shutters down and you've lost em for another day.

Yeh, yeh, thinks Tama. Here we go again.

Coldiver helps himself to a seat that creaks with strain beneath his considerable weight, his buttocks swimming over the edges. Meanwhile, we perch neatly on the corners of Tama's desk, our thin legs twining like creepers.

– Before you open your mouth, the answer's no, says Tama, enunciating the words precisely. She's a handsome woman, is Tama, hovering somewhere in her forties, although you'd never be rude enough to ask. Her thick hair is tucked away in a tightly-executed French pleat and she fills out her denim pinafore dress very comfortably. Her broad lips are painted a dark cherry colour that sets off her matt black skin.

– And before you think of opening your mouth a second time, she continues, rolling a piece of paper into an old-fashioned typewriter, I'm far too busy to listen you out today.

Sydney Coldiver makes a cradle of fat fingers behind his head and gives the bones a crack.

– Aw, Tammy, I may have skin as thick and pock-marked as an orange, but I'm a big softie at heart. You know I am. Who's yer letter to?

He leans in, the seat letting out a squeak of relief, and pushes his big bug eyes up close. He has a padded quilt of a face, patches of pink and purple and brown all thrown together. Worse, there's a smell of gravy issuing from between his full, wet lips. Tama's handsome features flinch away.

– My name is Tama, she says.

– Eh? Who's it to? Maybe I can help.

– None of your bloody business.

– Ha! That's my girl. You know, I'll make a rollickin woman out of you. I'll have you in charge of a hundred men on one of my new projects. You'll see. I tell you, Tam-tam, I'm gunna turn this town around. I know the bloke that's won the contract to build the new jails, he's a mate of mine, and he's gonna use my men. I know the blokes up at Lake Argyle, too – I'll send another bus-load to the mine up there. And if they get the green light for the tidal power station in Derby, I'll be the biggest provider of skilled and unskilled labour north of Broome. What are you writin? Is it a Government letter?

He tries to lean over far enough to read it, but she forces him back with her eyes.

– C'mon, Tabitha, give me a break. I've spent enough time with you blackfellas to know how to win your trust. Haven't you seen what a good rapport I have with those Abos, Emmeline and Arthur, out on the long grass? If you just hunker down a few feet from their flea-infested mattress, keep your eyes from catching theirs, and let yourself get into their rhythm

– because they know if you've got the rhythm, he says, suddenly lurching forward again, they pick it up, whether you have it or not – then after a while they'll speak to you, tell you things that give you an idea of what goes on up top. You'd be surprised how much old Uncle Coldiver knows.

Tama knits her brow again.

– Because they have it, y'know. Wisdom. It's all there inside their grogged-up temples. They remember the days when this arsehole desert and everything in it made sense. When everything happened for a reason. Jiss had to trust your instinct. Niver anything to fear in a world like that. Sounds pretty bloody perfect to me.

– It wasn't all apples, says Tama, shortly.

The seat lets out a despairing, muffled cry as Coldiver's buttocks crash down. He looks around vaguely for something he can use as a toothpick, experimentally detaching the lid of a biro.

– Who gives a bloody toss, anyway. It's now that matters. Look, I might gob off like Lawrence of bloody Arabia sometimes, but I'm right, Tammy. That's the irritating thing about me. You know what I could do for this town. Help me hire a goddamned receptionist, there's a good girl. I've got a roadhouse to run. I need cleaners, a bar man, someone to answer the phone. Your mob would be perfect. We'll all get rich with Uncle Sydney at the helm. Come in with me, Tambourine. I'll make a queen bee out of you.

Tama's eyes focus on something behind Coldiver's right shoulder.

– The assimilation programme has failed, Mr Coldiver. Please listen to what I'm saying. We don't want to join forces with you. Ah, look, garbo day today.

– Eh?

– We got two bags in the kitchen, if you wouldn't mind.

– *Eh?*

She looks levelly at Coldiver.

– Garbage bags. You niver heard of em?

Coldiver throws his head back and guffaws.

– Aw, Tamo, you'll be the death of me, dja know that? Jeez, I could use you on reception. Why don't you come and work at my roadhouse? Together we'll put this town on the tourist map. Whatja say? I'm gonna get a hire car business, take over the coffee shop and make it upmarket, pizzas and salads and stuff . . .

Tama bashes at the keys of the typewriter so hard that the loose paper clips in the desk tidy dance up and down.

– OK, OK, I'll leave you alone. But I'll be back, Tamo, just you see, and I'll win you round in the end.

He doesn't get up from the chair so much as get thrown off, the springs in the base projecting him eagerly forward. He helps himself to the biro that belongs to the lid as he goes, pausing a second time to take a fake red chrysanthemum from a vase and stick it through a buttonhole in his shirt. At the door he turns round and looks at her with an innocent smile.

– Hmm? What was that?

It is better than tennis, the little battle of wills that ensues. Tama folds her hands and looks at Coldiver, and Coldiver looks back at Tama, and from where we're perched on the desk we turn our heads between the two. The look on Coldiver's face as she gradually makes him understand what she wants him to do – and, moreover, *that he will do it* – is worth a whole month's welfare. This woman is as tough as an old boot, he's realising – no, *tougher*. She'd whip him all the way down the street with his arse hanging out. Thank Christ, he thinks, thank *Christ* I didn't invite her out for a bit of nookie – close call, because I think she's a bit of alright, even though she's not in the first flush, and it could've got sticky. What mincemeat she'd make of the wife.

We nod and chuckle. His multi-hued face turning a shade or two paler, Coldiver waddles dumbly into the back room, picks up the two bin bags and dumps them outside without a word, casting a sorry glance down the street to check he hasn't been seen. As soon as he's gone, Tama sits back in her chair with a weary sigh, covering her large dewy eyelids with her hands. It's only nine o'clock and she's already had enough.

She's startled by a tumult of screeching. It sounds like all the unoiled bicycles in town braking at once. Tama opens her eyes to see a flurry of feathers streak past – galahs, at least a hundred of them, turning the air into a pale grey soup with red streaks. She stares in mounting horror till the last one has disappeared. Broken, scattered feathers sink through the air in their wake. She covers up her eyes again.

An omen, if ever she saw one, she thinks.

From his seat on the grass Jimmi Rangi hears the ruckus too. He removes the cigarette from his mouth with a slow finger and thumb, turns reluctantly and watches the chaotic mob disappear down the street. Two narrow plumes are ejected from his nose. Deep down in his furrowed eyes, something flickers briefly – a snag of emotion.

– Want some breakfast, mate?

A shadow falls over his face.

– There's a nice little coffee shop down the road and Uncle Coldiver's feeling bountiful today.

Jimmi shades his eyes with a hand. Above him towers a bright red face, a pair of protruding eyes.

– You're new round here, aintcha? asks Coldiver. Niceta meet ya.

The hand he offers Jimmi is slick with sweat.

– G'day, mate, says Jimmi.

– I'm Sydney Coldiver. You can call me Syd.

-----

a fist flies out

T he two roos stand upright on their hind legs, face to face. Billy, crouching within a wattle thicket, holds his breath. He knows this is going to be more than a friendly bout of boxing. He can sense the aggression in the air.

The larger of the two whacks the ground with a hind foot. Billy can feel the vibration. The claws on the end of the foot are vicious – long black talons. He's read that an adult roo will balance its entire bulk on its tail and rip you with these claws.

Suddenly a fist flies out. A returning punch swings back. They fling their heads right back as they aim at one another's jaws. Billy recoils from the force of their blows, shunts backwards within the cover of the wattle. He feels vulnerable with his chest bare, and looks round for his T-shirt before remembering that it's tied around his head. He shields his chest with his hands instead.

The roos are making strange clucking sounds as they circle one another. In a single movement, one locks the other's chest in a forearm vice. There's a moment of near-motionless wrestling before they break free. Again they collide, wrapping their arms around each other as if in an embrace. Billy stares, wide-eyed, as the pair of them move closer to Billy's thicket.

They are batting each other so fast that their limbs are a blur. Blood sprays across pale chest fur. They are far too close for comfort now. Billy tries to back away, but the bush is too dense behind him. Suddenly the larger of the two leans on its tail and thrusts both hind legs into the other's belly. Billy shouts out. The roos freeze from the neck down, heads whipped in his direction. Ears swivelling.

His only option is to run towards them. One big leap from the wattle. It's partly out of habit that he decides to take the jump with feet together. They scatter to either side, and as they do he smells the gamy stench of their pelts. Perhaps they will see him as one of them, he thinks, fleeing from a separate, more serious threat. Perhaps they'll take flight with him. His whole body pounds from the jarring thumps of his feet – or is it their thumps, coming along behind? He's too frightened to look back and see. He hurls himself into a stand of acacias, ducking for a branch which scrapes the top of his scalp, tearing off the knotted T-shirt. Too bad. He keeps bounding, all the way to the top of the path, his thighs starting to complain now. Skids sideways on the loose scree, grasps the red box tree to stay on course.

As he slaloms down the path, he can't help smiling to himself, wondering whether he did it, whether he convinced the roos that he belonged.

He pokes a finger in a hole in the fly screen and slides inside the cool house.

The TV is blaring in the living room, although no one appears to be watching. He pads around on the kitchen lino, soundlessly. On the table is a plate of cold toast and Vegemite that's been left for him, but it has sat there since breakfast and he doesn't fancy it. He thinks he's hungry, but doesn't know what to eat. He slides dishes of leftovers to the edge of the shelf in the fridge, takes a suspicious sniff, pushes them back. From the next room comes a man's voice:

– *No deaths have been reported so far, but many houses have been flattened . . .*

An earthquake? wonders Billy, vaguely. A cyclone?

– *. . . went to Red Alert at midnight until 4pm West Coast time, when winds dropped to a hundred and seventeen kilometres per hour. Barry Jeffers joined Exmouth residents . . .*

He opts for a joint of ham, a half-inch of fat sludgy and damp around the top and sprinkled with bright orange breadcrumbs, peels back the al foil and scrabbles around under the rind with his fingers until he manages to pull off a solid lump, aware that he's spoiling the shape of the joint for slicing.

– *No chance mate. Ya couldn't even hear the bloody phone ring. I had to scream in me wife's ears . . .*

– You gotta go. He'll be here any minute.

Billy sticks the ham quickly between his teeth so that there's no going back, prepares to swing the fridge door to with his hip.

– You heard me. Skit.

Through the open door of the kitchen he sees a creature with four arms and four legs stumble backwards out of his parents' bedroom, across the hallway. A hand clamps the back of his mother's neck, pushing the thick, orange hair up into loops. Another hand rolls the cheek of her arse. She's wearing a silky, coral-coloured slip that Billy has never seen before. The creature trips clumsily over itself and staggers down the corridor, out of his line of sight.

Billy takes the ham from his mouth and puts it quietly down on the benchtop, shiny with saliva. He looks out of the kitchen window, his heart thudding, half fearful, half hopeful. Sees only bird shit splattered across the glass and beyond it an empty yard with oil stains spotting the grit.

Out of the corner of his vision a triangle of her slip appears and disappears in the kitchen doorway. This slip seems the biggest travesty of all to Billy: a possession she's hidden from them both. They are murmuring to one another, but the rush of blood is too loud in Billy's ears to make out any words. Suddenly the man steps into the doorway again, and with a shock Billy takes in the familiar stance, belly thrust forward, chest back, bare legs sticking out from his stubbies. The same old grubby singlet. There's a slick of sweat on his shaved temple and a sharpish, lemony smell to him that Billy's never noticed before.

Stevo smiles at Crystal. He raises two fingers to his lips – a goodbye kiss or a pact of silence, Billy can't tell which – and then he's gone, out the back door and down the steps, lighter footed than usual. He must be feeling good to have that spring in his step, Billy thinks. The fly screen bounces in his wake.

Billy looks down at the scratched vinyl benchtop and dabs at the crumbs with the pad of his finger, aware that he is old enough to understand what he's just seen, but not old enough to know what to do. His mind begins to formulate a sentence, something he could imagine someone saying to her, and he takes a breath but knows it won't sound right coming out his mouth. When at last he turns round she's leaning against the frame of the kitchen door with her eyes closed and her fingers rubbing between her legs with the same small movement she uses to rub at the ring of dirt around the bath. She hasn't seen him. He knows he's witnessing something he shouldn't, that afterwards he'll wish he'd turned away.

But staying where he is, hidden by the open door, is the only thing he can think of doing. He stares as Crystal pushes her fingers encased in the coral-coloured slip inside herself, pushes them in and out, then deeper in. She tips her head right back. A little bleating sound escapes her mouth. The arch of her neck seems enormous – a long, vulnerable expanse – yet muscular. She thrusts the fingers right up to the hilt and holds them there, her lips stretching right to the sides of her face. Then her chest collapses in on itself like a fire burnt through at its core and her body slides slowly down the door frame like bodies do in films when they've been shot, leaving a smear of blood on the wall behind them. She's left sitting spread-legged on the floor.

He waits for the sound of her breathing to steady. Then he bounces the fridge door to with his hip.

– Hi Mum.

Her startled eyes dart towards him, shiny and white. Billy turns his back on her, puts the piece of ham in his mouth and begins to chew, feeling the uncomfortable size of it, the stringy texture, tasting nothing.

– Billy.

– I just came in. F'something to eat.

– Didja.

– I didn't notice ya till just now.

For a moment there is nothing except the sound of her breath. And then, from outside, comes an unmistakable, whistled rendition of 'Waltzing Mathilda'. There is only one person that could possibly be. The banal notes pluck cleanly at the air. Billy hangs over the benchtop, loving this whistle, willing it towards them with all that it brings – the return of normality, or at least pretence. Whatever fragile equilibrium they will now exist within. He hears the Blunnies being pulled off, Crystal scrambling to her feet just as the fly screen opens. The unquestioning footfalls loping down the hallway, passing Crystal hurrying in the other direction.

– Jeez, I could use a cold beer ay.

Stan strides into the kitchen, ungainly hands reaching for the tap, the soap.

– Christ knows what 'e was on about, Stan is saying. Get out in the yard and have a squiz. Windscreen's gone and she's 'ad more bingles than I've had fried eggs. Belonged ter some hoon who didn't know you were sposed to drive around trees. Stevo said she'd be apples in a week or two, but who wants a bloody Nissan?

He rubs the big greasy hands together in rotations, grey suds splashing the benchtop and the floor. From down the corridor, Billy hears the bathroom lock draw across, the squeak of the shower being turned on.

– How's it goin, Billy? Passed Fred Frost on the road jiss now an 'e says 'e saw ya jumpin like a roo this mornin. Next we know you'll be sproutin a tail, I reckon.

Stan shakes his big hands up and down, looks at Billy properly for the first time, and gives him a delighted smile.

– Hooley dooley, wassup with you? You look like you just sat on a porcupine. Pass me the tea towel, ay.

---

full moon rains

Out on the sandstone plain, a white full moon rains down. The brushed cotton of a pair of pyjama legs is luminous as they meander between the termite mounds. The air is still, the wind tucked up asleep. Only a snake swishes its body out her way.

Red dust stains the cuffs of her sleeves as she climbs the path up the escarpment. On the top, the silhouetted outlines of trees are sharp against the grey sky. From somewhere comes the cool hoot of an owl.

She finds it easily. She unhooks it from its twig and presses it to her face. It is soft and warm and smells of soap powder and Billy's skin. The spirit child beams with pleasure. There is nothing more extraordinary or precious to her at this moment than this green T-shirt. It causes the earth to stand still beneath her feet. It creates a burst of sweetness like a honey ant's belly on her tongue. In a shadowy compartment of her mind she hears the voice of her grandmother, a soft hand stroking her cheek: *This is what you need to do* . . . But it doesn't last long. As ever, she finds it hard to remember.

She ties the T-shirt around her waist. Her little piece of Billy. Who needs a bunch of cockatoos? This will do the job so much better. She will hatch his love as if from out of an egg.

part III

he shivers and sweats

At night he imagines the infection climbing up his legs like a fast-growing plant, its tendrils in his veins. He shivers and sweats, throws a hollow *hey!* into the gloom of the ward every now and then. Sooner or later it'll land where someone will find it.

Eventually he hears footsteps – not plastic soles this time, but the muffled scud of leather. *Hey*, Billy says, more softly. He feels tearful, reduced to a child. The figure sits without a word on the edge of his bed, presses on his wrist with two fingers, lays the back of a cool, dry hand against his burning forehead.

Billy has no time to waste.

– They punished me for what I did to the kangaroo. You ask em. I hid underground for a long time but they found me anyway.

His eyes are frantic, darting. The figure on the bed takes a watch from a breast pocket, presses a button on the top to illuminate its face. A small green glow between them.

– Am I going to die?

– You're not going to die, Billy, he murmurs. You're hurt, but not that bad.

The fingers release their pressure on Billy's vein.

– The blood that came out was kangaroo blood. Taste it! You taste it, you'll see!

The junior doctor, James, says nothing.

– You don't understand what I'm sayin, accuses Billy.

– Tell me again.

James slips the watch back in his pocket and takes out a sharpened pencil and a small, spiral-bound notebook. In the light from a street lamp outside, the junior doctor's face looks older, jaundiced, but the features are still delicate and poised – carefully outlined lips, a long, fine nose – as if they had been drawn with the pencil he's using now. Billy listens to the rasp it makes on the page.

– I brought it on meself.

– It's not a wound you could have inflicted on yourself.

Billy flings his grey-green eyes to the side.

– You don't understand. They were only doing what I wanted.

– Who are 'they'?

Billy struggles to get control of his lips. – The ones that talk to me.

James looks up.

– I didn't want to hear them any more . . . Billy's voice has climbed up an octave. I ran away, went underground, but they came after me.

– Why did they come after you, Billy?

– Because of what I did to the kangaroo.

A bubble of snot pops at the end of Billy's nose. He sniffs it back in.

– And what did you do to the kangaroo?

– I maimed it.

James searches Billy's eyes for more. He shrugs. – That happens all the time, on the roads. It's hardly a crime.

Confusion floods Billy's eyes. – It was the worst thing I could do.

James raises both eyebrows, expectantly. He waits for Billy to say more, but already the brightness in his patient's eyes is fading, a shutter coming down. An alarm clock ticks on someone's bedside table. From the other end of the ward comes the squeak of mattress springs as a patient gets out of bed, irritably.

– Wish you'd bloody keep the noise down.

James waits for this woman to disappear into the bathroom, then flips the cover of the notebook over and slides it back into his breast pocket, reaching into the kidney tray behind him for a syringe. This is the third night the Saint man has mentioned hearing voices. He's convinced there is a psychological explanation behind the extraordinary wounds in his thighs. None of them have ever seen an injury of this nature on a white man; even on blacks it's becoming increasingly rare. Ann is reluctant to pursue the case any further, but James is convinced he's right.

He follows the line of Billy's arm to where it disappears under the sheet, calculates where to reach for his hand. As he injects the sedative he wonders what he should be feeling for this man. So far he has swayed between pity and annoyance, but now he has reached a new stage: gratitude. Billy is a gift of a case-study. He couldn't have pitched up at a better moment.

James uncaps a syringe of saline and flushes it through the canula, then tucks Billy's hand back where he found it. The way he moves Billy is confident, he realises. Even blasé. He must be starting to lose his self-consciousness when touching patients.

– D'you think you'll be able to sleep now?

He's loath to let Billy go now that he's discovered how to touch.

– If you're still awake in an hour, I'll give you a top-up, mate.

He runs his fingers up towards the shoulder, but the drowsy body offers no response.

The young doctor visits Billy every night for the next five nights. He looks different during these visits, the sallow skin lending him a maturity that his flushed, daytime look denies him. Billy stares up his nostrils with their tiny blue veins, like snips of cotton. There is something fragile and girlish about him, Billy has decided. If he holds onto his youthful dedication, he'll make a good doctor. Women will fall for his earnestness and for that sensitive nose. Men will believe what he says.

As the days pass and the infection in his legs is brought under control, Billy's fevers lessen. For a while he keeps talking, but a distance has crept in between them. On the fifth night, the junior doctor bites the end of his pencil and looks at Billy and knows that it is over, this short period of access to his patient's private world.

Edging back towards lucidity, Billy feels uneasy. A sense of wrongdoing hangs in the air between them. There is guilt on James's face.

– What've you been writin? Billy asks, the dent forming across the bridge of his nose. Nothing up here worth recording, mate. 'Sall a load of bull.

James gets up abruptly. – All pathology is interesting to me. I'm still learning.

Billy has the feeling he is being left before he is ready to be left. He has no idea what James has extracted from their strange, night-time rendezvous, or even what form these meetings have taken; but he knows that he wouldn't have spoken so much if he had been in full possession of his tongue. He can see that James knows this too.

But the junior doctor is getting good: he has learnt how to detach himself, how to give very little away. He sheds the guilt from his eyes with a single blink and looks at Billy as if nothing special has ever passed between them – as if he knows no more about Mr William Saint than he does the man who was wheeled in an hour ago with a chestful of broken ribs.

He runs his hands down the front of his white coat, as if to cleanse himself of Billy, gives a slight, empty smile and leaves.

*   *   *

He has his hands around Cecily's waist. With every breath he explores the smells that cling to her – antiseptic soap and latex gloves, her bed, her sweat, her pillow-crushed hair. He luxuriates in these private smells of hers. He likes to imagine her sleeping at the hospital, in her uniform, simply finding an empty bed in one of the wards and slipping between the sheets for the night, then in the morning pulling the curtains open and wiping out the sleep from the corners of her eyes and picking up where she left off. He didn't imagine she was the sort of person who needed a ritual to get herself started in the mornings – a shower, a cup of tea, toast for breakfast. Some people can just get up wherever they are and carry on with their lives, and Cecily is one of them.

He has been offered a Zimmer frame and a wheelchair, but he won't touch either. He'll only get out of bed if Cecily is there. He can make it from his bed to the end of the ward before his legs start to shake. Then he needs to sit on somebody else's bed before he can make it back. She comes at ten o'clock in the morning and then again at four for this twice-daily exercise. They do not have a physio available at present; this was explained to him by the yellow-crested doctor. He should get one later through his GP. The muscles would benefit from regular massage, stretching exercises, that sort of thing. It's vital he does this if he is to regain full strength in his legs.

Billy had nodded, knowing that there would be no GP, no exercises.

What Cecily is doing now is more for her sake than his own. He treats Cecily to this observation, but she doesn't bother to respond. Perhaps she detects in it a note of self-pity, a plea for attention. He doesn't care. He's in the mood for talking, so he goes on.

– The last time I walked behind someone like this I was five. A croco-dile, we used ter call it.

From where he's standing he cannot see the expression on her face. He suspects there is nothing much to see; she has turned professional on him again. He watches how her uniform buckles on the plateau of her arse.

– Then two kids would hold hands to make an arch, and we'd all traipse through.

They have reached the end of the ward. She takes hold of his hands and places them squarely on the frame of an unmade bed. He leans where she's left him, a bent stick of a figure, winded. He feels as if he has climbed up the side of a mountain.

– 'Sa load of bull, what they make kids do, ay. I don't know why they stand for it.

Cecily's eyes, as usual, are cast to one side. He wonders if she ever gets an urge to stare at a face full on. Perhaps, when all the patients are asleep, she goes down the ward staring at each sleeping face, long and hard – the warts and moles and scars, the slack cheek muscles, the badly shaven chins. He remembers how Yakka used to straddle him those evenings when he fell asleep at Stevo's, not wanting to go home yet. She'd wait for his eyes to open, her paws pinned to his shoulders, tongue lolling out. The jagged white zig-zag on her nose. You never knew how long she'd been there. As soon as you opened your eyes, she looked away immediately, feigning indifference.

– Whatja reckon, Cecily? Did they make you do stupid things at school too?

The eyes flicker up and down. It's not disdain exactly, she's just not reacting. Disdain would be giving him too much.

He laughs sharply. – You gunna talk to me today or what?

When he gets no response he sits on the empty bed. On his inner thigh, a curdled mixture of yellow pus and blood has seeped into the fabric of his hospital pyjamas.

– I'm jiss waitin to take you back to your bed.

– And I'm jiss waitin for you ter speak ter me.

She tilts her chin up.

– I got other patients to see. There's blokes mo' bad than you.

He thinks about imitating her, the way she spits the words out: *Blokes mo' bad than you.* But he thinks she'd probably walk away, and he wouldn't blame her. He picks up a card from the bedside table.

– *Dear Dad. Please will you come home for Christmas. Mum says it's not worth cooking a turkey for two. I promise to be good and not make you jacked off. Love your son Brendan.* Aw, that's plain tragic, that is. Have you seen this, Cecily? *P.S. Can I have the new Playstation for Christmas.* Jesus, they're fucken insensitive buggers, ain't they? When 'is dad nearly died of a heart-attack a week ago. Who'd wanna have a kid, ay.

Cecily plucks the card crisply out of his hand and puts it back on the bedside table. She stands before him and waits.

– Jesus, I get the fucken message. Where'd they train you nurses, in the Congo?

He leans on her more than last time, staring down at the graph-paper squares, imagining colouring them in with a felt-tip pen. Halfway across she covers his hands with her own and he thinks for a wild moment that she's going to lift them off and leave him without support in the middle of the ward. His heart leaps into his throat. He'd sink like a limbless man in water.

But instead she leaves her hands there, wrapped over his, the warm fingers gently meshing with his own.

Patients come and go. The man in the bed that Billy walks to every day is discharged with a strict warning to cut out the smokes, the booze and the red meat. Treat this one as your final warning, he hears the yellow-crested doctor say. Next time you're in here you won't be around to know it.

The man shakes Billy's hand goodbye.

– They're trying to turn me into Mother fucking Teresa.

Billy shrugs. – They're trying to keep you alive.

– It's a high price to pay. Too high.

When he's feeling stronger Billy submits to using the wheelchair to visit the TV room. He bums a cigarette off one of the others, pulling it from the pack with his lips. There's a mob playing cards in the corner, and they could've been airlifted from the Spini except that they're drinking Cokes from the soft drinks machine and they're in their bedclothes – ugly olive green or maroon pyjamas with stitching around the pockets, matted towelling dressing gowns, sleeves that have been dipped in their baked beans. Some wear plastic slippers with trodden-down backs, some have their big gnarled feet bare, tufts of hair sprouting from their toes. There are women whose nighties fail to reach their knees, swollen legs bulging out of tight support stockings. Those not playing cards are slumped in Salvo armchairs in front of the telly, their double chins bunching up, chest hair frothing out the top. Sitting between them, Billy wonders what they have done with their pride, these men and women, allowing themselves to be seen like this, the smell of sleep thick on their breath. He wonders whether any of them will acknowledge one another should they meet on the streets of the Alice once they're discharged, or whether they'll look away.

To begin with, some try to make conversation, ask him how he's going, but he feigns dumbness, waits for them to grumble Hev it your own way, mate, and shuffle off.

a vast, ancient heart

Mid-afternoon in the desert. A big, fierce sun crashes down. The red earth is strewn with the white spots of sun-bleached stones and the black spots of their shadows. All day the heat has built and built as if pumped by a vast, ancient heart, recycling an age-old sadness with its dull, leaden-templed beat. The horizon is delirious with heat, beset by a violent shimmer.

We lie as if felled by some mighty fist, our backs scooping out the air. Our throbbing feet hang limply over the sides of our hammocks. A crust of flies moves over our eyes and lips. Inside our mouths, leathery tongues inch around in search of a dab of moisture. We're too lazy to get up and find something to drink; in this state a body chooses to ignore its needs.

Look.

The rest of us raise our heads half an inch. What is it?

Over there.

An exclamation mark quivers like an arrow on the horizon. It becomes a torso that stretches and wobbles, part of the mirage itself. As it gets closer it starts to firm up. Eventually we can make out a pair of coltish legs hurdling the termite mounds.

Unbelievable! She never stops. Even in this heat.

Some of us drag ourselves up on an elbow to watch the little figure jumping and tottering in the molten air. As she gets nearer we see that she is clutching something to her chest. At one point she drops it, or a part of it, a handle connected by a springy coil. As it hits the earth there's the tinkle of a bell.

Her lilting voice sings out: Look what *I've* found!

She picks it up, only to trip over it once again a few steps further on. A delightful giggle rises up, free to travel anywhere it pleases in this empty expanse. Eventually we can see that what she is carrying is made of red plastic with tentacles, like some sort of deep-sea creature.

We stick out our lower lips and puff the flies away.

When she finally untangles herself and steps into the piecemeal shade of the snappy gums, she breathlessly holds out her new toy for us to admire.

It's a telephone, she announces proudly, flushed more from exhilaration than the heat. You can use it to have conversations.

We look at her morosely, rubbing our eyeballs with the heels of our hands.

We know what it is.

I thought it might help you to communicate with the people.

Despite our lethargy, irritation rises within us like sap.

We don't need a telephone to do that.

The spirit child twists from the waist, coyly.

I know you don't *need* it, but . . . Here, have a listen.

She holds out a handle with two bulges on either end. Tentatively, one of us bends down an ear.

Hang on, you've got it the wrong way around.

She turns the receiver for us. From deep down in the tunnel of the phone comes a familiar female voice.

– Mum? Hey, Mum. It's Estha.

We drop the receiver in fright.

Is it a spirit? we ask.

The spirit child laughs out loud. She picks up the receiver and urges us back. We approach cautiously, and for a few seconds listen again, as frightened as we are enthralled. Then we push the whole contraption away.

We don't need a telephone to listen to Estha! We can listen to her whenever we want. We can just go down to the coffee shop.

But that's exactly the *point*, says the spirit child. You *weren't* down at the coffee shop listening to her, were you, right this moment. You were lying here in your hammocks.

We squawk and twitter in incoherent protest, shuffle our feet in the dust.

This way, you can listen to her and anyone else you want without having to move, the spirit child goes on. What do you think? As a way of keeping in touch without having to leave the camp – don't you think it's effective?

We eye one another, begrudgingly impressed but trying our best not to show it.

It's up to you, she shrugs, her bare feet easily finding a grip on the smooth, pink-tinged bark of the snappy gum. It's yours if you want it. I'll wire it up and leave it here in this tree.

The next morning, she shakes us roughly by a shoulder.

It's time for my lesson.

What?

There are some things you should teach me.

She stands above us, expectantly.

Are you serious?

I'll get you lot breakfast, if you like.

She knows us well, the spirit child.

OK then.

With a flourish, she produces a bunch of bananas from behind her back.

Dnah!

Don't s'pose you've got coffee as well?

Don't push it.

We manoeuvre ourselves upright and share out the bananas. She leans against the trunk of a tree, arms folded.

What sort of lesson do you want?

A sex education lesson.

Beg pardon?

You heard me.

May we ask what *for*?

So that I can understand this business with Stevo.

We eye her sceptically.

That's got nothing to do with you.

I didn't say it did, she says. I just want to understand it.

You're just after the gossip, we say. You're just as bad as all the others.

We gobble the bananas quickly, defensively, as if at any moment she might ask for them back. She clicks her tongue, crossly.

OK, then, I'm asking because of Billy.

We stop mid-mouthful.

Billy's *our* concern. Hands off.

She looks away, taps her foot irritably.

You can't expect me not to take an interest.

We say nothing, our mouths too full of banana.

Well? she says after a while. Are you going to tell me or aren't you? If you don't, I'll only go and ask someone else.

We sigh, drape the empty banana skins across our thighs.

You want the whole story?

The whole story.

Alright then. Here we go. We take a breath. It started when Crystal was bringing in the washing one day. Suddenly Stevo turned up –

She holds a palm in the air.

Stop! I want to be able to *picture* it. Go back to the beginning.

OK, OK. F'Chrissakes. We wriggle around, making ourselves more comfortable. She was wearing a yellow cotton dress – you know how nice she looks in yellow. You could see the outline of her undies beneath it, the sort with the stringy straps around the hips –

Blood smarts in the spirit child's cheeks.

I don't need –

You say you're old enough for the full picture, so you're getting it. Shut up and listen. She was unpegging T-shirts, a row of them, on the outer wire of the Hill's Hoist. They were large and shapeless, these T-shirts of Stan's – unlovely garments, soiled with engine oil. He's had them ever since she's known him. Crystal's feet in her rubber thongs shuffled sideways down the line, a few hardened scraps of dark red varnish left on her nails. Those long, freckled legs as slender as ever . . .

The spirit child is fascinated now.

On the next row was a big stripey sheet –

I know the one!

– and behind the sheet as she grappled it down and wrapped it over her arm was –

Stevo from the servo!

She claps her hands together.

No prizes there. Crystal gasped, which was complicated by the fact that she had a peg between her teeth. Stevo was staring at her with blatant intent in his hungry brown eyes – shamelessly, insolently. It was impossible to misinterpret such a look. There was no get-out clause in there at all. Not that Crystal's the sort to fend someone off with nervous small-talk. Strewth, no. Crystal has been getting fidgety for a while now. She's been fantasising about something like this.

I know.

Stevo took the peg out her mouth and used it to attach the sheet up on the line behind her, so that now it hid them both. Behind this sheet, some twenty paces behind, Stan's Blundstones stuck out from beneath a car.

Poor bugger.

Mind your language!

Go on.

Crystal was immediately aroused – perhaps by his insolence, perhaps by the stories she'd heard about his wonga, as he's known to crudely describe it. Within one another's orbit, the force-field between them was strong. He was hard as a crowbar beneath his stubbies and yes, bulging like a fist. A tidal wave of lust rose up inside Crystal. Her vision swam. Her lips fell open. Stevo, a trickle of saliva worming its way out his mouth, moved in, and suddenly his lips were jammed against hers, a hot, vigorous tongue reaching ravenously for the back of her throat. It was surprisingly rough and dry, this tongue, but perhaps that's how it was with Aboriginal men, Crystal thought – who knows – there was so much she was about to find out. He tasted of Capstan tobacco.

The spirit child's eyes are wide. She's gulping down every word. Guiltily, we cough and attempt to rein ourselves in.

. . . and?

Oh, you can guess the rest, we mutter.

No, I can't!

Yes, you can. That day behind the sheet it was just a bit of groping. It left them jumpy, desperate to finish it off.

Finish *what* off?

You *know*. Every damned weekend since, the telephone rings about eight o'clock in the morning. *Tell Stan I've found a new one.* Derby, Broome, even as far as Port Hedland. *Tell Stan it's much better than the last one. Unmissable. He'll regret it for iver if he doesn't grab it today.* Stan hasn't smelt a rat yet, but most of the other people in town have caught a whiff by now, seeing Stan charging off with a tow bar on his ute every Saturday morning, Stevo pulling out of the servo in his Land Cruiser and heading north the minute Stan's out of sight. Those brown eyes of Stevo's looking undeniably shifty behind the wheel. He'll raise a finger in greeting but he never stops to talk.

And no one's breathed a word to Stan?

Not yet. To tell you the truth, most of them are pleased Crystal's getting a poke. At least someone around here is, they say. That Crystal Saint's a looker, they say, no doubt about it. Quite a catch for old Stevo. Living up to his name.

Didgee gooda, the short-necked turtle?

No, the one that Estha made up. The solar-powered sex machine.

But does Crystal like this . . . *poking*?

Oh, you know Crystal. She thinks she deserves it, doesn't she, after all this time. She's not in love or anything, but she gets turned to jelly by the thought of those dark hands pinning her wrists to the bed, the wiriness of his chest hair as it drags across her breasts, the rough tongue frantic in her ear. She even likes that firm, insistent potbelly, the whole heavy, sweating mound of him crushing the wind out her lungs. It makes a change after tentative Stan, all shaky fingered and whispering declarations of ever-lasting love and, oh yes – let's not forget the wonga. The sheer girth of Stevo's wonga breaks her open like a quartered fruit. It leaves her trembling all over. That never happens any more with Stan.

The spirit child stares at us, open-mouthed.

Well, that's everything you need to know and then some, we growl, gathering our discarded banana skins together and hurling them away from the camp. Do we have your permission to get on with our day now?

Alright, she says vaguely, gazing at the banana skins and for once not nagging us to go and tidy them up.

the pink cockatoos

Billy stands with his back to the ghost gum, his shoulder blades fitting neatly into the hollows of the trunk. He waits for the mob of pink cocka-toos to settle back down in the branches and forget he's there. He'll wait for however long it takes – until he becomes a part of the tree if neces-sary, his veins growing into the wood, the wood splitting apart to make room.

– I knew a man who rubbed his wonga against a tree, Stevo had told him once. 'E liked the smoothness of the bark. And fuck me if the tree didn't blossom more than all the other ones did.

The cockatoos strut and titter. Their nervous *quee-eers* are brittle in what would otherwise be the hard-boiled silence of midday. Billy watches them fan their crests, preen their fluffed-up chests with their beaks. He presses himself deep into the trunk, imagines the bark resealing over his face. He might be here for hours. It doesn't matter: it's Sunday and Crystal's not expecting him home. With his finger and thumb he peels back a piece of bark, feeling the soft creamy dampness underneath.

After a while the heads of the cockatoos sink downwards, their necks compressing. Billy sees how the branches cut the sky up into jigsaw pieces of perfect blue.

He counts slowly down from ten. And then he does it.

– Yaaaaaaaaaaaaahhhhh!!!!

The pink cockatoos rise up in one big, alarmed squabble of bashed wings and knocked branches, their screeches mingling with his. When he runs out of breath he tops up his lungs and begins again, half ripping off the back of his throat. Feathers rain down as if from a burst pillow. Billy screams with delight at the chaotic mess of it all, the sheer idiocy of what he has done. Staggering, dizzy, he flings himself through the storm of feathers to the ground. He's motionless now but the earth still carries on spinning. Feathers land on his face.

Hey, Wallamba! Over here.

At first he can't tell if it's the echo of the cockatoos or something inside his head. He lies still, panting.

Wall*amba*.

He scrambles onto all fours. It's a new voice; the voice of a girl. He whips around in a clumsy circle like a dog chasing its tail. He sees a figure standing on the top of the escarpment – a taut little body, braced against the breeze. Could it be her that spoke? She's black, though not a full-blood. Messy hair with a hint of brown in it. She looks younger than him, though she's slightly taller. Her floral cotton skirt is blown by the wind so that the line of one skinny leg shows bluntly through. It's a straight-up leg, no muscle on it at all.

Billy stares, heart thudding, as the girl fills her lungs. Then she opens her mouth and starts to sing. The sound that she makes is sure and strong with the force of her small lungs behind it. It pours from her like a liquid, although it's a discordant song – rugged, full of unexpected corners.

Billy has never heard anything like it. She doesn't have a pretty voice, he decides, just as he later tells himself that *she* isn't pretty, with that prominent forehead, the wide nose, the huge eyes sunk in deep. He knows at once that what he's hearing is too big for him, too much. Even his own yell had nothing of the primitive force that shudders through her small frame, cracking the dryness in her throat. The words make no sense and yet they sear right through, jangling up his insides. He doesn't like the feeling. It makes him want to run away.

The voice climbs up, cracks on a high note which she holds for what seems like an eternity and then, wavering on the tail end, she lets it go. Billy can see her little rib cage rise and fall rapidly as she looks out over the plain. She seems to be surveying the landscape much as he does, seeing things in places where others see nothing.

A nameless fear lodges in his chest. He tells himself not to be stupid.

She is just some half-blood kid, no different to him or the kids at school. He has no reason to be afraid of her. He watches her slide off the steepest part of the rock, jumping the last bit down to his level. She looks him directly in the eye.

– Hello, Wallamba.

She knew he was there all along.

– You've been listening, she says.

Her dark gaze belies the playful tone of her voice. There is something fierce about her. She's younger than him, he's sure of it, but it's as if she's never heard of shyness. He gets to his feet, awkwardly: at least he can match her stance. Meanwhile she gathers up her untidy hair with a scoop of her hand and twists it as she strolls over. She has longer eyelashes even than the Brahmin cows, thick and feathery, curling up at the ends. With a jolt, he notices that she has his T-shirt tied around her waist. She's stretched the sleeves in order to make the knot – or maybe they were stretched already. She lets out a mischievous cackle.

– Here. Have it back. I've finished with it now.

She unties the T-shirt and holds it out. Billy takes it. She stands there, chewing her bottom lip, amusement flashing in her eyes.

– I just sung you up.

She smiles to herself, twisting the hair in its rope.

– What are you on about? says Billy, trying to invest a note of cockiness in his voice.

– You'll know soon enough.

He stares at her, blankly. – You can't make anything happen by *singing*.

– Where did you learn that?

She drops the rope of hair and it springs open a little, then holds its twist. Billy searches her face for some hint of weakness, eventually detecting a flicker of curiosity in her eyes – curiosity about him – and he clings to it. She averts her gaze immediately. She knocks her bare toe against a tuft of rat's tail grass. Billy knows he should make the most of this small moment in which he seems to have the upper hand.

– Why dja call me Wallamba? My name's Billy.

He tries to dredge up some power in his voice. But he only succeeds in making her laugh, her full lips unsticking to reveal surprisingly big, gawky teeth with gaps between them. Her torso is flat beneath her old, shapeless T-shirt.

– You don't know *anything*, do you!

Billy blushes.

– It means kangaroo boy, she says. That's what I call you.

Billy's limbs tighten, instinctively. – Have you been watching me?

She finds this funny too and lets out another cackle, deflating him even more. – There's no hiding from me, Wallamba, she says with a glint in her eye.

When she walks on, he finds himself following, dumbly.

– Might as well get used to having me around, she says, looking back at him over her shoulder.

She's treating him like he's her little brother, Billy thinks, irritably. They are taking the path that he has always thought of as his own, except that she is leading the way now, jumping from stone to stone with her flat feet as if it had been hers all along. Her feet hold the smooth rock with a stability he envies, her toes gripping as if they were lined with suckers. He does his best to keep up. Halfway down she stops abruptly, the long eyelashes resting on her dark cheek. He almost bumps into her. Up close, he can see how the upper and lower lashes knit together. He has an urge to brush them with his finger to see if they're as soft as they look.

– You'll love me for ever now.

Her voice is barely a whisper, but Billy's sure he heard her right. He stands motionless, to one side. Straight ahead he can see the pitching roof of his house within its stand of scraggy cabbage gums.

– That's stupid, he whispers.

She picks a stem of grass and runs the end through her teeth.

– You're cleverer than that, Wallamba. You've got a brain in there, somewhere.

She looks at him mischievously, and then she runs off toward the dirt road, her yellow soles kicking out behind her.

Billy rubs his nose with the flat of his hand, not knowing what else to do. He isn't ready for her to leave just yet. After a moment he chases after her. She hears him coming and speeds up. They both skid at the bottom of the path, but she rights herself more quickly and streaks ahead. When she knows she's safely ahead she spins around and walks backwards.

– Love-sick already?

Billy stops abruptly. He shakes his head.

– You better go home then, Wallamba. Your mother will be waiting for you.

She's swaying her hips from side to side, teasingly. He can see the shadowy outlines of her thin legs within their floral tent. She winks at him, then walks on.

– What's your name? he calls out.

She stops and looks over her shoulder. She's as surprised as he is by the boldness of his question. For a moment she hesitates, as if considering her answer. And then her square teeth flash in a decisive smile.

– Maisie, she says.

She smiles again, more kindly this time, then tosses her hair as she runs off down the track.

---

lace-trimmed bra and matching knickers

In the half-light of the bedroom, Crystal sits on the edge of the bed in a turquoise lace-trimmed bra and matching knickers. She's freshly bathed, with almond oil rubbed into her skin. Her toe-nails are painted burgundy. Even her hair is clean and brushed, an orange frizz bouncing lightly around her freckled shoulders.

He doesn't seem to notice at first – or maybe it's just that he doesn't dare show that he's noticed. She can hear him unclip his watch, the plunk of it landing on the chest of drawers. A pause, perhaps while he's checking the sight of himself in the mirror, or maybe he's looking at the reflection of her back. She's always been proud of her back, the length and straightness of her spine.

She twists around, the wires under her bra cups digging in. There he is, oblivious, staggering on one leg as he tries to pull off his sock.

There was a time when she couldn't get enough of Stan's body. In the middle of the night she'd brush against the curve of a bicep or buttock and she'd want him, waking him with her hands, gentle at first but within moments grasping him urgently, hauling him out of unconsciousness and transforming his sleep-soft torso into one strong enough to withstand the push and pull of her own. Their shouts would fill the night, knowing only this room, this uneven darkness, the epicentre of this touch, until just as abruptly they fell back to sleep again, light-headed, sticky thighs still meshed.

Now she looks at him and sees the mechanical operations of the muscles in his neck, taut with the concentration of balancing as he tugs the sock from the toe rather than sliding a finger down from the top. What she sees before her is a workhorse's body, too lacking in grace to be convincing in a sexual sense. Yet without sex, what was there left between them?

He takes his jeans off, then stops to inspect a blackened fingernail. He drags a thumb over it, checking it'll hold overnight. Only then, in the stillness of that moment, does he feel her eyes on him.

She turns away from him quickly. – Thought we might play around a bit, Stan.

There is a long, taut moment.

– Pardon?

– I want you to be rough with me. Push me around.

– You're sure?

His voice bleeds with distrust. Crystal twists around to face him.

– C'mon, Stan. I don't ask for it very often.

– That is certainly true.

Already she is struggling to keep a handle on her irritation. Her eyes roam over Stan's body. His shirt is hanging over his naked buttocks; she can just see the end of his penis drooping down. She has begun to despise this habit of his of taking his jeans off first. It's such an undignified way to undress. At least he could have the grace to wear underpants. He would probably say there's no point – his jeans needed washing every day as it was, that he was only trying to save her the trouble.

– You want *me*?

He points a vague finger at his own chest. She only just manages not to laugh. Instead, she looks around with wide, mocking eyes.

– There doesn't appear to be anyone else in the room, Stanley.

Stanley. His blue eyes cloud up. Now he'll be searching in the bewilderment of his mind for why she should choose to claw him with that name.

– Are you sure about this, Crystal?

Crystal shakes her hair from her shoulders, looks down at her pale, freckled thighs. Sometimes he seems determined to dig his own grave.

– Oh, you'll do, she says softly, echoing the way they used to tease one another years ago. She had meant to relax him, but it brings a twinge of poignancy into the air. For a while neither of them moves. Then she hears him pulling his shirt over his head. The mattress caves in behind her. She tenses, sensing his anticipation.

Stan clears his throat nervously.

– Lie down, then.

It comes out tentative, a mere suggestion. He tries again.

– I said lie down.

Crystal snorts and lets herself fall back into the bounce of the mattress. Jesus. This is turning into a farce, but she'll have to go along with it now. There he is, kneeling above her, his erection poking out like the spout of a bloody watering can – except without the floret on the end, more's the pity – his eyes bulging, fighting to wipe the gratitude off his face.

She closes her eyes, yanks her knickers down, and lets him get on with the rest.

She wakes early to the sound of hammering on the tin roof. At first she is confused, but then a spring of jubilation erupts in her heart. She's had sex with her husband! This is her reward. After seven unbearably long, hot months – all those interminable, listless days, the pressure building as much inside her head as in the surrounding air – they have rain.

It is the answer to her prayers. Within days there'll be a riot of tender green grass. The trees will come into bud. Stan will turn up for his meals with a twinkle in his eye and she will get her old appetite back. They will fuck all afternoon. The river will flood and send a sweet, drenching lake over the flats. She won't need Stevo any more. Flowers will appear like a scattering of confetti: pinks and whites and yellows and crimson reds. An Eden. A bloody great Eden, and about time too.

But Stan is getting up and pulling back the curtains with the air of a man who knows something isn't quite right. He knows even without looking at the pre-dawn sky. Crystal watches him prod the air with his big nose, peer at the expanse of pale grey and scratch his buttock, before getting back into bed. His cold shin brushes hers, and he pulls it back quickly: just because of what happened last night he knows it doesn't necessarily mean he can touch her whenever he wants.

– What is it, Stan?

– It's beetles.

Crystal's chest stalls, the jubilation quickly draining away. Of course. What was she thinking? That she could have fooled God as well as herself and Stan? This was a punishment, not a reward. If it wasn't fires in this place, it was cyclones. If it wasn't either of these, it was some monstrous type of insect. A biblical plague. They'd had them once before, thousands of beetles falling from who-knows-where and somehow finding their way through gaps in the tin roof, chewing through the Artex ceiling and crawling all over the furniture, between the sheets, in the bath, even floating belly-up in the dunny. You couldn't hide from them. They were like the truth, popping up everywhere you looked: *Crystal has a lover*. Last time she'd chased the little buggers with a broom for days, thwacking their brittle backs and creating sticky red stains on the lino.

Oh, God, it will be a torment. She can't bear to think about it. She hides her face in her pillow and pulls up the sheet.

– Don't worry, says Stan lightly, feeling suddenly superfluous in his own bed and getting out again. He sits on the edge, pulling on his socks, merrily oblivious of his wife's plunge into gloom.

– With a bit of luck the mudlarks will eat them as soon as the sun comes up, he says.

---

little brother to ayers

The telephone is balanced precariously on one pair of knobbled knees. On another sits the *Yellow Pages*, spread open between Machinery Dealers and Marriage Guidance Counsellors. Our fingers run down the names.

What about that one?

What *about* him?

He sounds nice, that's all.

He doesn't sound any nicer than any of the others.

Or this one. Kimberley Bobcat Hire.

They'll just want to talk about bobcats.

What about Kununurra Diesel Services?

Bor*ing*.

From her pew in a branch above us, the spirit child gives a loud sigh.

I *told* you – just pick up the receiver and see who's there. I've fixed it so you can hear all the conversations going on in town.

We swap nervous glances.

You first.

No, you.

No, you.

Eventually we lift the red plastic receiver and hold it out between us, bodies bending inwards from the waist. Behind us the white cable dangles down to the ground and wiggles off across the desert floor, fully intent on its own business. There's a bit of pushing and shoving as we jostle for the best position.

– Coldiver's Roadhouse, g'day? says a voice.

– Very nice, Jimmi! You're a natural.

Ah, the wowser again. We don't seem to be able to get away from him.

– That's me, boss, says Jimmi.

We beam at the spirit child. Success!

– Good boy, Jimmi. Now listen.

One of us grabs the receiver and a little squabble ensues as we tug it back and forth.

– Hang on, hang on, Jimmi. I just got to get me sausage roll out the microwave. There we are. Lovely. Jimmi, I got an idea. You're gunna be a tour guide, take people out to that rock.

There's a pause, during which we can make out the sounds of Coldiver munching on his sausage roll. A gravelly cough as he clears masticated flakes of pastry from his throat.

– Still there, mate?

– You mean the rock that's split in two, boss?

– That's the fella.

Another silence. We twiddle the phone cord around our fingers.

– It's sacred, boss.

A weary sigh from Coldiver. – Get over it, Jimmi. You say this rock is sacred, but to the eyes of any sensible whitefella it looks like, well, a bloody great sandstone boulder split in two. Dja get my drift?

– Boss, I –

– You gotta think canny, Jimmi. Like the whitefellas do.

There's a long pause.

– Look. I'm a good Aussie bloke, says Coldiver. Got a decent brain, uni educated, my wife's got Grade Five on the piano and my son probably knows how to ask for a packet of frenchies in Japanese, and unless this lump of sandstone pipes up and tells me to sod off, then we might as well make the most of it. See the way I reason, Jimmi?

There's the snatch of Jimmi's cigarette lighter.

– Yeh, boss, I do.

– Good. See if you can rig up a poster. NEWLY DISCOVERED SACRED ROCK, LITTLE BROTHER TO AYERS or something along those lines. Any guests yet, Jimmi?

– No, boss.

– They'll come, they'll come. Now if you'll scuse me, Uncle Sydney's got a date.

There's silence, and then a low buzzing. We stare at the little black holes.

What happened?

The spirit child reaches out and takes the receiver.

He's hung up.

Hung up? On what?

The spirit child gives us a withering look, then replaces the receiver on its cradle.

You'll get the idea eventually, she sighs.

---

stretching his shadow

Y ou can't see me! a mischievous voice sings out. But I can see you!

Billy stands on the edge of the escarpment. The late afternoon sun is stretching his shadow twenty paces over the ground. Before him, the low, startlingly white branch of a ghost gum sweeps majestically to the side like the prologue to a bow, bobbing heads of grass around its base. Beyond is the stand of trees and bushes where the kangaroos come in the mornings.

He turns around. Squinting in the low light, he rakes the craggy flank of the escarpment where it tapers steeply away below him, the sinewy little box trees craning their necks into the void.

Not *there*. Over *here*.

He turns again and there she is, clasping the trunk of the ghost gum as she circles it. Her hair is pulled back in a stubby ponytail and tied with a faded pink ribbon.

– Maisie?

She lets out a childish giggle.

– Did you hear about that boy from Watery River station? Not your mate Jon-Jon, the stutterer. His big brother.

– Ted?

She wipes her nose on the back of her arm.

– Yeh. He bought a Fergusson tractor last week and wanted to know how long it'd run on a tank of fuel, so he drove it around and around a tree for eight hours, till there was a gutter *that* deep, and when at last the engine conked out, he stumbled out, really dizzy . . .

Billy laughs into his hand.

– Dizzy as a newborn calf . . .

She lets go suddenly and staggers in imitation of Ted Frost. The leaves of the ghost gum rattle in the wind. She stops laughing and stares up at the tree and waits for the breeze to die down. Then she brushes the flecks of bark off her hands.

– Had your tea yet?

He shakes his head.

– Good. Come on, Wallamba.

Along the edge of the escarpment there is an overhang of rock below which is a narrow, protected shelf. There's just enough space for two people to sit with a view out over the plain. Maisie climbs in first, steady on her feet as ever. By the time he joins her she's delving into a large, hessian bag stowed in one corner. She holds out an orange. It's dazzling against her dark skin.

Billy takes it shyly, waits for her to find one for herself before digging his thumbnail through the thick rind. A spray of juice hits his cheek. He doesn't know where she got them from, or how she dragged them here, or why the ants haven't found them already: none of it makes any sense, but he has a feeling she doesn't want him to ask. He peels the skin in an unbroken helix and is about to offer her half when he sees that she is biting into hers whole, the teeth breaking through the bitter rind as if it were an apple.

He rests his orange on his knee and watches as she wrenches the peel from her mouth, tears off the remaining flesh, then bites in again. Juice runs freely through the sluice of her fingers and drips onto her bare thighs. To think of eating an orange like that! Without taking his eyes off her, Billy puts a single segment into his own mouth. It is sweet and sharp and he winces on the insides of his cheeks. The tartness floods his nose. A scratch on his hand he didn't even know he had starts to sting.

– Whatja do with the pips? he blurts out.

She turns in surprise, her eyes wide with the business of eating.

– Pips? She finishes chewing, swallows, and then, seeing the surprise on his own face, she smiles delightedly, strands of pith trapped between her teeth. – Aren't you sposed to eat the pips?

Billy gets out a carton of milk and fills two tall glasses. From the living room comes a burst of canned laughter.

Maisie stands uneasily in the shadow of the kitchen door, half merging with it, the whites of her eyes shining. She'd been reluctant to come back to his house, but he'd persuaded her. Now she has the look of an animal about to bolt.

– Billy, is that you?

Maisie freezes at the sound of Crystal's voice. Billy puts a finger to his lips and hands her a glass. She takes it uncertainly. They drink, each watching the other from the sides of their glass. Billy watches the level of milk in her glass go down, draining into shadow. She drinks all the way to the bottom and then comes up for air, a white moustache on her lip.

– There's sausages under the grill, shouts Crystal. We already had ours.

Maisie gives him her glass which he puts on the benchtop, and they creep into the hall. A slice of brightly coloured television shows through the hinge of the living-room door. She makes no sound at all with her feet. Once they're both in his room, Billy pushes the door until it clicks.

Dark hairs show through her milky moustache. – Sure she won't come in?

Billy shakes his head. – She only ever comes in to clean.

She seems unconvinced, but after a while her curiosity gets the better of her. She looks around the room, pausing at each pair of guarded eyes staring back at her from the walls, the pile of unironed T-shirts on the chest of drawers, the scrapbook on his bed. The bed itself is unmade, the sheet snarled up against the wall. She gazes for a long time at the saucerful of dead beetles on his bedside table, but she doesn't make a comment. When she reaches the shelf with its line of stones, her eyes hover over each one, then move backwards and forwards along the line.

– You c'n have one if ya want.

She looks at him in surprise. – Which one?

He goes over and chooses a piece of layered quartzite. Once in her palm, she pushes the soft tip of her finger against its jagged edge.

– It's really sharp, she murmurs. It could cut you.

– I c'n polish it if ya want.

She shakes her head, folds her fingers over the quartzite and pockets it. Then she looks immediately at what else there might be for her. She stares for a while out of the window at all of Stan's junk. Next to the window hangs a mirror. When her eyes meet it she gives a jump and steps backward. Billy laughs. He goes over and stands beside her.

They are stark opposites. She is like his shadow, he thinks, dark where he is light. She doesn't seem to have grown since he met her and he's almost a full head taller than her now, but her face and the individual features on it are all so much bigger than his own.

– Did you hear about the bloke whose totem was a bush potato? she asks suddenly.

Billy looks at her eyes in the mirror. He shakes his head.

– He ate it by mistake.

Billy stands awkwardly beside her, not knowing how to respond.

– Someone put it in a sandwich and he went munching in – yum yum, this is good, never eaten anything like it, totally unfamiliar yet strange how it reminds me of myself . . .

She giggles with horror, bringing a hand to her mouth.

– What happened to him? asks Billy.

– When they told him what he'd done, he got a knife and hacked into his stomach, delved inside and pulled out whatever he could, all this yellow gut tangled like rope in his fingers . . .

– Ew!

Billy is laughing now too.

– The poor bugger didn't know where to stop.

– Poor bugger! echoes Billy.

– He died, of course.

She shivers involuntarily.

– That's a terrible story!

– Not really. It was only to be expected.

In the mirror they both watch her hand reaching around his back. Her fingers are sticky with orange juice. She grips his shoulder tightly. She has such stern, deepset eyes, but the white moustache is still there, comical on her dark skin. Billy breaks into a smile.

– Hello, Maisie, he says.

– Hello, Wallamba, she says, smiling back.

After she's gone, he lies on his bed and listens to the sound of Crystal washing up, handfuls of cutlery being shoved into the plastic drainer, the TV still blaring in the other room. He doesn't want a word for what he's feeling. Whatever it is, it's a sense of fullness, like air pumped into his veins. When he holds his breath an excitement bubbles in his throat. He closes his eyes and imagines he's being sung to from the inside, as if she had slit him open that first morning and tucked her song inside, leaving it there like a second, bleating heart.

Maisie. *Maisie.* It's an old-fashioned name but he likes it.

the chasm

One evening, with nothing better to do, the wind scours the plain, gathering the loose red dust and rolling it up like a carpet.

It shapes the dust into a series of long, sculpted dunes which, from above, lace the earth with a network of bones beneath the skin, a skeleton that may one day rise up and take shape. For now, though, this creature lies buried, and the rhythmic motion lulls the wind with a sense of peace.

Ahead rises the sheer eastern face of the escarpment, the beginning of the Hann plateau. The wind never fails to be astonished by the adamance of this escarpment, nor the stunted box trees latched limpet-like to its flanks, pushing their scabrous roots into minute cracks and crevices, forming their own topsoil by breaking down the rock as they go. When it has finished with sculpting ridges, the wind weaves among these trees, exploring the ledges and buttresses of rock, ever hopeful of triggering a spot of trouble, but not managing to do much more than send a handful of stones cascading down.

Rounding a bend, it comes to the immense sandstone boulder cleft open from top to bottom. Whether the boulder had once been attached to the escarpment higher up and had split like an egg as it fell, or was battered by a blow from above, the wind has never been able to tell. But it loves this sandstone boulder because when it looks right through from one side to the other it can see a perfect keyhole of sky.

The wind eases itself inside the chasm gently. At once it is swallowed up by the cold, ancient shadow of the rock. Sheer, dark-red sides soar upwards, teetering over at the top and trapping the rock's dank, mournful smell, the sourness of fetid water caught in a niche somewhere. To the wind the chasm is primordial, lost, abandoned, as if the heat of the desert has failed to ever find it and bring it into the present day.

Emerging into sunlight again on the other side, the wind sighs with relief, but can't help turning around for another look. Such a perfectly shaped keyhole of sky! It might be dark and weird in there, but oh – how the keyhole beckons! How it *begs* to be chased!

The wind takes a few steps back. Sucks in air, and runs.

Slapping the side of the boulder, the wind is forced into the shape of the chasm and passes through the cold heart of the rock. It takes no more than a few seconds. When it's spat out the other end, a soft, breathy note spills out with it: an eerie, haunting sound. The voice of the rock itself.

The wind stares at the rock, astonished. Never has it made a noise like that before! There's nothing for it but to try again. This time the wind starts further back, gathering more momentum. Bruised by the initial impact, it rips through the rock in a long, thin stream, so that the whistle too is drawn out – a high, piercing cry this time with a hint of yearning in it.

After that the wind cannot get enough. Again and again it rears back and hurls itself towards the keyhole, slamming into the rock so hard that only a terrorised, seared part of itself gets through. The cry becomes a scream – keening, awful, anguished – until it is an almost human screech of angular intensity, a cry from the very edge of nature. And suddenly, as if at this pitch it has nowhere else to go, the note takes a cue from the rock itself and splits in two.

Tumbling head over heels, the wind picks itself up and spins around. Could that really have happened? A dissonant semi-tone splintering off from the first? The wind brushes down its tattered extremities, puffs itself back up to size, and is about to try again when it hears a ghostly echo.

Yes, there it is! A distinct second note. The wind is practically hyper-ventilating now. It has never heard anything like it.

On the next attempt, the second note steps further away from the first and becomes a different note in its own right. Again the wind runs through the rock, and again, until semi-tone becomes tone becomes third, then a dissonant seventh, one screeching high, one low. Each time the two notes move around one another in a different way, sometimes playing, some-times arguing. Back and forth the wind rushes, so that the notes sing out over and over, overlapping in layers of chords and echoes, a chaotic two-note ensemble that bounds from key to key.

All right long the wind plays with the sandstone boulder, and the voice of the rock screams out across the desert, filling the air with the ache of something that has been trapped inside since time began.

part IV

the longest serving inmate

Some patients leave; more arrive. The speed at which a bed is filled seems to suggest that arms are broken and spleens ruptured whenever news gets through that a patient has been discharged. There's a steady stream of heart attacks and strokes, swollen appendixes and suspect tumours: a world of injury and illness which Billy had had no idea existed. He had never really questioned where men went when they disappeared from the shift rota. Now he knows.

Visitors – husbands, wives, girlfriends, boyfriends – stiffly dressed and trailing clusters of uneasy, foot-swinging children, peer at Billy unashamedly as they're filled in on ward gossip. They munch on the biscuits and fruit they brought with them as gifts.

– See that one over there?

– The one with the piercing eyes?

– Yeh. Had a run-in with some Wongis. Got himself a taste of black-fella law.

– You're kidding.

– He never gets any visitors.

– Shall I take him some grapes?

He's the longest serving inmate now – it's been four weeks since they brought him in – and this dubious honour invests him with a certain authority. He has his own armchair in the TV room, can leave his smokes unattended when he goes to the bathroom and they'll still be there when he gets back. Every day he is the first to be handed a plate of food by the lunch boy, with Cecily pointing at the menu card and dictating what he wants.

One night with the curtains drawn around his bed he hauls himself into the wheelchair, his bare feet resting on the cold metal slat. He is starting to get used to his wheels. He moves about so much faster, he almost prefers them now. According to the yellow-crested doctor, he has every chance of recovering ninety per cent of his normal movement and strength, although Billy was taken aback when he heard this. Only ninety per cent? The inflammation has made itself at home in your bones, the doctor explained. You'll never shuck it completely. Wind up somewhere cold and damp and you'll feel a stiffness setting in. Like rheumatoid arthritis.

Great, thought Billy. Fucken great.

He makes his way down the sleeping ward, attended by the ever-present *eek, eek, eek* of his wheels. He punches open the double doors, then propels himself through before they have time to slam back. It doesn't take long to call the lift; nothing much going on at this hour of the morning. When the doors slide back, there is a woman in a voluminous quilted dressing gown in one corner with her arms clutched across her chest: another night-time wanderer. He gives her a nod but she chooses not to acknowledge him. Afterwards it occurs to him that she might have been sleep-walking.

He takes the lift up to the tenth floor. The woman stays behind as he wheels himself out. A long, unlit corridor stretches away before him, windows along the left-hand wall. He can't tell if there's anyone around to hear his wheels complaining. Halfway down the corridor he stops and from a sitting position is just about able to lever one of the windows open. These are the only windows without bars that he's found in the hospital. It pushes outwards and the warm night air rushes in, heady with the smells of heat-roasted earth, the tang of saltbush, eucalyptus musk. His head swims, intoxicated. Below him a stretch of saltbush pans out behind the car park, quickly becoming indistinct in the darkness. Above it a heavy, violet sky.

For a long time Billy sits there with his eyes closed, listening to the scratchings of the cicadas, lapping hungrily at the night air.

In the morning he locks the bathroom door behind him and wheels up to the bath. Draped across his thighs is a towel and a tablet of soap.

– Lemme in, Billy.

– Leave me alone.

– Lemme in.

He bends over the armrest to reach the taps, gets a good hot gush going and dangles the plug above the hole by its chain. It skits to one side in the rush of water so he turns off the tap and waits for the plug to be sucked down.

Cecily takes advantage of the momentary silence.

– Sister got a master key for these locks. Dja want me to go and get it? Cause I will.

He's about to drown her out with the hot tap when she speaks again.

– Billy, when are ya gunna grow up?

He hovers for a moment, unsure whether to be shocked or amused by this. Eventually he decides to plump for the latter: if it's no more than a decision, then why not make it? With a wry smile he wheels around and lets her in.

Ignoring his eyes, Cecily locks the door behind her and lowers her backside on to the edge of the bath. Then she twists around to work the taps for him.

– Carry on, I ain't looking, she says.

– I thought you had better things to do than give me baths, says Billy. I don't need ya.

– I know that.

She lets her hand hang in the stream of cold water, the fingers giving shape to the flow.

– So . . . ?

But she won't be hurried. He realises his mistake and gets on with the complicated business of undressing, rolling the pyjama bottoms down slowly over his hospital underpants, over the bandages. There is less seepage these days, but the wounds are still unsealed, slowly healing from the inside out.

– I c'n take that thing out now.

She's motioning with her dripping hand towards his canula. Edging along the rim of the bath, she takes hold of his hand and slides the needle out, capping it before tossing it into the surgical bin. Then she reaches up to the cupboard, finds a bottle of disinfectant and upturns it on a wad of cotton wool, two big up-and-down shakes. All this she does without having to get up from her pew. Both of them study the curiously shaped bruise that has mushroomed on the back of his hand, the colour of worn jeans, or a faded tattoo. She dabs it with the wet side, then the dry side, one or two wisps of cotton sticking around the hole which she picks at, carefully.

– That Dexter J. Kramer bloke.

Billy looks up, sharply.

– What about im?

– E's a sticky one.

– What's happened, Cecily?

She shakes her head. – Them Americans, any chance they get to earn some money.

– He's gunna sue, is that it?

Cecily swishes her hand in the water and turns off the cold. – 'E wants you ter do some tests.

– What sort of tests?

She dries her hands on the corner of his towel, peels the backing off a large square plaster and smooths it down with her thumbs.

– Keep that out the water, she says.

Billy tries to scrutinise her face, but she keeps it lowered.

– What's 'e tryin to prove?

For a moment her gaze travels across his face and then away, allowing only the briefest of contact with his eyes.

– Mebbe 'e can sue the hospital for not locking you away sooner, she suggests. I dunno.

– Ah. A schizo on the loose, ay.

She lets go of his hand, turns the heavy mass of her brow to one side.

– How is the fella, anyway? asks Billy. Has 'e gone home yet?

– Yeh, ages ago. He looked diff'rent by the end. Thinner. You rearranged his teeth.

Billy can't resist a smile. – Poor bastard. 'E didn't deserve it.

– 'Is wife, bloody angry one that one. You shouldda done it to her instead.

Billy chuckles.

– Or that James bloke, Cecily adds.

– Ah! Turning on your own, now?

– You shouldn't've talked to im, she says.

Billy looks at Cecily, then down at his lap. He starts unwrapping the tablet of soap.

– I know. 'E caught me out. Diminished responsibility 'n all that.

– Yeh, well, you know better now.

– I do.

Cecily waits for the moment to pass, then takes a breath. – Dja miss em?

– What?

– Y'know, the voices.

This startles him even more.

– I don't know.

– You know.

Billy looks up.

– No, I don't miss em. Well, maybe, one of em. A bit.

Cecily nods. She uses her hands to haul herself upright. At the door she pauses.

– Want new sheets?

– Had new sheets two days ago.

– I'll make you new sheets.

– Thanks.

– You turn that bath off. More than enough water in there.

She unlocks the door, then manoeuvres herself around it.

---

tonight's main headline

The light is fading. Dust hovers in the air. We take a deep, luxuriating drag, wistful in the knowledge that this will be our last for the evening, and pass the beautiful toke to the next set of waggling fingers.

Looks like madam's pitching up.

What's she got this time?

We shake our heads, slowly.

It's a bloody invasion.

Wish she'd just leave us in peace.

Now, now. That'll happen soon enough.

She is levering something large and square over the ground in zigzags, first one corner, then running around to heave the other. We rub the muzziness from our eyes and noses, the sweet-tasting smoke curling languidly around our heads, our lungs.

Yoo-hoo! calls out the spirit child.

One of us stands up and hollers: Whatever it is, you can take it straight back! We don't want it!

Determination has apparently given her the strength of a full-grown man, for within a short while she has the cumbersome object sitting ten feet from us, a big hulk of a machine with a grey glassy eye and an ugly metal halo hovering over the top.

This, she says, is going to change everything.

A television set, presumably, we say drily, aiming to steal her thunder. We pass the surreptitious spliff behind our backs. What in the world are we supposed to do with that?

Watch it, stupid.

This is the way she speaks to us now – no respect.

But we can see anything we want to already, we snap.

Her supplicant palms shoot out to the sides in exasperation.

There's not very much to see from the vantage point of a hammock! she cries. Now you can not only hear their voices, but see them *live in action* too! And all without moving an inch.

We shuffle, uncomfortably. One of us flicks the end of the spliff in the dirt.

At the rate you're cluttering up our camp, we're going to *have* to move.

She ignores us, busily smoothing out a patch of earth to one side of the stand of snappy gums to make a viewing area. She untangles the long cable that snakes out behind her towards the town, like the telephone line, plugs it into the back of the machine and fiddles with the metal halo. The black-and-white fuzz on the screen sharpens, warps, turns to fuzz again. Then a picture springs into being: a red Buick parked in a shabby front yard, a tall man in stained blue overalls attempting nonchalance by leaning an elbow awkwardly on its bonnet.

Isn't that Stan Saint?

Those of us still sleeping jolt awake at this comment and peer blearily over.

– *Your friendly Kimberley panel-beater!* chirps the television set.

The spirit child giggles, then checks the bulbous digital watch she has taken to wearing.

We're just in time to catch the end of the six o'clock news.

We know the news already. It's boring.

Something hardens in the set of the spirit child's lower jaw.

Don't be so quick to dismiss it! Sometimes it's a little bit saucy, the stuff they show on TV.

Saucy?

That's what I said. Sometimes there's even some *poking*.

We mutter amongst ourselves. No one's immune to a bit of sauciness from time to time – it keeps the mind active – but we'd rather not have to admit it in front of the spirit child.

Go on, then, if you must.

Not if you don't want it, she says. I can always take it away again.

Put it on, or you won't get any supper!

Unable to suppress a smirk, she presses a button on the remote control and with a low, begrudging *bumpf* the picture switches to a woman in a smart jacket sitting at a table. Her lips are painted the same orangey-red as her jacket. She has a perfect, symmetrical smile, a line of square white teeth, and curly auburn hair packed neatly around her head.

– And back to tonight's main headline, she says in a tin-bright voice. *Prime Minister Paul Keating has made a public declaration of his ongoing love for his ex-wife Annita. He says he'll always love her for making him a cup of tea when he got home from branch meetings at eleven p.m. and (I quote) 'a bit of a cuddle as well', if he was lucky.*

Ha!

We look around at one another in delight.

That's nothing! cries the spirit child. It gets much saucier than that. Now, check this out.

She presses a button on the remote, and there, sitting in what looks like an aircraft hangar but is actually the inside of his house, is none other than Stevo from the servo, staring at a screen perched on the top of his fridge. In front of him is a stack of white toast cut on the diagonal, each layer soggy with the margarine from the layer beneath. Around him on the floor are squeezy bottles of tomato sauce, spilled sugar cubes and half-drunk mugs of milky tea.

– What, no sex? Poor bugger, murmurs Stevo, looking up at the still shot of Keating on the screen. He has a smear of margarine at the corner of his mouth.

And this!

The spirit child presses another button and a second dim interior appears. This time there's a shadowy figure nestled in an armchair, the soles of two feet looming large in the foreground. To one side, someone is curled up on the sofa in a blue dressing gown.

– At least he gets a cuddle, mutters Stan, swapping the cross of his ankles and hurling a resentful look at Crystal.

We stare at the spirit child, completely baffled.

Isn't it clever? she exclaims, not bothering to hide her pride. I've rigged it up. Secret video cameras tucked inside their television sets, transmitting back live pictures by satellite. Whoever you want, whatever time of day, you just need to press a button –

She looks from one pair of eyes to another, desperate for our approval, her face alight with hope that any moment now we will shower her with the praise she so yearns for. What a brilliant girl! However did we get along without you? What other clever things can you do?

We stay quiet. It doesn't take long for the hope to die away.

Next morning, the wind flings itself over a branch like a sheet left out to dry, and sighs and groans with each inconsolable breath.

Cut it out, will you? we cry. We're sick of listening to your wretched snivelling.

But I'm *hot*.

So what, so are we.

But it *hurts*. I feel deflated. Completely worn out.

Have you been playing at the sundered rock again? It's your own fault for exerting yourself.

At least I've been *entertaining myself*. I'd have thought you would be pleased.

Then just accept that you have to pay for it afterwards.

If I'd known I was going to feel as terrible as this . . .

Unable to take to any more, we get up and dust ourselves down.

We're going to the coffee shop, we announce. To take advantage of the joys of air conditioning.

The wind looks up in alarm and gives a hysterical shriek.

Air conditioning? Isn't that *man-made wind?*

Such a clever idea, we say, shaking our heads respectfully. Wish we'd thought of it first.

You bastards! cries the wind, hurling itself back over the branch. You thoughtless, *thoughtless* bastards!

Estha ties the strings of her apron behind her and flicks a switch on the wall. Three rows of fluorescent lights transform the room into an artificial midday. She kicks a plastic wedge beneath the door and hauls yesterday's bin bags outside. It's Saturday and the garbo men aren't due until Monday, but what else is she supposed to do with all the left-over chook legs that have started to let out a stink?

On the forecourt opposite, Yakka twitches in the shade of the Diesoline pump, nose tucked between parallel paws. Estha whistles, a quick, upwards curl of a whistle and Yakka looks up and wags hello.

We troop in behind her through the open door, and by the time she comes back inside we've made ourselves comfortable, scattered around the tables.

Morning, Estha.

Estha doesn't hear us but she nods at Rossco and Gerry who come in shortly afterwards, spreading their newspaper out between them as usual. Estha gets to work with making the cappos.

There's a single, pleading yelp from over the road. Estha leaves the machine steaming and goes to the window to see Stevo marching purpose-fully across the forecourt towards his battered Land Cruiser.

– Wrap-around sunglasses, she murmurs. Whatever next.

– Fancies himself something rotten, does our Stevo, agrees Rossco, looking up. Can't think what he sees in imself.

Yakka, poised on four trembling legs, sneezes in the flurry of Stevo's exhaust. Estha watches the Cruiser turn left, heading north. Off to the Saints' house again, and it's not to play with Billy. She shakes her head and wanders back behind the counter.

The bell pings again and a large, looming shape appears in the doorway. Coldiver blinks, takes in the empty tables, then heads for the one nearest Estha.

– Black coffee and a chiko roll, darlin.

Estha carries on drying a large frying pan. Rossco and Gerry swap a look, then get back to their paper. Gerry rubs the freshly cropped bristles on his scalp. We gather around and peer over their shoulders. On the page they've got open is an advertisement for a holiday house on the edge of King Sound, the photograph taken when the tide was in so that the water laps up to the edge of the lawn. House with Beautiful Sea View, it says. Swim from your Back Yard.

– Look at this, Rossco, says Gerry. There'll be a Sydney-sider come all the way over to Derby for the summer: what a hot property, a taste of WA. Dreams of streets lined with mango and palm trees. A family of four taking up residence for a month . . .

Behind his smeared lenses, Rossco's eyes light up. He licks his lips and takes the baton on.

– While the owners of the house drive their caravan two kays down the road . . .

– But not so far away that they can't come back and piss their pants when they see the looks on the city folks' faces as soon as the tide goes out . . .

– Because there, stretchin before them, will be two slick miles of grey mud flats, crawlin with salties and stinkin of stranded fish left behind by the tide!

The two men slap the table as they laugh.

– A grand old beach house, ay!

– It'll be as much use to em as tits on a nun!

We raise our eyebrows. It amazes us how they find the same stories funny year after year.

Gerry turns the page. Rossco's head bobs up and down like a harnessed horse to make room.

– Here's another good un, Rossco, says Gerry. *Six Federal Polys Come to Town*.

Rossco peers through his smeared glasses. They're so dirty he's finding it difficult to see. On this page there's a photograph taken down a residential street in Derby. A series of wooden signs outside people's houses are proclaiming 'Yes to Tidal Power'.

– That'd put an end to the teasing of Sydney-siders, having a fuck-off power station on the mud flats. Whatja reckon, Rossco?

– I reckon there'd be –

– Jobs for life, for all of ya.

They look up. The guts of a chiko roll spill onto the table as Sydney Coldiver's big lips chow down. He dabs up limp bean sprouts and other spilt innards with a finger.

– No more going to Derby to sit on the end of the jetty, throwing dead squid at the crocs, is what I was going to say, finishes Rossco steadily.

Coldiver brings his fat fist down on the table, hard. A couple of bean sprouts jump up.

– Whatja want from your lives, fellas? he roars, a little piece of something flying out his mouth and hitting one of us on the side of the face. You wanna be a load of unemployed bludgers with more time on your hands than a fucking tortoise, or do an honest week's work and get a pay packet on Friday night?

We share a smirk and a chuckle. Good old Coldiver. Never lets us down.

– And come home too knackered to shag the wife, points out Rossco.

– And have to hurry down the street in forty-five-degree heat, adds Gerry.

– And niver have time to throw dead squid at the crocs, insists Rossco, shaking his bearded face.

All at once, Coldiver's cheeks ignite as if they had been drenched in petrol. Behind the counter, the normally impervious Estha, adding two sugars to the saucer of Coldiver's coffee, looks on, marginally interested.

– What sort of a life is *that* to show your kids? Coldiver barks.

– A good life is what it is, counters Rossco, calmly. Y'know, Gerry, I always like goin out on that jetty in the evenings, jiss to sit there, lookin at the Southern Cross tilted on its axis, how low it is on the horizon. Did I tell ya? My little boy Reggie saw a shooting star last night. Two streaks of light, like tyre tracks behind, 'e said. Kept jumpin up and down going, Right over there it went, didntcha see it, Dad? Didntcha?

– Didja tell him he could make a wish? asks Gerry.

– I did. 'E squeezed his eyes tight shut. I wonder what 'e wished for, ay.

Coldiver, his face still burning, blinks in disbelief.

– I wonder, ay, echoes Gerry.

In the little silence that follows they all get in on the act: Estha, as she carries the coffee over to Coldiver's table, Gerry and Rossco as they stare blankly at their paper, all wondering what *they'd* wish for. A sixty-pound barra for Gerry. A two-week package to Kuta beach for Estha. A big house down on One Arm Point for Rossco. No – a win on the lotto, thinks Estha, changing her mind on the way back, then she could afford to go to Bali *every* year. She could buy that cream sarong and the studded leather sandals she saw in the shop in Broome. She could ask one of those beautiful Kuta cowboys to give her a massage on the beach. In the evenings he'd take her out for pineapple daquiris. Walking hand in hand down the beach in the moonlight with the waves gently lapping at their feet.

Rossco tries to guess what his little boy Reggie might've wished for – something clever, no doubt, something sensible, something that would take him out of this town and into the wider world.

A blow job from Estha, thinks Sydney Coldiver, taking a sip of coffee, because she's not bad-looking for a boong.

– I'd wish for some bloody changes in attitude around here, for a start, he says out loud, putting his coffee cup down with a clatter.

Gerry shakes his head. – It's a fine place ter live, this town. I wouldn't want ter live anywhere else.

– Me neither, says Rossco, scratching his beard.

Coldiver bunches the soiled greaseproof paper from his chiko roll in his fist, every part of him angry.

– You could learn a trick or two from the blackfella I got workin at the roadhouse, he roars. Jimmi Rangi. More business sense than the two of ya put together. A rollickin business partner, 'e is. But I'll get you bludgers eventually. There ain't no gettin away from an honest day's work, you'll see.

Rossco and Gerry share a wink and jerk up their noses as Gerry turns the page.

Estha goes back to drying the pans and wonders what it'd be like to feel the cool ocean lap over your toes.

the learned professor

At 10.59 on the dot, a shrill *beep-beep-beep* punctures the stillness. The spirit child presses the little button on her digital watch then skips over to the square of levelled earth in front of the TV, swiping a pad of paper and a pen from under a hammock en route.

Bumpf.

In the middle of the red spinifex plain a man with wild grey hair hunches over his desk. The circles of his glasses have turned to pearl in a shaft of captured light.

The spirit child wriggles her feet into cross-legged position and stares at the man on the screen. She can almost smell the delicious mustiness of his study – the smell of knowledge, of solitude in the early hours of the morning. Midnight blue ink blots his page. But there is tell-tale dirt trapped beneath this man's fingernails, and peeping out from under his professor's black cape are a fashionable pair of runners. The spirit child knows his secret. She bites her lip.

In one practised movement, the professor swivels around to face the camera and looks up.

– *Good morning out there! Today in* Anthropology for Everyone *we are going to travel back to a time before any of you were born, before many of your grandparents had even set foot on this pristine, beautiful continent . . .*

Speak for yourself, points out the spirit child.

– *. . . before modern technological advances brought us the telephone, the radio, the television and fast, efficient means of getting from A to B . . .*

As he's talking, the learned professor gets up and starts to walk towards his bookcase. The spirit child chews on the end of her biro in suspense. This is the bit she likes best. As he gets closer to the bookcase the edges of him turn to jelly. First a hand, then an arm, then a foot is sucked into the books –

– *when the natives used what we might call* psychic powers *to communicate with one another . . .*

For a while there is nothing but a disembodied voice issuing from within the dusty rows of leather-bound books with their gold lettering and peeling spines. And then, *dnah!*, we are on the other side, and those same limbs are emerging one by one. Except that they have undergone a transformation while going through his bookcase, and instead of a billowing cape, there's a cotton shirt and khaki slacks and masculine, hairy arms.

The spirit child spits out the broken shards of biro plastic and looks around for one of us. She'd like to be able to tell us what she's just worked out: that the learned professor's ability to walk through bookcases and find a different geographical and temporal region on the other side is not just a way of entertaining the audience with gratuitous special effects – oh, no. It illustrates the fact that books can take you *anywhere in the world, including backwards and forwards in time*. This realisation has filled her with a sudden hunger to read voraciously – anything and everything that she can get her hands on.

But she doesn't want to miss any of the programme trying to find us. She flips over a page of her pad, and writes:

Homework for tonight: the use of special effects as symbol of mental process. Discuss.

Back on the screen, the learned professor is busy orientating himself within the red sandstone plain in which he has found himself – a landscape not unlike the spirit child's except that the enormous, hulking bulk of Uluru looms in the distance.

– *. . . and indeed what better place than the Red Centre, with its vast tracts of uninhabited land and nothing but the call of the butcher bird to impinge on the silence for a gentle spot of meditation?*

– *G'day, mate.*

A conveniently placed elderly white bushman, sitting cross-legged on his swag, shades his vague, sun-faded eyes with a veiny hand.

– *What are you doing?* asks the learned professor.

The blue-eyed bushman gives a leisurely smile.

– *Thinking, mate.*

The professor turns to the camera and raises his eyebrows as if to make a point. Then the camera swings around to find an Aboriginal man squatting on his haunches a few feet away, his big feet slapped squarely before him, chewing the end of a stick. His shirt is unbuttoned at the top, revealing parallel ridges of scarred skin.

– *And you, sir?*

– *I'm sending a message, prof.*

Without taking her eyes from the screen, the spirit child scribbles frantically to keep up, her letters big and unruly on the page.

Has the ability to communicate psychically been lost? Discuss.

Next the professor sets off through the bush, the long, loping stride of the cameraman giving the impression of an animal stalking its prey. The grass in this place is yellow and long and whispery. Ahead there are splashes of crimson in the tips of bauhinia trees. There's a hissing noise, cicadas maybe, or the wind in the grass, or maybe it's the rattle of the heat.

The learned professor crouches in the grass as if he's about to pounce. Into view come a mob of women, bare feet lifted high to clear the stalks of grass, some sort of song in the air between them. It's early morning and their shadows are long and pointed. Each woman carries an object: a boomerang, a fighting stick, a yellow handkerchief.

– *And so they leave their camp and their menfolk behind them*, the learned professor whispers, while th*ey attend to 'women's business'*.

Fighting sticks, flung into the air, spin head-over-tail against the sky. The younger women rip handfuls of grass and drag long branches by one cumbersome end, laughing and joking all the while. A group of older women sit on the ground with their legs stretched out to the sides, skirts gaping obscenely. A blur of skin passes too close, then comes into focus, a glistening, fleshy stomach with a vertical charcoal line plunging thickly downwards from the navel.

– *Me sing that one, me sing that* mari!

And then they start to dance. At first they move in a crocodile, one behind the other, their knees and backs bent like long-legged birds pecking at the ground. A sideways shuffle, a little half-skip at the end. The older women look on solemnly. Some of the younger ones have never done this dance before, and copy the moves of those in front, getting the steps wrong, then doing them double-time to catch up. They turn their heads over their shoulders and flash one another big grins. The whole thing is a great, delightful game.

What's this? we roar.

All the while we've been creeping up behind her. The spirit child leaps to her feet and dashes to the screen, guiltily covering as much of the picture with her spread-limbed body as she can.

None of your business! she shouts.

Don't order us about.

This is private! I'm busy! Go away!

We peer down at the abandoned pad.

What's this? Taking *notes*?

She stares, caught between fierceness and fright, between wanting to hide the screen and wanting to snatch back the book. We pick it up and flick the pages over.

Psychic powers . . . Initiation ceremonies . . . Love magic. What on earth are you doing?

We glare at her. The spirit child stares in panic.

I've got to learn about it from somewhere! she shouts. You never tell me anything.

We glare back at her, angrily.

But . . . the *television*?

It's *Anthropology for Everyone*. It's great. The learned professor, that's the bloke hiding in the grass there, he can walk through his bookcase and come out anywhere he wants –

We stare at her in disbelief.

But this *learned professor* is a whitefella . . .

The colour rises in the spirit child's cheeks.

Look, if you don't want me to listen to him, you'll have to buck up and take more responsibility. Who else am I supposed to turn to?

We glare at her haughtily, but the truth is we have no answer. Spotting her chance, the spirit child snatches the pad from our hands and storms away, maintaining enough foresight to grab the remote control as she goes.

Bumpf!

The picture of the women shrinks and dies.

Drrinng drrrrinnnng! Drrinng drrrrinnnng!

It's more a desire to put an end to the awful noise than any real curiosity that forces us to shinny up a snappy gum and pluck the receiver from its cradle. We press it to a whiskery ear and listen.

– Jimmi?

That Coldiver again!

– Boss?

– I've got bloody awful news.

We beckon the others over. There's a pause as Coldiver swigs from a bottle, the tell-tale clink of glass against teeth.

– Our first coupla guests are comin on Monday.

A prolonged silence from Jimmi.

– I know, it's disappointing after all this time of having the roadhouse to yourself. But think laterally, Jimmi. You might meet some pretty girls.

Jimmi laughs. – This good news, boss.

– Remember to put up an advert about the rock tour, Jimmi. Make up some creation story about it being a giant eagle's or a lizard's egg or some-thing. Them poms'll lap it up.

There's the snatch of Jimmi's lighter.

This way, says the wind.

Up the tree?

The wind nods.

We complain that we've already been up and down trees answering the telephone all morning, but the wind just shrugs. One by one we monkey up the white flank of the ghost gum, smooth as a well-sucked bone. Some of us straddle the strongest branch, while others sit hunched and hawkish in a fork, waiting to be convinced of the need for this exertion.

Keep going, hisses the wind, motioning frantically. Further along the branch!

But it's hard work in the heat of the day, we moan.

Keep going! Keep going!

And then, from the far end of the branch, comes a shout. Pushing a mop of silvery-grey leaves aside, a brown school-bag is hauled out.

We catch one another's eyes as we have our first inkling of what this might all be about. We stack up one behind the other along the white bough and peer over shoulders as the bag is opened and the contents taken out and passed from hand to hand down the line. A round of Coon cheese sandwiches. Three Tim Tams wrapped in foil. A packet of salt & vinegar crisps. An orange. A lined exercise book filled with mathematical equations. A black furry pencil case. A bouncy ball made of rubber bands.

Another shout, this time from behind. At the far end of a second branch a pair of runners have been discovered, hanging from their own knotted laces, perfectly placed so as to be concealed from the kitchen window and the road.

He calls it the hiding tree, explains the wind.

After that we explore every remaining inch of the tree, scrambling along to the perilous ends of scrawny branches, lifting and shaking every mophead; but there is nothing else to be discovered. And then there's a third shout.

Look at this!

We tumble down to the ground, in too much of a hurry to do it gracefully, landing on the corrugated track with a series of soft thuds.

On the track, stones have been arranged across the dirt in careful lines. It doesn't take us long to make out the individual letters.

BILLY SICK TODAY.

He's sent us a message at last! we cry.

It's not for you, you pack of galahs, sneers the wind, loving this opportunity to be the one with the knowledge for once. It's for the driver of the school bus. So he knows to drive on, not to bother tooting the horn.

But what's wrong with Billy?

Nothing's wrong with Billy! Don't you see? He's wagging!

As understanding dawns, we look around at one another. Our confusion gives way to wide grins. The scenario tickles us. We can just picture it: the school bus slowing down, the driver taking in the sign, then picking up speed again. From inside the house Crystal, listening to the sound of the bus's engine, would hear nothing different than if Billy had been picked up.

He's quite a kid, our Billy, we say. Perhaps he's gone off somewhere with Jon-Jon.

The wind looks at us scornfully.

He's not with Jon-Jon. He's with his *girlfriend*.

What girlfriend?

Don't you notice *anything* these days? They went off together an hour ago.

We stare at the wind in confusion.

For Chrissakes, says the wind. What are you, a load of bloody ostriches? She's befriended him. She's trying out all her half-baked knowledge of Aboriginal law on him. She's trying to initiate him. She's –

We have started to tremble now. We hold onto the ghost gum for support.

Go after her, we command the wind. Go and find her and bring her back!

---

a real dunny

He grazes his knee more than once on the way up, miscalculating the height of the rocks, rushing it. His composure isn't what it used to be when he came up here just for the roos. At the top he sits hunched up from the cold, waiting for the sky and the land to cleave in two, for the horizon to make itself known. A shiver bounces down the knots of his spine.

Suddenly, from out of the rock appears a silhouetted elbow, a triangle of sky wedged within it. The chafed edges of hair, the bend of a knee. She extracts herself from the rock as if she had been locked inside it all night.

His surprise rescues him from his usual shyness.

– How long've you bin there?

She shrugs, barely acknowledging him, a casualness that forces him back into shyness again.

– Where's the car?

– Back at the house.

– Have you got petrol in it?

– Yeh.

– Good, Wallamba!

Her tone is condescending, but the big square teeth shine from a smile that seems genuinely pleased. Billy's heart balloons. It doesn't take much these days.

– C'mon then, Wallamba.

The rocks are just beginning to turn red as they make their way down, the huge, soft sky opening up behind them. In the yard Maisie stares, hands on hips, at the line of pristine vehicles: the jacked-up Snipe, the Kingswood, the Holden, the panel van, the Oldsmobile, the Buick.

– Which one shall we take?

– The ute.

– Why not this one?

She runs her hand down the glossy flank of the pale blue Kingswood, its lacquered surface without a single blemish, the chrome iridescent in the pre-dawn light.

– He never drives that.

– Why not?

Billy shrugs. – Don't know.

– Let's take it, Wallamba.

– It's too low-slung.

– But it's so *cool*, this car, Wallamba! I've never driven in a car like this!

She locks him with her large, black eyes. Blinks those feathery lashes.

Billy looks at the Kingswood. He's never had much time for these cars of his father's. They'd always seemed to him more like toys than anything useful.

– Dad'd have a heart attack.

She leans against the pillar of the shed, her skin looking darker than usual in the dimness. He can already imagine the black skin of her thighs against the cream leather seats.

– Go on, Wallamba.

– Hang on, then.

In the hallway he holds his breath, listening. He opens the little door of the key cupboard. There they are, hanging neatly in a row, each one carefully labelled. The keys are cool in his hand.

Back outside, he brushes his hand against her arm without meaning to.

– Climb in. Release the hand brake. You steer, I'll push.

She smiles at his attempt to sound like he's in control. He busies himself with heaving the Kingswood out of the grooves it has cut for itself in the hard-packed ground. She climbs in and steers in a big loop towards the drive. The car hobbles up and down over potholes.

Only when they are far enough from the house does he jump in beside her and start up the engine, looking back anxiously at the bedroom window for a flicker of life.

She knows tracks he has never heard of, let alone driven down. They head towards the coast. There was a community out here in the 1950s, she tells him, maybe earlier. A hundred blackfellas and a handful of whites – a missionary, a teacher, a doctor. Prospectors passed through sometimes, brought them pens and ink, bags of flour and sugar. The prospectors never found anything worth digging up, but it wasn't for lack of trying. Recently a mob from Wangkatjungka came by and found a complete skeleton arranged neatly on the earth, not a single finger or inner ear bone out of place, an iron bar running down the length of him that must've held up the tarp of his tent.

– How dja know all this?

She shrugs.

– Must've been lonely, dying out here, says Billy.

– Depends how much you like your family.

She darts him a mischievous look. He doesn't know how to respond to some of the things she says. When he's with her he feels like a piece of string pulled taut, almost too taut to breathe. He laughs, though, happily, still wonderstruck that this is happening at all, that she seems to want to spend time with him. Sometimes he thinks they're kids playing at being adults, sometimes they're adults playing at being kids. Most of all, Billy can't get over the fact that he's driving his dad's beloved old Kingswood – Stan's pride and joy – with this girl his parents know nothing about sitting on the seat beside him.

Maisie, on the other hand, looks as if she's been driven around in cars like this all her life. She stretches her slender arm out of the wound-down window, catching at seed heads, her chin resting on the frame, the breeze lifting a clump of her hair. Billy perches in front of the wheel, wiping sweat from the fuzz that's beginning to grow on his upper lip. Every so often he glances across at her dark thighs spread out on the cream leather.

The track is strewn with boulders. Billy takes it slowly, letting the car tilt and right itself. He hauls it over a jump-up, down the other side. So far so good. The sun is fully risen now and lights this new country with long, yellow shafts. They drive through a narrow gully where he expects the axle to drag, but it doesn't. He finds himself wanting to sing out: Hey, Mum! Dad! Guess what I'm doing! Exhilaration perches high in his chest, like a pip. His face breaks out into a grin.

They drive through waist-high cane grass dried to straw, some of the stems snapped and pointing horizontal, making hexagons and cubes which trap the sunlight as if in a web. Stems splinter and hiss against the sides of the car. Broken stalks pile up above the wipers. Grasshoppers land on the windscreen and bounce off, squirting pale faeces.

– It go up like *that* if you put a match to it! she shouts above the din. Like what happened to *them*.

Approaching on the side of the track is the burnt-out hull of a bull buggy. She had timed her comment precisely; she must have known what lay ahead. They get out, making a circle of the debris. Billy finds himself imagining what his father would say had he been there. Several dollars worth of good scrap aluminium in there, mate. Strewn over the ground are ugly pieces of metal twisted beyond recognition. The radio dangles by its wires. Further away are objects thrown clear by the explosion: beer cans, a potato masher.

– They were mustering cattle back here. A generator on the back, the buggy bouncing around, dry grass everywhere. All it took was a single spark.

She is talking in that teachery way she has, as if she wants to educate him. Perhaps she has this whole trip planned; all her speeches worked out. It makes him want to show her that he is the bigger and stronger of them now, although he has no idea how to do it. He watches as she stoops to look beneath the chassis.

– Did anyone die?

– None of the men did, but they had two dogs tied up beneath the buggy, out of the sun. It must've been horrible. The dogs barking, flames everywhere. They had no way of cutting them free.

Billy looks at her as she brings her head back up: this slim girl who can still seem like a stranger. He doesn't smile at her. She's open-mouthed, breathing from the top of her chest. There's a screech and they both look up. A pair of red-tailed black cockatoos fly out of a tree with long, loopy wings, swerve to the right and then at a harsh *kree* from one of them swerve to the left. When they pass in front of the sun there is a momentary, speckled darkness: a cockatoo eclipse, thinks Billy. Two shadows cross their faces, one hard on the heels of the other.

For a while after that, she doesn't speak.

– These are black basalt outcrops, he tells her, back in the car. He is looking for ways to redress the balance now; he knows plenty of things that she doesn't, after all. – That is high white sandstone, over there is red Leopald sandstone.

He hates the sound of himself – such a know-all – but it is the only way he can think of.

– In the creeks you c'n pick up handfuls of sand and find bits of quartz in it, sparkling. There are pipis in there too. They nibble yer feet. They're as hungry as baby piranhas. It's kind of ticklish until they get rilly stuck in. Ya hev to be careful not to stand around for too long, or you'll come out with a toe missin.

She stares at him for a while, then bursts out laughing. – You're telling lies, Wallamba!

Billy bites his lip to hide his smile. – You believed me for a minute.

Later he slips a cassette in the machine and when she's not looking he turns the volume up. It's works to a tee: the voice of the Triple J presenter introducing the next song. She stares in wide-eyed surprise.

– You can pick up the radio? Out here?

Billy bubbles inside with his secret. He can't wait for her to click, to discover the brilliance of the trick, but he won't be the one to tell her.

He smiles and smiles.

The track divides, each path fanning out towards the edge of the estuary. Billy knows roughly where they are now: this is where the station men come to stock up on barramundi at the end of the dry. They've probably been here in the last week, if they're not still here now. He went with the Frosts once, a little way further along the estuary. It was him, Jon-Jon and Ted in one ute and Fred and his head stockman bringing up the rear, because the boys were out of spares and it was easy to get a flat. They camped for a week, caught nothing until the last day when the barras came in in one big, congested cloud. Fred and Ted had slapped their big grey and white catches on the table. Billy remembers how their red gills opened up like accordions, how they flipped their heads and tails in spasmodic, Herculean efforts to survive. Gabe, the Aboriginal stockman, had run his knife down a gullet and laughed when the little pod-shaped heart popped out. He'd put the fish in the fridge still alive, and Billy had timed it: it took thirty minutes to die.

He picks a track. As soon as they can see the estuary he stops and they get out, leaving the car doors open. Billy doesn't dare look at the paint-work on the side of the car. It must be scratched all over.

The estuary is wide and shallow, a tongue scooping out soft mud. The sun cuts the water up into a million, glittering pieces. The tide is coming in fast, surging landwards and uphill, defying the rules of rivers. Billy is struck by how strange it is to see a body of water move like this. And there is something else not right about it, too. The water seems thick and turgid, and it's not just the salt. He stands on the grass bank, trying to make it out.

– It's yellow mullet, she says, as if she can read his mind.

At first he doesn't understand, but then he sees them: the heads of the fish sticking up above the surface as if they have only just learnt to swim, the squirming of their frantic tails just visible beneath the surface. The whole thick sludge is alive and teeming with them.

– Are they swimming or being carried by the tide?

– I don't know. Maybe both. Come on, Wallamba.

Without waiting for him, she scrambles down the soft mud bank. Billy takes off his Blunnies and socks because he can see that she's sinking into the grey sludge up to her ankles already. It smells salty, fetid, bad. He plunges in.

– *Ow*!

The mud is searingly hot. Scalding. It has blasted the tender skin on the arch of his foot, and yet there she is up to her ankles in it and not a flicker of pain on her face. He backs off, clamping a hand around his reddening foot, blinking back the tears. The pain is so immediate it makes him want to retch. As soon as he can bear to take his hands off he inspects the damage: bright crimson scrambling over the skin like a birthmark.

– Maisie!

She's out of sight already, somewhere down there on the bank. With a rush of alarm, Billy reminds himself that this is sea water. There are probably crocodiles in there. Salties. For a moment he is panicked enough to start pulling his boots on over his blistered foot and run down to find her. But then he stops. Most Aboriginal kids know what they're doing out bush. She'd only laugh at him, this girl who acts as if she owns the place, who seems to know the stories behind everything they pass.

He rips his boot off again and the pain in his foot makes him suddenly angry. It'd teach her, he thinks, stupidly. Losing an arm or leg to a saltie. Maybe she'll listen to him after that. He grabs a flagon of water from the car and limps towards a clearing between the trees feeling sorry for himself, throat clenching, eyes packed with tears. There's the remains of a fire left by the station men, a rickety grill thick with white lumps of hardened animal fat and a two-lane highway of ants motoring to and from an abandoned tin bucket which is emitting a loud buzz. He gulps from the flagon, pours a little over the side of his foot, but it's not cool enough to be a balm. He stares at the buzzing bucket, knows what he'll find inside it without needing to look, but goes over and peers in anyway. The sight and stench of it knocks the wind from his gut. It's rancid with grey scales and filmy black eyes, an inch-thick layer of flies, and he retches again, stumbling backwards over a tangle of rope.

– *Maisie?*

He is furious with her now. He doesn't care if she sees him close to tears. He doesn't like this place, and it's her fault that they're here. Another rope hangs from a tree – the remains of a bush shower perhaps – and he clambers up it. Perhaps he'll be able to spot her from up here. The branch creaks uneasily as he swings. The smell of rotten fish is still in his nose and another wave of nausea churns up his stomach. All he can see is a beaten path through the dry grass heading away from the water, and he jumps down and follows it, picking up a stick to lash in front of him to scare away snakes. A cluster of flies scribbles around his face. Ahead of him there is more buzzing, even louder, and when he rounds the corner he sees a patch of flattened grass and in the middle a white dunny with a black plastic seat. There are flies everywhere.

He's so surprised he forgets about his sore foot. A real dunny carried all the way out here! What a load of softies the stationmen are! There's even a twig nearby with a roll of toilet paper stuck on the fork, down to its last few sheets, wrinkled and thick with ants, but perfectly dry.

He lifts the lid of the dunny with his stick, turning his face away. He'd expected the stench to be terrible, but it's not too bad. Ants scatter around the edge of the bowl. A nasty quagmire of black shit lurks down in the darkness. He props the seat up with the jut of his hip, undoes his flies, and squirts the ants off the rim of the bowl. Then he lowers the seat and drops his trousers. His gut gives an angry twist. He closes his eyes and all he can see are the platinum scales, those gaping mouths, the dull black staring eyes. He remembers Fred Frost picking up a hook and piercing the gills of a mullet, the flesh tough as leather, and a hot shiver runs up from his stomach. Sweat prickles all over. Jesus, I've gone and got the runs, he thinks. His bowels churn and out it comes with an all-too-easy splat, the texture of whipped cream, plopping down into the black hole. He feels the sweat run up and down his arms, across his forehead. He shivers, despite the heat of the sun, waits till it's all done, finishes the last few sheets of paper, then sits there a while to make sure. When he feels the tickle of a fly crawling over his buttock he decides he's sat there long enough and pulls his trousers back up.

The rope has stopped swinging in the clearing. Billy pushes it, absent-mindedly, wondering what to do now. Probably he should go and look for her on the bank, but he's still angry at her for leading him there in the first place. Besides, his limbs are weak and shaky, and he wants to stay here in the shade rather than face the sparkling water and hot sun again.

– Wallamba?

He peers through sweat-bleared eyes. It takes an effort to make her out on the edge of the clearing; she is standing with the light behind her.

– Maisie? Guess what I found. A dunny. A real dunny!

She doesn't answer. He screws up his eyes against the sun and holds an arm across his face.

– Come and look if you don't believe me, he says.

She still says nothing. He starts to realise it may not be her. He takes a step to one side so that the bough of the tree blocks the sun.

– Maisie?

And then he sees. It's Maisie alright, but she's naked and there is thick, grey, estuary mud smeared over her skin. Her face is caked with it, as is her torso, her arms and her legs. The mud reaches right up into the roots of her hair. Even her eyelids are clogged with it. Billy can see where she's wiped her nose and sent a bit up one nostril.

He gives a nervous laugh. – Maisie, what've you done?

Only the whites of her eyes and the pink of her tongue show through.

– What did you do with your clothes?

She must have lain down in that mud, he realises, in that scorching heat, rolled her entire body in it. He stares at her, unbelieving, his eyes coming to rest on the two tiny nipples poking through like thimbles, the small mounds of her breasts beneath. He feels his penis harden. She is walking towards him. Something makes him steel himself against her. He takes a step back.

– Take your shirt off, Wallamba.

Her eyes are shining in a way he has never seen before – although, if he's honest with himself, he knows that that look has always been there, beneath the surface. It's an irrefutable look, a command, an implicit condemnation of anyone who might dare to refuse her. He has never argued with her, he realises now. He has always allowed her to get her own way.

Fingers shaking, he undoes the buttons of his shirt and throws it on the ground. She's nearly close enough to touch him now. He takes another step back.

– Now your jeans.

There is a deadly seriousness in her voice. Billy does as he's told, stepping out of the legs one at a time, almost losing his balance as she closes in.

– Underwear, Wallamba. Don't forget your underwear.

– You want me in the nuddy? He tries to laugh. – What's this all about, Maisie?

– Do it.

He does as she tells him and is left standing there with his hands clamped over his withering erection. She is close enough now that he can smell the mud on her. He veers between terror and desire. The mud is starting to crack around her eyes. She turns and walks into the yellow grass.

Come on, Wallamba.

His heart is beating so loudly in his ears that he's no longer sure if her voice is inside or outside his head. As he follows he sees that she has something shiny in her hand. He doesn't recognise it until she moves her thumb against the sharp edge. It's the piece of quartzite he gave her.

– Where are we going, Maisie?

This way, Wallamba. You'll see.

– Maisie –

Ssshh! Follow me.

---

the air is spiked

A black thundercloud rolls in front of the sun. The air is spiked with tension. The wind ruffles itself, uneasily.

How much further is it going to be, anyway? it mumbles to itself.

A bough swoops across the path like a skipping rope. The wind hurdles it and collides mid-air with a naked boy running in the opposite direction. The wind is thrown into a spin. The boy drops a hand to the ground to keep himself steady, then plunges on into the tall cane grass, thrashing at the sharp stalks with bare hands to clear a path.

– Billy! screams the spirit child from further down the track.

The wind stares at the back of the naked boy. Yes, it's Billy. There are smears of dried mud all over him but you can still see the pale skin showing through.

– Billy, *wait*!

The wind turns around in astonishment. Here comes the spirit child, racing through the path that Billy has made in the bashed stalks. Mud breaks off her in clumps, her matted hair sticking out stiffly. She is staring straight ahead with eyes that are fierce but stricken.

The wind steps aside to let her pass.

– Billy, don't go! *Don't go!*

The shiny blue doors are still flapping like an emu trying to take off as the spirit child reaches the car. There's a screech as Billy lets off the clutch, slams the other foot down. The spirit child hurls herself at it, managing only to catch the edge of the doorframe before being thrown to the ground. Grass hisses against the paintwork. The wind hovers, unsure what to do. Billy's terrified face slides behind the spattered windscreen, his muddy backside failing to find purchase on the slippery seat. The Kingswood lurches, stalls, restarts and lumbers off over the uneven grass.

He got away! He got away! squeals the wind, uselessly.

The spirit child picks herself up, the mud crumbling around her. She wipes a hand over her face, trying to dislodge it from her eyelashes. In the other hand she clutches the piece of quartzite. She stares wretchedly at the space where the car disappeared, unable to contain her dismay.

I so nearly had him! she cries. Just five minutes more . . .

The wind shivers and looks up. Dark clouds are piling on top of each other in great, towering castles. In the distance there's a flash of lightning. The wind's pulse begins to pick up.

I'll transform those tree-tops into whirling dervishes, it hisses.

The spirit child looks at the wind for the first time.

You won't do any such thing, she says.

Yes I will. You wait and see.

The wind starts to gather itself together, excited now.

I'll have the branches whipping and snapping. The twigs will be smashed to splinters.

You won't do anything till Billy gets home. *Is that clear?*

The wind catches the look in her eye. For a second it holds out hope, but then it lets out a weary moan.

Spoilsport! Why does it always have to be about Billy, anyway? Billy-Billy-Billy-Billy-Billy! What about *me*? What about the *rain* and the *storm*? It's already moving in from the coast, we can soon catch up, we can chase him all the way home –

The spirit child holds her ground, firmly.

Listen to me, she says. You'll leave him alone, OR ELSE.

the existence of frogs

In the front yard, Stan watches leaden banks of cloud traipse laboriously in from the west. Clouds have been blowing inland every morning for the last two weeks, only to dissipate by midday. But these are different; these are low and dark. These cut off the sun and transform a bright midday into a gloomy netherworld. They stop the birds singing and make the leaves whisper, revealing their pale undersides.

– 'Sgunna rain some. I don't know how much.

He has said it to himself; there's no one else out here but him. At his feet, the cracked mud of the yard is divided up like a web. He narrows his eyes at the fine pillars of haze in the distance.

– 'Salready started over there, he points out with a bounce of his large nose.

Moments later a pellet hits the back of his neck. He swats it as if it were a fly. Another thuds the bulbous toe of his Blunnie. And then there are splashes all around him, the topsoil in the flower bed with its bedraggled, barely alive petunias rising up in little sooty explosions. Stan's nostrils fill with the sweet, mustardy smell of rain on hot-baked earth. Within seconds it has become a downpour. Red dust secreted in the creases of his elbows runs in dirty streaks down his arms, draining off the tips of his fingers.

He looks up, receiving darts of rain in his face. These drops are big; they sting through the fabric of your shirt. They bound waist-high off the hard-packed ground, pound the roof of the lean-to with the insistence of dried-up gum nuts. Stan retreats with drunken, backward lurches to the shelter of the verandah, grinning at the outlandishness of this instant drenching, the utter insolence of it. On the verandah he is soon deafened by the noise of the rain on the tin roof, his vision blocked by the clean sheet of water cascading off the edge. It feels like he's standing in the breach of a waterfall. Spider plants and ferns in the hanging baskets jostle in alarm. Bullets of red earth are fired at his shins.

He takes a handful of sopping shirt and wipes his eyes and nose.

– 'Scoming down dead straight! There's no wind in it yet!

He has to shout now to make himself heard. He barely registers the creaks and bangs of Crystal releasing the metal props from the windows and slamming them shut. He brings his hands up to clap, but his self-consciousness gets the better of him, and he lets his fingers run through his hair instead, causing it to stick up in tufts.

What makes Stan especially gleeful is the knowledge that, within a few days, every rust-coloured puddle and bucketful of water will be thick with teeming tadpoles. A few days after that there'll be frogs all over the place, hopping in amongst the old tyres and under the cars – one hundred, five hundred of them – *batchup, batchup, batchup* they'll go, a whole darned chorus of them conjured out of nowhere for the occasion. He has always loved the suddenness of the existence of frogs.

– Ahoy there, frogs! he shouts, bringing up his arms again. *Ahoy!*

The fly screen slams behind him.

– For God's sake, Stan, have you gone *mad*?

She's as bedraggled as he is, her hair splattered tight against her head so that you can see how her much her ears stick out. Her eyelashes are strung with beads of water.

– Our son's disappeared with a bloody useless car and you're talking to the fuckin *frogs*?

Involuntarily, Stan's eyes lower to examine the way her wet T-shirt clings to her chest.

– In half an hour the rivers will be raging and how's he gunna get through then, ay? Have you bothered to think about that?

Stan hangs his head, feeling like a man caught guzzling cakes at a funeral.

– B't you love the rain, Crystal, he stammers. He makes a useless gesture with his arm. – The rain –

– That was *before* –

– But still, it's a relief – you've always looked forward –

– Do ya think I care about the bloody weather right now? Jesus, Stan. Y've been more worried about yer bloody car than yer own fucken son.

– That's not fair, Crystal.

– Too bloody right, it's not fair.

She shoots him a look that could stop a clock. Meekly, he follows her inside, nose and ears dripping.

– I'll go and look again, he says, leaking onto the lino as Crystal collapses in a chair. I'll drive further this time, down to Derby, to Broome – wherever.

Crystal buries her face in her hands. It takes Stan a while to register that she is crying, and when he does, he feels almost glad. It's years since he has seen her soften up enough to let go. With a tentative finger he parts the damp hair on the back of her neck, clearing a patch of pale yellow skin. He thinks about kissing it.

– Cryssy . . .

His voice is like butter.

– At least we don't need ter worry about him gettin thirsty, ay.

For a few tense moments he watches this triangle of skin for a sign of her reaction. The colour mounts quickly from yellow to pink.

– I didn't mean ter sound too jokey. I meant – y'know – I meant ter sound –

She grabs his arm and rams her head in his armpit, shaking with sobs.

– It's all my fault! she gasps.

The whole of her scalp has reddened beneath the sodden strands. He strokes her hair to the sides, uncomprehending.

– You're jiss stressed out, thassall. Over-emotional.

Her sobs come harder. Stan stands awkwardly where she's pulled him, not wanting to move a muscle even though his back is caught at an uncomfortable angle. After a while she peers up, her eyes bursting with what looks like a plea. Her nostrils are quivering.

– Stan, there's something I need ter tell ya.

– Ssssh!

He smooths her curls down with his palm, as if by keeping the external parts of her in place he might also be able to keep down whatever she's trying to say.

– I'm having an affair. With Stevo. It started three years ago.

Stan keeps smoothing the curls, pressing them flatter and flatter.

– He'll be home soon, Cryssy, he says as if he hasn't heard her. – You'll see. Everything will be right as rain. Hey! Dja geddit? Right as rain!

She looks up at him with waterlogged eyes. Stan clamps her face to his stomach. It's something to relish, he thinks. The chance to hold her tight and close. To feel her weakened body against his.

the perfect arc

Billy hears the drum-roll of thunder as if it comes from the edges of a dream. He sloshes into water without any idea how deep it is. There's a moment of stillness while he finds out if the car will sink or swim. The back wheels spin on the edge of the bank and for a while anything could happen. Mud flies up, splats the windows. A surge in his own desperation seems to make the difference and the vehicle hauls itself onto dry land.

Through the noise of the thunder her voice rings shrill in his head: *Wallamba, Wallamba, Wallamba!*

All around there is water. It's coming out of the air at a slant, rising up from the ground in streams and puddles that reflect the uncertain light from the horizon, the dense black clouds above. Sometimes, when the wheels are skidding sideways, he has the feeling that the elements have merged – air, water, earth, all one wet, unstable world. He could be careering through sky. On the horizon is still a clear belt of light, the sun itself netted like a ball in the grasping hands of the treetops.

Don't go, Wallamba! Don't leave me!

He has no idea where he is, which direction might be home. His concern is only to keep on the track – whatever track it might be. The wheels of the Kingswood swing and slide and he slams the steering wheel hard to the right. Then he slams to the left. Clods of mud fly up. The car feels weighed down with it, wedges of dirt piling up around the fenders and along the sides. There's a rattling from within, like he's got a box of spare parts hurtling around in the back. The low sun flashes semaphore at his windscreen, and for a while all he can see is a bird's eye view of an estuary and all its muddy inlets: silvery blobs wiggling at the edges where the wipers do not reach. Up ahead is the stolid bulk of a boab, squat and stunted, and he swerves to avoid it, but the boab moves too, and he sees the first stage of a leap – somehow finding time to admire the grace of it, the perfect arc that it draws in the rain-shriven air. But he doesn't yet know what it means.

There's a massive jolt as it hits the bumper. Billy slams his foot on the break. It isn't a boab at all. The car spins in a wide circle and a large, heavy body is deflected first upwards, then inwards. The windscreen bends like a wave. First Billy sucks air through his mouth, then he sucks in glass. A chunk of skin is gouged from his shoulder. There is a tremendous ricocheting within the car: powerful limbs thrusting in every direction, slashing the soft leather seats, smashing a rear window. Water runs down his face. Billy slides into the foot well, whimpering, arms wrapped around his head, and cowers there as the creature thrashes and claws above and around and behind him, the car rocking from side to side as if it were caught in a cyclone.

Wallamba! Don't leave me! Don't you dare!

He has no awareness of how long this terror lasts, how long it takes him to generate enough presence of mind to locate the door release. When he does, he slams his fist down hard then hurls himself sideways, sliding into the mud. The wound on his shoulder stings madly. He lies on his side with the rain washing over him, terrified. The frenzied car still rocks and sways behind him. He can hear the battering against the framework as the creature misses the exit every time. He gets to his feet and slides around the car, opening all the doors, his bare feet skating wide. Suddenly, it is out – *honk-honk-honk* – a terrible noise Billy has never heard before as its massive form shears past.

It happens quickly but the picture locks in his mind: the roo's mighty rear leg sticking out at a grotesque angle, the lopsided, giddy arc that pitches it into the trees.

----

a filthy puddle

The wind back-flips around the snappy gums, sweeps up a trunk, then nose-dives back to the ground.

– To give vent after all this time! it cries, climbing up for a second go. I can't tell you how good it feels!

We huddle miserably in the mean patch of shelter provided by the snappy gums, water dripping down our backs, our mangy shirts clinging to our wasted limbs. Even our beards are saturated; when we wring them out, a dirty stream drains over our toes.

Can't you go and do that somewhere else? we snap.

Kill-joys.

This is hardly the time to call us names.

Don't tell me you're upset about Billy. Such a *silly* billy.

Oh, shut up and go away.

The wind makes a pantomime of shutting its mouth manually, then cartwheels around us, relishing every minute. The spirit child, shivering forlornly in her wet blanket, looks up. The rain has washed the worst of the mud off her now, but she's sitting in a filthy puddle.

What will you do to Billy? she asks in a tiny voice.

We refuse to look at her.

You should be more concerned about what will happen to *you*, young lady, says the wind.

The spirit child looks at the wind, then turns beseechingly back to us. We still won't meet her eye.

You know perfectly well that Billy will get exactly what he deserves, says the wind. And don't imagine you'll be able to argue them out of it. They've had it up to here with your meddling.

The wind pauses, savouring the moment.

They're afraid they'll lose him completely now, it adds.

The spirit child keeps her fearful eyes on us, but we have turned our backs. She is dreading the extent of our fury, but we're too wet, too angry, too wretched to deal with her now.

I loved him too, she whispers.

There's a long, low whistle from the wind. The spirit child bows her head. Her lower lip trembles uncontrollably. After a few seconds she lets out a fat sob. She grips the useless, sodden blanket between her fists. When another sob threatens to spill out of her, she stuffs the blanket in her mouth.

---

the whole bloody axle

Stan doesn't recognise it at first. It's not just the poor light; it's the way the bonnet has buckled up into a harelip. There's the metallic scrape of something being dragged along underneath – the whole bloody axle by the sound of it – and there's nothing left of the windscreen except a few jagged teeth.

The car grinds to a halt in the middle of the drive. Something whirls past Stan, splashing in the mud. Stan watches, dumbstruck, as she yanks open the car door, throws her arms around the crushed figure on the front seat and starts pulling. Even then it takes Stan a moment to register what this is all about. Rain pours into his open mouth. Blow me, he thinks. Pummel me into the earth.

– For God's sake, Stan. Come and help!

They take one arm each and drag Billy into the house and down the hallway, his stumbling feet insisting on going through the motions of walking, even though they can't keep up.

– Bathroom, bathroom, directs Crystal, wondering what in the world she will discover when they wash the dirt away. It's been years since she's seen him naked, let alone held him close like this. In her head is an all-too-familiar refrain: I told ya so, didn't I tell ya, one day you'd not come back . . . And yet he *was* back, and she bites her lip to stopper the useless barrage.

In the bath she cradles this sixteen-year-old boy, her son, as if he were a baby again. Stan directs the shower nozzle as Crystal explores him gently, discovering grazes, bruises, the flap of skin hanging off his shoulder. He has a dozen little nicks on his face with glass embedded in them. She takes these shards out with tweezers and drops them into the basin. It is only as the water begins to run clear that she notices the beads of fresh blood floating to the surface of the pool between his legs. She tries to touch his genitals but he won't let her.

– Oh, *Billy*. What've ya done to yerself? Are ya tryin to be like Stevo, is that it?

She doesn't expect an answer – at least, not yet. She turns her appalled face on Stan.

– Get me soap, disinfectant, cotton wool.

Stan opens a fresh packet of soap and hands it to her in heart-thumping silence, then tries to unscrew a bottle of TCP and ends up leaving it on the side of the bath with the top still on. His hands are too big for this job. Or his heart is too weak – who knows which. In any case, he doesn't want to be there when she unearths the worst of the damage. He goes into the hallway and pulls down towels from the cupboard, tugging at whatever he can find and ends up setting off an avalanche, towels of every colour tumbling on his head, on the floor, his hands shaking as he fights them off. Oh, all he wants is the job of wrapping one of them around Billy when he gets out the bath! Let me help him, he finds himself whimpering. *Let me help him*. Stan stands there, bleeding with pity and confusion in the heap of towels. And then it comes to him: soup. He could make soup. Tomato, or chicken and mushroom – one that Billy likes. In the kitchen he finds a box of sachets, shakes it so that they spill all over the benchtop. Ham and pea, ham and pea, ham and pea. All the bloody same. His hands still shake as he scrabbles between them, searching for one that isn't there. He's barely able to see through the brimming tears. We don't even have his favourite soup in the house! he mouths, silently.

Then, from the bedroom, comes shouting.

– Stop it, Billy. Jiss *stoppit*.

Stan lets a mug crash to the floor before rushing down the hallway.

– Hooley dooley, Crystal, what is it?

– Jiss stop it! *Please!*

She is waving about an unlit cigarette.

– What is it?

– Look at im!

Billy's lying flat on his bed, a towel beneath him, his arms and legs jerking strangely. The spasms seem to shoot down from his chest. Stan squats down by the bed.

– Whassup, Billy?

He rests a palm on Billy's forehead, searches the scratched, bruised face for clues. Crystal's got halfway wrapping his shoulder with a bandage and laid a wet flannel across his genitals. A blood stain spreads slowly from its centre.

– 'E can't control em, says Crystal. 'E says 'e doesn't know what it is.

Stan puts his other hand on Billy's chest, exerting a gentle pressure.

– Is it the pain?

Billy shakes his head. He keeps his frightened eyes on Stan.

– You can't stop em comin?

Billy shakes his head again, knees jolting.

– I can't watch, says Crystal.

– Is it because you're cold, mate? Shall I get another blanket?

Another shake of the head.

– I can't watch, says Crystal, leaving the room.

– Get another blanket, orders Stan.

They hear her pick up the phone in the hall. Stan finds a blanket at the end of the bed and tugs it up.

– Or maybe you're too hot. Is that what it is, Billy? You're too hot?

He whips the blanket off again.

– He's having a fit. A seizure. You know, like an epileptic, they hear Crystal say down the phone.

Stan catches Billy's eye and they listen.

Crystal's voice rises in pitch. – I know that, but what if 'e swallows 'is tongue?

Stan winks at Billy. – She'll give him what for. Jiss you wait.

– Oh, *fuck* that, fuck it all, fuck this goddamned place! What's the point of having a flying doctor if he won't fucken *fly*?

Crystal slams the phone down.

Stan chuckles and Billy manages a small smile back. I've got him now, thinks Stan. He has his big, clammy hands resting on Billy like presses. Already the body has started to still.

– Take a big breath. Nice and deep.

Billy does as he's told. For a second he seems to get the upper hand, his muscles relaxing, but as soon as his lungs are empty the spasms judder through again.

– Bloody 'ell. It's like 'e's wired up to an electric shock machine, mutters Crystal from the doorway.

– Gently does it. You're in shock, thassall, says Stan.

His voice is low and soothing. Billy closes his eyes but keeps his head turned towards his father, as if to show he's listening.

– Let the jolts come, don't fight em.

He runs his thumb over Billy's brow.

– Didja see the rain, Billy? Didja see the way it came down? Built up good by midday, and they was black too, them clouds. I never seen it break so sudden.

The jolts become weaker, more like twitches.

– I dunno where you've been, Billy, or what took ya. Off kangarooing, I 'spect. It's happened to plentya fellas, they've charged off huntin somethin or other and got themselves completely befoodled, not known where they ended up. I giss you didn't realise how far you'd got. Was that it, Billy?

The eyelids flicker.

– Yeh, right. It happens, these things happen. Nothin on God's earth you can do about it. It niver did happen to me yit, but I'm a stickler about not driving at dusk, like I told you since you was little, and I know you're a good boy Billy, and normally wouldda kept to the rules, if at all possible . . .

Stan rubs the back of his hand around his nostrils, chasing an itch.

– But *Jee*zus, Billy. The *Kingswood*.

Billy turns his face away.

– Of course, I c'n get it fixed up in a jiffy, Stan says quickly. Bit of straightenin up to do, few stitches inside . . . But Lord knows what you ran that axle over, I mean *Jesus* Billy, it's practically torn in two. I niver seen anything like it.

Another tremor judders through Billy's chest.

– But even that, y'know, it ain't a problem, Stan adds.

The body lies limp and small on the bed. Billy's breathing is still shallow but he seems a little calmer now. Stan runs his thumb across the damp forehead, over and over.

– I hit a roo, says Billy. His voice is barely audible.

– Didja, Billy? A big un?

Billy nods.

– Mid-air. I caught its back leg. Got flung on the bonnet –

– Came in through the windscreen?

– Yeh.

– Right in? Right into the car?

He nods.

– Was 'e a big fella, Billy? Didja wipe 'm out clean?

– No. 'E was still alive. But 'is leg was mangled.

Stan is open-mouthed. He can barely bring himself to ask.

– The leather seats?

Billy hesitates, then nods again.

– *Je*sus, Billy. And did 'e run off with yer clothes as well?

A spasm practically lifts Billy's torso off the bed.

– It's OK, Billy, says Stan. I'm jiss bein a silly arse. You don't need to tell us everything if you don't want to.

Billy's hair is almost dry now, wisps fluffing out around his face. Stan smooths them down with his big, knuckly hand. He wants to make everything alright. He lays his hands on the boy's thighs until the muscles relax. Then on the bony ribcage. He finds he has the power to do this: every muscle softening beneath his ordinarily clumsy touch.

– I've got to get out of here, says Billy softly. Before they find me.

From behind them comes the sound of a lighter and Stan looks around at Crystal, leaning in the doorway, her own hand still trembling as she tries to get the tip of her cigarette to take. She is utterly bedraggled, like a cat someone didn't quite manage to drown. She inhales and looks up and Stan sees that there is something new in there: surprise – amazement, even – as if she can hardly believe this display of tender strength on Stan's part, that he's got it in him still. Stan gives a little snort. God knows she's done her best to stamp it out of him these last few years. He watches as she takes a deep drag, then another, the gorgeous heady poison that she loves so much rushing to her temples and making her head swim. No real idea what goes on in that head, he thinks. But then, neither does she of what's in his.

– A pair of bloody pies, ain't we? he says.

– What?

– Oh, nothing.

Billy is breathing more deeply now. His narrow lips break apart.

– That's it, Billy, says Stan. Far better off asleep. As we all would be.

part V

quite some yarning

Three doctors stand in a line at the foot of his bed: Ann Gould, James and the yellow-crested Dr Mayer, who appears to be the one in charge of this impromptu gathering. Occasionally they look over their clipboards at Billy in his wheelchair, as if their view of him were changing as they digested the notes on their charts.

– Of course we'd be happier if it hadn't come to this, Dr Mayer is saying. But it's in your interest for us to give you an official diagnosis of schizophrenia. Mr Kramer's lawyer is extremely tenacious, and such a diagnosis will stamp out his case before it ever gets to court. The statement you gave the police was sufficiently bizarre and full of contradictions, so there's no problem there. In fact, the cop who interviewed you wrote 'belligerent nutter' on the bottom of your statement.

The skin around Dr Mayer's eyes wrinkles up in amusement. He is a tall man with a weathered walnut of a face, liver spots around the temples, a hawkish nose. Nobody else seems to find it funny. Hand on hip, Ann is knocking a pen against the clenched barricade of her teeth. Dr Mayer ignores her agitation. He is the only one of the three who seems not to find it necessary to pronounce a personal judgement on Billy.

– You say these voices never urged you to harm anybody, or to harm yourself? Dr Mayer asks.

Billy raises his arms up in an exasperated shrug. – What dja want me to say?

James coughs obsequiously into his fist. – Dr Mayer –

– Hmm?

James clasps his hands behind his back and tips his body forward, deferentially.

– This problem of the lack of schizophrenia medication in Mr Saint's treatment record. I have an alternative document – more anecdotal, but persuasive, none the less.

He hands Dr Mayer the spiral-bound notebook in which he took notes during Billy's first week.

– With Mr Saint's permission, of course, he adds with a flutter of a hand in Billy's direction.

The yellow-crested doctor opens the notebook to the first page, his eyes scanning a line or two at random. He flicks to a page further on.

– Quite some yarning, you blokes've been up to.

Billy picks up the newspaper on his lap and thumps it against the bed. Ann stops tapping her teeth and looks at him quizzically, as if her interest in him has been snagged for the first time since his arrival.

– It includes quotes from the patient, describing in graphic detail how the wound was inflicted, James says.

The yellow-crested doctor looks intrigued. – Does it name the perpetrators? I'm assuming there were more than one.

James bobs his head a little, pausing for dramatic effect.

– He says he heard only their voices.

They all look at him then, three pairs of eyes allowing themselves to be openly curious about the life of their patient beyond this ward. Billy detects a morsel of shame in James's eyes. He runs a hand through his hair, outrage budding in his chest. He knows he cannot allow these private ramblings of his to be submitted to public scrutiny. He clenches the arm of the wheelchair, eyeing the proximity of his crutches. Surely with an element of surprise on his side it wouldn't be hard to do. There will be consequences, of course – sedation, the loss of what little trust in him they have. No doubt they'd get the notebook back again eventually. Or perhaps they would decide to let him keep it, hand him over to Dexter Kramer and his lawyer and wash their hands of him completely.

Either way, he cannot sit there and do nothing. He readies a fist but an almighty crash from further down the ward startles them all. The three doctors spin around to face flying bottles, broken glass, a barrage of kidney trays. Pink and white pills scatter like pennies. A woman is crying out in pain: a petite, curly-haired nurse who is pinned to the floor beneath a heavy trolley. Dr Mayer, James and Ann run to help, along with several nurses and those patients who are able to move, although these pyjama-clad helpers are quickly shooed away.

From his wheelchair, Billy stares at the mêlée. Ann has picked up the telephone in the corner of the ward. Dr Mayer and James are on their hands and knees by the prostrate nurse. Billy doesn't notice Cecily until she detaches herself calmly from the group of nurses hauling up the trolley. She rolls her hips slowly across the empty space. As she passes Billy's bed, she plucks the dropped notebook from the floor as if it were the most natural thing in the world, not so much as glancing at him as she slips it into her pocket and continues on down the ward.

The lift doors open smoothly. He throws the creaking wheels forward with generous sweeps of his hands. He has been meaning to ask for some oil, or another wheelchair, but he only ever thinks of this when he's alone.

It is always the same window that he stops at. Today he levers himself out of the chair to work the catch, stickier than usual, and it takes the weight of his whole body to budge it. Once his head is hanging out, he is not sure whether he is doing the gulping, or the night air has swallowed him whole.

It only takes a moment of this drug before he hears it. Harsh and reedy, tormentingly beautiful. He stands up straight, looks out into the darkness and meets her eyes. He can always find them. Two tiny flecks of white, bobbing in the darkness. She knows she has him. There'll be a smirk tugging at her mouth. She is just playing, of course, playing with something half remembered and barely understood. You sing him up and then he loves you for ever. Love magic, they used to call it.

As the emotion rises inside him, he feels the need to move, quickly. It doesn't matter in which direction. He contemplates climbing out the window, tumbling down into the musky night. He is ten floors up. He looks down. The darkness looks soft as a pillow. He can do it; he has the strength in his arms. He feels the air whip past, the smash of bone as his knees and chin hit the bitumen. His chest buckles. He drops back into his chair. The fear subsides.

All this is memory; he knows that. You cannot spend your life being haunted by something which isn't there any more. But if it's true that she's no longer there, then what? Surely that would be worst of all: that she wasn't there to undo this thing that she's done.

Cecily sits on his bed, a luminous graph-paper apparition. A mother, a lover, a nurse. She pumps air into the Velcroed strap that's wrapped around his upper arm.

– Of what. What are you scared of?
– Of the claim she has on me.

Their eyes edge around one another's, taking in only the curve of a cheek bone, a blurred frizz of hair, tiny hairs on a neck. It leaves a space between them for speaking.

– Your heart is not in you any more, Cecily says.

It is a statement, not a question. For a moment she stares at her watch, the job taking over.

– Alright. Not bad.

She reaches around clumsily for the clipboard and fills in a figure in a box. Then she rips open the Velcro armband, unwinds it down to the flesh. She makes as if to haul herself up but he grabs her wrist.

– Cecily –

It is the first time he has used her name and it shocks him, the unfamiliar intimacy of it on his tongue. It is more of a shock than the touch. He looks at her mouth, knowing this is as close to her as he can get. The black lips are firmly sealed.

– Cecily, will she come back?

He cannot keep the urgency out of his voice. Cecily expels the air quickly through her nose: half grunt, half snigger. Clearly, he thinks, the answer is too obvious for her to bother with. She shakes her wrist free and stands up, tugging her dress at the hem.

– You're the one who decides that, she says, gathering up her equipment and dumping it on the trolley. You tell me.

– But I'm lame now, he finds himself saying, idiotically, in a harsh whisper that hurts the back of his throat. He is trying not to wake the people in the neighbouring beds. – Perhaps she won't want me. They say I'll always walk with a limp.

Cecily smiles at this. – You're not nearly as lame as you were before.

She gives the trolley a sharp kick to release the break, then sweeps a handful of curtain aside.

– Your blood pressure's down, she says. You're almost completely well.

a feed like that

Two parallel trails of smoke meander up from the bar at the Spini, plateauing below the reach of the ceiling fans like a layer of smog. Rossco pushes his metal-rimmed glasses up his nose. Gerry picks at the dirt around his nails. Clay leans against the wall behind him, his mouth stretched into a lazy grimace. No one has said a word for half an hour.

There's a sharp whistle from the kitchen. Clay rocks himself forward and troops through the curtain of ribbons.

The outside door swings open. Standing in the rectangle of light is Stevo, his big belly thrust forward. He comes in, dragging his slipper-thin thongs. Following behind is Stan in his blue overalls.

Rossco and Gerry turn to see who it is then go back to their glasses of beer.

– Ow y'goin mate, orright? says Stevo.

Neither Rossco nor Gerry manage more than a grunt.

– What's 'appened to you fellas? cries Stevo, hoisting himself onto an adjacent stool. Lost your tongues along with yer freedom? Ha! Now that you're Coldiver's boys.

– Fuck off, mutters Gerry.

Stevo laughs. – Hey, Stan. Sit down here.

Clay reappears, plastic ribbons trailing over his shoulders, and slams two blackened T-bone steaks on the bar. Arms folded, he looks between Rossco and Gerry and the T-bones and back again.

– You'd fight for a feed like that, he prompts.

Both men jab their arms forward to free their elbows from imaginary shirt sleeves, and clamp the steaks down with their forks.

– Ain't no fight left in em, says Stevo. They bin workin on the new jail at Halls Creek. First day's work in – what, ten, twelve years?

– Wondered what was up with em, says Clay.

– They're gunna do a string of em, Stevo goes on. Wauchope, Hermannsburg, Alice. There's a lot of work to be 'ad, according to Coldiver. 'E's bin tryin to get me signed up an all, but I ain't playing cop. Twenny years' work stretching ahead for ya, ain't there, fellas? What a prospect, ay.

Rossco and Gerry, cheeks bulging, make no comment.

– They don't know what's 'it em, do they? laughs Stevo. Completely bushed.

He grins at them, delightedly. Clay snorts, rubs the bar down with a square of green and yellow towel.

– Shouldda got the blackfellas doin it, it's them that's gunna live in em, says Clay.

– Bloody 'ell, don't you start on that, says Stevo.

– Trouble is there ain't no decent young blackfellas left. Only the old buggers. An we all know why *that* is.

Stevo pulls his cap down over his eyes. Clay looks at Stan instead. Stan returns the gaze dutifully – even his eyebrows are raised. The barman pinches the end of his hairy nose. Then he holds up an index finger.

– Aw, Jesus, Jesus, mutters Stevo, pulling the cap down even further. 'Ere we go.

– That's yer old boy, Clay says, ignoring him. He jabs his finger in the air. They cut it down this way, then they cut it that way. They do it with a tin can. That means you're a man. Don't it, Stevo? The younguns have got more sense than to sit around and git their whistles pricked, and I for one don't blame em.

He stands back, nips his nose again. – They circumcise the women too.

Rossco lets his fork drop down. – For Chrissake, mate, I'm eatin me tea.

– They fuck em first, adds Clay.

Stan gazes longingly at the rectangle of light at the door.

– I'll tell you what, says Clay. The meaning of reconciliation. I've worked it out. It's the blackfellas who should forgive *us*. Reconciliation means the Aborigines should be reconciled to what's happened, and forgive *us*. Ain't that right, Stevo? And then we'll all live happily iver after.

He starts to laugh, chest heaving.

Rossco pushes his plate away. – Aw, Christ, Clay. Yer full of shit. And this steak's as tough as a fuckin boot, ay.

– At least it's given you yer tongue back, says Stevo. Who's shoutin Stan? Or is it me as usual?

Clay fills two glasses to the brim and stands them on the bar.

– Might as well pour me another straight away, says Stevo, launching into the first. I got a thirst you could photograph. Stan?

Stan looks up. – Oh, no more for me, mate. One's enough.

– Christ, Stan, what's wrong with ya? Quick, get some more air in that glass! Brighten yerself up!

– 'E don't like his beer much, do ya, Stan, chips in Rossco.

Clay pricks up his ears. – Who doesn't like 'is beer?

– 'E says it tastes like piss, says Rossco.

Stevo throws his head back, slapping his bare thigh. Stan shifts uncomfortably on his stool.

– 'E'd rather have a coke, ay, adds Rossco. Wouldntcha, Stan? He confessed to me jiss last week.

Everyone joins in with the laughter now. Stan reddens. What a good joke he is for everyone, ay. He doesn't know where to look, so he stares straight ahead at the wall behind the bar which is covered with banknotes from all over the world. New York. Lisbon. Cape Town. Dublin. Below them is a shelf with a row of old-fashioned brown pill bottles, their labels typed with a manual typewriter: *VIRGIN AGAIN*, he reads. *Iron hymen pills. The miraculous invention of Dr RU Tighter, Newbeaver, Virginia. Bring back that first-time feeling every time. (Delicious cherry flavour).*

  – We gotta gettim in practice, mate, says Stevo, jerking his head at Stan. Whatja say, Clay? Free beers all round?

  – I need practice too, volunteers Gerry.

  – And me.

  Clay looks at them irascibly. – You're bloody criminals, the lot of ya.

  He slips his fingers in the tops of four new glasses and starts filling them anyway.

  – You don't 'ave to drink it, mate, Stevo whispers to Stan. I'll drink it for ya.

  – I'll drink it, insists Stan.

  Gerry watches this new round of drinks being set down.

  – You c'n tell a lot by the way a man drinks his beer, he says, thoughtfully. Long drafts means a satisfied man, sure of getting laid every night. Little sips is a man you don't trust, a man you don't sit your wife next to. Ain't that right, Rossco?

  Stan sloshes the remaining amber liquid around the sides of his glass, leaving a scum behind.

  – Stan, you're sippin.

  – Drink up, Stan, I'm halfway through me second already, says Stevo. I'll be gettin us another in a minute.

  – This'll be heaps for me.

  – Aw, come on, Stan. Let yer hair down for once, ay. Do ya good.

  Stan looks dubious. – I don't know why you keep saying that.

  – Cheer you up.

  Stan snorts, tips the glass up for the final gulp. – Reckon I need cheerin up, do ya?

  Briefly, he catches Stevo's eye.

  – Maybe, a bit, says Stevo, looking away. Anyway, it's me birthday tomorra. I gotta celebrate.

  – No worries, says Clay.

  – Thirty-three again? suggests Gerry.

  – Fuck off.

Another whistle from the kitchen. Clay disappears off to see what it is. Rossco scratches his beard. It sounds like a cat testing its claws on a carpet.

– Y'know, seein as it's a special occasion, there's somethin I bin meanin to ask ya, Stevo, says Rossco.

They all look at Rossco expectantly.

– Yeh?

– What Clay was saying about circumcision, Rossco begins, halteringly. Didja –

Stevo stares at him bluntly. He's not going help the man out.

– Y'know what I'm gettin at, Stevo. Didja –

Stan looks from Rossco to Stevo and back again. He licks away a line of froth from his lip. – Sure 'e did, he says.

Stevo tips back on his stool, giving his big, taut belly more room. He rubs his hands up and down his thighs, takes a breath, then looks down at his hands.

– Did it hurt? asks Rossco, wide-eyed.

– What dja think, mate? Stevo mumbles, embarrassed.

– Then why dja let them do it?

Stevo lets the two front legs of the stool drop back down. He shoots an uneasy look at Stan.

– Ask any Aboriginal woman, he says.

Stan stares at his glass, his face hatched with distress.

– I ain't asking for the facts of life, says Rossco. I got them from me dad. I wanna know what difference it makes.

– Like I say, you ask –

Stan lets out a big, noisy breath, sitting as upright as he can on his stool. Rossco, noticing his discomfort, dips his head apologetically.

– Sorry about this, Stan, he says. But we gotta know.

– Yeh, echoes Gerry. We gotta know.

Stevo gives a sigh and slaps his hands on his thighs. A little cloud of dust rises up.

– Alright then, fellas, he says. Let's get it over with. Ya know ya foreskin?

Stan manages a tight little laugh. – We're not complete beginners, mate.

– No. Well. They cut that off first.

– I knew that, says Gerry quickly.

– That one's a matter of hygiene, Stevo goes on. A few years later, they make another cut, lengthwise this time, which causes ya wonga to swell up sideways at the top. Like so.

He bunches his hand into a fist. Stan gulps audibly.

– No woman worth her salt wants a man with an uncut wonga when she can have one with meat on the end of it, does she? says Stevo bluntly.

Rossco and Gerry avoid looking at Stan.

– So, says Stevo, unsure whether to be embarrassed or allow himself a touch of pride now. So there it is.

– But the big question is, says Rossco, leaning forward eagerly, can anybody get it done?

Stevo throws his head back and hoots with laughter, his tongue ululating like jelly in the cradle of his mouth.

– Jeez, you wanna be initiated into Aboriginal law? You wanna be blackfellas? It's rare but not unheard of. One thing I should warn youse though. Get it done and you'll niver piss in a straight line again.

The night is cool, chiselled by cicadas. Someone is peeing against a tree. Stan hears it and wants to go too, but nothing's going to make him open his fly in front of Stevo tonight.

– I'll walk, he says, bumping into a boab tree and veering sideways.

– Bollocks you will. Get in.

Stevo swings his Cruiser out onto the road without looking. There's hardly ever anyone coming anyway. The headlights forge a tunnel, throwing the rest of the world into shadow. Stan keeps his eyes pinned on this light in an effort to control his bladder and the growing nausea in his gut.

– 'Eard from Billy? asks Stevo.

Stan shakes his head, not daring to open his mouth in case he's sick.

– Hard world for a sixteen-year-old out there, muses Stevo, shaking his head.

Stan bumps and jolts in the seat beside him. – Seventeen, he says.

– Wha?

– He'll be seventeen by now.

Stan shuts his mouth again quickly. Stevo shakes his head.

– Hard to imagine your Billy as a fully grown man. God knows what came over him, walking out like that so sudden.

– He's not the first young man to leave home, Stan says, defensively. Won't be the last, either.

– Yeh, but it was so sudden. *I'm going now*, isn't that what 'e said? Jiss like that. *I'm off*. As if he'd jiss been kippin at your place for a night or two, instead of 'is whole bloody life.

He glances at Stan. Stan looks away.

– An to think 'e 'ad it all lined up, a glorious future as a panel-beater stretching ahead, 'is name in lights, famous through WA . . .

He throws Stan a consoling wink.

– I'm only kiddin, Stan. 'Snot as if I c'n talk, after all.

When he still gets no response, Stevo sighs and turns the headlights off.

– Fuckit. Who needs em, he says.

Stan's not sure whether Stevo's referring to headlights or children. He's right if it's lights: the whole landscape is visible now, the skittle-shaped boabs on the sides of the road hoary in the moonlight, their shadows striping the ute as they pass. The moon itself, spliced up by their branches, looks as delicate and mottled as a circle of rice paper with an edge shaved off. They pass the snaggle-shouldered ridge of a cow standing stockstill on the side of the road. At one point they hit a pothole and bash shoulders painfully.

Stevo puts an arm around Stan, grasping the bony edge of him.

– Y'know what, mate?

– What.

– We're managing this orright, ain't we?

Stan says nothing.

– Crazy innit? Stevo goes on. Never thought you an' I would be able to look each other in the eye, let alone go out drinkin on me birthday.

They hit a stretch of particularly bad corrugations in the dirt road. The contents of Stan's stomach are thrown into convulsions.

– Crazy, innit?

Stan says nothing.

– Life, ay, says Stevo, slapping the flat of his hand on the wheel.

He glances sideways, takes in the peaky face.

– You know, I wouldn't've said all that back there, about me wonga. Only they kept on . . .

Stan turns his face away. – It's OK.

Stevo's face is glum now. – Dja really think so? Jesus. I don't know.

– C'n you stop a minute?

The sudden breaking throws Stan forward and he lurches out of the Cruiser with stomach heaving, the acrid tartness of beer erupting at the back of his throat. He doesn't try and stop it; it's a relief to bring it up.

When he straightens, half of it's caught in his nose still, hurting like a bee-sting. He sniffs hard, swallows a foul-tasting lump back down. Then he pees against the wheel.

– Awful waste, says Stevo, shaking his head as a sheepish Stan gets back in. They catch one another's eye. Stevo lets out a chuckle.

– You don't 'alf look crook, mate.

Stevo's laugh picks up. He doesn't seem able to stop. Soon it's turned into a high-pitched wheeze. Tears stab at his eyes.

Stan starts to smile too, despite everything. – Stop it, will ya?

But Stevo is shaking his head, helpless with laughter now, thudding the wheel with his hand. He looks at Stan with streaming eyes. Stan grins, clutches an arm across his raw-feeling stomach. He hasn't a bloody clue what this is about or why it's funny, but he can't help joining in.

They skid to a halt in the oil-stained yard. The house looks like a brown cardboard box with its lid wedged open. There's a light on in a front window. Stan's nose casts a long, knobbled shadow over his face.

– Fuck! he hisses, eyes stretched wide in alarm.

– What is it, mate?

– Fucken fuck. I'm in the poo.

– *What?*

– It's blady Crystal. She's still up. She'll chuck a berko if she sees me this wrecked. We'd better creep in good and quiet.

– Speak for yerself, mate. I'm not comin in.

Stan gives him a desperate look. – You have ta, Stevo. I'm not goin in there by m'self. I won't make it up the bloody steps.

– You gotta be jokin, Stan. I'm not comin in with ya.

– She'll roar the shit outta me.

Stevo stares at the house. The light goes off in the bedroom. He sighs. Shaking his head, he gets out the Cruiser and shuts the door as quietly as he can behind him.

– Christ. I can't believe I'm doin this.

He opens the flyscreen door and helps Stan down the hallway.

– Billy's room.

– Orright, mate.

Inside the small room, Stevo hoists Stan off his shoulder and sends him sprawling on the single bed.

– Boots.

– Wha'?

– Get me boots off.

Stan lifts his feet up one at a time while Stevo tugs obediently at the heels of his Blunnies.

– Shocks!

– Eh? This is bleedin crazy.

Now it's Stan's turn to giggle, although the terror at the thought of Crystal in the next room, swearing at them under her breath, flits over his face from time to time. A hiccup escapes, and it sets him off again, the laughter curdling his insides. He rolls on his side in case he's sick a second time. Next door the bed thumps against the wall.

– Blady Crystal.

– You shouldn't talk about ya missus like that.

– Like hell I should. Blady Crystal. *Blady Crystal*.

– *Stan!*

– She'll be that pissed at me when I go in there. You've no idea what I'm in for.

Stevo stares at the wall that separates the two rooms. Billy's posters still cover the walls: the large black eyes of kangaroos looking distrustfully down. Two more thumps on the wall.

– She's jacked off orright.

– You go in there, suggests Stan in a sudden burst of inspiration.

Stevo's eyes grow wide. – No, mate, I'm not goin in.

– Go on, it'll cheer 'er up.

Stevo stares at Stan, dumbfounded. – Don't be a pig's arse, Stan.

A shrill kettle whistle has started up in Stan's head. He sighs, his face hanging off the edge of the bed.

– Truth is, Stevo, she duzzin think either of us are much chop.

– Eh?

– Not just me. You neither.

– Piss off.

Stevo plonks himself on the bed beside Stan.

– No, I mean it, insists Stan. She duzzin think much of any of us.

– What are you talkin about?

– Y'know, *blokes*. The male species. Stan closes his eyes. The room has started to spin. – She thinks we're not much more advanced than animals, ay. He gives a derisive snort. The bed has turned into a merry-go-round and he clutches to the edges of it, trying to lift himself above the nausea. The blurred figure of Stevo comes and goes.

– Well, we're not, says Stevo.

– Ay?

– Any more advanced than animals.

Stan props himself up on an elbow. For a short, hopeful moment sobriety seems within reach.

– None of us are, Stevo is saying. How could we be? We *are* animals. Predators at that. There's no getting away from it. Our sole reason for existing is to reproduce.

Stan eyes him dubiously.

– Crystal included, of course, Stevo says drily. She's an animal too.

Stan lets out a sharp guffaw and and claps Stevo on the shoulder. – Christ, Stevo! I niver knew you was a joker!

Stevo smiles weakly; he hadn't intended to be funny. Behind him, Stan swings his legs to the ground. He rubs the tip of his nose with the base of his hand.

– Well, I giss one of us'll jiss hev to show 'er, eh?

– Eh?

– Show 'er what animals are made of!

Stevo looks unsure. – You goin in there, mate?

– I am.

Stevo feels Stan's weight lift off the bed. His heart sinks a little as he realises what this means, although it's mingled with relief.

– Hooley dooley, Crystal, cries Stan. Here I come!

Halfway through the night, Stevo wakes to find himself still in his clothes. He has crêpe paper where his tongue should be. A regular hammering in his head. He turns onto his side. A slight breeze lifts the square of pale curtain at the window.

Jesus. Where the fuck is this?

He looks around him and the eyes of a dozen kangaroos look back. Oh fuck. There's a sweetish smell about the room: Billy's smell. He'd know it anywhere, though he'd be hard pressed to find the words for it.

He plumps the pillow and lies back. He wonders where Billy is at this moment. He has an image of him in Perth, walking down a bright, sunlit street. Suburbia: neat houses made of bricks and tiles with gates in the walls and garages just for cars. He's wearing a denim jacket and carrying a clutch of hard-backed books under his arm – library books with letters sellotaped to their spines. Geology, zoology, botany. No reason he shouldn't have made it to uni by now. There he'll be, sitting at a desk with an Anglepoise lamp at one elbow, poring over his books. He'll be like the man who came into the Spini once who could name a bare stick without buds or leaves or gum nuts on it – Acacia *dunnii*, Acacia *cowleana*, he'd gone. They'd all thought he was a genius. That's what Billy will be able to do with rocks.

The breeze from the window flutters the edge of the sheet. Stevo clambers underneath it and pulls it up to his chin.

Maybe he'll be a teacher. Or a reporter on the local paper. Or even better, an *environmental consultant*. Isn't consultancy where all the money is these days? Perhaps they'll call him the Rock Man. We'll get the Rock Man on board. They'll slap him on the back and drive him around their building sites, show him how they're cutting up the earth here, dumping it there, redirecting the course of the river from here to here, and he'll nod and listen, spend the whole day taking it in, and then he'll shake his head: No way José. Ah, that's my boy, Billy! The power of his authority! They'll make him an honorary professor at the university in recognition for his contribution to earth sciences. There he is, sitting on a big leather chair all proud and grown-up, while they put a necklace of gold coins around his neck like a bleedin mayor. Maybe some Aboriginal leader will come up and shake his hand and say, Thank you for protecting our land. You are its ally, its friend.

The thoughts spin around in Stevo's head, one chasing the tail of the other. From out of the end of the sheet a worn-out rubber thong drops to the floor.

He's envious of Billy in a way. He never had a chance to get out into the big wide world himself, take his pick of the different lives on offer. He had to look after his old mother in Halls Creek, her and a bevy of fat, ageing aunts, always getting him to fetch and carry, do this do that do the other. By the time the last of them died he already had the first girl knocked up, and he's been dodging the child support people ever since.

If he'd had a chance to get out there and embrace the world, a chance like Billy has now, stepping out with open arms instead of having to be shifty, keep half an eye on whoever's chasing at his back, then he might have made a better man of himself. A big, honest, generous-hearted fella with a nice word for all the ladies.

Returning the wary gaze of the roos on the walls, Stevo feels a strange lump in his throat. Maybe it's not too late, he dares to think, although this intrepid voice is barely more than a whisper in his head. Maybe he can still make a bid for freedom. Have an adventure. Go and find his dad is what he should probably do, if the old battler's still alive, still eking out a living from the pokies in Perth. You never know, he might have something half sensible to say to his son by now.

He swallows at the strange lump in his throat, but it doesn't go down. Even coughing won't budge it. Either he's having an emotional crisis or he's got throat cancer, he decides. He's not sure which'd be worse.

In the morning Stevo sits on the edge of the single bed, moving his stiff neck cautiously from side to side. He listens out for signs of life. With a guilty pang he remembers Yakka. She won't have got fed last night. He hears the clatter of a pan being slammed on the hob. Waits a few minutes, hoping to hear the flyscreen door snapping shut. If just one of them would go out, he'd be able to handle it. He doesn't really mind which one.

The minutes pass. He looks at his watch. He needs to get back to Yakka. Estha will've noticed, no doubt. She'll find the poor mite with her ears flopped down, sniffing around the servo forecourt, and curse at his hopelessness.

There's nothing for it: he'll have to face them both. What a way to start your birthday. With a sigh, he scuds on his thongs and steps out into the hall.

In the kitchen Stan's face hangs mournfully over a large plate with the scrappy remains of a cooked breakfast on it, dark shadows pouched beneath his eyes.

– Hooley dooley, Stevo, you look rough as guts. Didntcha get any sleep?

– You don't look so hot yerself.

– Pull up a chair, why dontcha. Bloody pair of derelicts we are.

Stevo casts an apologetic glance at Crystal, who is staring at him in alarm over her mug of tea. He looks over at the frying pan. His stomach feels as if it's about to collapse in on itself.

– Give im the works, ay, Crystal.

Crystal flicks a venomous glance at Stan. – What, yer legs won't stand up?

Stevo, sensing the enormity of the tension contained within the tight, seething coil that is Crystal, swallows hard around the lump in his throat. She'll never forgive him for this.

Stan, seemingly unfazed by the situation, shoves a triangle of buttered toast into his mouth and scrapes his chair back.

– Take a seat, Stevo, like I said.

Stevo does as he's told. He stares glumly out the window, wondering how many times he's sat at this table without Stan in the house, relaxed

and sated after a frenzied romp in the double bed across the hall. An image
from the night comes back to him: Billy getting university degrees and
lording it over everyone. Christ, what was *that* all about? And himself going
on some sort of wild goose chase, like a teenager pumped up on raging
hormones. He shakes his head, a smile curling at his lip. Jesus, what a load
of baloney. One thing's for sure: no one who's come out of this town will
ever amount to anything worth getting excited about. He leans his head to
one side and gives his ear a shake, as if he could tip the nonsense out.

– Happy birthday, mate, says Stan, dumping a cold wedge of omelette
in front of him. It's a little grey around the edges, but it tastes alright.

Crystal's eyebrows pucker.

– Aw, yeh, smiles Stevo. Thanks, Stan, you're a mate. Didja get me a
birthday present?

– No, but at least I remembered, says Stan.

– That's right, says Stevo, pleased. You did. No worries. No worries at
all.

west of sydney

This morning there's a buzz of excitement at the coffee shop. A white
girl with sleek brown hair is sitting at the table nearest the counter, and
has asked for a coffee and a dingo pup in the poshest pommy accent you
ever heard west of Sydney. Every now and then she casts her eager, friendly
face up at Estha, clearly desperate to forge a link.

Estha's having none of it, of course. She keeps her eyes down, intent
on working up more smears on the stainless steel units. She doesn't trust
other women much, especially not good-looking ones from out of town.
We decide it's the least we can do to keep the poor girl company ourselves,
and gather in a cluster around her table – although our attentions are
entirely wasted on her, of course.

Nice to meet you. It's not often we get visitors here.

She responds by hauling her rucksack up onto the adjacent table and
emptying out half its contents: dog-eared paperbacks (*Songlines*, of course,
Oscar and Lucinda, one by a bloke called Dalai Lama), rolled up T-shirts,

several bottles of contact lens solution, crushed packets of tampons, a Maglite torch, a tin opener. There's so much detritus we're soon forced back onto our feet. At last she finds what she's looking for: a hard-backed notebook and a pen.

Her name, we gather from the airline tag attached to her rucksack, is Rebecca Hetherington. And according to the notebook – the pages of which are turning in the draft from the air-con – she's a twenty-six-year-old nurse from Nottingham, England. She's staying at Coldiver's Roadhouse – not because the *Rough Guide* says this town is worth a visit, but precisely because it doesn't. In fact, the town and the roadhouse and everyone in it might just as well not exist as far as the *Rough Guide* is concerned; but Rebecca wants to do things differently, get off the beaten track. She's brave enough now that she doesn't care if people stare at her when she walks into one of these outback dives by herself.

She's brimming with energy, this Rebecca Hetherington, and to be honest we're enjoying lapping up a bit of it ourselves. She thinks everything in this country is wild and totally brilliant. She wants to absorb it through her skin, let it penetrate her soul – the landscape, the people – oh! she especially loves the people, so funny and feisty and bold. Most travellers have half their minds on whether there'll be a toilet on the bus or how their sun tan's developing, but she's broken free of these petty concerns. She's practically feral by now.

– Is it pretty around here? she blurts out suddenly. Her eyes are wide and full of hope that this Aboriginal girl behind the counter might help her unlock a spiritual treasure chest. Unfortunately, she couldn't have picked a more reluctant accomplice. Seizing the opportunity to slam that eager face shut, Estha bangs the upturned coffee scoop on the edge of the bin.

– Pretty desolate, Estha says, twisting the scoop back into place with a grimace.

– Well, *I* think it's pretty, what I saw from the Greyhound, insists Rebecca, privately thinking that you only really appreciate beauty when you see it for the first time, with fresh eyes, like a child. She gives Estha a big smile. – I'm thinking of going out to visit that sacred rock near here. D'you think it's worth the journey?

Steam shoots and squeals through the cappo machine, frothing up a jug of hot milk. Estha takes her time with it.

– Where you expectin ter hire the four-wheel-drive? she shouts over the racket.

Rebecca motions confidently towards the street.

– Oh, the nice man at the roadhouse, he takes tours there.

– The wowser?

– Sorry?

Estha turns the steamer off. – You mean Mr Coldiver?

– No, no, the Aboriginal guy. Jimmi.

Estha stops what she's doing, wipes her hands on her apron. – Jimmi Rangi's gunna take you to the rock?

– Yes. He organises tours there in his ute.

Rebecca smiles again. When it's not returned she opens her journal and flattens the pages out. She clicks her pen. She's been writing in this notebook every day for the last two months. As she touches her pen nib to the paper, a greasy plate with a solitary dingo pup rolling around on it is unceremoniously dumped on the clean page. Rebecca looks up, affronted, but Estha's already turned her back.

We can't help giving a little chuckle. Rebecca stares in horror at the battered creation before her.

– Pretty hot outside, says a voice.

Rossco and Gerry are both looking over, politely. They know Estha can be tricky with other women and, like us, they feel it's the least they can do to be friendly. Rebecca takes in the two men, one tall and with an enormous red beard and glasses, the other short but bulky, with a tattoo of a snake around his neck. She makes a show of having to put down her pen.

– Oh, I'm used to it. There's a trick to it. You have to stop resisting it. You have to *revel* in it. Every once in a while I rent a room with air-con and have a really good night's sleep, but otherwise I haven't minded a bit.

The big red beard gives a nod. – Is that so.

Rebecca gives a wide-mouthed yawn. – The flies, though, now they're another thing completely. All those little legs and feelers clamouring to get at the corners of your eyes and up your nose. You only have to open your mouth for a split second and one of them flies in. And swallowing a fly is possibly the most *revolting* thing I've ever done in my life.

Rossco gives another nod. – That'd be about right.

– But that's forgetting the mozzies of course, Rebecca goes on. At Kakadu I woke up one morning and my eyelids were so swollen with bites I could barely see.

The English girl shudders and shakes her hair, so that it spreads thickly over her shoulders, then gathers up the escaped strands into a ponytail. The two men watch, unblinking, not wanting to miss a single second. When she's formed the ponytail perfectly, she lets it fall again.

– You like travelling, then?

Rebecca flicks her gaze at the shorter of the two men, the one with the buzzcut and snake tattoo. She sighs, tips her head on one side.

– Well, put it this way. It's four weeks now since I've put on any make-up. There's no point – your mascara smudges as soon as you start to sweat and your lipstick just melts in your bag. And that's really liberating. It almost doesn't matter where I am – I could be in Timbuktu, for all I care. Wherever the hell Timbuktu is.

She knows she's got a flush on her cheeks today. According to her diary – which makes for pretty saucy reading – two nights ago she fucked an Australian boy called Troy in the back of his shaggin wagon. Beautiful, she says he was – a bronzed-up surfer from Bondi, doing the tour like her, only nineteen years old. *Sometimes*, she's written, *I wonder if I do things purely because I know they'd shock my mother*.

She moves the plate with the batter-wrapped sausage onto the next table and settles back down to write.

– Don't get koalas in Timbuktu.

She looks up irritably. – What difference is it going to make to my life whether I've seen a koala bear or not? It's not going to change my soul.

A muscle twitches on Gerry's taut cheek. – What the bloody heck's wrong with yer soul?

– Gerry, warns Rossco, putting a hand out.

– It looks fine from where I'm sittin, don't it to you, Rossco?

The beard opens up to make way for a smile full of crooked teeth. – Certainly does.

– You came to our town ter change yer soul?

Rebecca sighs, wondering how she got herself into this mess. – Actually, I came here to write my journal. If you don't mind.

Gerry gives a low whistle. – Keep yer hair on.

Rebecca puts down her pen and dumps her forehead in her hands.

– I'm sorry, only I didn't get much sleep the last two nights and you know how it is when you're travelling – no time to yourself.

Gerry gives a nod. – Sounds tough.

The two men turn back to their paper. Rebecca picks up her pen.

It's sort of weird, this town I've landed in. I've just been trying to explain to these two inbred blokes who are trying to chat me up in a café, it isn't so

much about seeing the country, what matters is that by the end of three months,
you're like a different person. No one back in Nottingham will recognise me. I'll
tell them I've changed my name to Sheila!

But she can't relax any more. She packs away the notebook and takes
a few dollars from her purse and leaves them on the table. As she swings
her rucksack onto her back, clouting one of us around the head, she gives
Estha a last, brave smile.

– Nice meeting you!

Estha manages a nod. As soon as she's out the door, Gerry and Rossco
lean out of their chairs so they can watch her walking down the street.

– Strewth, she was bloody gorgeous, says Rossco.

– Her norgies weren't much chop.

– They were a bit on the small side, true.

– And she was full of shit, adds Gerry.

– That she was.

– Estha's norgies are better.

– You're right, mate, agrees Rossco. Give me Estha's any time.

Estha turns her back to hide her smile.

----

your little tin heart

Stan's nose rises from the pillow in a perfect triangle. His mouth has
fallen open at one end in the shape of a spanner. The pillow next to his
own is still freshly plumped. Crystal's taken herself off to Billy's room
again, says she's unable to sleep with him fidgeting all night.

He wouldn't be fidgety if she didn't keep going off to sleep in Billy's
room, Stan wanted to say, but didn't. He'd be fine if she stayed put in
their bed.

Poor Stan. He is genuinely bewildered. He has chosen not to hear what
she's saying to him, not to notice the despair taking root behind her eyes,
and now nothing around him makes sense.

We climb onto Crystal's side of the bed, stretching our dusty limbs
out beside him, fighting over the spare pillow. With our faces right up
close, we can see flakes of rough skin on his lips, blond eyelashes in

amongst the brown. Inside his ear sits a big glob of wax, waiting for the far-off day when he will think to clean it out. Here's where it all happens, we think, staring at his big, heavy skull. Where the night-time agonies unspool. Where a little boy still clamours to be heard.

Crystal, the little boy whispers. Tell me what you want me to do.

You really want to know? asks Crystal.

Yes! An exasperated hunch of the shoulders.

Well, alright then, I'll write you a list. A list of things to do, and a list of things not to do.

Oh, if only it were that easy! Off he'd go with his two long lists, one black, one red, and he'd potter around with his tins of nuts and bolts and tick the items off one by one. *Fix the hinges on the kitchen cupboards, store your fishing rods somewhere I won't trip over them, stick down the kitchen lino, scrub out the toilet bowl for once in your bloody life,* and when he'd got to the end of the list he'd hand it back again with a proud, loving smile on his face.

Done it, Cryssy!

Great! That's really wonderful. Oh Stan, I must be the happiest woman alive.

Ah, but it's not as easy as that, is it Stan? She wants things from you that you don't know how to give. A touch of poetry. Physical confidence. A wonga shaped like a fist. How can you possibly hope to make her happy ever again?

A mosquito buzzes through a gap in the fly-screen and whines in an aggravating crescendo around the room. One of us swats it against the ceiling.

In Stan's dream he stands at the edge of the yard, looking out into the bush. A big, defeated man. Oh, he *feels* a lot but it's all twisted up and it never comes out in the way he means it to.

They're at breakfast now, a shining kettle, a plateful of eggs – not scrambled, but perfectly fried, golden yolks floating in a sea of unblemished white. The sort of eggs he's always wishing she would make. His favourite.

Happy? she howls, incredulous, with a cruel little hoot of laughter. You want to know what would make me *happy*?

Yes!

She puts down her knife and fork. Alright then, Stan, I'll tell you. What would make me happy right now is to drive away from this shit-hole town and have a night out at the movies. I'd like to see an old

American classic with Greta Garbo in it, or the young Marlon Brando or whatsisname with the doggy eyes, Humphrey Bogart. And afterwards I'd like to lie on the edge of a swimming pool shaped like a cashew nut and have Humphrey feed me lychees, peeling them with his fingers and putting them on my outstretched tongue. Can you sort that out for me, my sweet?

A big, troubled sigh wobbles through the spanner-shaped mouth. Stan rolls over onto his side, tucking his hands, prayer-like, beneath his temple. We edge ourselves a little out the way.

Quite handsome, really, our Stan – in a big, cumbersome, sun-blasted sort of way. Though that nose does dominate the skyline rather. Some women like big noses, of course, suggesting a stoutness of character and, of course, that their owners might be big in other places too. Stan isn't badly endowed, we know because we've had a peek – oh, don't give us a hard time for looking, his fly is always half undone anyway, and as you know he doesn't wear any underpants – but what use is it if she doesn't find him sexy any more?

Look at him, his palms pressed together like that. Such a meek, gentle spirit. Look at the anxious grooves around his mouth. Those scabby lips that cry out to be kissed. Look how everything's bundled up behind that tortured brow – throbbing, unable to get out. It's rare to see such intense concentration on his face, even during waking hours. Normally he just ladles out dollops of banal goodwill onto everything within smiling range.

Oh, what a mess he's in.

He opens his eyes. They gape wide, staring in terror just over our shoulders. The winnowing dawn is beginning to lighten the window. His heart starts battering against his ribs: the start of another day. Good God. What further humiliations lie in store?

We look into those eyes, right through to the big, soft, maggot-eaten soul that lurks behind there, licking its cuts and bruises, hoarding the love that's come back, returned to sender, nursing the bewilderment, the grief. Oh, he had so much to give, did Stan, once upon a time. A whole great ocean of love with beautiful white ships sailing on it. A body rots from the inside out if no one wants that love.

As dawn breaks we get up stiffly, one by one, file quietly down the hallway and out into the front yard. In the smoky dawn the world looks ancient and perilous, a newly unearthed jewel. The outlines of the cars under their shelter are just beginning to form. A hub cap glistens with dew. A lonely magpie carols from its perch on a telephone cable.

No wonder Billy Can flailed around as he did. There's no comfort to be found in a father so lost himself. Now Billy's gone and that was another rejection to deal with, another hammer-blow to the heart. It's enough to make you weep, seeing a man so broken; but it makes us angry too. It makes us want to yank his big nose out of that exhaust pipe he's always sticking it down and tell him to do something for once. You can still save your marriage if you want to, Stan Saint. She's a good-looking sheila, your Crystal, but bored as hell and that ain't a good combo – worst you can imagine, in fact. Why don't you mop up that great, craven tank of a nose with a hanky and think about how to earn back her respect? Why don't you take her off to Sydney for a week? It's time to ring the changes, Stan Saint. This crazy domestic set-up of yours is breaking your little tin heart, and if you let it carry on any longer, it'll be more than even a panel-beater can do to knock it back into shape.

In the morning Stan can hardly believe his eyes. Plump in the middle of the table is a plate of fried eggs. Six of them, each one a perfect yellow island lapped by a pure white sea.

– Fried, says Stan, rubbing his hands together. Oh good. He pulls out his chair and sits down, not taking his eyes off the eggs. What's the occasion?

Crystal's hair is hoiked up with a couple of clothes pegs, a stray orange ringlet dangling down.

– I'm eight weeks pregnant, is what.

A knife clatters to the floor. Stan leaps to his feet, pushing his chair over and lets out a whelp like a dog that's had its tail trodden on. He clutches at Crystal's shoulders with his large, knuckly hands.

– Hooley dooley, Crystal! That's wonderful, ay.

Crystal attempts to wiggle out of his grasp. – Thirty-nine this year. Niver thought I still ad it in me.

– Let's pray it's a little girl this time. I reckon I'd like a girl. He gazes at Crystal, doe-eyed. – Oh, *Chryssy*!

This is more than Crystal can take.

– Stan, you do realise it's not –

– It doesn't matter. I don't care.

Crystal looks down at her lap. Then she starts dealing out the eggs with a spatula. Stan is left standing, unsure where to put his hands. When the yolk of a balanced egg breaks and dangles through the prongs, he tries to grab it from her. For a moment they wrestle with the spatula, and the rest of the egg slithers to the table.

– Oh, for God's sake, barks Crystal. Don't wet your pants about it. There'll be enough of that in seven months' time. Will ya sit down and let me do it.

Stan looks at the broken, bleeding egg as if he has no recollection of what it's for, let alone that this is his favourite breakfast. His eyes are burning brightly. He's had a glimpse of something. He tightens his fist around it. Whatever happens, he won't let it go.

Crystal sees this determination of Stan's and stalls, her already questionable appetite draining away completely. She drops the spatula, slumps back in her chair, and automatically looks around for her pack of Horizon 50s.

– Jesus, she says, remembering. No more smokes for *seven fucken months*.

She lets out a wretched moan.

----

it is dark and dank

Rebecca Hetherington takes out a water bottle from her backpack. She swigs from it, tucks a loose strand of hair behind an ear. Looks around.

– This it?

– Yeh, miss. This is it.

She wanders over to the huge sandstone boulder with its jagged cleft down the middle and steps inside. It is dark and dank, bone-penetratingly cold. She touches the side of the rock with her hand and it meets the sponginess of lichen or mildew, oozing with water. She shivers. You'd think the air in there had never seen the inside of a human lung.

She steps back out into daylight. – Coming in?

Jimmi, still sitting in the driver's seat, shakes his head without looking up. That's odd, she thinks. He was so friendly on the drive out, all dressed up in his Mambo shirt, showing his beautiful white teeth in flashes as he spoke, that mop of corkscrew hair jiggling and jumping whenever they hit corrugations in the track. Now he's treating her like a complete stranger.

He's not even interested in the rock they've driven all this way to see.

– Suit yourself, she says starchily, trying to ignore a gnawing anxiety in her belly.

She waits a moment longer, fiddling with her water bottle. But he's still sitting rigidly in the ute, showing no sign of wanting to move.

– I'll see you back here in half an hour then, she says, and marches defiantly into the chasm by herself.

Get a grip, Rebecca, she commands herself as the walls close darkly around her. Remember what this trip is all about: pushing your limits, discovering your own resources.

There was no denying it, though. This rock was downright creepy. Not only was it claustrophobic, but there was something hostile about it. She takes a few more steps in and looks up, sees a sliver of pale blue sky. She pushes on, deeper into the chasm, keeping a hand on either wall. The air is like a clammy fist in her chest. For some reason she keeps imagining the two halves of the rock closing in and crushing her. Making her into a fossil. She shudders. They'd never discover your body. Things get lost in places like this, she thinks, swallowed up in the murkiness, and are never seen again. She should have brought her Maglite.

From somewhere overhead comes the steady *drip-drip-drip* of water on rock. Where there is water there is life, she thinks. Microscopic algae, perhaps, strange prehistoric larvae dividing and sub-dividing. She would swear she could feel the eyes of small creatures staring at her as she passes. She unscrews the water bottle and is about to take another swig when the bottle is snatched from her hand.

– *Hey!*

Her body is pitched sideways, her shoulder slamming painfully against the unforgiving wall. A tidal wave of warm air rushes past her, slapping her hair across her cheek and pinning her limbs to the rock. Stones ricochet off the walls. She screams and the sound is ripped from her mouth and carried away like the scream of someone on a train hurtling into the distance.

And then, from within the rock itself, comes an answering shriek.

Eeeueueueueeueueueuehhhhweeeeeeeeee!

It is the strangest, eeriest sound she has ever heard. It echoes around the walls of the rock, gradually fading away – but even now, as she begins to peel herself off the rock again, she somehow knows that this tyranny has only just begun. As the last echo peters out, she heaves her mauled body forward and stumbles with outstretched hands towards the light.

– *Jimmi? Jimmi!*

But already she can feel the wind mustering itself at her back, ready for the next assault.

Jimmi wakes with a start, his mind racing. Heat pours in through the wound-down window. His mouth is dry and tastes of rancid meat. He turns the heavy gold watch hanging on his wrist, clunky as a bracelet.

It's very late.

His hands are almost too sweaty to grip the steering wheel. Her bag is still where she left it on the passenger seat. He struggles to swallow as he peers out through the windscreen. He takes care not to look at the rock.

Too many hours have passed.

He starts the engine and slams his foot hard against the floor. A ball of red dust tails him all the way. He has difficulty swallowing with such a dry throat. When he reaches the main street he doesn't stop at the road-house but drives on, snagging the tyre on the kerb outside the ATSIC office. He leaves his engine running.

Tama gets out of her chair as he charges through the door. She has her big fleshy arms open, but he puts out a hand to prevent her from touching him.

– Bad thing happen.

– What bad thing?

Jimmi holds out the English girl's backpack. Tama stares at it, blankly.

– I'm listenin, Jimmi. I c'n listen all day.

---

the signal to jump

Stevo gives Yakka a decent scratch on the muzzle. He offers her a biscuit from the tin. She gobbles it up gratefully, then watches him, head on an angle, poised for the signal to jump.

He coughs nervously, and for a second Yakka thinks that's it, does a false little leap with her two front legs, then checks herself. She twists her head once more.

Stevo hurls his swag into the tray of the Cruiser. Then he squeezes his belly behind the wheel and slams the door. On the forecourt, Yakka lifts one paw. Her plaintive eyes are on him and he can hardly bear it.

Without a backward glance he revs the engine and pulls out onto the street. Why does it feel like everyone's watching him this morning? They're all used to seeing him driving down the Great Northern Highway in his Land Cruiser; but the whole bloody world seems to know it's different today. The lights are green and he speeds towards them, but they change just before he can make it and he's left idling directly outside the coffee shop. Exactly what he'd hoped to avoid.

There she is, such a slight figure in her training daks and short-cropped T-shirt, skin a shade or two darker than his own, sweeping the floor. As he sits there, she wedges open the door and sweeps the dirt out onto the street.

She clocks him straight away. Sometimes it feels as if she's always on the look-out, following his every movement. Even now he catches those eyes flicking to the tray of the Cruiser and back again. No Yakka? The question planting itself on her otherwise expressionless brow.

He raises a hand but offers no explanation. The lights turn green and he's off.

From the start, he misses Yakka something awful. It's humid, cloudy, and the road is long and straight and boring. The sandstone plain with its cityscape of termite mounds rolls on and on.

He tries to lift his mood by slipping a tape in the deck. Chisel should do the trick. Blast those cobwebs out. He turns the volume up, noticing the way the music invites the landscape to lean in, to become the sound-track to his film. *Stevo Pike's Big Escape.* He turns the volume down and watches the landscape shrink back, become impersonal. Then he turns it up again.

In the middle of nowhere he spots a hitcher with a sign chalked Perth, a lanky whitefella dressed in sandals and baggy old shirt. Twists of leather around his wrists. A bloody leftie if ever Stevo saw one, but he reckons he could do with the company. He scuds the Cruiser into the dirt.

– Orright?

– Alright.

The hitcher slams the door and sits on the edge of the seat, nervy and full of twitches. He scratches his greasy hair as if he has lice. Stevo dislikes him instantly and decides to ignore him.

– Where are you from, mate? drones the leftie.

Stevo motions with his head. – Back there.

– Aw, yeh. The leftie nods in slow motion. And where are you heading?

Stevo flicks him a look. Where does he bloody well think?

– South, mate.

– Aw, yeh. The leftie nods again. And what d'you do for a living?

Stevo lets out a sigh. What's the betting the bloke won't like heavy metal? He slips in a bit of 'Kross Culture and turns the volume up. The raucous chords blast out. Stevo senses the hitcher flinch, and he chortles internally. If he dares to start talking again now, Stevo will put Brain Haemorrhage on. Or Angry Anderson. That'd be a laugh, eh – he hopes he has them with him.

The leftie looks out of his window, miserably. Stevo settles himself more comfortably into his seat. Ha! Rebelling, pissing people off – that's what having an adventure is all about. Too tied down, that's been his trouble. Ignoring his own needs too often. And the last thing he needs right now is to be a father all over again.

They drive on. Stevo looks happily around him. Funny how after a while you lose sight of the shapes, he thinks, and see only the colours: the red and the green and the blue. Always the red and the green and the blue. The salt mountains of Port Hedland have just stuck their tips above the horizon and introduced white into the mix when Stevo has to slam on the brakes for a pair of emus that have taken it upon themselves to stalk across the road, heads held high and mighty.

– Just take your time why dontcha, fellas, he grumbles.

He has to swerve to miss a little one, bounding along after the event, gawping stupidly.

– Bloody emus. If I 'ad a gun I'd shoot the lot, he says. Roast em for me tea.

The leftie looks at him with all the shock and disdain of a city boy for his backward country cousin.

– What're you talking about? The hippie drone is forgotten now; instead the voice is like a mozzie in Stevo's ear. – They're beautiful, graceful birds. Should be left to recover their numbers. There's plenty of beef and chicken on the planet, so why do you need to kill emus, for God's sake? In fact why eat meat at all? Do you know how much protein there is in a single lentil?

Stevo looks out of his side window.

– Don't preach to me, mate, he says. There's nothing graceful about an emu. They're pop-eyed, ugly, foul-tempered and mangy, with a kick that could crack more ribs than you knew you owned in the first place, and anyway if one runs across your path it does so with the express intention of you popping a bullet in its pea-sized brain.

The leftie looks out of his own side window, appalled, but Stevo's just warming up.

– And I'd shoot a roo too, if one of them sprung by, he goes on. They're just overgrown grasshoppers anyway. They need to be culled. They'd be boundin over everything if you let em. Besides, I had lentils once and they weren't fit for me bloody dog, turned up whole in me shit for the next seven days, no kiddin.

This is an out-and-out lie. He's never had lentils in his life. But he'll say anything he thinks will piss the bloke off now. Stevo takes off his cap, uses it to mop up the sweat tickling his scalp, then flings it on his lap.

– I think you'd better drop me off, mate, says the leftie, abruptly.

– I think I will, mate, no worries.

Stevo slams the Cruiser onto the verge and the leftie spills himself out, notices there's nothing here but bush and Port Hedland way off in the distance, and looks back at Stevo sheepishly.

– No hard feelings, mate, the leftie says, clearly angling to be let back in.

But Stevo's already turning the wheel and he doesn't even look at him.

– Whatever feelings are there are there, he says shortly. No point pretendin they're not.

The leftie has no alternative but to push the door to, disappointment pulling on his long face. Stevo drives off in a victorious swirl of dust.

Shit, thinks Stevo, glancing in his rear mirror at the figure standing wretchedly on the empty blacktop. Leaving a bloke on the road in the middle of fucken nowhere. Didn't think you 'ad it in ya, mate.

There are whines in Estha's ears for several minutes before she looks up. She thinks it's the cappo machine about to spew a jet of hot black coffee over her apron. It wouldn't be the first time. But when she finally slams her palm against the steamer button, silencing it, the whines are louder than ever.

– Yakka?

Stevo's collie is standing on the pavement outside, her lead in her mouth, as if she might make herself less of a bother that way. No doubt she'd have brought a few tins of food and a can-opener across if she could've found a way to carry them, Estha thinks.

Estha can't remember when she last felt such a rush of love. She flings open the door and takes the creature's bony jaw in her palm. Yakka drops the lead like an offering, and looks away, humiliated. She gives a single, unconvincing wag of the tail.

– 'Salright, girl, whispers Estha, lowering her face so that Yakka can lick it when she's ready. You c'n stay with me. It won't be long till the old solar-powered sex machine has someone else chasin him back again, ay.

---

the oxley moron

The sound of clapping rises to a peak then fades away. Out of bleary, squinting eyes, we make out the spirit child sitting cross-legged on the red earth, her face just a few inches from the screen.

Turn that bloody thing off.

But it's nine o'clock in the morning!

Exactly. Some of us need a full nine hours. You're sitting too close, anyway. It's not good for your eyes.

Stop nagging, will you? This is my favourite show.

Not the learned professor again?

No, I've gone off that. It's *Good Morning Australia*.

Even more of a waste of your time.

Don't be such snobs. I like it, and everybody's got a right to an opinion.

Not in *our* opinion.

If you don't like what they have on the show, you can always phone the presenter, Bert, and suggest something else. You know where the phone is.

We let out a jangling chorus of sighs. Clearly, there's not much hope of a lie-in today, so we get up and plop ourselves on the ground around the telly, lounging on our elbows and stretching the slack skin of our distended bellies. A few gut-clearing burps and breezers spice up the air.

What are they talking about, anyway?

The election campaign.

Bloody oath. Is that Bert? He looks like a bloody owl.

If you're going to watch it, can you at least keep quiet?

We grunt and turn our attention to the screen. A middle-aged man in the audience wearing a green V-necked jumper has his hand up. Bert leans over with the microphone.

Didn't know they did audience participation.

It's a special edition for the election, the spirit child hisses. *Ssssh.*

– *You, sir, what's your name?*

– *Dave Dent. And I'd like to say hello to my mum.*

– *Hello Dave's mum! Which party are you supporting, Dave?*

– *I'm supporting that woman, whatsername, the Oxley moron.*

– *Pauline Hanson?*

– *That's right. Don't look at me like that. She's not so bad as they make out, you know. I find myself agreeing with her in private, an I'll bet my bottom dollar I'm not the only one in this room who does.*

There are a few jeers from the studio audience, a splash of claps in one corner.

– *You've got to give her credit for not minding being hated. It takes a tough cookie to stand up in front of all them disapproving do-gooders. I take my hat off to her, I really do. Who wants to go out to dinner and find their tucker's been cooked by some slope-head, anyway? Or their job taken by one, for that matter.*

More murmurings.

– *Well, Dave, some people would say –*

– *It's good to see a woman making the most of herself. She's what I call a thinking man's crumpet, she always makes sure she's got make-up on and her hair do's in place, which is more than I can say for whatsisname, you know, the one with the slugs for eyebrows.*

– *Mr Howard?*

– *Right. You'd've thought all them women's libbers would be happy, having a powerful woman speak up, but they're never satisfied, it's like the pommies and Maggie, always complaining she wasn't a woman's woman, more like a man than a woman – never satisfied, whatever you give em. Their problem is they don't want to be happy, that's what it's always been with them poms, bunch of miserable* bleep!

There's a burst of hearty applause.

– *Well, thanks for your opinion, Dave. Let's move over here –*

We turn around and stare at the spirit child, horrified.

Is this the level of political discussion among the man and woman on the street?

The spirit child shrugs. You have to understand –

We hold up our palms. No, no. We understand! We're truly heartened and proud that free speech is alive and thriving in this country.

Free speech is very important, the spirit child says.

Absolutely. We couldn't agree more. Long live free speech. Hooray.

We climb back into our hammocks. Our limbs cry out with relief. Our bodies feel ancient these days, the bones sore and stiff as rusted hinges.

Who needs love for their fellow creatures when they can have free speech? we mumble, rolling over and burying our faces in our blankets. The unmistakable stench of urine rises from them.

We ask you. Who needs love any more – ours or anyone else's?

We can feel the judder of the spirit child's feet as she stomps crossly away.

Suddenly the spirit child is running – running so fast and fluidly that her feet seem to spin just above the surface of the earth. Pigtails whir behind her like a pair of propeller blades.

Turn on the telly!

Oh, for goodness sake.

Just *do it*!

Good Morning Australia has finished, and it's not time for *Oprah* yet.

She slams into a snappy gum, using her hands as brakes, then clambers over the hammocks, throwing back blankets and tossing old runners over her shoulder.

Hey, what is this, a bloody inspection?

Who's got the remote? she demands.

It's there somewhere. Stop messing everything up.

Turn on the telly. *Quickly!* It's important.

We haul ourselves out of the hammocks, disentangling our limbs from where they've slipped through holes in the mesh. Behind us, the television springs to life with a *bumpf*.

– *They'll be our ruin, one way or another, the bloody Abos*, growls a familiar voice.

We trudge reluctantly over to the television set, more from a sense of duty than a genuine desire to find out what this is all about. On the screen, dozens of frowning faces crane angrily around a furry microphone. There are television cameras on wheels, a jostling of journalists trying to get a better position, white lights flashing and making everybody blink.

Isn't that the coffee shop? Isn't that Emmeline and skinny old Arthur? And Sydney Coldiver?

– *All I'm trying to do here is make an honest dollar, provide jobs for good, straightforward Aussies – family men, all of them,* Coldiver is saying. *I'm trying to build a decent business. I'm trying to put this town on the map.*

His blustering face fills the screen, the pink-rimmed eyes bulging more than ever.

– *How are we going to encourage tourists to come to this area,* he goes on, *when there are half a dozen Abos snoring in the long grass on the side of the road, and when one of them has just been charged with abduction and murder?*

The camera pans out to take in the figure at Coldiver's side. We scarcely recognise him at first. He's still barefoot, but he's dressed in a colourful Mambo shirt and reflector sunglasses which make it impossible to see his eyes. An ostentatious gold watch hangs on one wrist. On the other hangs a handcuff, attaching him to an adjacent police officer.

– *There's nothing honest about what you're doing,* a voice shouts out. The camera swivels round to find the huge red beard that is Rossco. – *You're an opportunist, Coldiver. Admit it. You made this man defy his own traditions. You paid him to do it. If it was in your interests to let the blackfellas drink grog, you'd pay them to do that too.*

– *You shut your face,* Coldiver roars. *And don't bother to turn up at work on Monday morning.*

– *Thank god for that,* mutters Rossco.

– *You should show some respect to the blackfellas,* hurls in Gerry, standing by his side. *Leave em to make their own decisions! And you c'n fire me too, if you want.*

Coldiver is weak with rage. – *I don't need to listen to you bludgers. Go back to your fucken ice-age of a coffee shop and stick your heads in the blender.*

– *No, you bloody listen to us for once,* storms back Rossco. *We were doing alright in this town before you came along!*

– *There are people here who need jobs!* spits back Coldiver, incandescent, punching the air with his fist.

– *I've had a job an' it near-on killed me,* moans Rossco. *And look what it's done for Jimmi!*

Coldiver throws his hands up in despair, exposing two big circles of sweat that have stained his loud pink shirt beneath the armpits.

– *You think I don't belong here, doncha?* he says. *That I'm a city man who has no idea how it works out here in the bush. But I'll have you know I*

*come from a family in New South Wales who've been working the land for
more than a hundred years. Eighteen ninety-six they took their first sheep
down there. Nobody ever gave us anything for free, not my dad, nor his dad
before him. This idea of giving the Abos handouts – it's not realistic, and it's
not good for em. And on top of that, it ain't* bloody fair.

– *Look there, boss*, says a voice.

It is Jimmi who's spoken. He has taken his sunglasses off and his handsome black eyes are blinking up at the sky.

– *What?* demands Coldiver irritably.

Jimmi motions with his nose. The crowd gathered outside the coffee
shop looks up, as does whoever's in charge of the camera. There's a good
deal of murmuring from people offscreen as the picture jerks giddily
around in the sea of blue until it hits on a possible target: a tiny speck,
almost invisible to the naked eye. It zooms in to find a bird.

– *What are you on about, Jimmi?*

– *Dat bird. He tell me. I bin make big mistake.*

The cop attached to Jimmi takes this as a sign that it's time to take his
charge away. Jimmi twists his neck to stare at the bird for as long as
possible. The crowd opens for the two men reverentially, as if for a body
of water. When they reach the police car, the policeman puts a hand on
Jimmi's head to make sure he clears the roof.

Coldiver, staring after the head of curly black hair as it ducks, clenches
and unclenches his fists.

– *Oi! You owe me money, you rat!*

Jimmi halts. He questions the policeman with his eyes, gets a nod back,
and with the officer's help, slides the gold watch off his wrist and throws
it towards Coldiver in a casual, under-arm arc. Then he folds up his
sunglasses and they follow suit. Coldiver catches them with messy, two-
handed slaps. Next Jimmi unbuttons his Mambo shirt, exposing his honed
black chest, but the cop refuses to take the handcuff off his right wrist, so
the shirt stays dangling from the arm. A barechested Jimmi and the cop
slide into the back of the car.

A journalist with a microphone steps in front of the camera.

– *And so we leave the inhabitants of* –

We point the remote at the screen. The picture fizzles and dies.

Wowee, our town on telly! chortles the wind, kicking up dust. We're
on the news! Did you know Jimmi Rangi was going to be arrested?

We shrug our shoulders, turn our backs in irritation. What of it?

He'll probably spend his life in the jail that Gerry and Rossco have been building, the wind says, unsure whether to be thrilled or appalled by the thought.

Somewhere behind us the spirit child is banging a crushed Emu can with a metal spoon.

The wind suddenly stops running around the TV and looks at us in astonishment, as if it has come to a decision.

This is the most dramatic thing that has happened here in years, and you didn't even *know* about it? it asks.

Yeh, well, it's not *that* bad, we say, touchily.

Yes it is, mutters the spirit child.

What do *you* know? we snap.

You should never have let it happen.

We didn't *intend* it to –

Then your methods are clearly not working, she says.

So why don't you tell us what would be working better? Go on!

You could advertise on telly, she says, looking up, a sudden sparkle in her eye. They all watch it, you know. Two hours a day, on average.

We clasp our hands to our foreheads, let out an agonised cry.

We're not advertising for people's souls!

It may be the only chance we've got.

It would be tantamount to giving up!

It feels like you already have.

She jumps to her feet, hands on hips.

Want to know what I really think?

We shake our heads glumly. Not really.

Well, I'm going to tell you anyway. I think it's *useless* what's going on around here. You laze about all day, too stoned to do anything practical, numbing yourselves against reality, staving off the day when you finally get it into your fuzzy heads that nobody – not *one single soul* out there – is listening to you any more. Don't you get it? Those days when everyone tuned in on a daily basis are over. Done! *Finito*! It won't be long before there isn't anyone alive who believes in your existence. They won't even know you *used* to exist. Life will go on, but with no reference to you at all. Do you understand what I'm saying?

That's enough, we say sternly. You're speaking out of turn.

Some issues do need to be raised, interjects the wind, hesitantly. A little healthy discussion . . .

You keep out of it! we shout. What's going on anyway? Are you two ganging up? Both of you should shut up and mind your own business.

The spirit child stamps her foot. I won't shut up! she cries. If necessary I will take it into my own hands –

Oh, *will* you now? And what happened the last time you did that. Eh? You thought you knew best, but what a bloody great disaster *that* was.

If you'd let me finish –

He ended up running away and we *all* lost him!

If you'd let me take charge –

Take *charge*?

Yes, take charge –

Where the hand comes from no one knows. We are suddenly aware that she is sprawled on the ground, arms thrown out to the sides, skirt riding up around her hips. She is too shocked to cry out. Gingerly, she touches her face, then inspects her palm for blood.

We turn away, mortified.

You hit me.

Yes. We're sorry.

You *hit* me.

Please. Get up. We won't do it again.

She looks at each of our faces in turn. The wind is too stunned by what it has just witnessed to speak. We shuffle around one another, not wanting to be the one left in front. Moving like an old woman, the spirit child climbs shakily to her feet, brushing a tear off her cheek. Her skin is swelling up and the white of her eye has turned pink.

Unable to bear the tension, the wind runs up a tree trunk and rustles a fistful of leaves. In the confusion, we are barely aware of her reaching out for our hands.

We mustn't lose faith in each other, she says quietly, drawing us into a circle. She sniffs. If we do, then we have allowed what is happening to the people to happen to us as well. Maybe, one day, we'll look back on all this and laugh . . .

She smiles through her tears, although it clearly hurts her to do so. The blood vessels smart in her eye.

Or have I been watching too many Hollywood movies? she giggles, hunching her shoulders coyly to her chin.

a new skin

On a stiflingly hot night Crystal gets up and stands in the bath with a sheet wrapped around her and turns on the creaking shower. It's nowhere near as cold as she needs it to be, but it's better than nothing. The tepid spray spills over her upturned face, hits the sheet, and battens it down until it sticks to her like a new skin, redrawing the outline of her body.

She stays under for several minutes and then she drags her sopping train after her back to Billy's room and flings herself onto the bed. The sheet presses heavily down. It's almost like another body lying on her but actually it's more comforting than that – it blots out the world and buries her. She could let it stifle her if she wanted.

She tries to relax, all too aware that she must make the most of this short period of coolness and get to sleep, because in fifteen minutes she and the sheet will both be bone dry again.

There's a movement in her womb. She peers beneath the tent as if she might see a sign of life. Do that again, she whispers. It's me. Your mother.

Mother. Just thinking of the word triggers an avalanche of emotions. There is panic, dread, regret. Guilt, of course. And a terrible, tumbling sadness. But there is also hope mixed up in there somewhere, and this is the one she clings to. She's been aware of it amassing tentatively inside her for a few weeks now, as if this new baby had spied the few last shreds of optimism on the far-flung edges of its mother's existence and lured them back to her core.

In this action of her unborn child, Crystal glimpses the potential for love, a narrowing of her loneliness, a new-found energy. This pregnancy is nothing like the first. This time she feels ready. This time she will give herself – wholly, completely, gladly – to the tiny creature inside her. Every ounce of love she can muster.

She turns to face the grey square of light at the window. The curtain moves against the sill. Inside her chest a tight sob is gathering momentum.

Oh, Billy, Billy, Billy, she thinks as it bursts out. It's too late, this love, I know. It's come too late for you.

who stole my batteries?

T he spirit child slides the cassette into the hungry mouth of the VCR, good eye gleaming. Ah! The sense of anticipation never lessens, even though she has watched every film in her collection a dozen times by now, can strike several famous poses on demand, and execute a Yankee accent to a tee.

She presses play, but the screen before her remains resolutely blank. She presses play again, harder, although she already knows that pressure makes no difference.

Go *on*, she cajoles, but the little red light in the corner of the remote, she now realises, isn't responding. She shakes it. Puts it against her ear and listens for signs of inner activity. Shakes it again. When the back panel slides away beneath her thumb, she jumps up in a fury and marches over, her little fists digging into her ribs.

Who's got them? she demands, indignantly. Who's the culprit?

We open red-lidded eyes.

Uh?

Who stole my batteries?

Your batteries? What use on mother earth would we have for batteries?

I don't know, but I wouldn't put anything past you.

With one good eye and one all but swamped by her swollen, green and yellow shiner, she surveys the mess of crushed Emu and Coca-Cola cans, the pizza boxes, the cigarette butts scattered around the camp. With her good eye she follows the tangle of wires spanning out from the fridge, the telly, the hydrogen lamp and the telephone. And then she spots the tell-tale, regular motion of a head gently bobbing up and down, a finger lifted lightly to each ear. Now we come to think of it, there's been a background throb in the air for an hour at least. We'd mistaken it for the buzz of an insect, but actually the *de-boomb-boomb, de-boomb-boomb* is unlike any of nature's own rhythms.

The spirit child grabs the wires and yanks.

What the –

Those are my batteries!

A surprised face, lapsing into a guilty smile.

Aw, lighten up. We just wanted to listen to some techno. Here, have a listen.

Even in her fury, she is unable to curb her curiosity for all things technological. She fingers the soft foam ear-pieces.

Go on. Put them in.

De-boomb-boomb, de-boomb-boomb.

Several minutes go by. There's a twitch of pursed lips. A softening around her jaw. Eventually a little smile steals across her mouth. Fingers clicking over her head, she juts her hip to one side and starts to dance.

We look at her in delight. Have you ever seen the spirit child dance before? we whisper, behind our hands. Not bad, is she? Look at the angles of her shadow against the red earth. And the wide smile scooped out of her face. She's quite a little mover.

Gradually we take to the dance floor around her, the late afternoon light striping the rust-red earth with long shadows. Welcoming us with her arms as we venture into the open, the spirit child takes out her left ear-piece and offers it to one of us, joining two heads with one beat. *De-boomb-boomb, de-boomb-boomb*. Shadows of the trees pass over her face as she moves, the two bodies carving sinuous mirror images of one another in the air.

A liquid curve, triggered by her snapping fingers, ripples down her arms and out to her shimmying hips. She charms us as if she were a hypnotising snake, her oscillations stirring within us a seductive memory that we don't quite dare grab hold of.

She'd grow into quite a woman, if she ever got the chance, we whisper. Which she won't, of course, as long as we're around to remember.

We suck in our cheeks as we stand around the edge of the dance floor, at last allowing ourselves to feel the all-too-familiar mixture of love and grief and pity and dread which her presence has always inspired in us.

noises

Darkness. The moon has whittled itself away to a thread. Lying on the cold, hard ground, the spirit child has a sense that she's the rabbit beneath a magician's heavy black cape, thrown over to quieten her down. The stars are punctures, little bursts of laughter and delight coming from another world.

We hear the *pad-pad-pad* of small feet.

I can't sleep.

We stir in our hammocks, emit little grunts of irritation.

Why?

It's too dark, and I can hear noises.

What sort of noises?

I don't know. Just noises. They're coming from over there, where the Saints' house is.

It's probably just the wind. Go back to sleep.

She stands her ground, unappeased.

Can I climb in with you?

The whites of her eyes glow in the darkness.

Bad for your back, we say.

What about *your* backs?

Our backs don't matter any more.

Still she stands her ground, a slight little thing, looking over her shoulder from time to time. She gives a pathetic sniff.

I don't like living out here any more, she says. It gives me the creeps.

We sigh. What on earth is there to be frightened of? Nothing out there can hurt you.

The dreadful lie shames us even as we say it, stabbing our hearts with guilt. But it is better this way; her lack of memory serves her well, and we're not going to remind her. We avoid looking one another in the eye.

And then, in the distance, we hear an unmistakable sound. Every ear tunes in. The spirit child clutches the side of a hammock.

There! Did you hear it? Over there amongst the cabbage gums!

We nod. There's no escaping that sound. It strikes a hammer-blow to our hearts. It's only a matter of time till they shatter again.

What is it?

A baby crying.

The spirit child stares into the darkness. There is nothing to see except the hesitant stars in the sky. The cry builds and builds, until it's an outraged wail.

Why is it crying?

Some of us let out a groan and roll over, turning our backs. We don't want to think about what this means. We want to go back to sleep.

The spirit child shakes a hammock roughly.

Don't go to sleep! Tell me what's wrong! Is it Crystal? Has she had her child?

Yes. That's it. It's Crystal's baby. That's all.

She stops agitating the hammock.

If it's only Crystal, why are you looking so frightened?

Another shriek pierces the darkness: a different voice. This time we sit bolt upright.

What was *that*? she gasps.

That was Crystal yelling at Stan.

The spirit child puts her thumb in her mouth, terrified.

I don't believe you. There's something going on. Something bad happened here once.

She throws her neck back and looks up at the sky. The stars seem larger than before, holes growing in the heavy black cape. She shivers down the length of her spine.

Go back to sleep, we say.

She stares at us, thumb wedged firmly in her mouth.

You're becoming cold and hard, she says around the edges of it.

We feel around for the blankets that have slipped away, draw them up defensively around our bony shoulders.

You will too when you've lived as long as us.

You're keeping something from me.

The spirit child looks at us for a while and then, when she gets no response, strides off. As soon as she's gone we wish she hadn't.

Where are you going? we call out.

Bed.

You might as well sleep with us now!

But she shakes her head firmly, disappearing into the darkness. We strain our eyes in vain for a glimmer of her white pyjamas. With a sigh we wriggle back down in our hammocks, pulling our threadbare blankets around us. With luck we'll be able to slip straight back into that deep vein of sleep that she wrested us from.

But our composure is ruffled now.

At least she hasn't worked out what happens to her, we reassure each other, disembodied voices in the darkness. At least she can exist in ignorance.

We listen to the sound of each other blinking. There's an occasional heart-weary sigh. Anxious eyes wander around in the darkness. At one point the wings of an owl whirr by and several of us sit up in fright. Embarrassed by our jumpiness, we make a fuss of lying back down, getting comfortable again, complaining about who stole whose blanket.

Then, from out of the darkness, we hear her small, meandering voice:

Nothing out there to hurt me. Nothing at all.

part VI

nowhere in the landscape

A sudden wind swipes the car from the west, splatting an uncertain, light squall onto the windscreen. Billy turns on the wipers, dried out from lack of use, manages only to smear the dirt and grease across the glass. Cold rain lashes at a slant, the sky one vast expanse of grey cloud that reaches down to the salt lake and turns the whole world a uniform, dirty white. Nowhere in the landscape is there a single splash of colour.

The first time he crossed Lake Lefroy, Billy had the sense that it absorbed everything – sound, emotion, colour – a huge, muffling expanse, letting off a numbness as hot or cold might let off steam. These days he allows events to happen to him and they are neither good nor bad. The forming of opinions is of no interest to him any longer. He's not sure any more whether it was the lake that did this to him, covering him in its grubby shroud, or whether he was already like this when he came, seven years ago.

He likes the monotony of the lake. It suits him. A planeload of Finns arrived in the 1950s, according to Harri, lured by a government needing labour for its fledgling mining industry, and when they first saw the salt lake they couldn't work out why it hadn't melted in the 45° heat. They weren't the only newcomers to mistake it for ice, to see it as a trick of physics or meteorology, and so reveal an underlying distrust of the desert and all things in it. Even without the sun the salt is blinding: fifty square kilometres of brilliant white pancake that tears at the eye. After the rain, stagnant water collects in unsettling green pools. In the summer, the lake crusts up and sends back the blue of the sky with a slap. Nothing grows around the perimeter except low saltbush.

Billy sits up tall to get behind the broken sunshade, groping on the seat beside him for his regulation eyewear. They turn everything to ochre but as soon as he's got them on the muscles around his eyes relax and he no longer needs to squint. Then he puts his headlights on – not because he needs them, but because he's on the lease now, and it's a way of countering the imperious glare of the lake. Every communication must be countered, he has learnt, if you want to protect yourself.

The Hunt, Revenge and Intrepide orebodies all lie beneath Lake Lefroy. The stark tombstones of exploration rigs rise up from the salt. A monstrous black pipeline bisects the lake, pumping water from Perth. On the horizon is a blue ridge of mullock waste. At the midway point he averts his eyes: an upside-down gum boot sticks out of the salt just here, and further along a black triangle poses as a shark's fin. The antics of some late-night sparky. Funny on the first day, but he must have seen them a thousand times since then and he can't bear to look at them any more.

By the time he reaches the other side of the lake the rain is driving almost horizontal. A truck tips its load of crushed mullock on the edge of the road as he gets out, heavy grey slabs thundering. Billy snatches at the hood of his raincoat, hunkered down, jamming his elbow on the handle of the steel door, taking in the sign with one quick glance: PLANNED FIRING TODAY, TUESDAY 11 NOVEMBER, 12 NOON.

– William Saint, he says, pushing his dripping hood back.

The entry guard is short and dumpy, sideburns wrapped around his thick face like a muzzle on a dangerous dog.

– Mine and job? asks the guard.

– Franki, bogger operator.

He knows this guard, but the man refuses to recognise him in return – or any other of the miners, as far as Billy knows – using this small rebuff to establish his uniqueness, their uniformity.

– Single men's quarters?

There's rainwater dripping off the end of Billy's long nose. He squeezes it between a finger and thumb.

– I thought I'd dump me swag in the women's quarters, ay. I like the sound of those new geos. They got degrees.

The bulldog gives him a dead-pan once-over, taking in the serious face with its scattering of white scars and strangely piercing eyes. He's a tall man, intimidating if you looked at him for too long.

– I like my women to have brains, adds Billy.

The bulldog blinks. He has to crane his neck to look up at Billy's face.

– You wouldn't understand, Billy says.

The bulldog gives a snort. – Where are you sleeping?

– At the caravan park. I missed the bus in this mornin.

– Why dja miss the bus?

– None of your fucken business.

They lock eyes, though Billy refuses to reward the bulldog with anything more than a look of casual boredom.

That snort again. – Papers, passport, documents.

Billy pulls a sheaf of papers from his back pocket, curled into the shape of his buttock and still warm from sitting on them. The bulldog puts his elbows on the table, wedges his head between thick wrists, studies the papers with slow movements of his eyes across the page.

– You bin at the Superpit for three years before?

– Yeh.

– You left the Superpit to go underground?

He looks up at Billy, a flicker of curiosity in there now, as if he has spotted the chink in Billy's armour. Billy takes his time cleaning his protective sunglasses on the ends of his shirt, holds them up to the light at the window to check for smears. He lets his silence do its work. The rain outside has stopped now, and the tracks of water running down the windows are lit with greasy rainbows.

The bulldog shuffles the documents together.

– Reckon you must've gone a bit troppo, mate.

Billy looks at the bulldog. His smile has snagged at one end, a mark of private amusement. He puts out his hand for his tag.

– I wanted to be inside the earth, he says.

The bulldog looks at him in confusion.

– Don't worry, mate, says Billy. You wouldn't understand that either.

His nipper is Sim, fresh from a potato farm in Scottsdale, Tasmania. His small, swarthy body is strong but the eyes crouched behind the generous dollop of black hair are furtive, as if somebody once told him that nothing and no one should be trusted in this world.

They all reckon he looks like a potato with that squat white body, and smells like one too – the milky, earthy smell that comes off when you're peeling them. Often when Billy comes to pick Sim up in the single men's quarters, he finds him sitting in his underpants crosslegged on the bed, the insides of his thighs a raffia mat of dark curls, a book on agricultural practices propped open.

– How're ya goin, Spud? Schoolin up on yer bintjes and pinkeyes?

Sim is unable to hide the fact that this offends him.

– You'd hev to be a mainlander to talk about bintjes and pinkeyes as if they were an interchangeable potato!

Billy suspects the kid was sent here by his parents to toughen him up and bring some ready cash back into the farm after a three-year stint – and perhaps he'll make it. Perhaps he'll be the one man around here to save his two thousand dollars a week instead of spending it all on grog and girls. For some reason Billy has taken an interest in Sim, as if to get this raw boy through his three years unharmed and sent home richer will make it all worthwhile. He doesn't want him to end up like so many others, the ones that hang on for another five, then ten, then twenty years, until all that's left to do is wait for silicosis to eat away their lungs and get dusted off on a pension. They have no idea where home is by the time they're told to go there.

There's no sign of Sim in his room today. The sheets on the cot bed are crumpled and a pair of grey boxers are draped over the back of a chair. On the small desk are heaped piles of the *Golden Mail* and *The Kalgoorlie Miner*, a cold hot-dog on a plate balancing precariously on top. Billy picks up the hot-dog without waiting to ask but baulks before the first bite and brushes a thick layer of salt off with his finger.

Sim appears in the doorway, a towel wrapped around his waist, another wound turban-fashion around his head. Billy can smell the damp frowstiness of the towels, wonders when they last saw the inside of a washing machine.

– Dja hear what happened to me yissterday? asks Sim, unwinding the towel on his head and rubbing at his wet hair.

Billy stands there chewing.

– Fuck. I near on died and ya didn't hear about it?

Sim's eyes brim with the neediness of a boy who's used to the daily attentions of an anxious mother. He throws his short body up onto the bed, puffs a pillow behind him. The towel gapes at his crotch.

– I was off-siding with Pete. The level we blasted for the first time Sunday. Something was up with the jumbo, making a noise like a bloody donkey. Anyway, Pete wasn't happy about it. He called the fitter, an 'e sent me to get a grease cartridge out the back of the ute. So I got it out and just as I turned around –

– Whatja wanna put all that salt on for? You'll have a heart attack before you're thirty-five.

Sim holds his short arms out, the weight of his story in them. – Chrissakes, mate, I'm telling you about my near-death experience and you're harping on about salt? It's not your fucken hot-dog anyway. I was gunna have that for me breakfast. Listen. This humongous boulder lobbed down, smashed the bonnet, bent the bull bar, and the headlights popped clean out like a pair of fucken eyeballs.

The picture makes Billy laugh. He shoves in the last bit of hot-dog, giving Sim a full view of the half-chewed contents of his mouth. Sim watches critically.

– I was an inch away from being under it, he says quietly. An *inch* away.

The boy stares unhappily at the empty hot-dog plate with its neat dollop of tomato sauce. After a moment he wipes up the sauce with a finger.

– An I still get lost heaps. You go in sitting on the end of the ute looking backwards and how're ya sposed to tell which tunnel you're in when it's time to come back to the surface? They all look the bloody same.

Sim keeps the tomato sauce finger in his mouth. Billy brushes his hands together, looks towards the plate to check he didn't miss anything else and swallows down the last mouthful.

– You git hungry enough you'll find yer way up eventually, he says.

He picks up Sim's hat and slings the overalls over his shoulder.

– Hey, I need to put them on!

– Jiss trying to save ya time, calls back Billy from halfway down the stairs.

They leave their ID tags on hooks at the shaft entrance. A rumble and screech of pulleys announces the cage to be a dozen floors away, maybe less. Sim, still tugging at the crotch of his overalls, looks around as if trying to nourish himself with this last sight of daylight and surface activity. The hatched bars of the cage emerge uncertainly from out of their dank womb. There's a dozen men ahead of them and space for only one more. Billy takes it, by grace of his seniority.

– Catch a lift in the truck, he suggests to Sim, nodding to where one is driving towards the vehicle entrance.

The men in the cage all face the same direction, too self-conscious to stare into one another's eyes at such close range this early in the day. The outlines of the levels flick past. Ten storeys down, everyone but Billy gets off. He closes his eyes, welcoming the sense of sinking deeper into the belly of the earth, his stomach lagging slightly behind. At last the cage hits bedrock. He slides the mesh door open with a clank and steps out.

He is the first one down. He walks a few paces then turns off his cap-lamp and stands in darkness. He can't even see his own feet. The air is dank and sits on his skin. There are foul pockets of staleness, although he barely notices these any more, accepting them as he accepts the changes in the smell of the other men during the course of a shift.

For these few minutes before the others arrive Billy revels in the solitude, the sensual deprivation. He catches himself making an initial movement towards his breast pocket. If he could light a cigarette down here it would be perfect. Faintly, he can hear the sound of subterranean water dripping onto the tunnel walls. Add a macaw or two, the shriek of a monkey, and he could be in a rain-forest at night.

Too soon, there is the clamour of steel on steel, the cage door sliding across, footfalls behind him on the hard-packed rock.

– Who's there?

The beam of a cap-lamp crosses Billy's chest, comes back to find him. He switches on his own, springing himself into being.

– Saint? What the fuck are ya doing standin in the dark?

The voice is stone-muffled, flat.

– Just takin a smoko, says Billy. Without the smokes.

Harri eyes him edgily. – I could give ya a written warnin for not keepin a low beam on. Are yer batteries flat?

– Everything's in order.

In the unforgiving beam of the cap-lamp, Harri looks terrible. There are deep clefts around his mouth, as if his entire chin could be slid out in one removable chunk. Even the acne scars throw shadows. Billy smiles; he has no need for this show of authority. Harri runs his hand over his mouth, apologetic. He can't be bothered with it, either.

– Anyway, we're setting up. Get Sim to unpack the truck. You do the checks. Blasting's at noon. Drilling in an hour. When we fire this cut, we'll be into nickel.

– I c'n start sooner than that.

– No need to, Harri calls back.

– If I start sooner, I'll do more holes by noon.

Harri turns around. He looks at Billy sceptically, rubs the oily wreck of his chin, his eyes beginning to wake up.

– Why do more than you 'ave to?

Billy shrugs. – You're the boss. He brushes past Harri, heading back in the direction of the others.

– Why so keen?

– I c'n teach Sim.

Harri's irritated now that Billy is walking away from him.

– Well, you c'n bloody clear the extra rubble, the two of youse, after. Don't make us late up. I don't want ter be late up tonight.

Billy turns round, carries on walking backwards. – Got a date?

– Laura. The monthly visit.

– She reckons you're worth comin all this way for?

– She's a good bird, ay.

– She'd niver put up with you f'more than once a month, that's the truth.

– That's probably the half of it, says Harri, grinning.

Billy sets the bit against the dolorite and wedges the upper part of the airleg against his armpit. Once the massive steel starts to rotate, the vibrations feed into his shoulder, his throat, his chest. Soon his teeth are buzzing and his bowels churning: no atom of his being is left in peace. After the first twenty-minute stint he can't stop his teeth chattering and his fingers and arms have turned numb. He will do another five stints like this before the morning's up. After each one he drinks a plastic beaker of water which Sim hands to him, then wipes out the fine coating of black dust from inside his protective glasses.

At morning smoko, Sim brings him his coffee. The quivering from Billy's hand passes into the liquid. If he spills it, the other men pretend not to notice, or feign indifference, one of them carelessly tossing a cloth in his direction. This is the lot of diggers, and they respect a man who can absorb the physical assault on a daily basis. More than that, they're sobered by the sight of a man in his early twenties turning old before their eyes.

At eleven o'clock he turns the airleg off and steps back, still trapped in a slow-motion, soundless world. He lifts off his ear-muffs and only after the ringing subsides does he become aware of the groaning and beeping of the trucks as they manoeuvre around the rises, and that the men who are looking at him and moving their mouths are also making sounds. As Sim packs the airleg away, Billy turns back one more time and claws at the rock face with his gloved hands, scrabbling at the loose rubble, delving deep into the private recesses of the earth. Every handful that he can bring out himself is a private victory. Grime runs with the sweat on his face, clogs up the creases around his eyes. When he blows his nose, the mucus is black. One day, the void they have created down here, a kilometre beneath the surface, will cave in on itself, eaten from the inside out. Up above will be a new landscape, man-made and lacking in natural reasoning – artificial hills made of mullock that would shift and erode if they weren't sown with hummock grass, wattles and saltbush; waterless hollows that the annual rainfall will never be adequate to fill. It will be like a boxer's face – the same eyes, the same skin, but with something shifty about the bones underneath.

– Saint!

Two hands grab fistfuls of Billy's overalls and hurl him onto the ground. Harri's scarred face is more astonished than angry.

– Leave off, can't ya? Ya fucken lunatic.

The face is charged from the top downwards with ammonium nitrate mixed with diesel. The charger is a man named Francis Jacobs, a sinewy creature with a perfect mullet of a hair-cut: red quills standing upright on top, as if from the force of all the blasts, a greasy ponytail snaking down his neck. He has shadowy clefts beneath his high cheekbones. The other men call him the powder monkey.

They leave him working while they go to the crib-room for lunch, rolling waxy togs of foam between their fingers and pushing them deep into their ears. Conversation peters out as the sound of pumping blood takes over. They are deaf mutes now, left to follow the familiar routine, touching more than usual – a steadying hand on the back of the man in front as he steps out of the cage, a shove in the direction of an empty table. Sometimes they'll throw a stone or a teaspoon at someone to get their attention.

Beneath them, Francis Jacobs turns the detonator key. He's not conscious of the tic high up on his narrow cheek where the bone appears to be dented. He glances around, ostensibly to check that he's alone, but on some other level wishing that there were someone here to appreciate the accuracy of his circuit.

Above, the men drag chairs on concrete. Pete Monday, the jumbo operator, hollers to one of the nippers to bring him his mouse-proof crib-box. They blow ripples across the surface of their thin machine coffee, then take a sip and scald the tips of their tongues. They don't think of the digital figures on the clock down below.

Francis's freckled hand hovers over the detonator button as he goes through the paces of his solitary countdown. A red light springs on in the darkness. At 11.55 he pushes the button and leaves.

The blast forces the men's ear-plugs in, then sucks them back out, the wave passing through them with the force of a small earthquake. Pete Monday unscrews a thermos of strong-smelling chook soup, oblivious to the destruction going on beneath them. Even Sim, the new nipper, shows no sign of having registered the blast, too intent on seeing if his meat pie has finished in the warmer. Billy bites down on a corned beef and sliced gherkin sandwich, knowing that this is what he came for, this place where there is no silence, where the voices can't reach.

They've been working together for long enough now that they each know their role within the group. Only Sim still has to prove himself. When he first arrived, no one told him where the toilets were. Complicated underground directions led down stopes with no exits; above ground they led into kitchens or the private office of some big cheese. *Aw, sorry, mate, I thought this was the bog.* Once he found himself in the room reserved for testing urine samples for traces of alcohol and drugs. He was young, but he had to go through it, like anyone else. On one occasion, slick-fingered Francis removed the watch off his wrist while he kipped on a row of chairs at crib, and when Harri noticed that he was going under without a time-piece, he said he'd give him a written warning. Three written warnings and he'd be out. Harri only backed down after Billy intervened on Sim's behalf.

They eat without talking – largely because most of them can't be bothered to take their ear-plugs out. At twelve thirty they begin to collect their belongings together. Pete Monday picks up a stack of napkins, grates back his chair.

– You know, you shouldn't use that much.

Pete stops dead in his tracks, takes his time to turn around.

– How dja know what I'm usin em for, mate?

– It's bad for the environment, says Sim.

Pete looks to see who else has overheard this little dialogue with the nipper. Several of them are smiling behind their hands.

– Spud's worried about conserving paper! And 'e works in a bloody nickel mine! Pete announces.

– There's things they could do different here if they were more aware of conservation, whines Sim, the colour rising in his cheeks.

– Mate, this is where Australia's wealth comes from, says Wojciech, the sparky. Let them worry about conservation back in Queensland.

– At least they're recyclin the polypipes, says Harri, diplomatically. Hev ya noticed? They use em as roadside markers. They're better than timber posts. No one need know you iver went off the road with a bendy polypipe.

Pete places his wide face directly on a level with the young nipper's eyes. His skin is the colour of uncooked sausage meat. He rounds his shoulders, aggressively.

– No one's gunna tell me how many napkins I need to wipe me arse, he says.

– You might think different if you had to pay for em, insists Sim.

– Listen, mate. Pete fills his lungs. Takin a dump is the best part of me day. I put in enough fucken hours for this company that they can let me wipe me arse properly. If I were loaded I'd buy quilted paper an all. I'd be the happiest crapper around.

– 'The possession of the greatest riches does not resolve the agitation of the soul nor give birth to remarkable joy,' trills Francis, suddenly. He has come in without any of them noticing.

The others look up in surprise.

– Ar, Jesus, mate, fuck *off*, you're the one who's agitatin me fucken soul now, cries Pete. Now, if it doesn't put anybody out, I'm goin for a dump.

– OK, Monday, laughs Harri. See ya in a couple of hours.

They go back down to find great heaps of broken ore and mullock spilled onto the floor of the drive. They bar it down, then load it on the trucks with the bogger, watering the face with hoses to keep back the dust. Billy shows Sim how to install a line of roof bolts. When it's done, Billy crouches on the ground and tosses two chippings in his hand. They are heavy, dark grey flecked with gold, a shine to some of the facets indicating the presence of nickel. Harri will be pleased: positive news to report to the site manager.

There was a time when Billy would have tried to take possession of these pieces of the earth; when his head would have swum with the thought that they had not seen daylight for however many million years. Now he throws them down as if they were litter. Within a few days the nickel they dug today will have been railed to Kwinana. In six months it will be part of someone's stainless steel sink in Wagga Wagga. If he thinks about it at all, he laughs at the ease of it, how simple it is to dismantle the earth, piece by piece.

On the surface they tag off and Sim swipes Billy's keys and beats him to the driving seat.

– You're in no state, Sim says. Why didntcha get the bus this morning, anyway?

– Couldn't get up. Missed breakfast an all.

Sim turns the key in the ignition. – Good sleep, ay?

– Beaut.

Sim flashes him a boyish smile. – Sexy?

– Nah, mate. No dreams.

– Sa pity.

Billy looks out of the window. High up there's a brown speck circling in the blue: an eagle, biding its time.

– Nah. No dreams is why it was good.

They follow the fume-belching bus back across the causeway, weighed down with its load of tired but freshly showered men. There is a pink sheen to the lake now. Long, low shafts of light slice through the cloud as if through a door left ajar. Billy's spent forearms lie in his lap as if someone else had dropped them there, his fingers curling up like the legs of a dead beetle.

By unofficial agreement the bus pulls over outside a building with windows frosted up to shoulder height. A sign on the door advertises three skimpies. Men from Schmitz, Thunderer and Sirius, as well as the Lanfranchi shaft, spill onto the pavement, shielding their weakened eyes against the last glare of the day.

The Federal Arms offers them a reassuring sensory continuity – dimness, cigarette smoke in place of dust, the growl of male voices in place of the jumbos – easing them through the transition from life below to life above. Stump, the six-foot-five-inch owner, takes in the faces of the men as they come in, amending his complex mental chart with each one's arrival and departure time, the quantity of beer he's consumed, any fights won or lost, any rumours of disloyal visits to neighbouring watering holes. If grief is given to one of his skimpies, there's a heavy black strike through the entry: relationship terminated.

A large hand lands on each of their shoulders: Harri, steering them to a table. Francis Jacobs is already sitting there, sliding out the ingredients of explosives from beneath his battered fingernails.

– Does Laura do the cobwebbing when she comes, Harri? Francis asks as they sit down.

– If I let her out the bed.

– Dja think she'd come and do mine?

– You gotta learn to do that shit yerself, mate. No self-respectin woman will bed a man who can't keep his own house clean these days.

– I c'n cook a mean chilli mud crab, says Francis. You iver tasted my chilli mud crab?

– Where dja get the mud crabs out here?

– Oh, I ain't done it in years. But I useta, back home.

– That'd be why we ain't tasted it, then, Francis.

Harri's in the habit of shouting his crew a jug at the start of the evening, and one by one they pay him back with glasses, a ritual that leaves the men with the sense that they are obligated to Harri more than he to them, whereas in fact it's the other way round. He can put away more than any of them, somehow managing to sit bolt upright while the liquor plays havoc with his insides, slurring his speech, blurring his vision.

One of the skimpies comes over to pour out the drinks and the men are silent as they let their eyes travel over her smooth belly, the curve of her hips, the bright pink nylon of her panties. The fabric is a little baggy at the back where she fails to fill it. The bristles of Harri's moustache turn a shade darker with their first soaking of beer.

– Playing tonight, fellas? The skimpy holds the emptied glass jug against her tummy, her belly button temporarily magnified in all its intricate twists. – Stake's up to seven hundred and somethin.

Their eyes swim in the distorting glass. She raps the lid of the Chase the Ace box with metallic, inch-long nails.

– *Fellas*?

– Course we wanna play, says Harri, rousing himself.

They tear off corners of the paper tablecloth and scribble down their names. Harri tosses his scrunched-up paper towards another skimpy leaning on the bar.

– Don't duck! I'm aimin for yer cleavage, sweetheart!

– *Guys*. You gotta *fold* them, else whoever digs their hand in will know which ones are his. They all gotta be *folded*.

A shadow falls over them – the hulking form of Pete Monday, pulling up a chair. He sits down heavily, commandeers the entire surface of the table by spreading his thick arms on it, mopping up the puddles of beer.

– Youse fellas see me underwear yit?

– Aw, Pete, we don't want to see yer underwear, mate, says Harri. Not after that scene today.

– You're gunna.

– Someone hand me a peg for me nose.

Pete Monday starts undoing his shirt buttons. – De-nah-nah-nah . . . They watch, despite themselves.

– Oi, Petey, ya fucken gorgeous, yells someone from over the other side of the room. Ya gunna have them girls on their knees!

– I'd like that. Pete grabs the edges of his shirt. – Ready?

– As we'll ever be, mate.

– Sure you c'n handle it?

– Jesus, Pete, get it over with.

He wrests back the shirt and pumps out his chest. A T-shirt underneath reads A WOMAN'S PLACE IS ON MY FACE in black letters.

– That's enough to make you a feminist.

– I think I'm gunna throw.

– It's great, innit? A mate of mine from back home has started 'is own factory in Geelong, prints up whatever you want. I reckon he's whippin up a fortune.

– Didja come up with that bit of poetry yerself?

– As a matter of fact I did. He scratches at the rough stubble around his jaw-line. – It deserves to be the first line of a song dunnit? I'm gunna show them fellas over there. It's somethin else.

– What's the difference between God and a jumbo operator? asks Harri when he's gone. You heard that one yet, Spud?

– God doesn't think he's a jumbo operator.

– That's me boy, fast learner.

– Two kids an all, 'e has, mumbles Francis, looking over at Pete, helping himself to a chair at a table in the corner.

– Been underground too long, that's Monday's problem.

– How long? asks Sim.

– Seventeen, eighteen years.

– Don't take much sense to make a kid. In fact, more sense you got, the less kids. Dontcha reckon, Billy?

– Don't ask fucken Saint, says Francis. He wouldn't know how to make a kid if you paid him.

Harri raises a scruffy eyebrow at Billy. – That Jackie's soft on ya, I reckon. He tosses his head towards the skimpy in the pink bra and knickers who brought their beer. Standing at the bar, she has one hand on her hip, and with the other she slides a cowrie shell along a silver neck chain.

– See? says Francis. He hasn't even noticed her. It's wasted on im.

– It's not wasted, he's jiss waitin for the right one, entcha Billy?

Billy takes a cigarette and sticks it between his lips. He picks up his lighter.

– If e'd fucken defend imself, then I might believe it, says Francis. He waves a hand in front of Billy's face. – Cooee! We're callin you a Vegemite-driller!

Billy lights the cigarette, leans his body back into the give of the chair, narrows his eyes.

– Betcha never even –

– Francis, growls Harri.

Francis looks rattled, jumps to the edge of his seat. – I ain't saying anything unflatterin. Look at them big hands, that straight nose. He's built like a bloody Greek! The women here'd die to get a suck of his cock.

They both look at Billy. He takes the cigarette from between dry lips. After a while he can't help it: the edge of his mouth cracks up.

– There, see! Francis looks around excitedly. – See? 'E knows it himself. 'E's a fuckin spunk and it's wasted!

Harri is laughing now. – Maybe 'e's jiss tryin not to show the rest of us up. That right, Billy? If word got round, all our women would bloody leave us and start queuing up at your caravan door.

Billy runs his finger around a circle of beer on the table. He smiles.

– Aw, look at im, for Chrissake. No way in, no way out.

– Whatja guarding, Billy? laughs Harri.

– The privacy of his soul, that's what, says Francis. The privacy of ya fucken soul. I tell ya, it better be good. It better be fucken good.

– Me name's bin drawn! Me name's bin drawn!

They look up to see Sim's beaming face at the bar, far more delighted by the little scrap of paper in his hand than by the proximity of Jackie's cleavage. A second skimpy in a leopard-skin bustier tied with red ribbons shuffles a deck of cards with deft fingers. A hush falls on the room as Sim runs his eyes over the fanned cards. Smoke rises quietly to the ceiling. Sim lifts his hand as if to take a card but stops, distrusting this first impulse. He hovers near another one, then pauses again, undecided, his instinct apparently offering him nothing now that he ignored it the first time. Then he plunges in at random, snatching a card quickly from the middle. Even before he's turned it over he looks unhappy with his choice.

– Four of clubs. *Shit*!

The disappointment overwhelms him. As the light fades from his eyes, he searches out Billy from among the sea of faces. He makes no attempt to hide his neediness. Most of the men turn back to their beers, embarrassed, but Billy freezes, his cigarette halfway to his mouth. He hadn't realised just how much Sim wanted to escape this place. The nipper looks stunned, as if a door has just slammed in his face, and behind this door all that exists are years and years spent tunnelling underground. It is as if he can think of no worse fate.

Perhaps he should feel pity for the kid, but what Billy feels instead is envy. Envy that there is another life calling Sim, another life he yearns to live.

– Never mind, Spud, Harri is shouting, coming to the rescue as ever. Come back ere and bring another jug with ya. The tide's going out in these glasses.

---

thirty kays south

On the edge of the highway thirty kays south of the town, a pair of feet stick out of the tray of a battered Land Cruiser. As a triple-rigged road train charges past, a dozen wild eyes light up the bulging outline of a stomach on the Cruiser's tray, stark against the grey night sky, a lumpy head propped on a rolled-up swag, hairless as a turtle's. Hands folded neatly on the belly.

The wind has dragged us all the way down here to see this sight, but now that it's here it seems to have forgotten the point of the excursion. All it wants to do is race from side to side across the highway, seeing how many times it can cross before the road train slams past. There's a rush of air and a scattering of pebbles, the last pocket of air bursting with a bang that whips our beards across our faces.

Phew! Close or *what*.

A little shaken by just how close that was (though doing its best to hide it), the wind comes over to watch us climbing into the tray of the Cruiser. We squat on our haunches around Stevo's snoring frame. Up close we can count the dozens of little beads of sweat clinging to his scalp. We haven't failed to notice the strap of a coral-coloured slip hooked over one ear.

Ran out of petrol. Ironic, really, seeing as he used to run a servo.

Shuffling around on our haunches, we look up at the broad stretch of sky above. It's not a bad place to sleep, safe from snakes and dingos, although you'd get mashed to a pulp if one of those road-train drivers let their concentration lapse for a second or two.

Stevo opens his eyes. Without moving he stares straight up, apparently struck by how much clearer the stars are here than back in town. A beautiful sweep of them arch overhead, popping and sizzling in their black frying pan.

Stevo's lips move silently, as if he is testing himself. There's the Saucepan, that's easy, and the bright one over there, that's easy too, although he can't bring the name to mind this very minute. The tight little cluster over there is the Seven Sisters. Where the bloody hell is the Southern Cross? Must be too low in the sky. That box shape, that's Pegasus, and the A over there is Taurus . . .

He trails off, failing to identify any others. He blinks at the surrounding bush, his brown eyes muddied with tiredness. He didn't find his father down in Perth. Instead he found the empty Hume cement pipe the old man had been living in for the last twenty years. Some other bagman was living in it now. He'd mumbled something to Stevo about a waiting list and hurled a hunk of stale bread at him to send him packing.

Stevo studies the constellations he can't name – by far the majority of them – trying to join the dots into a familiar pattern. There's something resoundingly lonely about these stars with no names, he thinks. Chances are he'll never find out what they are, either. They'll hang there, unacknowledged, unloved, for the rest of his life, like so many fatherless children, until someone else comes by, some better man than he, who does the decent thing and looks them up in a book.

With his neck arched back, the lump that's been bothering him for so long sits uncomfortably high in his throat. He nearly chokes when he tries to swallow. He brings his chin down and swallows hard, three times in a row, but it still won't go away.

Bloody 'ell, he thinks. Jiss my luck to get cancer now, when I think I've worked it all out.

<hr />

go, cathy, go!

In the stifling heat of midday, the boom box slams out its insistent beat: *DER DER DER DER*. Somewhere between the heat and the beat, a keening, synthetic melody insists upon itself, over and over, broadcasting its mesmeric trance.

Flat out in our hammocks, the beat gives orders to our pulse. We are at its mercy, completely surrendered. Blissed out. Head over heels in love.

Oi! What's going on?

Her shrill voice pierces the soft membrane of our subconscious. We reseal the wound, allow the beat to pump the blood back around our heads. All we want is to exist within our limp bodies, slide around inside our sweaty cocoons. Remain in this semi-conscious state for ever.

WHAT'S GOING ON?

The music stops mid-beat. Hearts flutter in confusion, though the drumming echoes on. Struggling for breath, for control of our weakened limbs, we peer out from under sweat-drenched blankets. Moisture dribbles down our temples.

We thought you *liked* techno music, we croak, hearts still skipping like lunatics.

She is looking at us, open-mouthed, her hand resting on the switch of the boom box.

You were dancing to it the other night.

There's a time and a place, for Pete's sake! she cries. It's forty-three degrees out here!

Sheepishly, we extricate our shaking limbs from our hammocks, the mesh imprinted on our skin. There's a crackle of stiff knee joints, sighs as we ease back our shoulders, but we can't help swapping little smiles, nonetheless. It was heaven there for a while, alright. For a while we forgot that anything else existed.

We limp and hobble into open space, sore eyes squinting in the sun. Something even brighter glints from a tree – a flash like some sort of signal.

What's that doing there?

Nothing gets past that girl.

What's what doing where? we ask innocuously, although one or two · of us are giggling behind our hands.

You know what I'm talking about.

Oh, *that*!

We make a big show of noticing it for the first time, slapping our numbskull heads, hoping to distract her with our extravagant pretence of innocence.

Oh, it made an *excellent* head-dress! You should've seen it. Look, this is how we wore it, like that, on a slant. You missed a *brilliant* night. We danced around this big wheel, played poi with balls of fire. It was amazing –

The spirit child is looking distinctly unimpressed. She holds out her hand.

Give it back. I want to watch the race.

Hmm?

The race. Don't tell me you've forgotten.

Oh, the *race*! Yes, yes, of course!

We scratch our heads in an effort to pep ourselves up, go around shaking the hammocks of those still sleeping.

Come on, you lazy buggers! we shout. You good-for-nothings. What do you think you're doing, sleeping during the middle of the day? Quick, get up, it's the race!

Eyes are rubbed. Mouths stretch wide around yawns.

The race? Are we going to Sydney?

No, you idiots, what d'you think we've got a TV for?

The aerial requires a bit of twisting back into shape, but nothing we can't handle. We fetch some beers from the fridge, lay out bowls of crackers and dry roasted peanuts. Soon there's a buzz in the air. We've been looking forward to this race for months. Years, even. In the viewing space, the spirit child draws a line on the earth in front of which no one is allowed to sit. She bounces from foot to foot, then stands still with one ankle twined around the other. Then she starts running on the spot. She can hardly contain herself.

Are you sure we're on the right channel?

It's on One, right?

No, no, it's on Seven. Give me the remote!

If only we were watching it live.

Your fault for taking that E last night.

We swap embarrassed glances, but the spirit child is too engrossed with the remote to notice. *Bumpf.*

Wouldn't it be great to feel the atmosphere of the crowd? I bet some of the others have made the trip.

Look! Isn't that the mob from Arnhem Land, doing laps of the running track?

Clearly, they haven't got a telly yet themselves. How behind the times is *that.*

I wish we were there. What a vibe there must be!

If you'd all shut up, maybe we could generate our *own* atmosphere.

Hear hear. Pass the grog, will you?

On the screen the athletes mill around, the bright colours of their outfits flashing in the sun. They stretch their hamstrings, close their eyes for a silent meditation, look around the stadium at all the people. She's easy to spot, in her flamboyant green and gold hooded one-piece.

It's a bit different to what the local women wear to aerobics.

Have you been hanging out at the Fitness Centre again?

Just look at the muscles in her thighs! Phwooar!

The spirit child sits up close to the screen, brushing the girl's face with her finger. The static of the screen is furry beneath her touch.

We're watching you, Cathy, she murmurs.

Get back behind the line, you're blocking the view.

Is lane six the best lane?

All the lanes are the same, dumbo.

But is it her favourite?

She doesn't have an opinion; she can't afford to let such things put her off.

Cathy, can you hear me?

The girl in the green and gold one-piece looks over her shoulder, briefly.

She heard me!

She was probably just looking for her mum in the crowd.

Oi, that's my armchair you're sitting in.

Who says?

It's always mine.

It's not any more.

I went and got it from St Vinnie's.

I thought we didn't believe in personal possessions.

The spirit child sits on her haunches and sticks her thumb in her mouth.

I think she heard me.

It must be pretty terrifying, running in front of that crowd. How many people d'you think the stadium holds?

She *definitely* heard me.

Not to mention the millions glued to their television sets all around the globe. From Andamooka to Yambacoona. Just think!

They're all cheering for her. She'll use them to give her strength.

The spirit child leans over the line in the dirt and touches the athlete's runners: red, yellow and black, the colours of the Aboriginal flag. She strokes the hunched-over back, the fingers that lightly brush the ground.

Out the bloody way!

The spirit child springs back, does a little nervous jump and turns it into a game of hop-scotch on the spot, unable to bear the tension.

I *know* she heard me.

I wonder what she's thinking now.

She's imagining herself winning, of course. She's thought through every stride: how each one will take her a little bit further ahead of the others . . .

How she'll leap across that line, pride swelling out her chest . . .

How she'll lift her hand triumphantly to the crowd . . .

The athletes lift their chins up.

This tension is almost too much.

Have I got time to pee?

The gun cracks.

They're off!

The spirit child starts sprinting around the television set, thrilled by the roar of the crowd.

– *And Cathy Freeman is out. Cathy Freeman is in lane six!*

She's got off to a good start, no tripping.

Look at those streamlined eyes, fixed firmly on the finishing line.

She has *such* a beautiful body.

Stop going on about her bloody body.

– *And the pressure is on her. Lorraine Graham is moving into position* . . .

Look how the loose skin on her cheeks wobbles up and down.

Look at those mighty calf muscles.

We did a good job, ay.

Not that we can take *all* the credit, of course. She had to do the training. But we can take *some* of it.

Of course if we hadn't spiced up her dreams, told her she could really *be* something . . .

Oh, yes. That made all the difference. Telling her she would always win.

That other girl's in the lead!

– *Jamaican Lorraine Graham in the black is making up her stagger, but Freeman picks it up a notch* –

Go, Cathy *go*! screams the spirit child, on her fifth lap of the TV.

Didn't we give her the idea for that tattoo on her right shoulder, as well? I'm sure we did. *Cos I'm free*. Ha! Such a good little phrase. Everyone around the world likes it.

No, she thought it up herself.

Caaarn, Cathy! screams the spirit child. Faster-faster-faster-faster-faster! She's in the lead!

Get out the bloody way!

She's in the lead!

– *Katherine Merry from Great Britain is there. But Cathy Freeman goes into the lead –*

She's winning!

You can do it, Cathy!

Beat that pom!

Get out the bloody way!

Did she win?

Get back!

Who won?

Listen to that crowd! They're going mad!

Bloody hell, did anyone see who won?

– *Well, Cathy's just put Aboriginal Australia right in the spotlight,* says the commentator.

She's lying on the ground!

Is she dead?

Who cares? She won!

– *And now she's donning an Australian and Aboriginal flag tied together for her victory lap . . .*

She won!

– *Australians are calling it a defining moment for reconciliation. For the benefit of viewers abroad, we should explain that the concept of reconciliation is a highly charged political debate in Australia. Many Aborigines want a formal apology for past government injustices, including land seizures, government-enforced assimilation policies –*

You did it, Cathy!

– *Do you think she'll be running in Athens in 2004, Bruce, or do you think she might go into politics?*

– *Well I think it's a little early to spec—*

I'm *sure* she heard me.

– *I suppose to appreciate why the use of the word reconciliation is so politically charged, we have to understand why Australians feel the need to be reconciled to each other. Tell us about the Aboriginal people, Professor.*

Hey! It's my favourite –

– *Oh, dear me. Well, they're about 2.3 per cent of the population –*

– Right. And these are mostly people who – how shall I put it? – have not done very well in modern Australia. The assimilation programme did not work for them.

– It's not that they haven't done well, it's just that their achievements are different. Many are accomplished artists and leaders within their own communities –

– Yes, but they did not react well to the government's attempts to assimilate them into the mainstream after the Second World War –

– Well, no, but remember that assimilation meant having your every move controlled – where you could live, who you marry . . .

– Really, gosh. Let's bring the conversation back to Cathy Freeman's triumphant race today. When there is a minority at odds with mainstream society, Professor – that have a historic grievance – is there a danger that we might latch onto models, such as Cathy Freeman, which we find comforting and reassuring while turning a blind eye to the rest of those people?

– Inevitably, yes, but Cathy Freeman is very politically aware, and I believe she will cast her victory in a political context. She will no doubt raise such issues as the stolen generations, which is a major cause of shame for many Australians living today –

– The stolen generations?

– I am referring to the Aboriginal children who were forcefully removed from their families under government policy from the nineteenth century through until as recently as the 1970s under the policy of assimilation. You can read all about it in the report by the Human Rights and Equal Opportunity Commission . . .

– Oh. Right. But can you tell us how many children were taken, Professor?

– No one knows for sure. The estimate runs between one in three to one in ten.

– Wow, that's quite a number. Thank you, Professor, now back to the stadium where the hero of the day is most definitely Cathy Freeman . . .

The spirit child gazes around at where we're sprawled on the ground.

These stolen generations, she says. Why haven't you –

And then she sees that we've nodded off to sleep.

from deep down rossco's gullet

−So ya didn't take to Perth then, Stevo? Or did Perth not take to you?

Light-headed from too much caffeine, Estha is attempting to dole out slinky noodles which keep slipping from the ladle and back into the pot. She spies a lone piece of chicken floating in the broth and makes chase.

− Aw, nah, done with Perth.

− We thought you'd gone inta smoke, didn't we Rossco? says Gerry. You gunna stay put now? Open up the servo again?

Stevo flicks a guilty glance over at Estha. He nudges his cap down over his eyes.

− Thought I might try East Timor, he says.

− Jesus, Stevo. What dja wanna go there for? It's not somethin ter do with that bloody wowser, is it?

− That's right, it's to do with that bloody wowser, says Coldiver, looking up from a mug of tea. He's thrown everyone off by sitting at a different table today, near the window instead of up by the counter. − There's shit-load of building going on in Dili. You should come too, Rossco, Gerry. Uncle Sydney's prepared to give youse another chance. We're gunna have ourselves a ball.

Rossco mumbles something unintelligible, sips his coffee, sets it down.

− Shit, these buggers are playin hard to get, says Estha, chasing another piece of chicken − or perhaps the same piece.

− Not as hard as some other buggers I could mention, grumbles Coldiver. Estha, darlin, why don't you come to Dili too?

− Not bloody likely. Why would I want ter go and work in some third-world town without a sewer system? Now, if it's Bali you're offerin, that's another question . . .

− You leave off Estha, growls Stevo.

Estha puts a bowl of chicken and noodle soup down in front of Coldiver. − Two dollars to you.

− Yeh, and one fifty to everyone else. What's wrong with Estha comin, Stevo? Equal ops an all that. It'd be an adventure for her. She c'n earn six times as much as she's earnin now.

Stevo stretches out his legs and slumps back in the chair. He scratches at his chest through his singlet while unfamiliar emotions battle it out on his forehead.

– Estha doesn't want ter git mixed up in any of your schemes, he says.

– What's good enough for you is good enough for Estha. She can't stay here all her life. Anyway, I'm jiss trying to keep the family together. Uncle Sydney has a heart, you know.

Estha goes very still. Gerry spurts coffee out his nostrils. Stevo pulls his cap down even further.

– We'd had us six inches by this time last year, says Rossco loudly.

– Don't change the subject, says Coldiver.

– Fred reckons he'd had eight, says Gerry, wiping his nose with a napkin.

– That's Fred for ya, ay.

– Right. Over-optimistic bugger.

Estha slips back behind the counter.

– You should take advantage of these working opportunities, fellas, says Coldiver. You should take life a bit more seriously, like Stevo here.

Stevo takes his cap off and looks out of the window, miserably. Rossco gives Gerry a conspiratorial wink.

– Ah, ya gettin serious now, are ya, Stevo? What was it I heard you was up ta down in Perth? A website, weren't it, Stevo? A website for the building trade?

– Yeh, we heard about that, says Gerry. What was it again? Double-you double-you double-you, whogivesashit dot com.

Rossco and Gerry thump the table and laugh. Then they look at Stevo, the crease carved by his cap giving him an extra line on an already furrowed forehead.

– What's wrong, Stevo? Coldiver buy yer sense of humour?

– I don't know why I bother, mumbles Coldiver.

– Nor do I, says Gerry. Me and Rossco got it all worked out, haven't we, Rossco? If you wanna make money, you gotta find a way of connin people. Make more money that way than doin a job.

– Yeh, that's right. Only we can't think of anyone we want to con yet.

Coldiver looks mildly impressed. – That's very promising, fellas. I didn't think you had it in ya. Stevo c'n probably give you a few handy hints on pullin the wool over somebody's eyes. In the used car markets, at least.

Stevo rubs the sweat off his face. – Jesus. Give me a break, will ya? That was a long time ago.

– I'm only pulling ya leg, Stevo. Pretty little monster I heard she is, too. Fair like her mother, an all.

– Leave off, growls Stevo.

– Didntcha have a plan of growing lychees up there on the high ground before Walcott Inlet? interrupts Gerry. We 'eard about that one, too. We reckoned you might be onto somethin there. You'd hardly 'ave to even clear it. They'd pay anythin in China to have lychees on their table at Christmas, the fucken rich ones.

Stevo looks up, puffs his cheeks out, uncomfortably. – Aw, yeh, an I was right too. I jiss couldn't get the cash stumped up.

– What is it, Rossco? says Gerry suddenly. You're turning purple, mate. Rossco, his fist up by his mouth, shakes his head.

– Is it yer ticker, Rossco?

Gerry's half out his chair, reaching for Rossco's brow.

– Gunner do a big burp, Rossco mutters. I c'n feel it.

Gerry flops back down. – Strewth Rossco, you 'ad me worried there for a minute. Should we be sendin Estha out?

– Comin, says Rossco softly.

– Christ, it's a biggun, ain't it, Rossco?

Coldiver gets up and slams his empty soup bowl and mug on the counter. Just as he passes Rossco's table, a drawn-out, sonorous belch erupts from deep down Rossco's gullet. Gerry collapses into waves of delighted laughter.

– Fucken unbelievable! he hoots. Where dja get em from, mate?

A smug smile plants itself on Rossco's face.

– Sa job producing bewdies like that.

– Ya see, mate? This is why 'e don't want any of that nine to five shit. Too busy workin up numbers like that.

– I love me burpin, Rossco admits.

Coldiver stands in the doorway, shaking his head.

– I'll see ya in the mornin, he nods to Stevo. We'll both be outta this town in two weeks, if we're lucky. No need to iver come back.

From under the peak of his cap, Stevo sneaks another sideways glance at Estha. Sure enough she's watching him, her pretty face shorn and blank. As soon as their eyes meet, she looks away.

– Don't count on it, mate, says Stevo, keeping his eyes on Estha.

– What?

– You 'eard me. I still might change me mind.

– Oh, don't you bloody start. What is it, somethin she puts in the coffee?

– I won't hear a word against Estha's coffee, mumbles Rossco.

– Oh, for Chrissake, snarls Coldiver. Get me outta here.

---

more noises

W e pinch soft flakes of tobacco into a ridge along the fold of paper and crumble a dark snowfall on top. The quietness has a thickness to it tonight, as if it is made of many layers. A deep red flushes the sky. The moon rising through the black branches of the snappy gums is the only pure white object to be seen.

What time is it? asks the wind.

We have to crane our necks to see the clocks hanging in a line down one of the trunks. We've stopped relying on the sky.

New York, Sydney, Perth or London?

Here will do, thank you.

Nearly nine o'clock.

A whoosh of wings passes overhead. We look up, filled with a sudden hope, but it's only a nightjar. Disappointment floods in its wake.

What day of the week? asks the wind.

It doesn't really want to know; it just wants to talk.

Tuesday.

Are you *sure*? I could have sworn it was Wednesday. I'd have bet my life on it.

The calendar's ticked off.

We bring the cigarette paper to our lips and moisten the edge. From beneath the hammocks comes a congested sniff. We had forgotten she was under there.

For Chrissakes, we scold her. Use a hanky.

Haven't got one.

A piece of rag dangled over the edge of a hammock is snatched roughly from our fingers. A few minutes later the nasty sniff comes again. She wants us to ask her what's wrong, of course, show her some sympathy, but we're not playing ball.

Eventually she can't hold it in any longer.

I miss him! she blurts out, giving way to tears.

Yesterday I was *convinced* that it was Tuesday, insists the wind.

We light our spliff, take the first few drags. The crying drones on and on.

It's because of you that he went away, remember, we say after a while.

The sobs rise to a wail. If you'd only let me finish what I'd started –

Oh, don't start that again. Billy's moved on. He's grown up. He's probably forgotten all about us now.

I wish *I* could forget, she wails.

We allow ourselves to feel a tinge of pity at that. Oh you will, we murmur. You will. No worries there.

Wake up!

We lie still, holding our breath.

Wake UP!

Unfooled, she shakes us roughly by the shoulders. There's a crack as a neck is put out of joint.

Ow!

We open our eyes. She stands before us in the gloom, straws of black hair escaping from her night-time plaits, eyes flashing.

You'd better have a bloody good excuse.

More noises.

Her nostrils are wide and quivering with the cool night air and the whites of her eyes are like two polished coins. We roll over. Overhead the boughs creak.

The baby again?

The spirit child shakes her head. These are *different* noises.

There's a fidgetiness about the way she stands, as if she is ready to break into a sprint within a split-second's notice if required. Her breath comes shallow and fast.

You're still over-excited from the race. You're probably still hearing the screams of the crowd.

The spirit child shakes her head again, eyebrows joining in a fierce knot.

No. These are *children*. Little children, like me.

Her voice is scolding, filled with the impatience of a child who knows she should be better understood.

Babies have a way of growing up, we say.

She looks out into a thick, tarry darkness, nothing to modify it in any direction – no distant yellow points of light, no pockets of greater density where buildings or trees might be.

When she speaks, her voice prickles with fear.

The cries . . . they come from all around me!

Grazing our cheeks, the wind sidles by, picking up her words on the sly. Before we know it, it has hurled them like boomerangs into the emptiness. A moment later they come back, hollow replicas of themselves: *all around me, all around me, all around me!*

We close our eyes, willing her to leave us alone. All we want is to snuggle back into the cushiony down of sleep and bury our faces in it for ever. It is the only thing that brings us any peace these days.

Go back to sleep, we murmur.

Not until you tell me who they are.

Where has she learnt such stubbornness? Surely it wasn't from us?

Do as you're told.

No.

We nuzzle our pillows. Perhaps if we just ignore her she'll get bored of waiting. One of us tries emitting a loud snore.

Don't leave me.

The voice is small and querulous – the sort of voice that would break our hearts if they hadn't been broken already, and by this same child too. We've lost count of the number of times we've grieved for her, then stuck the pieces of ourselves back together again and soldiered on. Our hearts are tough as resin now. Such is the curse of memory.

The hammock sags beneath the weight of her knee. Her hair drags over our chests. Soft puppy fat is pressed against our shoulders. Before we know it, our skin is wet from her tears and slimy with snot. There's the tang of Vegemite on her breath.

We resist the temptation to put an arm around her, though that is clearly what she's after. There's a moment's hesitation, then tiny fingers reach gingerly around our chests and pull us to her, press our bony, unforgiving spines into the softness of her sweet, warm belly.

grog

– Gimme some grog, says a voice.

Estha looks up, stares dumbly at the long mop of unkempt hair, the gaunt cheekbones, the unshaven, silver-pricked chin.

– Jimmi? Is it really you? she says, astonished. You've come home?

– I want some grog.

– Jimmi, it *is* you!

In her delight Estha reaches across the counter but stops just short of touching him. He shows no sign of even knowing who she is.

– Grog, he says again.

– I c'n do you a coffee, mate, says Estha, composing herself. Or a mango smoothie, maybe.

– Jiss grog.

She frowns, leans forward with both hands on the counter. – What did they do to you in there, Jimmi? This is a coffee shop, mate, not a pub. You need to go to the Spini if you want a beer. Or the bottleshop.

Jimmi just looks at her blankly.

– It *is* Jimmi under there, right?

He responds by looking at his feet.

– Have you been in to see Tama yet? asks Estha. Does she know you're back? She worked so hard on your behalf, mate. She'll be rapt to see you.

– There's Stevo, pipes up Rossco. He'll sort Jimmi out. 'E's on 'is fore-court, doin 'is washin.

Estha lifts the hinged counter and goes to the window to look. Yes, there he is in all his glory: naked to the waist, rinsing his singlet under the outside tap. She opens the door for Jimmi, then carries on watching as Stevo twists his singlet, shakes it out with one hard thwack, and puts it back on, careful not to dislodge the rolly stuck to his lip.

– Y'know, 'e niver thanked me for giving Yakka back, murmurs Estha. I'd hev liked to keep her, but I didn't.

– But then 'e never asked yer to look after 'er in the first place, points out Rossco.

– That's true, 'e didn't, agrees Estha. Jesus, 'e's a sook when it comes to these things.

*   *   *

Seeing Jimmi approach, Yakka bounds over to greet him. She sniffs his bare feet to discover where he's been, checks hands and pockets for titbits of food. Once the appraisal is over, she goes back to the shade of the diesel pump.

Jimmi stands by the four-star, waiting for Stevo to stop pulling at an unravelling thread in the hem of his singlet and notice him.

– I need some grog, he says as soon as Stevo looks up.

Stevo peels the rolly from his lip. He leans back a little to balance the weight of his belly.

– Don't we all, mate.

Jimmi waits in silence, his face giving nothing away. Yakka tucks her paws in more neatly under her jaw. Stevo sucks on the near-gone stub till he gets a decent glow, all the while scrutinising the dark eyes buried in Jimmi's face.

– I wouldn't recommend four-star, mate. Can of Fosters?

– Sure. No worries.

Stevo contemplates the Aborigine for a moment longer, trying to decide why this situation is unnerving him, then shakes the feeling off and goes inside. Moments later he reappears with a couple of cans. There's a worrying absence of pleasure in the black man's face as he takes the proffered beer, rolls it between his palms, transferring the cool lick of moisture from can to skin.

– Cheers, says Stevo brightly. Welcome home. Pleased ter hear about the appeal.

Stevo fires his pull-ring, stepping back to avoid the froth. Yakka looks up and barks once. Jimmi looks up too, apparently surprised by this abrupt burst of energy from so small and unlikely an object. He watches Stevo take several uninterrupted gulps. Then, without a word of thanks, turns and walks towards the long grass on the side of the road.

Stevo watches him go.

In the shade of the giant boab on the side of the road, Arthur and Emmeline sit back to back on a mattress, passing a bottle of sherry to and fro above their heads.

– Proper big mess you look, says Arthur, as Jimmi walks towards them. He takes a swig from the sherry bottle.

Jimmi's not sure if the old man is talking about him or Emmeline, who is none too well groomed herself. He decides to assume it's the latter. Standing well back, he pulls the ring on his can and brings the cold rim to his lips.

– Oi! Wait!

All three look up to see the burly figure of Stevo running down the street, the impressive belly holding itself surprisingly firm above his thin legs. Yakka tumbles at his heels, barking excitedly. It's a while since she's witnessed her master moving at speed.

– Gimme that beer back!

Jimmi pretends this is nothing to do with him either. He turns away, hugging the can to his chest, his face shutting down.

– Jesus, I'm a fucken idiot, gasps Stevo, puffing hard. Gimme it, Jimmi. You ain't tasted grog before and you ain't gunna start now.

Jimmi shakes his head at Stevo, his eyes filled with a child's obstinacy. Stevo tries grabbing the can.

– Go on, Jimmi, please.

Jimmi shakes his head again and doesn't notice the hand that pulls at his shoulder, swinging him around and making space for a second fist to fly at his jaw. He staggers, reels to one side, and practically passes the can to Stevo in his attempt to stay upright.

– Hey, you bully!

Emmeline, none too steady on her feet herself, has hoisted herself up and is charging straight at Stevo, gigantic breasts swaying from side to side.

– Why you hit im, you bully!

– I've got good reason, says Stevo.

Emmeline kicks the nuisance at her feet that is Yakka and throws a leaden side-swipe at Stevo. Stevo bars it, believes himself out of danger and turns his attention back to Jimmi, giving Emmeline the opportunity to pound her fists on his shoulder blades: *bam-bam-bam-bam*. Stevo buckles under the barrage, spluttering, and a frantic Yakka yelps and growls and pounces at her master's attacker.

– Aggh! Git yer bloody fists off me!

Jimmi, seeing stars, looks on, unsure of his place in this mêlée that he has somehow started. Seeing the can in Stevo's hand, he lunges at it, managing only to knock it into the grass where Arthur, without needing to get up, quietly claims it. Emmeline, pausing in her pummelling to catch her breath, spots the old man drinking.

– You better gimme that can real quick.

For a moment, everyone stares at Arthur, who is making the most of this chance to pour beer down his gullet as fast as he can. Jimmi is the first to react, swiping the can from Arthur's hand, but then Stevo grabs it off Jimmi and that brings Arthur to his feet, bouncing on his spindly legs like a true boxer, seemingly prepared to fight to the death for this single can of Fosters that was momentarily his. Arthur throws little smacks into the air around Stevo's jaw, while Emmeline holds Stevo still by wrapping both arms around his middle.

– Stoppit, all of ya! yells a voice.

The group on the grass look up. Estha, Rossco and Gerry are spilling out of the coffee shop. It's Estha who shouted, her voice surprisingly authoritative, while Rossco stands behind Gerry, encouraging him to intervene with little pushes. Gerry stretches his bulging arms, then makes quick work of them all. He grabs Arthur and Emmeline by their clothes and swings them out of the way. Jimmi and Stevo are flattened with a deft punch each to the gut.

– Everyone leave off! he shouts, dazzled by his own effectiveness, forgetting that it was in fact Estha who paved the way.

– Im take our grog, Emmeline whines.

– A man's got a right to a drink, mutters Jimmi.

– 'E's not in any state to know, Stevo gasps, winded, trying to get up but instantly collapsing again. 'E doesn't know what's good for im.

Estha, finding herself called on to arbitrate, glares at Stevo.

– An who you think you are goin round telling people what's good for em, she says, Christ only knows. Ya never gave *me* any advice. Never there when *I* needed ya. You need ter git yer fucken priorities right.

Clutching the old boab, Stevo stares at her, panting hard.

– Ya think ya so good, lookin after everyone else, dontcha, she goes on. But the truth is ya niver look after yer own. Ya couldn't give a rat's arse about me, ya bloody arsehole.

Estha looks as astonished at herself as everyone else is, but now that she's started she sees no reason to stop.

– You're a fucken hopeless piecea – piecea –

She flings out a wildly gesticulating hand.

– Chook shit? suggests Rossco helpfully, still being careful to place himself squarely behind Gerry.

– Chook shit, yeh. Whenever ya git yerself in a corner, what do ya do but run away and wait for the fuss to die down, then ya come back and expect no one ter say a word. Well it's about time you stood up and looked at yerself. Right fucken loser you are.

Stevo, looking more alarmed now than he had when Emmeline and Arthur were attacking him, stares at her, completely confounded. For a while there's a tense silence, then a growl from Yakka that melts into a confused little whinny, as if she can't decide whose side she is on.

– Hey, you're really spewin, Estha, observes Rossco, respectfully. Norm'ly it's Gerry doin that.

Estha looks at them all with unblinking brown eyes, astonishment and anger etched across her usually immobile face. She pulls a strand of hair from her mouth and firms up the line of her jaw, slowly becoming aware from the looks the others are giving her that there's a new, ferocious dignity on display, and it's hers.

– Good on ya, Estha, Gerry agrees. I'da bin proud of that roarin meself.

Estha takes a big breath and lets it out as a strangled noise, part laugh, part sob. They all wait for this noise to pass, then turn expectantly to Stevo.

– She really had ya packin the shits, didn't she, mate?

– Look, ya legs are tremblin!

Stevo still can't take his eyes off this defiant woman standing before him, her head held high, nostrils flaring. So many of her features are smaller, neater versions of his own. Who knows, she's probably got his own shapely legs beneath those baggy daks. He adjusts his feet, finding his centre of gravity, tries to clear his clogged-up throat.

– You want me to give ya a piece of advice? he croaks.

She looks unsure at first, but gives a nod.

– Don't you iver . . . Don't you *iver* . . . He pauses, noticing the difference in his voice. The irksome lump in his throat seems to have gone. – Call me a piece of chook shit. *Iver* again.

– What'll I call ya? she snaps back, not missing a beat.

There's a moment in which nobody dares to breathe. Stevo swallows, a magnificent, clear-throated swallow.

– Dad, he says, softly. Why dontcha call me Dad.

---

the language of the underworld

Billy works a row of five nights, has twenty-four hours off, then a row of five days. After that he has five full days off.

He no longer takes much notice of the sun. Sometimes when he's a kilometre down he can't remember whether it's daylight or darkness on the surface. He comes up expecting to find cool, sweet air sawn by cicadas, and instead is struck by a brain-boiling heat, a deadening midday.

He grabs sleep whenever and wherever he finds himself immobile – on the bus, sitting on a chair at crib, a partially eaten sandwich before him. Even at the Feddy with his head knocking back against the wall and his mouth hanging open, cigarette biting his fingers. During a twenty-four-hour break he'll sleep for twenty in one go, a bucket beside his bed so that he doesn't have to get up to piss.

– You have to forget about your old routine, he teaches Sim, who misses the long evenings out shooting with his brothers, the comfort of being called in for lunch and tea. The boy has huge, dark shadows under his eyes. Billy puts an arm roughly around his shoulders as they troop down the stairs, and Sim drinks up the human contact, especially coming from this aloof man whom, for some reason, he has chosen to trust with the faith of a blind, unweaned animal.

In the middle of the day, when half the men are on a shift and the other half are sleeping, there is barely a flicker of life in the caravan park. A dog has keeled over in the shade of an awning, its hairless, teated belly throbbing, a scribble of testy flies around its glistening nose. Billy's orange overalls, once the colour of a kumquat but now paled almost to straw, hang exhaustedly by pegged cuffs from a washing line that cuts a diagonal between the corner of someone's caravan and the high wire fence. A dark band of moisture shifts its way down the legs.

More overalls hang elsewhere in the caravan park – eerie, disembodied skins peeled from the bodies that lie inside the darkened caravans. It is as if the men need this outer layer to survive when outside. The names of the shafts are stitched in green or white or black lettering across the backs: Schmitz, Lanfranchi, Argo, Orchin, Sirius, Cave Rocks, Intrepide, Thunderer, Junction, Silver Lake. The language of the underworld, Billy likes to think.

In the caravan opposite, a metal bed-frame knocks regularly against the fibreglass wall. Billy ignores it. He doesn't envy its occupant; nor does he envy the men who are sleeping, even though he should by rights be sleeping too: he has to start at seven tonight and won't get home till six in the morning. But instead he prefers to sit on the steps of his caravan and smoke one careful cigarette after another, tapping each against the packet before loading the tip between his lips. He exhales slowly and evenly. He follows each swill of smoke with an injection of bitter black coffee. In the distance he hears the sound of a motor turning over and failing to catch. The sound reminds him of his father, though he doesn't think about him for long. The nicotine beats a track through the fug in his brain. Across the park, a man whose name he doesn't know is lying in a deck chair, his feet plunged in a washing-up bowl of water, a rabbit-skin Akubra cocked over his face.

There is no end to Billy's tiredness. Whole years of sleeping would be needed to make up the deficit. It has got to the stage where a few hours here or there barely make a difference. He no longer yearns for it like he used to – as he can see that Sim does still. On an afternoon like this he'd rather stay awake, craving the time to himself more than he craves the sleep.

On the first of his five days off, Billy gets in his car and drives out of Kambalda. Tall salmon gums come into view, sparse but poised, their thin trunks slicing up the sky. Beneath them a blur of sage-green saltbush, red earth showing through the gaps. A large sign claims to be 'Greening the Golden Mile'. The giant headframes of defunct mines are the last thing to disappear from his rear mirror, peering faces watching to see where he's gone.

He tunes to Goldfields Hot FM, inhales the fresh, overground air blowing in, spiced by sun-warmed saltbush. Some hit song from years back is playing – one which he remembers hating at the time, but now he feels nothing about, one way or the other. He takes the turning to Kalgoorlie, skirting to the east and out to Boulder, parks outside Freerange Supplies and gets out.

The shop windows are filled with stacked boxes of ammo, the latest lines in country casuals hanging on rails behind. Billy walks beneath the squeaking Swan On Tap sign at the Broken Hill Hotel, passes the scruffy, apologetic building housing the Australian Workers' Union, a tattoo parlour with a hackneyed selection of blue-taloned eagles and thorn-entwined roses, a trash 'n' treasure sale in a disused shop with three plastic tailor's dummies, the colour of newly born piglets. At the Old Palace Theatre he goes in, tells the woman at the window his shoe size and hands over a ten-dollar note.

He has never done anything like this before. Half of him is amused, the other half is anxious that he won't fit in. He joins the river of people in the corridor – kids mainly, with parents in tow. Nervousness gets the upper hand. There's a clatter of school about the place, all those high-pitched voices. He files through a doorway which opens out into what feels like a miniature sports stadium – high ceilings, tiered seats – except that a powerful blast of cold emanates from its heart. He imagines this is why most people come, at least to begin with – to know what cold feels like in the middle of the day.

He finds himself a bare strip of bench, pulling at his laces while he furtively takes in the scene below. The rink is circular and gleams just like the lake, except that this one is exactly what it seems to be. Most of the figures glide in one direction, as if they were caught in a current; only two or three rogue skaters, intent on anarchy, zigzag against the flow, forcing others to dodge out their way. Some move singly, others in gaggles. Together they make a complicated weaving of patterns. He had thought it would be peaceful, but the volume of noise is startling: the carving up of the ice, the shouts, the orchestral soundtrack blaring from scratchy speakers.

Billy wraps the excess cord around his ankles and ties it in a bow at the back – tight, strapping in his nerve. He tries to stand and immediately has to grip the back of the bench in front to stop his ankles turning. He grits his teeth and wobbles self-consciously down the steps.

At the edge he hesitates. Bright spots of colour flash past – woolly hats, fingerless mittens – clothing he has never seen before in this town. He wonders where people even buy such garments. The cold air climbs up his legs, invigorating, and all at once he glimpses a trickle of some old boyhood confidence. He snatches at it, launches himself into the middle of the rink, his body rigid with the determination to hold itself upright. If only the men from Franki could see him now, he thinks.

His first attempt ends in a panicked dash for the other side, little crystals of ice flying up around his shins. He clings to the edge, his head full of the sound of ice being splintered. He glances around. No doubt he looks ridiculous. But the rest of the skaters fly past, seemingly unfazed by his cross-rink dash. For the first time he is struck by how beautiful some of them look. The grace of limbs thrown nonchalantly back, the triangular motions of the feet scoring the ice. He spots a woman with very fine, pale hair flying out behind her, the ends cropped in a line, straight as a scarf, and he decides to follow her, lurching awkwardly from side to side as he returns again and again to the handrail. He knows he'll never catch up; she does an entire lap before he's gone ten paces. As she passes the second time, he half runs, half slides into her wake, hands spinning at his sides as he tries to balance. She twirls in a tightly drawn circle and laughs.

He doesn't know whether the laugh was aimed at him, or someone else. Everything happens too quickly here; it's too full of commotion. But it makes no difference. If he's making a fool of himself, so what. What he thinks instead is: I've done it. I've let go.

how to eat a cow

With her face so close to the screen that the static lifts the fine down on her upper lip, the spirit child traces the horizon with her finger. Then she shifts her head to one side of the screen and follows the exact same line, moving her finger through the air. Left, right, left. Screen, reality, screen. No doubt about it. The same horizon. The same red sandstone plain.

She presses pause. Buck Dacey's face freezes in unsteady chevrons of eyes and nose and teeth – that much-talked-about jaw jutting sideways ridiculously. She bursts out in a cackle of laughter. What a hoot to leave him so disarranged! She levers herself up and tip-toes around the back of the television set.

Draped around the snappy gums, some of us dangling our legs from an upper branch, some leaning against the trunks, we watch her. Clearly, she's hoping to discover the real Buck hiding around there.

Even if he *was* there, he wouldn't be worth finding, we say. It's a terrible programme.

She gives us a dark, sidelong look.

Smore interesting than talking to you.

She aims the remote at the screen and presses the upward arrow, recoiling slightly as if nervous it might cause the entire set to blow up. The volume rises and rises until it is sure to drown out anything we might say. There's an ugly blast of folk guitar – *ti-wang ti-wang!* – and the roar of a blazing fire. Large white letters zoom up against orange flames. She presses pause again and the letters skid to one side, the music veering off-key in its lower ranges.

Turn that bloody thing down!

THE BUSH CHEF: HOW TO EAT A COW.

No! It's my favourite programme!

With his half-boy, half-man looks, the perfect square jaw speckled with a hard-won stubble and an incongruous glinting ring slicing one eyebrow in two, Buck Dacey is the sort of grubby bitser that we particularly despise – part city-boy slicker, part outback crusty. Neither camp would willingly claim him. He has on khaki moleskins, Blunnies with no socks and a Save the Whale T-shirt, all topped off with a white chef's hat – a pretty dubious combination, in our opinion. We do our best to show our disapproval, but the spirit child is smitten and won't hear a word against him.

Today he's in a desert identical to her own. Beside him is a dead cow with its legs sticking up like an overturned table. The spirit child sniffs the air for a whiff of dead animal flesh; she still suspects that Buck is somewhere nearby.

– First off you'll need to find an unsuspecting steer grazing in a paddock and shoot it. As my dad taught me, a cow'll taste different depending on what it's been eating – spinifex or sorghum, Mitchell grass or bundle-bundle grass – and you'll soon learn which you prefer. Ideally, hit it smack between the eyes, like I did earlier with this poor baastid. Then slash the throat with a sharp knife and bleed the carcass out.

The spirit child sticks her thumb in her mouth, her forefinger curling over her nose. She loves listening to Buck's smoky, outback drawl. She gazes at his innocent, mother's-boy eyes, follows the way the jaw bone slides beneath the skin.

– Get on with the butchering straight away. The sun makes pretty quick work of a 'killer' like this, and if you hang around, you'll not only have a load of stinking green beef on your hands, but you'll have a few unwanted guests inviting themselves to dinner, too – crows, ants, scorpions, flies, maybe even a dingo or two. I've bin doing this since I was four years old an I should know.

The camera hones in on a fly already helping itself to the gunge around the creature's glassy eye. It dips its front legs into the goop and rubs them together.

Umm, delicious, we say.

Ssssh!

The bush chef tucks the cow's head beneath its shoulder.

– Take your knife and slit the skin all the way from the throat, following a line beneath its belly round to the back legs as if you were unzipping a suitcase

– that's the way, see how a nice little sawing action helps to get through the hide. You'll find the skin folds back quite easily – there, what a bewdy. Strip as much of the hide as possible up the legs – that's the fiddly bit. This can get pretty messy, so make sure you're not wearing anything too nice.

No danger of that for you.

Shut *up*!

– What now lies spread before you is a mouth-watering steak buffet. Each cut varies in tenderness, taste and quality. Here at the thigh we have the round, the silverside, and the topside, great steaks for whacking on the barbie. The rump – (he gives it a thwack with the flat of his hand and little drops of blood spurt up) *– is the tenderest bit, nice and fat and juicy if done a little rare. Makes my mouth water just to look at it. These forelegs – known as shoulder or blade steak – are tough. Only eat those if you put taste before tenderness and don't mind getting things stuck between your teeth.*

What's he think toothpicks are for? we shout.

– The head, left whole, is the bit the Aborigines on my Dad's cattle station liked best: they roasted the skull with all its meat on. You'd be surprised how much flesh there is on a good-sized bullock head. Euurgh! Got a fly up me nose!

Serves you bloody well right.

Even the spirit child laughs at that.

– The sweetbread is this gland here near the stomach – see, that little white critter. Fry it in butter and flour as soon as it leaves the body. The liver and kidneys are nice sautéed for breakfast the morning after.

On the fire crackling and splintering in the background, a saucepan lid jostles on a rim of bubbles. Watery brown liquid oozes down the sides and makes the flames spit.

– Always remember to garnish your steaks with sauces. What we've got here is a nice peppercorn sauce, perfect for disguising any bits of beef that may have gone off. See Teletext for the recipes at the end of this programme. But my favourite way of all to eat cow is salted brisket, otherwise known as corned beef.

Suddenly he is walking through a sparkling studio kitchen, shiny chrome cookware hanging from the ceiling, a gleaming gas hob, white plates stacked on a rack. He's still wearing the blood-spattered clothes, but his voice is softer now, more intimate.

– Put either brisket, silverside, round or tongue into brine. All the better if the muscles are still twitching – it helps distribute the salt through the meat. Leave it for a few days, then boil it with bay leaves, brown sugar and vinegar. You can either eat it straight out the pan with white mustard sauce – ummm, delicious! – or cold with boiled cabbage and spuds. If you're gunna do cabbage,

watch out for the blowies – they'll come flying from miles around. Cut it in nice fat slices with a big knife. There. Lovely. Sometimes – (he wrenches something from between his teeth) – *it's a little bit gristly*.

He raises a bottle of VB to his lips – *Cheers!*

The spirit child pretends to pick up a bottle herself and take a swig.

---

who's a pretty boy, then?

Billy slides his softpack into the back pocket of his jeans and heads out of the caravan park. At the gate he turns right and walks in the shade of a majestic eucalyptus. A few vacant lots have timber-framed structures going up: two men banging in nails at tree-top height are stark outlines against the blue sky.

When he reaches the shops, he ducks beneath awnings to keep himself out of the sun.

The streets are wider here than anywhere else in the country – another useless fact that came courtesy of Harri. He tells everyone when they first arrive: it's all because a camel can't walk backwards. He explains in his fatherly fashion how in the old days the miners used camel trains to carry their gear, and the only way they could turn the whole train around was in one big, sweeping circle. Harri finds the story hilarious, every time. He says he reckons the camels knew exactly what they were doing, that the joke was on the miners. Billy reckons the camel story has kept Harri going for years.

He passes no one except a young couple no more than Sim's age – the age Billy was when he first shipped up here himself – mashed up against the glass of the butcher's shop window with their hands under each other's shirts. On the other side of the window sit fat-wrapped joints of beef. Billy walks past them and all the way down the main street until the shops give way to houses again, squat timber buildings set back within their own staked-out yards, a few dusty grevilleas and bottlebrushes out the front. He picks a side road at random. Squares of corrugated iron painted pale pink and blue act as a fence. Peeling timber doors understudy as outdoor tables. Old towels converted into home-stitched curtains drape over unwashed sills. A woman's voice rings out at the end of the street, tapering up into a question – a couple of women yarning no doubt – but as he gets closer he can see only one figure, a woman in dark denim jeans and a tucked-in shirt, her hands resting on her knees. It looks as if she's talking to a tree. Then she puts two fingers in her mouth and gives a perfect wolf-whistle. An identical whistle answers back. She whistles again, and a little duet ensues. Billy can hardly tell one from the other, the intonation is so similar. As he watches, a curtain of pale hair swings over her profile and hides all but the tip of her nose.

He stops walking and looks up. Directly overhead is a semicircle of moon, left behind by the night. To one side an aeroplane cuts through the blue, its trail like creamy stuffing spilled from a rip. He takes a deep breath and walks on.

– Who's a pretty boy, then? shrills a voice.

Billy takes the cigarette from his mouth, flicks ash onto the road.

– You've taught him well, your cocky, he says.

The woman jumps, draws herself upright. She's probably in her late twenties, Billy guesses, but she looks older. There is something watered down about her, the hair falling in dirty-blonde clumps around her shoulders, a little lank. Her eyes are grey and narrow. She hunches around the concave of her stomach, shrinking behind childishly small breasts.

– 'E's not my cocky.

Her fingers are pushed through the mesh of a six-foot-high bird cage in someone's front yard. The fat white cockatoo picks up its feet and puts them down again, yellow crest sliding to and fro.

– Watch it, shrieks the cockatoo.

– You're the girl from the ice rink, says Billy.

Her pale forehead creases up, not recognising him.

– I'm the one that's always fallin over on my arse, explains Billy, tossing his cigarette towards the gutter.

– What's yer name then? screams the cocky.

– None of ya fucken business, retorts the girl sharply. She untangles her hand from the cage and Billy sees that her fingernails are bitten off, like his, no whites on the tips at all. The cockatoo hangs its head, sullenly.

– It don't look like it'd cushion ya much, yer arse, the woman says to Billy.

– What's the cocky's name?

– It's not my bloody cocky, orright?

She looks away, more irritated than ever. The cockatoo sways from foot to foot on its thin bamboo pole. Then it grips the cage with its hooked beak and rattles it dementedly.

– Fuck 'er up the glitter, suggests the cocky, and side-steps to the end of the pole.

They catch one another's eyes, and Billy laughs, but she still won't give. He can't tell if she's annoyed at him, or if she's always this prickly. He watches the way her hair separates into chunks either side of her shoulders.

She folds her arms defensively across her chest. – Are you chattin me up?

– No, says Billy.

Her eyebrows, plucked to within an inch of their lives, register a quiver of surprise at this. She slides her fingers into her jean pockets.

– Will ya teach me how to skate? Billy asks.

He tries to find her face behind its swinging curtain. When he does, a blue vein pulses through the delicate skin beneath her eye. Billy has the feeling that he'd leave a bruise behind on her skin if he so much as cupped her cheek in his hand.

– I remember ya now, she says, nodding. You've a look aboutcha. Like you're capable of something, ay.

Billy looks at where his cigarette still smoulders on the slat of the gutter.
– Of what?

– I dunno. Like you beat your wife or somethin.

– I don't have a wife.

She gives a little laugh – or not so much a laugh as a rising scale, three or four dry notes. There's no humour in them at all. – That's a start.

– So. Will ya teach me or what?

Her thin lips are almost the same colour as her skin. – What are ya, a fucken freak?

– No.

She gives that nervous three-note laugh again. Then she picks up a strap of hair and tosses it over her shoulder.

– Well, it ain't a euphemism for somethin, is it? It's just, you get a lot of pervs round here.

– I jiss want to be able to skate, sort of free. Like you do.

Free. The word registers, lightening her eyes. He can see that there's life in there, buried beneath the tiredness.

– I did all my three Rs at school, Billy says. Readin, writin 'n' rootin. He gives her his crooked smile. – Well, most of em, anyway.

Her eyes latch on the upward hitch of his lip.

– I'll be there this Saturday at noon, she says.

– FUCK 'ER UP THE GLITTER! screams the cocky.

At last she lets go with a genuine laugh – still the ascending scale but with vigour this time. A couple of dimples pepper each cheek.

By Saturday his limbs seem to have lost all memory of how they achieved their uncertain balance last time. The only sign that he's been here before is a dull ache around his knees and a twinge in one of his ankles.

He makes painful lurches around the edge of the rink, grabbing the hand rail every few steps. When he's gone around three times, his eyes flick up to the clock: twenty minutes past. The realisation that she might not come doesn't alter his mood – or if it does, it's only for a fraction of a second, a switch flicked up and down. But there is a fraction more diffidence to the way he launches himself onto the ice the next time. He manages a full circle without needing to hold on, his muscles gradually relaxing so that he's able to stand a little straighter. Nearly *homo erectus*, he thinks. He's on his fifth or sixth circle when a pair of hands grab him around the waist.

– Keep goin.

Her voice is gentler than he remembers it, and for a moment he wonders if it's actually her. He tries to turn around and look. His feet stumble over each other, self-consciously.

– Don't stop, mate. Balance on one foot and then the other. It's not that bloody hard.

That's her, alright. He does as he's told, and gets it for the first two paces, but after that he loses the rhythm, and ends up letting her propel him forwards.

She moves her hips in closer, prompts his thighs with her own. He feels the press of her groin against his buttocks.

– Let's get a rhythm going.

She has a fresh smell about her, like slices of cucumber, some sort of delicate handcream. He wants to close his eyes and concentrate on this smell, let his feet go wherever she pushes them, but the self-consciousness won't leave him.

– Relax, wontcha?

– I can't.

– Don't be an idiot. Course you can.

She lets go without warning, taking his hand instead. As she sweeps alongside him, he almost doesn't recognise her: she has on pink-framed sunglasses and white ear mufflers, not so different from the ones he wears at the lease, and her hair is tied up in a knot. She looks altogether stronger in this element, her unpainted lips the only thing to link her to the girl he met on the street.

– How'm I doing?

– Not bad. You need to relax more, though, mate. You're practic'ly pullin me arm out its socket.

He bends his elbow, but still holds her so stiffly that he jerks her sideways with each lurch.

– Let go of me.

– I'll fall, he warns.

– No ya won't. Just keep your weight forwards.

She extricates her fingers and he immediately flounders, tipping back from the waist. He legs shoot out in front of him and he lands hard on his backside.

– Jeez!

But she's already off, a spray of ice in his face. He sits there with his palms flat on the ice, watching the strips of her steel blades slice the air behind her.

Later, staggering up the steps with no strength left in his thighs, he watches her from above. Her name is Janelle, he has discovered. She has kids. She wouldn't tell him how many – just screwed up her eyes, mimed counting, said, Oh God, I lose count, too many. Every now and again she throws him a glance, then kicks her feet behind her as she picks up speed and leaps into a twirl. She's good – the best on the rink – and she knows it. Once she shoos the back of her hand at him as if to tell him to look away, and he gets up and totters over to a refreshments booth. There's too much choice here – Sprite, Coke, cartons of orange juice. He realises he has no idea what she might like to drink. Finally he orders a coffee and a Coke, then at the last minute he notices that they sell fairy floss.

He regrets it instantly. The sugary smell is overpowering and he doesn't know what to do with the two mountainous sticks of pink floss while he's waiting for her. He feels absurd, as if he has now proved to everyone that he doesn't know how to behave in this place. He rests one fist on each knee, spots her tearing through the ranks of skaters and tries to wave with the fairy floss in his hand, but either she doesn't notice or she pretends not to. For a moment he lets his head rest against the wooden ridge behind him. You're a fucken drongo, Billy, he thinks. What are ya doin here? Within seconds his head has lolled to one side and he's fallen asleep. The two sticks flop against his jacket and the fairy floss starts eating into his clothes like a billowing pink fungus.

not unless dogs can fly

Gun-shots. They rebound off the walls of the buildings along the street, echoing dully in the heat-heavy air. One by one, figures run onto the pavement and freeze. Another blast goes off.

– Yakka? Yakka? Stevo runs across the forecourt, cap flying to the ground behind him. – Yakka! If they shoot Yakka . . . *Yakka?!*

Tama is standing quietly nearby, looking up at the sky.

– It ain't dogs this time, she says, carefully. Not unless dogs can fly.

Following the direction of her gaze, Stevo sees a cluster of tiny white feathers scuttle down the slanting roof of his own galvanised shed. Another shot rips through the air. There's a garbled squawk, and from high above the paddock behind the roadhouse, a little round object plummets swiftly to the ground.

Stevo runs straight back inside his hangar and emerges seconds later with a .22 in his hand.

– Gimme that, says Tama.

Stevo stares at her. – No fucken way.

She puts out a hand, undaunted.

– Why d'you want it? he insists. I'm only givin it to ya if yer prepared to use it.

– Oh, I'm prepared.

By the time Stevo and Tama reach the paddock, piles of bloodied black and white feathers lie dotted all over the dry grass. In the far corner stands the beefy figure of Sydney Coldiver, a rifle clamped to his shoulder. Behind him, Shane and Judd, Emmeline and Arthur's larrikin sons, are delving into a hessian sack. Shane pulls out a new bird and throws it, creeching, into the range of Coldiver's view-finder.

Tama levels the .22 with both hands and points it at Coldiver's head.

– Shoot one more cockatoo and you're dead, Mr Coldiver.

Coldiver drops his rifle in alarm, instinctively raises his hands. – What the –?

– There'll be no more shooting of cockatoos.

Coldiver casts a glance at Shane and Judd to see if he's being ridiculed. He senses he probably is.

– Don't tell me you blackfellas have a monopoly on them too, he says.

– For God's sake, why can't you use clay pigeons like everyone else? shouts Stevo.

Coldiver, recovering from the initial shock, wipes the sweat popping on his forehead with a rolled-up striped sleeve.

– Because cockatoos make a bloody racket is why. And they take a dump on me whenever I leave the house.

– So you're jiss gunna shoot em until there aren't any left? cries Stevo.

– I don't see why not. Bloody useless buggers.

With that, he lifts his rifle again and attempts to line up with a black-feathered bird that's flapping with hectic beats towards a white-trunked gum. Tama releases the catch on her gun. She replants her feet firmly on the ground. From where Stevo is standing he can see determination narrow her eye. He strides into the middle of the paddock, between them both.

– Ain't no one shooting anything any more in this town, he says firmly.

– Stevo, get out me way, warns Tama.

Coldiver ignores them. – Shane, throw up another bird.

Shane does nothing. Coldiver's face flares up. – *Shane!*

– There ain't iny left, boss, mutters Shane.

– I'm pulling the trigger, says Tama between gritted teeth. Stevo, get out me way or I'll shoot you too.

Coldiver throws down his rifle in fury.

– This is *my* roadhouse, he roars, and that means *I* own the bloody paddock, an *I* can do what *I* want in my paddock.

– It's not yours any more, says Tama, lowering her gun. Stevo's gunna buy it off ya.

– Am I?

– He can't afford to buy anything off me, snorts Coldiver.

– He's applied for a grant from the government, haven't you, Stevo?

– Bollocks he has, says Coldiver. He wouldn't know how to run a road-house as a profitable concern in a million years.

– Too bloody right, chips in Stevo. I'd close it down again, if it were up to me. We always got along fine when the roadhouse was closed down. Tama, have you really got me a government grant?

– It's not for sale, anyway, Coldiver says quickly. I like it here.

– Land rights, Tama tells Stevo. It'll be yours by the end of the year.

– Then I can build a house for Estha?

Tama smiles. – Don't see why not. She motions with her gun. – Get walking, Mr Coldiver. I'll see you back to the roadhouse.

Stevo joins in the ushering with little wafting motions of his hand. – C'mon, Mr Coldiver. Now get off me paddock. *Skit.*

<hr />

put yourselves in our shoes

Where's she hidden that damned thing?

We clamber around the trees as the shrill cry of the telephone sears out across the plain, feeling in the armpits of the branches. *Drrinng drrrrinnnng! Drrinng drrrrinnnng!* The cord is long and tangled but even-tually we discover the receiver on the other end. We drag it down to the foot of the snappy gums and press it against our ears.

Yes?

There's a babble of voices on the other end, as if we have picked up all the phone calls in town at once.

Yes? *Yes?* What is it?

There's no response. We look at one another, unsure.

Say g'day or something, urges the wind.

We clear our throats. Oi, you!

The babble gets louder.

Oi, you, listen up!

Still the senseless babble.

Just keep talking, says the wind. They have to hear you eventually.

We nod. OK. Listen up, folks! We have something to say, and seeing as you're not listening to the silence any more, we're trying this way instead. We'd like you to put yourselves in our shoes just for once. We've been sending you messages every day – cockatoos of every colour under the sun – and what do you do? First you ignore them. You get a bloody great black cockatoo shitting on your head – oh yes, we gave up on subtlety long ago – and then you carry on blithely about your day, acting as if nothing out of the ordinary is going to happen.

For a moment, there's a pocket of silence, an air bubble caught in a pipe.

And then you bloody well go and shoot them. What on earth does it take, we ask you? A cyclone? A tidal wave? How obvious do you want us to be?

From down the wires comes a laugh, and then the babble starts up again.

If you were to get smashed to smithereens by a road train tomorrow, you'd rant and rail because there were so many things you wanted to do, places you wanted to go, children you wanted to have, television programmes you wanted to see. Don't try and deny it. You'd say you weren't ready, you weren't expecting this just yet, for God's sake you're only forty-five, you've got a son of eight and he needs a father, all this Hollywood schmaltz you'd give us, whatever happened to love and under-standing, and haven't we heard in the Western world that life expectancy for a male is now seventy-four?

We pause, catching our breath.

Well, we'd reply. Don't say we didn't warn you, because we did. You just didn't notice the signs.

On the crackling line someone laughs again.

Frankly, it's getting boring being a spirit, we say.

The laughter goes on, oblivious.

In the old days, every post-pubescent on the continent would sit and close their eyes and allow themselves to receive whatever message we wanted to send them. Presentiments, forebodings, birthday greetings. Oh, the dreams we used to trickle into their ears! We'd have a laugh scaring the new initiates, creeping up behind them as they slept on a grave surrounded by fires spitting goanna fat. You could soon tell whether they had balls enough for the job. We'd cut them open, take out their entrails, put different ones back in. You should've seen the looks on their faces the next morning. Some of them couldn't take it, ran back to their mummies crying that they wanted to be normal and just get married like everyone else.

The babbling is getting louder now.

Maybe we took it a bit too far, because now we're horribly neglected. Did you hear about the young drover, not even a full-blood, and his dying uncle wanted to pass on his knowledge – how to read people's minds, suck illnesses through the skin, all that sort of thing – what an honour! – and yet the drover turned him down. He *turned a dying man down*. He said: Yes, I am willing to stand back and allow your knowledge to die with you, knowledge that can never be rediscovered, bye-bye all that wisdom, forty thousand years' worth, because you see I want to *assimilate*, I want to go down the pub with the other blokes and have a VB like everyone else. Let's be clear about this, he said to his uncle. You wouldn't let me drink if I took over your wisdom, right? You'd worry I might blab a secret while out on the piss. Yes, I thought as much. So you see, I'd rather not take the job on, ta for offering anyway.

We pause, the voices at the other end of the line fading a little.

And you know, as the drover made his way home that night he saw his uncle's totem, a wallaby, pounding alongside the ute. All along the road the creature kept pace, before whisking off into the darkness, gone forever. Another link between man and the spirit world irretrievably lost.

A deep, numbing silence.

So you see, we have every right to be jacked off. Some day soon we'll show it. Oh yes, we can rant and rail too, you know, we're not above temper tantrums. Some we gave up on long ago, but you, our precious children with your beautiful matt-black skin, our first-borns and our favourites, with your finely tuned senses and your infallible instincts – we had high hopes for you.

There's a pause, and then the line goes dead.

A blackened tree trunk swims in a bright red sea. Termite ships go sailing past. As the heat and humidity bear down, flattening everything with their steam-iron press, we struggle to get enough air. Every lungful we take is drugged with the lure of sleep.

The wind stares balefully into the molten distance.

What next? it croaks.

What does it look like?

The wind turns to look at us. Our limbs are dangling over the edges of our hammocks. Heads loll to the sides. Our torsos bend and blister like cellophane in the heat.

It looks like you're lying low to me.

We lift our outstretched palms – *there you are then* – but the hands fall back before properly making their point.

What about me?

Go and look for the cockatoos again.

They're dead, says the wind. Just like the dogs before them – the ones you thought were man's best friend. You thought they'd listen to the dogs, but you were wrong about that, and you were wrong about the cockatoos too.

Maybe some of them escaped.

The wind says nothing. It finds a couple of pull-rings, uses one to flip another – an impromptu game of tiddly-winks. Amazing. Even now, in the depths of heat-raddled inertia, the wind finds the energy for play.

What do you think of the pool table? it says, suddenly enlivened.

We glance over at the full-size, green-baize table standing on the fringes of our camp. We've been playing in the cool of the evenings these past few weeks.

Actually, we're getting rather good at it. The trick is to –

And what about the Hoover?

We bring our attention back to the immediate vicinity. All around us, debris clutters the ground: discarded items of clothing, old tin cans, bones that we've sucked clean with our toothless gums.

Waste of time.

The wind flicks a pull-ring high into the air. It spins, creating a painful flash of silver on the edges of our vision.

And what about the mobile phones? Do you think they will help?

We shrug.

Maybe. Eventually. Possibly by the time it's too late.

The wind shivers, despite the heat.

I suppose everyone's so busy these days, it sighs. It must be a struggle to earn enough money. I've heard they have to buy their kids the latest runners every few months.

An even higher spin of the pull-ring.

It does look cool, though.

What?

The way you huddle in doorways and on street corners, sit in the crooks of the gum trees or cadge lifts on the backs of utes with your mobiles flattened to your ears. *Hello? Hello? Is anybody listening?* It's like you're conducting an international covert operation.

We're not doing it to look cool.

I know, I'm just saying.

The wind hauls in a troubled breath, swells unevenly like a bloated witchetty grub, then shrinks back down again.

Well, you've just about been made redundant, haven't you, the wind says, rudely.

We sigh.

It's beginning to look that way. Soon we might cease to exist.

The wind looks up in horror. You shouldn't joke about something like that.

It wasn't a joke.

The wind stares at us, stunned. Then it springs to its feet, in full cajoling mood.

But you can't give in as easily as that! It would be a disaster! A disaster for the human race!

Thank you for pointing that out.

The wind starts pacing up and down, distractedly. So you admit it would be a disaster?

Irrefutably.

In that case, you won't let it happen.

We shrug. Perhaps we have no choice.

The wind stares at us for a moment, then goes back to its pacing. How did you ever let it come to this? You should've seen it coming!

There is a quiver in its voice.

We *did* see it coming. Look, calm down, will you? You're tiring us out.

I'm only trying to help.

It's not working.

What *will* work?

Sleep. Forgetfulness. Drugs.

The wind stares, agog. And then, without warning, it slams itself hard into one of the snappy gums. The hammocks rock wildly, so that we have to clutch onto the sides to stop ourselves falling out. The wind rears back, then slams the trunk again. The hammocks rise up like waves, spilling some of us to the ground. Others leap clear and wrestle with the wind, pinning it to the ground.

Stop it, will you? What do you think you're doing?

I'm trying to wake you out of your stupors! screams the wind. Just because you're going through a bad patch, you don't have to give up completely. What will happen to everyone out there if you do? Eh? What will happen to all the ones that you love?

Stop making such a goddam racket.

But the wind has worked itself into a panic now. It wheedles out of our clutches, leaps up into the tops of the trees and spins, a little cyclone of ferocious emotion. Wrenching off a branch, it lashes it at the hammock ropes. There are yells as the rest of us are thrown to the ground, others making a last-minute jump for it, grabbing at favourite shirts and pants and wads of left-over hash to get them out of harm's way.

Keep your hair on, will you?

The wind rips one of the hammocks loose and blasts it into the air. Its ropes flail wildly as the wind kicks the hammock high, thrashes it from left to right so that it bucks and strains, noisily.

That's *enough*!

For a few frozen seconds the hammock hangs suspended in the air. The wind pants hard. And then the AWOL hammock drops down, landing heavily at our feet. The wind looks away, more emotional than we have ever seen it. For a moment we wonder what it will do next – is it just collecting its energy for the next round? Or is the outburst over? We watch it closely, our possessions gripped to our chests.

What will happen to the children? the wind spits through clenched teeth. Its fury has made it pulse like a disembodied organ.

The children? we cry. Ha! That's rich, coming from you. Since when did you start to care about the *children*?

The wind flings itself against the ground, scooping up a litany of previously unseen pull-rings and causing them to bounce and scatter like the beads from a broken necklace. Billows of red dust swirl around, gritting our eyes and mouths.

Are you going to abandon them? Just like you abandoned Billy?

We didn't abandon Billy!

Bullshit! cries the wind, hurling handfuls of grit in our faces. He's probably still lost and scared and just as alone as ever. Yet all you do is go around blaming *him* for neglecting *you*. Did you really think that getting a white child to listen was going to make a difference? Did you imagine you could win over the hearts and minds of the whole white population? I never knew why you bothered with him in the first place. It's done nothing but harm – to you lot and to him.

QUIET! That is en*ough*!

We raise our hands in the air. For a while, nobody speaks. We glare at the wind and the wind glares at us, wild-eyed and panting, but it knows who's in control now. In any case, its panic is spent. It has had a glimpse of its own capacity for despair, and no amount of energy can survive in the face of that. Wrinkling up, it slides down the length of a snappy gum tree, gathering in a dishevelled heap at its base.

We wipe the grit from the corners of our eyes, scratch it from our hair.

We will do what we can for Billy, we say.

The wind picks at the ground, sullenly.

That a promise?

Yes.

What will you do, exactly?

We'll punish him, in order to redeem him.

The wind looks unconvinced.

And then what?

Then we'll finish what the spirit child started. It will be our gift to him. It's what the spirit child wanted, and she won't be around to do it.

The wind nods cheerlessly, then looks away.

part VII

the outbreak of intergalactic war

The door is open, so Billy pushes it gently and steps inside. He finds himself in the living room. There's the warm toffee smell of baby shit, cartoon squeals coming from the telly, bright oranges and reds and blues flashing on the walls. A yellow explosion goes off.

– *WE ARE WITNESSING THE BREAK-OUT OF INTERGALACTIC WAR!!!* screams a voice.

Two children of about four and six look over at him expressionlessly, then turn back to the TV. They are perched on a worn settee that has been wheeled up close to the screen so that it cuts across the room at an angle. A fake fur throw, overlapping onto the floor, is strewn with the detritus of small children – a soiled bib, an unopened brown envelope covered in wax crayon scribbles, a sticky lolly. Billy steps over a toddler-sized dump truck with bulbous red wheels, wondering how to announce himself, when she appears in the kitchen doorway, another child in a nappy on her hip.

– Oh, you found me note, didja. I was just about to give em their feed.

The baby in the nappy watches Billy doubtfully, his eyes the same grey as his mother's. His pudgy fingers are tangled in a clump of her hair which he's attempting to push into his mouth.

– Don't mind me, says Billy.

She tugs at her hair.

– Want a beer? Cupper tea?

– See to them first, says Billy. I'll be right.

– I c'n put the kettle on. Thanks for the fairy floss by the way. I helped meself to what was left of it.

The hair swings around in its curtain as she goes back into the kitchen. She's had it cut since he last saw her. The untapered line is even harder. Later he discovers that she does it herself, combing it out so it's draped evenly around her shoulders and using a mirror behind and a mirror in front, her right arm twisted around her back and denting her skin as she guides the scissors across.

With her spare hand she fills the kettle, lights the gas, slams the kettle down – kitchen sounds which he hasn't heard for a long time. The baby twists his head to follow each movement she makes. Billy pulls out a small wooden chair with the blue paint flaking off and sits on the edge, convinced it's going to crack beneath his weight. There's a child's scale to the furniture here; a child's taste, too. The wooden dresser is packed with knick-knacks – a row of tiny porcelain animals that he vaguely remembers coming free in cereal packets years ago, a picture frame with a 'Love is . . .' cartoon inside, a teddy bear in a MY BEST FRIEND T-shirt. A couple of books lie on their sides and he angles his head to read the spines: *Gone with the Wind* and *Paving the Way: a Romance of the Australian Bush*. Automatically, his hands move to his breast pocket, and then he stops himself: perhaps this is not the place.

– It's OK, you c'n smoke.

– Nah. It don't seem the right thing to do in here.

She slides the child into a high chair, wraps a curved plastic bib around his neck and dumps a pot of baby food down. Billy has never watched such actions close up. He feels awkward: too big, too male for this place. Behind her, the kettle starts to scream. Billy picks up the pot and scrutinises the label. Stewed apple and apricot with custard.

– Do I jiss stick it in?

Janelle puts her hands on her hips, amused.

– Yip. And when he spits it out, you jiss stick it back in again.

She turns the stove off and leaves the kettle where it is, wanting to watch this effort of Billy's to be helpful. He dips the plastic spoon cautiously into the pot, scrapes the top against the rim to flatten the mound of yellow sludge. Nudges between the soft pink lips. The child stares at the strange face, too distracted to eat.

– 'Snice seeing men do these delicate jobs.

There is a pause while nobody speaks. Eventually the child opens his lips enough for Billy to slip the spoon in. Some of it seems to stay inside.

– Most men I know are too loud and brawlin, says Janelle. They don't get the babies calm. You know the sorta blokes, the ones that want ter steal the show. I c'n never get a word in edgeways. I always wanted to do the jokes, but you can't with men like that.

He doesn't know how to respond to this, so he carries on feeding the baby. After a while she gets up and makes them both tea, then sticks a handful of fish fingers under the grill. She uses the remains of the water from the kettle to add to a bowl of instant mash, whirring it together with an electric whisk. At the sound of the whisk, the two other children come running.

– Lemme, lemme.

Little hands reach for the counter. Billy concentrates on feeding the baby, unsure how to behave with these older kids. The bigger of the two has very straight fair hair; the smaller one has jet-black curls and olive skin. Janelle puts the bowl of smash on the floor and gives the larger of the two the whisk. Little bits of fluffed potato splatter on the floor.

– Keep it in the damned bowl, OK?

Billy notices the younger, black-haired child scooping up the spilt potato and trying to return it to the bowl. With her bare foot, Janelle flicks his wrist away.

– Don't put your hand in there, Athol. Not unless you're lookin ter lose yer fingers before you've even grown em.

The child clutches his fingers protectively.

– Here, Janelle says more softly. Lemme count em, check they're all still there.

Athol shakes his head and hides his hand behind his back.

– Who's that? The older, fair-haired child aims an accusing finger at Billy.

– That's Billy. Say hi, he won't bite.

Billy gives a small smile. The baby has snatched the spoon from his hand and is banging it against the highchair.

– At least, 'e won't if 'e's not hungry, adds Janelle.

The older child gets a handful of Athol's T-shirt and glares at Billy as he drags his little brother away. They retreat to the living room, the TV still blaring.

– Don't take it personal. They bin around a few guys in their time and now they're kind of wary.

– It's OK, says Billy. I'm not much used to kids meself.

– I should've introduced you. Them two are Thomas Joseph Brent Hall and Athol Paulo Baldisseri Hall an this little fella is Clyde Milos Plavsic Hall.

– Big names for little blokes.

– They each got their dad's names in there. They all got different dads. Want some of these?

She spears a fish finger on a fork. Billy shakes his head. She puts two plastic yellow plates on the floor and dollops out the mashed potato, upending two fish fingers in each pile. Then she takes them through to the living room.

– Don't draw on the telly Tommy, he hears her say.

She catches Billy checking his watch as she comes back in.

– I jiss gotta put Clyde to bed and then we c'n go. My friend Paula's coming over. She'll see to the others.

– No worries.

The baby screams when she lifts him out of the highchair. At the door she turns round. – Ever watched a baby go to sleep?

Billy shakes his head.

She gives a come-on-then flick of her hair.

Heavy drapes have already been drawn across the window. The air is stale. A double bed takes up most of the space, a white chest of drawers with gold handles standing at its foot so that she has to squeeze between this and the frame of the bed to get past.

She draws back a corner of the doona, revealing fuchsia satin sheets and pillow covers. Billy throws her an amused glance.

– The baby likes em soft, she says sheepishly.

She changes Clyde as he lies on his back, quiet now, looking into her eyes and trying to catch clumps of hair.

– He loves your hair.

– He thinks it belongs to im.

Billy motions towards the soiled nappy that she's folding up. – Want me to take that?

She hesitates. – If you rilly want to. There's a bin in the bathroom.

Billy takes it away and stuffs it into an over-flowing swing-bin and when he comes back she's lying beside the child, propped up on an elbow, stroking its cheek with the back of a finger. A soft smile radiates over her face. Dimples in her cheeks again. Billy sits down on the opposite side of the bed and picks up a framed colour photo from the bedside table. There's a boy in the picture, no more than twenty or twenty-one, leaning cockily back in a striped canvas chair with his hands behind his head, overalls unzipped to reveal a white string vest. The overalls sleeves have been rolled right up, perhaps to show off his muscular arms or to avoid a T-shirt tan.

– Who's this?

He's surprised himself by a rush of jealousy, although he's careful to hide it. It has nothing to do with Janelle; it's the boy himself – the wide, unselfconscious smile, the laughter in his eyes. He has the face of someone who's been loved all his life, and knows it.

– It says on the back.

A yellowed cutting from a newspaper is stuck down with Sellotape.

LEONORA TRAGEDY: Shot-firer's assistant Joe Brent, tragically taken at Sons of Gwalia mine, Leonora, during last week's incident.

Billy looks at Janelle. The hand that's pressed against her temple stretches the skin, making her eye even narrower.

He reads on: . . . *died last night after being hit by ventilation doors in a mine 30ks south of Kambalda. Brent had taken shelter behind the doors, 220m from the point of detonation, when they were forced off their hinges by the compression of air after the explosion. Brent had recently become a father.* She'd stuck a second clipping beneath it. *The fatal accident at the Leonora mine last year involving excessive use of explosives has led to the mining contractor being fined $20,000. The contractor was charged under the mine safety Inspection Act after investigation by the Dept of Minerals and Energy.*

– One of the boys' dads?

Her face is devoid of self pity. – Yeh. Thomas's. Thomas was two weeks old at 'is funeral. She smiles. – Look, he's gone already. 'E doesn't seem ter need to be rocked.

Billy looks up in surprise, but she's nodding towards the baby.

There's an early dusk. Clouds sit on top of the houses. An isolated gust of wind picks up an eddy of litter; otherwise the streets are quiet. There's only one place in town he knows to take her – De Bernales wine bar.

She's put on tight black jeans and a freshly ironed pale pink shirt with a frill down the front. Billy feels a little shabby in his ancient denims, softened and thinned from over-washing. A band is setting up in one corner. The keyboard player, a pallid man with a solid, chiselled block of dark beard, is wearing a black shirt, black suit and black wrapround shades. He's jabbing a connection wire at the edge of the keyboard.

Janelle sips her vodka tonic through a straw. – Look at im. Mr No Smile. Betcha he don't allow imself to smile, iver.

She slides her hand across the table and nudges the tips of Billy's fingers.

– Didja hear that bloke at the bar? she says. The one with the bald head? He offered that girl he's with a drink and she said, I giss I'll have champagne, and y'know what 'e said? 'E said, Giss again. The tight-arsed bastard!

She bursts out laughing. Her bitten fingers slap against her mouth.

– 'E did! 'E said, Giss again! Gawd, I'm in the mood for gettin drunk.

The band starts up a rendition of 'Black Magic Woman' and Janelle runs her fingers through her hair and shakes it from side to side. She's drawing the attention of other men at the bar, two young blokes who check her out then size up Billy too. Billy ignores them, raises an amused eyebrow at Janelle as she stoops to suck at her drink.

– *Black plastic woman*, she sings, loudly enough for the boys at the bar to hear. *Black spastic woman*.

Billy chuckles into his beer. – You're gettin to do the jokes now, he says.

– I am. I jiss need someone to laugh at em.

– I'm laughin.

She tips her head on one side. – Only laugh if you want to, though. I don't want you laughin if you don't think I'm funny.

– Oh, no worries.

– Promise me you won't laugh jiss because you feel you oughtta.

– I won't, OK?

– Alright, I'm sorry. Janelle shrugs. – It's important to me, thassall.

There's a shout from the other end of the bar.

– Hey, Saint!

– Aw, Jesus.

The powder monkey grins as he strides towards them. Shadows pool in the dents in his cheeks.

– Look at the two of youse!

– How're ya goin, Francis? says Billy.

The powder monkey just nods, looking from one to another.

– Shout youse both a beer?

Billy shakes his head firmly. – We're gunna eat.

– You'll be needin menus, then. Allow me.

Francis picks up two big sheets of shrink-wrapped card from the bar, and hands them out with a flourish. There's a look of dry amusement in his hawkish eyes.

Janelle takes the straw out of her drink and knocks what's left of it back, the ice chinking against her teeth.

– Thanks, she says. We'll call ya when we're ready to order. You c'n take my empty while you're about it, too.

Francis winks at Billy. – Didn't know the two of youse were going out.

– We're not, says Billy.

– Appearances deceptive, ay.

– She's my skating teacher, says Billy, his eyes locked on Francis's.

Francis laughs, the hollows in his cheeks shifting uneasily. – That's a new one, mate.

– Don't forget Janelle's glass.

Billy continues to look at him coldly. The jittery smile on Francis's face disappears. – I'll send the waiter over.

Once he's gone, Billy raises his eyebrows at Janelle. – You know im too, ay?

She stands the menu upright on the side of the table so that it shields their faces from view.

– 'E tried to get me in the sack once. He ain't half got a strange way of talkin. Take me to heaven, Ellie! Let's fly with the angels, fuck in honey –

– Fuck in honey?

– Allelujah! You're the best, baby! And then all this weird philosophy shit. I didn't have a clue what he was on about.

– Did it work?

She shakes her head. – It worked on one of me mates, though. She said 'e carries on like that all the way through.

Billy looks over at where Francis stands at the bar, his jeans tight around his narrow hips.

– Jesus. Fucken Francis. Who'd ave thought.

– Hey, look at you, Janelle says. Mr Smile.

The windows of the house are dark. The curtains haven't yet been drawn. Janelle stands at the open front door, one hand on the little black bag hanging over her shoulder.

– You c'n come in.

Billy is a little drunk now, too.

– Nah, I don't think –

– Just kip down. A night in a proper bed.

He follows her inside. The house is heavy with the presence of sleeping children. Janelle goes straight into her bedroom to check on Clyde, while Billy waits awkwardly in the hallway. He thinks about going into the living room. He hasn't watched telly in an age. Then he hears her whispering and he goes into the bedroom and stands beside her. She's lifted the baby up. His face is screwed up on the verge of a cry, and he's arching his back.

– I need ter pee before I feed im, says Janelle. Here, you take im.

She pushes the baby at Billy without looking to see whether he knows how to hold him. Clyde squirms in Billy's hands, launches in on a sustained whine. The toilet flushes next door. Janelle comes back in carrying a toothbrush. She holds it out.

– Swap?

– What's that for?

– Whatja think? Here, I'll give im is feed.

Billy hands the baby back and takes the toothbrush and watches her fiddle with the buttons on her shirt. She looks up.

– Go on, then, she prompts.

He feels just as out of place in the bathroom. There are dozens of little pots and tubes on the glass shelf above the basin. None of them look like toothpaste. The mirror is wet with splashed water. He finds a tube of children's milkteeth toothpaste folded over and over on itself, squeezes what he can out of it and bends over, keeping an ear out for her. When he's finished he sits on the toilet seat until he can hear her moving about. He comes back to find her naked from the waist up and undoing her jeans.

– Janelle, please don't –

– What?

– Undress.

– You want me to sleep with my jeans on?

– Jiss something.

She stands upright.

– Jesus, Billy.

She gives him a long-suffering look. Then, leaning over the bed, breasts dangling, she tugs open the top drawer in the chest.

– How old are ya, Billy?

– Twenty-three.

– Old enough not to be shy of a pair of tits, you'd think.

She tosses him a T-shirt and takes out another one for herself.

– There, can't get much less sexy than that.

Billy shivers, though it's anything but cold in here. He takes off his own jeans cautiously, as if his legs were made of china. When he's down to his jocks and T-shirt he gets in the bed, keeping as tight to the edge as he can. A small bedside lamp throws an orange circle onto the ceiling. Between them is the regular movement of the baby's rib cage, already asleep again. He can hear the drag of Janelle's eyelashes on her pillow.

– This OK for ya?

Billy nods.

– You don't say much, do ya?

She gives him a chance, but nothing comes back.

– I don't mean it as a criticism. It's better that way, I reckon. Not like me, blabbing on about whatever's in me 'ead. But when you're holed up with three kids it's nice to hev someone yer own height ta speak ta for a change.

– I like listenin.

– That's a start. Not many men do.

The drag of her lashes again. He imagines them leaving a smudge of black on the satin pillow.

– The gasbags are the worst. Expect you to umm and ahh at everything. As if I give a toss what they like and don't like.

He smiles.

– You come close to my idea of a perfect man, y'know. Tall, blond and quiet. It all goes on inside.

She reaches out a hand. He tenses, but the hand's not for him. She brushes it against the downy whispers of hair on the baby's head.

– I c'n imagine whatever I like aboutcha. I'll probably get it wrong, but I don't rilly care. Soon's you open your mouth, I'll find out you ain't like what I'd pictured at all. That's the danger with quiet men. You fill in the gaps with whativer you want. But I don't care about that yit.

Billy lies very still, keeping his eyes on the baby.

– So, dja like workin down the mine, then? she asks.

He shrugs.

– Dja do it for the money?

– No.

– Then you must like somethin about it.

He shrugs again.

She inches closer to the baby. She's looking at Billy and he meets her gaze, the baby reduced to a haze.

– Y'know what, mate? Somewhere, folded up inside, I think I know the secret to what makes a person happy. It happens sometimes, on a Saturday morning when the kids are playin in the yard and I put out the plates in the sun to warm 'em up . . .

The orange glow of the lamp catches a lock of her hair and makes it shine. She senses his eyes on it and tucks it shyly behind her ear.

– One day I'm gunna take the kids and go an live in Esperance. A nice house by the sea. It'll be a safe place to grow em up. They'll be teachers and lawyers and doctors, one day, my kids. They won't end up down a mine.

– Sounds nice.

– You don't believe me.

– Yes I do.

– I save what I can, unlike you fellas. I c'n make it happen, you'll see.

– I believe you.

– Do ya save what you earn, Billy?

– I don't spend it.

– So you're savin for somethin?

Her hand disappears beneath the sheet. He tenses again, but she's only scratching her leg.

– For God's sake, what are ya so scared of?

– I'm not scared.

– Like fuck you're not. I niver saw a man so scared.

– I'm not.

– Why dja flinch every time I move then?

Their eyes lock over the baby's nose.

– Do you think I'm too skinny?

– No.

– Then what're ya flinchin for?

He takes a steadying breath. – I didn't come here ter sleep with ya.

She looks at her pillow, scratches at something with her thumb.

– You know what I think? I think you're the sort that keeps imself to imself because 'e don't want to give anythin away. But ya can't expect to git anythin back if you don't give.

– I don't want anything.

The baby moves its arm up and down between them, unsticks its lips, blows a little bubble of regurgitated milk.

– Then what are ya doin here?

– You invited me in for a kip.

She sighs, lifts her elbow and rolls onto her back. – Jesus. Alright. I git the message.

She rolls away from him, the folds of her T-shirt forming an angry cross on her back. He doesn't know how this happened – who misunderstood whom; where the wrongdoing lies. She turns off the orange lamp. He hears her let out a sigh.

– Is there somebody else, Billy?

She twists her head back to look at him. He's lying very still. His eyes are focused on the sleeping baby, tracing the line of its profile, the button nose, the bulge of the veiny forehead. Gently, he prods Clyde's curled-up fist with his finger until the baby takes hold.

– Is grip's tight, ay, he says. Even in 'is sleep.

any picaninnies here?

T he bush chef grins from ear to ear, showing his perfect white teeth. The eyebrow ring blazes in the sun. Slanting across his chest like the strap of a school bag is a rifle.

The spirit child stares at him, captivated. He gets more good-looking by the day.

– *First you will need to get your hands on one of these. This one's a .22 magnum. It's pretty cheap to use. You get fifty shots for eleven dollars whereas the more high-powered .243 costs about a dollar a shot. Which is fine if you're Clint Eastwood, but most of us are a bit hit and miss, and roos can be pretty snappy movers. The other advantage of a .22 is that you don't end up with minced roo, as you would with a .243.*

There's the sound of a shot firing. The spirit child leaps to her feet. She *knew* it! Buck's been here all the time. Then she catches sight of us over by the blackened tree stump in fits of giggles, blowing up empty crisp packets and bursting them between clapped hands. With a puff of annoyance, she sits back down again.

– *To get a licence you have to either be an Aborigine, preferably not with an alcohol problem, or you have to get the signature of a property owner saying you can shoot on his land. Some property owners in WA are quite good sports; others you'll have to bargain with. Slipping them a few hundred dollars will usually do the trick.*

BANG! She looks up sharply. That wasn't a crisp packet. That was thunder. We look up too. It's raining out towards the coast and there's the musty smell of approaching dampness in the air. The spirit child picks up the remote and turns the volume up.

– *Otherwise of course you can run one down on the road. This is most likely to happen at dusk, when they're on the move, and you're half asleep. But there's a trick to it: you've gotta hit them in the head. If you hit them in the chest the guts get into the meat and it all goes bad.*

A shiver runs down her spine. Black clouds are building dramatically above the sandstone escarpment, the sun still fierce in the gap between the two. To one side, a gaggle of us bend over at the waist in silent laughter, stoned stupid.

– *For starters, you'll need to prepare a kangaroo-shaped hole in the ground like this, and get a nice big fire going inside. This one's been burning for about an hour. Gut the roo to check if the liver has got parasites in it – if it has, give the whole damned carcass to your dog. If not, drag the kangaroo over – they're heavy buggers – and throw it in. Then you pull the coals and earth on top, like that, until it's completely sealed, just the legs sticking up. Look at the way the claws are clenched, ay, like it's a pretending to be a tiger. Grrr! That smell – well, you can't smell it but I can – is the singed fur. A real stinker.*

There's another loud thunder-clap. The spirit child looks around to see us running, giggling, towards our hammocks. When one of us trips, several others go flying, and we roll about clutching our bellies, hysterical with laughter.

– Meanwhile, you can roast the tail on the coals. Do it in its own skin, like a banana. OK, it's pretty tough and not very appetising to look at, but the Aborigines on my dad's station used to say it makes you strong, it's their equivalent of spinach. I suggest you have a few beers while you're waiting, because it's gunna take a while. Cheers bonzas!

Lightning splits the sky in two. The spirit child turns the volume up as high as it will go, and then makes a dash for it, reaching the snappy gums just as the first heavy drops come down – long strings which bounce on the ground then coil up again, like yo-yos.

– THE LEGS, SHOULDERS AND TAIL MAKE A PRETTY GOOD STEW, MIXED WITH A FEW SPUDS AND ONIONS. YOU MIGHT WANT TO BOIL UP THE INTESTINES AS WE'RE DOING HERE. UMMMM, MOUTH-WATERING! ALTERNATIVELY, THE STOMACH, MILK GUTS AND KIDNEYS CAN BE

A second strike flares wildly to the ground. For a moment, we're all captured in open-mouthed, ice-white shock.

– SKEWERED THEY MAKE

There's a crack and one of the snappy gum boughs crashes to the ground. Yellow flames streak up a trunk. The spirit child screams and runs back into the storm. Within seconds she's drenched to the bone.

– MARVELLOUS KEBABS! shouts Buck.

By late afternoon the storm is all but forgotten. The sun has flooded the landscape in warm, yellow light, drying the earth, the hammocks, our hair and clothes. The spirit child unpegs her pyjama bottoms from the telephone line and cosies up in her blanket with her exercise book. The shadows lengthen around her. We take the telephone off the hook and roll ourselves a joint.

There's an hour or so of calm. The spirit child's pen moves across her page. Soon it has grown too dark to see. She closes the exercise book and, using it as a pillow, lies down right where she is.

Goodnight, she calls out.

Sleep tight, we call back. Don't let the bed bugs bite.

Some time in the night a gut-wrenching wail rips through the darkness. In one movement, the spirit child springs to her feet, heart racing. She's been on tenterhooks all this time.

That was *not* a dingo, she says, gasping for air as if she's been held under water. That was a little girl.

She twists the corner of her blanket. Silver fragments of moonlight glitter from behind the trees, picking out the frightened whites of her eyes. She runs to the shelter of the snappy gums, stumbling over the end of her blanket.

Did you hear it?

Sssh!

That cry —

Yes, yes. We heard.

There is a flash in our eyes too, and she sees it. She takes a step back, cowed. She covers her mouth with her blanket. Our rebuffs are familiar to her now, but she isn't used to our fear.

What is it?

Her voice is a hoarse whisper. She searches our faces, trying to read some sense into the deep lines carved around our mouths.

Is it a memory?

Ah! She's not stupid, the spirit child. We look away, distract ourselves with picking at threads in the hammocks. Since our spat with the wind the other day, the hammocks are looking more dishevelled than ever.

We don't want to talk about it, we say.

She stares balefully at the coloured threads, at the red and purple and dirty white, drawn together into their faded patterns. There is longing in her eyes, as if she'd like to believe in these threads, let them carry her away somewhere else entirely.

You have to tell me.

You'll know soon enough.

Even as we say it, the air turns chilly. Beneath our feet the ground starts to vibrate. The spirit child backs up against the hammocks.

What's happening?

Before we can answer her, a pair of headlights sweeps across the camp – so bright that we have to shield our eyes from their terrible glare. A big truck smashes through the bush, two shadowy figures behind the wheel. Strapped to the back of the truck is a large, rattling cage with a padlocked gate. Dry wood cracks as the wheels roll over the undergrowth, squashing it to a pulp. Crushed leaves emit a bitter scent. The truck lurches towards the stand of snappy gums.

The spirit child grabs whatever limbs of ours she can find, the hairs on her arms and neck bristling.

– Any picaninnies here? a voice calls out.

It's a man's voice, roughened, hollow. Devoid of tenderness.

– No, we got no picaninnies, we shout back out loud.

The spirit child stares at us, wide-eyed with horror, an awful question coming to the surface.

We give a slight nod, raise index fingers to our lips. She clings to us tightly, each breath rasping against the back of her throat. The headlights swoop in a circle, miss us by inches, career away. Red tail-lights recede into the darkness.

Who sent them? she asks in a tight little voice.

Mr Government.

What for?

To collect the half-bloods. They wanted to bring them up themselves, teach them the whitefella way.

She pulls her blanket around her shoulders.

Why didn't you stop them?

It's hard to remember now. It took us by surprise. We were probably distracted by something else.

You were *distracted*?

Her gaze hardens on us.

What's so outrageous about that? It happens! Just for a moment we turned away and –

We pick at the threads of the hammocks.

And *what*?

– and when we looked around they were gone.

Who?

Children. Thousands of them. They would disappear, suddenly – just like the dogs, just like our beautiful cockatoos. Most of them we never saw or heard from ever again. Their loss haunts us every day. There was one we particularly loved – she was a cheeky imp of a thing, always dressed in hand-me-downs. She wore a pink ribbon in her hair.

The spirit child's eyes grow wider.

Whose child? she whispers.

Her mother was from Wangkatjungka, her father was white – a station-hand maybe, or a cook, or a passing anthropologist . . .

A blinding light swoops back and shines directly in our eyes, catching us all in its beam. The spirit child screams. We clasp a hand over her mouth.

– Any picaninnies here? hollers the gruff voice again.

– No, we got no pic—

– What do you call *her* then – a dog?

The spirit child whimpers. Her snot is gluey between our fingers.

Can they see us? she whispers hoarsely.

You're flesh and blood in our memories. Just as you are to Billy.

The beam of a torch picks out her horrified face. A large pale hand reaches out of the darkness and grips her roughly by the hair. She screams in pain, and before we know it the ghostly white arm has scooped up her slender body. She yells and thrashes, arms flailing, feet kicking. She never was one to give in without a fight.

With all the commotion, the wind wakes abruptly, shouting out in confusion.

What is it? Is it happening again?

Yes! we cry. Our child! They are taking away our child!

We rush out into the open, glimpse the yellow soles of her bare feet slamming the darkness and cover our faces with our hands, as if we might prevent the terrible sight from entering our consciousness one more time. The wind zips back and forth, frenzied but powerless. We hurl ourselves at the dark figures, grabbing the hems of their trousers.

– Put her down! Give us our little girl back!

But we are nothing to these men. They swing their truncheons at random, and who cares if they find a scrawny torso, rupture a lung, crack a rib in two as if it were a chicken bone? So what if they get us right in the eye? The next day it will mushroom, billow over in heinous colours – but these men will not be around to see it. They bash our fingers where we attempt to reach for our child, until we are afraid that their truncheons will hurt her too. The cage door slams with a clatter and the bewildered, terrified spirit child pushes her fingers through the wire and stares at us in anguish, the snot running freely from her nose.

We chase after her, but the vehicle is travelling too fast, and one by one we collapse in the clouds of dust spewing from beneath its powerful wheels.

– We will civilise your child, the lean voice hollers back into the empty night. The cage rattles with the swaying of the truck. – Teach her to worship Our Lord Jesus Christ. You will see how we care for our own. We won't let her rot out here, surrounded by your dogshit and squalor!

Our wails fill the darkness. We pull out our hair, slash at our bare arms with sticks. Oh, for a physical pain that would shout louder than the pain in our hearts! We rush up to one another, grasp each other's quivering cheeks between our hands, unable to take it all in.

Is it true? we ask. Did they really take her again?

Yes, we say. It's true. She's gone. Now there's nothing left to do but grieve.

We fall to our knees in the dirt, sobbing. Oh, we still have tears to shed! Though we are frail and old and bitter, we are not bled dry. We fall to our faces in the dust, beaten by the grief which is ours and only ours to bear, consumed by the utter relentlessness of it all.

Eat the earth! we cry out to one another. Eat it till we are made of the earth itself!

We twist and writhe in the dirt, stuffing it into our mouths.

---

a load of bloody savages

T ama turns off the lights and pulls the door of the ATSIC office to behind her, the latch clicking into place. It's still light, but the street is empty. No doubt everyone's at the Spini.

She stoops to pick up her handbag and is still straightening up when a clammy hand grasps her arm. Startled, it takes her a moment to recognise the stewed face and froggy eyes of Sydney Coldiver, much closer than she would ever wish them to be.

– Jesus! Whatja think you're doin, givin me a fright like that?

– Tam*ara*.

The voice is wheedling, doughy. There is something sludgy about his eyes, as if he's been drinking, although all she can smell on his breath is the bitterness of coffee.

– For the thousandth time, my name is *Tama*. Either call me Tama or don't speak to me at all.

She shakes him off and starts walking down the street, her metal-studded shoes ringing out on the pavement, a purposeful zest in her stride. She won't let any man, however big and brainless, intimidate her. He catches up with a surprisingly long, galumphing stride.

– Tama, hold on, will ya. Listen, love. There's something I want ter ask ya.

– Go on, then, spit it out. I wanna get home.

He's got her stationary now. His face is burning. Surely, she thinks, surely he wouldn't dare to try anything on? No; there is something too laboured, too distracted about him. She softens, lowers her guard a little.

– I wanna know what it is about this place, Tama, he says. I know you c'n tell me. None of you have a brass razoo, but I'll be damned if I can eke a labour force out of this population. It's harder than musterin a swarm of mosquitoes. Stevo Pike was going to come to Dili, he knew he could make big bikkies, but now he's pulled out an all. Rossco and Gerry are hopeless bludgers. You know I ain't laid a finger on you, more's the pity, nor on that Estha either, so what has this mob got against me? Someone's spreading a bad word around, and I wanna know who it is.

Tama shakes her head. She feels like laughing – partly out of relief.

– You rilly don't have a clue, do ya?

He stands before her, his face a study in hurt and disappointment. If she didn't know better, she'd pity him.

– Mr Coldiver, she begins.

– Sydney. Please call me Sydney. Or Syd.

– Sydney.

She almost puts a hand on his chest, but stops herself just short.

– People around here ain't interested in money. It's meanin they're lookin for.

– But life's worth bugger-all if you haven't got food in yer gut and a roof over yer head! Coldiver blurts out, arms waving and spittle spraying. Tama openly wipes it off her face. – Are you tellin me the blackfellas were better off before we came along – all big guts an spindly legs, like Stevo? Them white do-gooders have told them how they lost a garden of Eden, how life was all peaches and cream, and they believe every single damned word. Those left-wing fucken bozos just want to make the Abos into some idea, use them to further their own high-falutin world view. They're sat around smokin bongs and the bloody blackfellas don't have any idea what they're on about.

Tama ducks to avoid a waving arm.

– Suddenly, everyone has forgotten about the malnutrition and the barbaric practices – the raping, the spearing, the medicine men putting the mozzers on everyone – bloody terrifying mob the Abos were! All those lefties say we should let the land go back to its pristine state, but I tell ya: most of you blackfellas wouldn't know what to do with a piece of land if you were served it on a plate. Within a week you'd run out of petrol and bullets to go and catch them turkeys with and you'd end up cutting the kidneys out of the fattest woman around and chucking em on the barbie. Load of bloody savages, you are, at heart! That's what we saved you from. Now, what everyone around here needs is a good, honest, nine-to-five job to give them pride and a pay packet on a Friday. Not a hand-out from Mr Government. I've seen some hard-working Abos up on the cattle stations: they can do it if they put their minds to it. I had ter earn my pocket money when I was a kid – fifty cents for sweeping the drive, a dollar for mowing the lawn. My old man knew how to instill a sense of pride in me.

He pauses to give his arms a break. Tama is looking up at him with a quizzical smile.

– Would you call that your religion, Sydney?

– What?

– The Protestant work ethic. Is that a religion to you?

– You c'n tease me, Tamarind, but I'm telling you, you lose your way without work. If what they need is meanin, I can give em meanin –

– By doing something which someone else tells them to do? She shakes her head, genuinely bewildered. – That don't seem to me the right way to go about bein happy, Mr Coldiver.

She peers at him up close.

– I'll tell you what's happened, Sydney. The country has been taken from our people, and without it they don't know where they're from, or why they're on this earth. They're empty inside. And don't tell me you don't know how that feels. Empty as a rusted old drum.

Tama swings her bag over her shoulder and carries on walking, her metal heels skudding the pavement. Coldiver breaks into a sweat trying to keep up with her, the shirt sticking down the middle of his back.

– Now you're soundin like one of those fucking hippy lefties, Tamala.

You see, they're jiss taking you over. You like your job, dontcha? You're about the only one around here with any sense, it seems to me. That's why I c'n talk to you. None of the others seem to get it. That Stevo Pike, 'e thinks like I do most days, only he won't admit it in front of the others. It's like everyone here's got the same disease.

– Ah, well, we all know where *that* came from. First you gave us smallpox, syphilis and the flu. Then we caught your lack of spirituality. Now we drink to fill the void, just like you, only we don't digest it quite as well and we end up with liver disease and diabetes. You iver heard of Shakespeare, Mr Coldiver?

– Shakespeare?

– Yeh, that pommy poet that they get so excited about when you're in school. There are more things in heaven and earth than you iver dreamt of, Sydney Coldiver. You remember the line?

– I'm in Shakespeare?

She swings her bag further onto her shoulder, half-closes her eyes like a disdainful cat. Nearby, someone slams a window. The blue, flickering light from a TV set washes over Coldiver's face and turns it the colour of mouldy cheese. Tama watches him take in a big, uncomfortable breath and let it out again, hands on hips, his stomach full and congested. He presses his wet lips together abruptly as if he were trying to stop himself belching.

– Maybe what it comes down to, Sydney, she says, is that you're simply in the wrong town.

– Eh?

She goes up close.

– Maybe you're barking up the *wrong bloody stump*.

She watches her words seep slowly into the fleshy fabric of his face, the colour paling a little as they are absorbed. She suspects she is witnessing the first moment in which Coldiver has actually listened properly to what someone else is saying. She stands back, feeling pleased with herself.

– Now. If you don't mind, I'm gunna go home for my tea.

the creaking of insects

T he moon looks yellower than usual, as if it has gone old and stale, or has been sealed in a waxy rind. It is full and round and wisps of purple cloud interlace across its middle. Behind, the sky is a dusty lemon-pink. We've trudged down to the river to indulge our melancholy and suck on the coolness of the night. The only sound is the creaking of insects and the faint lap of water curling in its soft channel alongside us, brown and viscous and warm.

A stone bounces on the water. *Plop, plop. Plop.* We listen out for a fourth bounce, but it doesn't come.

How was business at the coffee shop today, anyone know?

Five.

You heard a fifth bounce?

No. Five chiko rolls, fourteen coffees, one milkshake. Watched it on the TV satellite link-up she fixed up.

What flavour?

What flavour was what?

The milkshake.

Banana and mango.

Fresh?

Of course not. Out of a packet.

A spotted nightjar dives through the air, trapping an insect in its beak. There's the crackle of a brittle, tinder-dry body. An unexpected breeze lifts the tail-ends of our beards.

Thought you'd gone to bed, we say. You're normally comatose by this time.

Can't sleep, mumbles the wind.

We give a little lift of our chins in acknowledgement of our shared emotional state.

She'll be back, we say, not without tenderness.

I know, I know. The wind sighs. She'll just trip across the desert one day, a pretty, laughing little girl . . .

There's a splash as a fish plops out and back into the water. We strain our ears to hear more, but the night air has already pocketed the sound, and we're left gazing at the broad reach of delicately hued sky above us, the wisps of cloud thinning out, weaving and stretching like chiffon.

The sound that she made when she laughed, says the wind. It was just as laughter should be.

The wind is still now, although it injects the air with a certain heaviness.

It bubbled up like a fountain. When she got really carried away, it ended in hiccups. Do you remember?

There are smiles on our lips as we nod, silently staring at the vastness of the sky. The light is holding on around the edge of the earth.

Sometimes I think I can still hear her, murmurs the wind.

We cock our heads, sharpening our ears on a blade of cool night air. A pair of bats tangle over our heads.

Nonsense, we say suddenly. Pull yourself together. All this sentimental wallowing will get you nowhere.

One of us kicks a stone irritably. Half-heartedly, a foot returns it. Then it's kicked again, a foot steps out to block it, and before we know it a little game of soccer has taken shape – we may be old and depressed but we haven't lost our sense of fun completely, it seems – until it hops above a bare foot, rolls down the bank and plops into the river.

Five!

Five what?

The fifth bounce!

Outside the community gates the next morning, the grass looks greener and thicker than usual. The rains have encouraged new shoots. You have to get down on your hands and knees to fully admire the fresh green tips poking out of the barrel of last year's coarser sheaths. They are so vivid, these shoots – so juicy. The urge to nibble them off is almost too strong to resist.

The wind nudges us in the ribs. Look who's here.

We stagger quickly to our feet. Jimmi Rangi is getting out of his ute to open the gates. He's back in his flared trousers again, but this time with a Bob Dylan T-shirt on top. He swings the left gate open in a wide arc and props it back with a stone. Then he does the same with the right. Despite the fact that the gates are made of chicken wire, his action seems to have the effect of letting the air rush in and out, the air in the community mingling with the air in the town.

With a hand on the hot roof of his ute he slides neatly back into the moulded seat. As he drives past, looking relaxed and happy, he raises a hand in greeting.

He waved at you!

The wind stares at us, taken aback.

We are as surprised as the wind is, and the nod we give to Jimmi is hesitant, almost shy. Through the wound-down window we see something long and shiny flash on the seat beside him: Stevo's .22, by the look of it.

Uh-oh, says the wind. I thought we were done with shooting in this town. Do you think we should go with him?

The ute hasn't yet picked up speed. Despite our arthritic joints, we manage to lope up behind it and scramble onto the tray top, turning around to haul up the stragglers. The wind curls into a ball and somersaults alongside the wheels, over and over and over – a childish pursuit, anyone might think, but the wind never gets bored of such things. We make ourselves comfortable on an array of spare tyres and rolled-up swags, and take out some weed for a smoke. We might as well enjoy the ride.

Overhead, a perfect blue sky is scissored by electricity cables, crossing and recrossing the street. Turpentine wattles flick past, the mighty boab, and on another corner the resplendent crown of a flame-red coral tree is all the more glorious for the fact that the recent rain has washed the dust off its leaves. As we pass the servo Yakka rushes out in an excited tizzy of barking. She hasn't seen us out and about in a while.

How're you going, Yakka?

Jimmi hoots his horn to frighten her away from the wheels.

At the edge of town, the ute turns off the road and follows a track by the river. Jimmi drives with his head sticking out of the window, dodging potholes, termite mounds, rocks. A brown-winged pheasant shoots vertically out of the grass, squawking, its tail forked like an arrow.

– Hai!

The ute is still rolling as Jimmi leaps out and wades through the burnt gold grass with high stamps of his feet, the metallic flash of gun-metal at his side.

– Hai!

We bail out too and spread into a circle, eager to help. A goanna is crashing through the dead grass, leaving a tell-tale track of broken stalks. As we watch, it creates an inner circle of broken stalks. We close in. Jimmi signals at us with one finger, the gun raised ready.

– Hai! Hai!

He squeezes the trigger. A little explosion of frothed earth. The goanna hisses angrily and darts about in the crackling grass.

You're out of practice, mate.

– You wouldn't be any better, Jimmi growls.

The goanna is making a run for it, hurtling towards us with surprising speed. Soon we can see it: swinging its head from side to side and baring a row of serrated teeth. It's an aggressive old codger, leathery and tough. No good for eating. We stand aside to let it pass.

– Hey! Whatja do that for, fellas? cries Jimmi.

It was an old lady, we say.

Jimmi straightens up, wipes an arm over his sweating forehead. He puts his hands on his hips and looks over at where the vehicle has rolled on a few metres, the door still open. The sun is directly overhead, beating down on his shaggy black hair.

– Bloody goanna. I never liked em much anyway.

At the river Jimmi slips down the soft, muddy bank, fully clothed. Concentric circles fan out from his waist. Bent, angled fronds of pandanus dip their brown tips into the current, letting through shafts of light. With each step, silt mushrooms in the water.

He waits for the silt to subside, then lowers the bottom lip of a large plastic flagon into the flow. The rim of his T-shirt fans out like a skirt. There's a slight breeze: the tide must be coming in downstream.

When the flagon is almost too heavy to lift, he drags it back up the bank, then lurches in again, right into the middle this time, bending his knees so that the water swills over his shoulders, a soft, cooling lap around his neck. Then he bends further and the water seals shut above his head.

We bide our time on the bank. For at least a minute – maybe two – you would never know he's under there. A white-feathered corella rattles the pandanus. Another minute goes by.

Do you think –?

We're on the verge of jumping in after him when we see his magnified hands clawing the water, a stream of bubbles popping on the surface. He comes up like a crocodile, pausing with his eyes half in half out, the water licking in a bright white meniscus: a rigid, certain world on top, a wanton, shifting world beneath. Then he hauls himself back up the bank. His flares slap around his shins.

There's a satisfying crunch of dried bark as he flings himself down beneath the paperbarks. All around, the slim, mottled trunks soar up, their shadows striping his vision. Moisture tickles his skin as it dries.

– Why didn't you remind me how happy I am out here?

From high up in the paperbarks, we shower him with peeled bark pellets, torn between resentment and affection.

Don't blame us, we say. It's your own stupid fault for not listening all that time.

Squatting naked on the riverbank, he dribbles a little water into a pannikin. He stirs the sediment with a fingertip. The ochre spreads quickly, an orangey-brown stain lapping the sides of the cup.

There's not much give in the skin of this tightly muscled man. He makes a small dell in the blackness and leaves behind a perfect orange spot. From skin to pannikin, back and forth, the motion lulling both him and us with a drowsy contentment. The line of dots climbs an arm, crosses his neck like a yoke, freewheels down the other side.

He makes a second pannikin of white. Using his thumb this time, he smears a thick band across his nose. His lips he also paints white. He grins at his reflection in the river. His teeth look stark yellow in contrast, gums and tongue a shocking blood-red. Jimmi wags his tongue at himself, and in the wiggling mirror a white cockatoo flies out from a tree.

We can't help but admire the face that bends and buckles in the browns and blacks of the water. The thick, scruffy eyebrows, the way the bridge of his nose screws up. All in all, he cuts an impressive figure. Standing up again, he stretches his lean, knotty arms, the shoulder blades sliding together beneath the skin, clefts forming in the sides of his buttocks.

Not bad, we say. Not bad.

He stays on the bank for another few hours, decorating his lean torso, his legs, his arms, catching black hairs in the slick and setting them hard. Every now and then he angles his face to receive the ministrations of the sinking sun. He is lost to us now, oblivious, but we don't mind any more.

Flies zing and wrangle around his head, but he doesn't try to swat them away. A brolga flaps lazily through the last heavy minutes of the afternoon. We look out over the tops of the trees, over the sea of gold-flecked grass, this adoring, plentiful sea which has everything to offer this man, everything to give him that he needs, if only he knows to take it, and watch the giant, ruby-red sun burn into the horizon, a gush of cool air flooding the land in its wake.

as if a ghost has passed through

It reaches her first as a distant rumble, nothing more than a road train going over corrugations in a dirt road. Then the door rattles in its frame. Just after that a wave enters the house. It takes with it her stomach, her heart, her lungs – shifting them sideways before dropping them back down again. It is as if a ghost has passed through her.

After that the walls shake and the glasses and jars in the cupboards clink and sometimes one of the pieces of china on the dresser waddles to the edge of the narrow shelf and she has to put a hand out to stop it. Janelle holds onto the sides of the dresser, all the little mementoes of her life jigging around as if they had been brought to sudden, animated life. She steadies the dresser, steadying herself.

Afterwards, irritation wells up inside her. It's years since she's paid any attention to the blasts – except to set her watch by. But here she is again, biting her lip and wondering where he was when the explosion went off – whether he was down the shaft or in the cage or at this moment is stepping out into bright sunlight, tugging at the fingers of his gloves and nodding at someone he knows.

Surely if she'd learnt anything in the six years since Joe's death, she'd learnt not to put herself through this any more.

He turns up unannounced one evening just as she's going to bed, hovering in the yard like a moth drawn to light. She spies him from the kitchen and turns the light off, not wanting to give him the advantage. She can see the square outline of his white T-shirt. He's a full head taller than her, lean but with strong arms and legs, and she likes that. Eyes that look a million miles into the distance. She goes to the front door and lets him in.

– The baby asleep yet? he asks straight away, as if the question has been bothering him all evening.

– Sure.

A careful, considered nod. – Tommy and Athol?

– Yeh, they're in bed.

He rubs his jaw. He hasn't shaved in a week. – That's good.

– If you want to come in . . .

He doesn't kiss her. He goes straight into the kitchen and helps himself to a beer from the fridge. While he's there, he checks on the bottles of pre-mixed milk. Catching her curious look, he asks if she wants a cup of tea. She says no, but he makes her one anyway. Later, he follows her into the bedroom. He doesn't even look at her while she's undressing, so intent is he on the baby. He uses the toothbrush that she keeps for him now in a glass on the edge of the sink. He sleeps protected by the veneer of T-shirt and underpants, and of course the sleeping baby, a physical barrier between them, a harbinger of innocence. During the night he gets up without being asked, propping the wailing creature against his shoulder and gropes around for something to heat the milk. He rocks the baby on the sofa, surrounded by the mess of plastic toys, feeding Clyde in the crook of his arm.

In the mornings, stumbling through in a man's white shirt, she's confused by having slept the whole night through. Tucking one bare leg beneath her on a chair and yawning, she nibbles toast that he puts down in front of her while the older boys run around in a mayhem of stick-ups and shoot-outs. She watches him leaning over the baby with a spoonful of stewed apple, mopping up the spillage on his chin.

– You'll have yerself hired as a nanny if ya don't watch out.

Later, when she takes the baby off him, he sits there with his big hands flat on the table, as if he doesn't know what to do next. She'll come in half an hour later and find him where she left him, staring at the creases of his knuckles, a flicker of tension snagged between his eyebrows. She yearns to touch his face, smooth out that dent at the top of his nose, but there are invisible boundaries, unspoken rules – no sex, no contact, no holding of the eyes for more than is practical and necessary. What she most loves about him, of course, is this separateness, the very thing that keeps her away. She thinks of it as a vast tract of country that spans out from his body, forcing them apart, even in the space of the bed. You'd have to be brave to attempt to cross that open space; it would be an act of pure will, like walking on coals.

Sometimes she fools herself that this is what he wants her to do, and that he's simply too afraid to ask. Perhaps she should take the initiative, take off her shoes and socks and just do it, step over that heat-blasted ground, face the withering, dust-laden wind, and when she is halfway across she will wave to him – I'm coming, whether you want me or not. At first he will panic, shout back that he has nothing to give her, that she is wasting her time. But soon he will realise he has no choice – she's coming anyway – and eventually he will relax, smile, even stretch out his arms to encourage her the last few steps of the way. And she will start to run, gaining confidence now that there's a chance of being welcomed when she reaches the other side.

One day he drives her out to the lease. She's never been before. He tells her to close her eyes and when she opens them she's astonished by the glare of the salt lake. She stabs the crust with the heel of her boot. It is too rough, too uneven to slide on, as she would have liked to do, but she tries it anyway, a slow circle on one foot, the other leg bent like a ham ballerina. A passing car gives a toot, and she takes a bow.

She starts to run in long, sinuous curves, hopping over the tracks of the trucks that have driven out towards the headframes. She misses the gulping cold that emanates from the ice. This salt is impervious in comparison, blank, its glare so intense that she can hardly see for squinting. Hearing his footsteps behind her she speeds up, running from them just as she races from the sound of other skaters on the rink, wanting to be the first to take possession of the virgin space before her. Soon she slows down, puffed.

– Look! Roos!

She points at the blur of bounding shapes in the distance. A mob of grey boomers.

– They're beautiful, ain't they? she calls, looking back at Billy.

Billy makes a vague motion with a hand. – Nice soup, I guess.

– That's a horrible thing to say!

He pats his pockets for his cigarettes. – Go on, don't stop runnin. I'll catch you up.

But her moment has gone now. She watches him stroll back to the car, lean against the door frame as he gropes around on the back seat for his smokes. She looks back at the glaring salt lake, knowing she should make the most of it while she's here, but her hunger for it has worn off.

– Hey! Janelle!

She looks back at him, startled by the clarity of his shout. He is smiling openly.

– Your red skirt – it's amazing! he cries. The only colour for miles around!

the last *laaa*

On a tatty, torn mattress on the floor of his house, Jimmi Rangi thrashes restlessly, the bilious odour of rotten flesh in his nose.

Psssst!

He grunts. Shoulders us away.

Don't be rude, we say. We've got something for you. It's the last time we'll ever bother you so you might as well wake up and listen.

He swats us, as if we were flies.

We sigh and sit down on the edge of his mattress. Gratitude is clearly too much to hope for at this stage. Through the glassless windows, moonlight spills in two slabs on the floor, revealing the source of the nasty smell: a bloody, crimson flower blossoming on the concrete. He must've shot a bush turkey and dumped it there.

On a count of three we start to hum, just softly at first. At a prearranged signal we split into parts, some voices taking the bass, others the alto, one letting rip on the saxophone's glorious cadences – or maybe it will be an electric guitar solo – who knows? That will be up to Jimmi, should he choose to listen.

Gradually the body beside us starts to relax.

Need it again?

An almost indiscernible nod of the head.

This time we add the lyrics. There are also drums, and a tambourine – a last-minute addition which somehow brings the whole song together – and some of us are moved to get up and experiment with a few dance steps. We weave in and out of the patches of moonlight, our bodies fluid in the room's silver glow. It's almost enough to make you feel young again, the music drowning out the creaking of our bones. When it's over we giggle and collapse in one another's arms, our skin lustrous with a fine sheen of sweat.

Jimmi rolls over, buries his sleep-crumpled face in the pillow.

Oi, you ungrateful rat! How many times do you get offered something as good as this for free? Listen, this one's special. Don't let it slip away. We'll give you one more chance.

He brings his tongue out to lick his lips.

On the count of three.

The tambourine rattles. The saxophone swells. This time we sing it slowly and deliberately, tapping our feet on the floor, or our palms on our knees, watching one another for when to come in with our solos. The song fills the room, seeming somehow to displace the foul smell of the turkey, and we smile at one another. Softly, softly now. A beautiful tune, this is.

A look of concentration settles lightly on Jimmi's face. At the end we fade to grey, as if what he is hearing is the CD version, as played on the radio. A pair of clicking fingers is the last thing to go.

We wait in the afterglow. A fly buzzes through one glassless window and out another. We become aware of the quietness of the community beyond these four walls: the whole place sunk in sleep. Jimmi opens his eyes and sits up, slaps his hands on the floor for something to write with. Still woozy, he hums out the tune as he makes marks on the concrete with an old stub of pencil, a wiggly treble clef and then a rough rendering of the notes: a semibreve, a line of quavers, the occasional accented sharp.

– *Mmmm, m-mmmmm, menumenumenum naaaaaa.*

That's it! And the bass line – just to make sure.

– *Mm mmmmmm, mebbay bay bay bay baaaaaay!*

Oh, getting clever now, adding bits of your own.

– *Laaaaah. Laa-aaaah. LAAAAH.*

Very nice. Now go back to sleep.

– *LAAAAAA! Manou manou manou manou maaaaaay laa laaa* –

That's enough! Don't want to wake the neighbours.

A smile tugging at his lips, Jimmi stares at the marks he's made on the floor. Then he flops on his back, his jaw left open from the last *laaa*.

We wait a while, hoping for some sort of thank you. All we get is a throaty snore.

Not at all, we mumble as we get up to go. Don't mention it. Really. Please.

The following afternoon we wake with a start, heat-axed heads ablaze. According to the clock on the tree it's a quarter past three. That's what happens when you're up all night composing. Beyond our debris-strewn camp the land seems to heave with a deep, troubled sigh.

What was *that*?

We listen out for a clue as to what woke us. An oppressive silence weighs down. And then we hear it again – an ugly, triumphant maw. We scan the apparently empty stretch of blue, and then we see it: above the escarpment, in an otherwise innocent, cloudless sky, a crow turns once, then twice.

We give the other hammocks a rough shake, our fingers trembling.

Wake up.

What is it?

In the place where our fingers are pointing, the crow plunges into a stand of trees.

Where's the wind?

An unpleasant nausea has taken up residence in the pit of our stomachs. We find the wind wedged in the hollow of a snappy gum.

You go. Find out what it is, we tell the wind.

The wind doesn't even bother to lift its head.

No way. It's too hot and anyway, I'm depressed.

We look at one another, anxiety swimming in our faded eyes. There's nothing for it. We take a big breath and set off across the sandstone plain.

We haven't been to Billy's house for several years now, and our slow, careful steps over the blistered plain are heavy with reluctance. As we get nearer we throw furtive glances to the sides, fearful of discovering signs of our neglect. The tin roof with its patchwork of rusted browns and pinks still tilts at the same jaunty angle. And there, at the bottom of the drive, stands Billy's hiding tree, its white limbs just as graceful and imposing as they always were. We observe with polite interest a few new cars sitting under the lean-to.

Maaw!

We look up. A second crow has joined the first with a cry of ghastly delight. From this position we can see that they're circling a stand of ironbarks further down the track. Even as we watch, one of them swoops into the branches again.

We eye one another, still hopeful of an excuse that would allow us to turn back. But nothing interrupts the dread-filled silence.

Come on.

We smell him before we see him. By the time we have found the thicket, we are already pressing our shirt-tails to our mouths. The stench is ripe and sweet, enough to make you retch on the spot.

Oh! The colour of five o'clock wheat, he once told us, singing it up to a sky that was speckled with stars which danced then swam back into focus then went berserk again. He was reeling with drink and his spunk was still sticky in his jeans. She's trouble, we said, don't say we didn't warn you, she'll lead you up the garden path and you won't be able to keep her. What garden path? he hollered in a voice unfettered by his usual self-consciousness, bending his head so far back we thought he might fall over and knock himself out. I ain't got a garden path. An I c'n keep a woman down. I'll show ya. You wanna see what I got? No, Stan, not really, we said. We've seen it already, if you must know, and getting it out in public – oh, *Stan*, for Chrissakes, is that really neces- sary? Ha! he cried. See that? Course ya do, ya can't miss it! Anyone else wanna see?

Oh, Stan, Stan. It was a long time ago, but it seems like yesterday now that he's here with his jeans bogged down around his ankles once again. The crows have made mincemeat of his manhood, picking off the tender foreskin first, then tearing out the soft red flesh of his balls. The eyes went next, nothing but gouged-out sockets left behind, and where his lips once were, straddled with freckles and browned by the sun, there is a ragged hole, twice the size it was. A black, leathery tongue lolls out, rudely, childishly, as if disgusted by itself, or at the foul smell leaking from his gut.

We stand around in a bewildered circle, our heads bowed, wrapping the ends of our frazzled grey beards over our eyes and mouths.

For a while it had looked as if he was taking it all in his stride, we say to one another. Even the midwife was embarrassed when she saw that the child had much darker skin than his own. But he put on his bravest smile, did Stan, made it clear to anyone who came to visit that he saw nothing wrong with this new baby girl of theirs, nothing wrong at all. After that nobody dared say a word. He accepted her lock, stock and barrel. He gave her all the love that no one else had seemed to want. For a while it was all going fine.

And then Stevo came back to town. Suddenly it seemed as if there was too much love flying around. Stevo wanted to do the right thing for once – and not just in terms of money. For a while Stan stood his ground, but he was never much of a fighter. And Crystal didn't seem to be on his side. One day there it was, staring him in the face: he was going to lose this girl, this gorgeous little girl, who was nothing to do with him. First one child had turned his back, and now another.

We know what it is to lose a child. We understand.

He made a good job of it, we mutter absurdly to one another, not knowing what else to say. That good strong leather belt held out well. The empty oil drum lying lazily now in the grass was just the right height. And an ironbark – just the ticket! A quality job, he would say, if he could see it himself. The work of a craftsman. Something to be proud of, ay.

Behind our backs, the last, fiery rim of the sun slips from view. Coming into their own, thin wisps of cloud rake the sky in a dozen different shades, deepening with each passing second. Scarlet, orange, pink, purple, grey. The scythe blade of a new moon hangs patiently to one side, awaiting its moment.

It's time to go, we say.

The wind, curled up in one of our hammocks, raises its head and gives a protracted yawn. It doesn't take any notice until it catches sight of us standing in a line, dressed in the least threadbare shirts and trousers we possess, our sharpened spears at our sides. Some of us have even brushed our teeth.

What's this, the Law Men cometh? The wind gives a derisive snort. What the hell do you blokes think you look like?

We turn to the wind with grave, sober eyes.

Cut it out, will you? the wind goes on. You're making me nervous in all that get-up.

Do you think we're not frightened too?

The wind stares at the deep lines etched across our faces, the skin that tumbles away beneath our eyes, the eyes themselves eaten away by cataracts, or worn thin by the constant glare of the sun. It seems only just to have noticed how much we have aged in these last few years. Struggling to contain its mounting anxiety, it puffs itself out, self-importantly.

And where do you propose to go, exactly. Eh? Tell me that.

First we will visit Billy, as promised.

And then what?

Then we're leaving.

What d'you mean, *leaving*?

We won't be coming back.

What, not *ever*?

Never ever.

A barely perceptible tremor passes through the wind.

I thought you were supposed to go on for ever, it says, quietly.

The hardened lumps of our Adam's apples bob up and down.

That's what we used to think too. But if nobody believes in our existence, then we no longer exist. It is a simple enough equation.

What about Jimmi?

We shrug. One man is not enough.

The wind can no longer hide its rapidly mounting terror. It shudders, a mass of hot air, scuffling the dust at our feet.

Hang on a minute, it says. Listen up. It flounders around for words, knowing this may be the only chance it will get. What would the world be like without you? Eh? Think of that. A spiritless world – is that not too awful a concept to imagine?

The leaves of the snappy gums rattle, excitedly.

Oh yes, we say. It is.

The wind darts from one pair of eyes to another, searching desperately for a sign that one of us is wavering – a speck of doubt that it can snatch hold of and intensify. This is an argument it cannot afford to lose. All it would take is for one of us to falter – just one – and within half an hour it'd have us lying back down on our hammocks, as morose and grumpy as ever.

When it speaks, it does so slowly and deliberately.

Let me paint the picture for you, it says, seeing as your minds have clearly gone soft from too much pot. If you leave, the people will be trapped forever within the limitations of their meagre, earthly existences, searching for meanings that do not exist in places they'll never find them. Imagine how they'll gnash their teeth on empty air, scavenge like dingos in the vestiges of what you leave behind, desperate for something – anything – that will suggest to them that their lives are worth more than a random number of years snatched from eternity and then snatched back again. Oh, they will search high and low, but not even love will give them the answers they crave. Whatever bonds they forge with one another will seem worthless in the face of the eternal nothingness that awaits them. They'll see no point in living if they're not around to reflect on it afterwards. Day after day, year after year, their battered, tormented souls will cry out for you, terrorised as they are by the knowledge that when they die, they die for ever, and that in death there will be no recourse – no glimpse of the intelligence that once was, no chance to sit around and chat, have a beer, share the memories. Just think! All those lives, the countless heartbeats, the beautiful faces, young and old, the longings, the whisperings, the hearty guffaws, the stories told late into the night. The gossip, the dreams, the ambitions. The tentative embraces, the burning desires, the earth-shattering orgasms – all snuffed out in a split second and expelled to a place beyond existence – *vamoosh!* – like a rugby ball kicked high and wide and lost behind the heads of the crowd . . .

The wind trails off, exhausted by its own conjured-up vision. It looks at us, ashen-faced.

Chrissakes, you have a terrible way with words.

The wind drops to its knees. Don't do it! At least wait another day. See how you feel in the morning.

We shake our heads, smiling despite ourselves. You are a fool, you know. We've probably never told you that before.

What about the spirit child? says the wind, ignoring the insult.

What about her?

Don't you want to see her again?

Our hearts will break if we have to say goodbye to her one more time. We have suffered too much already.

What about your hammocks, cries the wind in desperation. Your pool table. Your telephone. Who's going to look after them?

You take them. Have anything you want. In fact, we solemnly bequeath you all our possessions, our odds and sods of underwear, the telephone, the fridge, the television set –

The boom box?

The boom box too. It's all yours. You can do with it as you see fit – have a party, get your mates around.

The wind stares at the ground in despair. The branches of the snappy gums are motionless. In the sky above the hulking escarpment, the first star springs on. We will let it be our guide. We start to walk.

Wait, the wind whispers, hoarsely.

We do him the underserved honour of a backward glance.

All this swagger. It's just empty threats. You have no idea how much you're frightening me.

This isn't about you, for once, we say shortly.

The wind jumps up and grabs at the tattered edges of our shirts.

I don't believe you. Just how do you propose to leave, anyway? Do you imagine there's some great cosmic cliff out there that you can just step over, one after the other, like a load of lemmings? Is that it?

Your imagination really does leave a lot to be desired.

Stop patronising me, you bastards!

A delightful way to speak to dying spirits.

Mustering every last ounce of its energy, the wind billows up to the height of the snappy gums. Dragging a trail of litter behind it, it careens around us in a circle, hemming us in.

And what if I try and stop you? Eh? What if I blow you back and smash you against your damned snappy gum trees?

By all means. Have a go.

The wind picks up speed. Pull-rings, flattened Emu cans, empty crisp packets and orange-juice cartons, rags of underwear and dried gum leaves are all drawn up in its wake. Soon a perfectly formed cyclone is whirring around us, shepherding us into its epicentre. The hammocks flap and strain at their bits. We admire the solid wall of junk that surrounds us for a moment – natural wonders haven't ceased to hold their charm – but our interest doesn't last. Pushing it aside like a curtain, we step through, our long limbs stretching out into the cool of the night.

Caught up, even now, in the excitement of its own creation, the wind doesn't even notice us go.

Over the escarpment, the first star watches us, a familiar, beady eye that hates to miss out on the action. We walk towards it, feeling calm and empty and lost, something faintly tugging at our hearts. Perhaps it is the last great void that beckons. Soon, perhaps, we will start to yearn for it too. Death, they say, has a way of reconciling those whose time has come.

We walk towards the town. Boabs shimmer like a row of empty bottles on the side of the road.

part VIII

a large fire stoked

One evening Harri hires a minibus and picks a group of them up at the caravan park. Sim and others from the single quarters are already in the back. There's an Esky on one of the seats and enough timber in the back to keep a large fire stoked all night.

– There's rib bones 'n bangers in the Esky, says Harri, proudly. Laura had nothing ter do with it. I shopped for em all on me own.

Pete Monday, Francis Jacobs and a group of men from Schmitz are lined up on the pavement outside the York Hotel, plastic grocery bags bulging at their feet.

– Here comes the Bundy and Coke.

The men troop on, ducking as they make their way down the aisle, bum cracks peeping above their jeans.

– Always strange to see em in their civvies, muses Harri, watching the men in his rear mirror. His own greying hair is dampened and slicked back, the skin on his cheeks hen-pecked from a closer than usual shave.

– Look at Francis with his skinny tight jeans, ay. 'E's got the arse of a twelve-year-old.

Arms fly over the backs of seats as men turn around to talk to those behind them. The aisle fills up with boots as those whose legs are too long for the cramped seats stretch out.

– Look – you can spot the single men. They're the ones without any clean socks to wear.

Harri is in high spirits after a few days in the Alice with Laura. He shouts a couple of insults into the minibus, cranking the men up as if they were clockwork toys.

– That'll do it, he says to Billy. Can't stand all this formal shit.

A well-scrubbed Sim comes up front and slides in next to Billy.

– Look, I brought me billy can, Billy, he says.

– You'll be on the tea, then, says Billy.

Sim pulls a face, then leans forward. – How's life on the property, Harri?

– It's good, ay.

– Good crop of olives this year?

– Aw, they're a mug's game, olives. Every year we get about a sugarbox full. The bleedin parrots get em the night before we're about to pick em. Come in and scoop the lot. We've got grapes too but they drop off the vine if I'm not there and the chooks eat em up and get drunk as hell. Sometimes I wonder why we bother.

– How many chooks've ya got?

From the driving seat, Harri throws back an amused glance.

– I dunno, thirty odd.

– I like chooks, says Sim. I've got em back in Tassie. I got forty-seven and I know every one of em by name. Feedin em is the best part of me day. I love being around those little feathery things. The bantams are rilly pretty.

Sim trails off. Billy smiles and closes his eyes.

– Didja know, says Sim suddenly, if you put salt on a chook's bum, it dies. I tried it once and it works. And apparently, if you give it aspirin, it explodes. I niver tried that yit.

Harri rubs his scruffy eyebrow with a finger. – That's somethin, Spud.

Billy's temple rocks against the glass.

Two-day-old tyre tracks already circle the patch of scrub: Harri's done his scouting in advance. Three ghost gums stand on one side, one of them with a big, blackened bite taken out of its trunk, blistering charcoal around the edges.

The men get to work, quickly finding themselves a role. Teamwork is something they're good at. Two build the fire, others empty the shopping bags and set up a board for the meat. Francis rips the wrapping off a stack of plastic cups and lays them out on the ground, adjusting them with as much care as if they were elements of a circuit.

– Only one nip for Spud, shouts Billy, hoisting a load of wood onto his shoulder. Don't want him chunderin. 'E's on the tea after that.

Sim aims a kick at Billy's shin but Billy's too quick and side-steps it. The dry wood crackles like splintering glass as it takes. Above the flames the air shudders. Someone sticks a branch in the dirt for cricket stumps, finds a thicker piece of wood for a bat and a stone for a ball, too small for anyone to see it. Ten runs at a time are lost while someone scrabbles around in the dirt.

– I got it!

– Bullshit. That's a diff'rent bloody stone.

Gradually the darkness shepherds them closer together. A narrow moon blurs through a visor of cloud. The fire is roaring now, yellow scars of flame tearing up the darkness. Harri prises the raw meat off the grill where it's sticking and flips it over. Billy slings a frisbee of white bread onto each plate. The cricket stone smashes a jar of mustard and the cooks let out a groan. Sizzling meat fat seasons the air and they begin to take their places expectantly, eyes drawn into the flames.

– I think we should go around and say our names, where we come from, where we went to school, that sort of thing, says Harri.

– What is this, fucken AA?

– Good practice for it, ay.

There's a deal of carping but they submit in the end, an awkwardness settling on the faces of each one as they speak. There's barely a corner of Australia left unnamed. Someone hands around a packet of Winfield Blues, and they smoke from the same pack.

– I can't remember where I went to school, says Francis. Went to so many of em. Got assholed from most of em.

– What for?

– They didn't get my sense of humour.

– These make me sick as a pig, says Harri, staring at the cigarette he's just lit.

Pete comes around with refills of rum, sloshing it over their hands. Billy watches a moth immolate itself in the flames of the fire, its crisp, singed body carried away on a curl of smoke. A blackened rib is flung on his plate. He picks it up, tearing off the meat with his teeth.

– How bout you, Billy?

– The Kimberley, he says with his mouth full. Me dad's a panel-beater. Me mum sits around an smokes all day.

– Bloody crawlin with coons up there, mutters Francis, reaching across to the crate of beers.

No one wants to reward him by rising to his bait. Francis burps to feed the awkward silence. – Jiss one more ale, then I'll have a feed, he mutters.

– Christ, Harri, I ain't been out bush in a year, barks out Sim. Jiss from my bed to the shaft and to the Fed, and that's about the whole of it.

– You oughtta get out more, Spud.

– Nah. Goin out brings trouble, says Pete.

– Last time I went out bush I got friggin lost and it was only me and the dog, ay, says Francis. Three days and there wasn't a fucken thing to eat. I ad ter nick im. Poor old Jack. There was a pile of bones – lovely bones – and I thought fucken ell, I wish Jack was here, he'd have enjoyed all them bones, ay.

The men laugh.

– 'Sa load of bull if iver I heard it, grumbles Pete.

– Blood oath, it's the truth.

– Fucken ain't.

– Fucken is.

– I always thought you looked a bit like a dog, says Billy.

– That's puttin it politely, says Harri.

– Didja hear that?

– Pete farted.

– Not that. A bark. A fucken dingo.

They listen, heads tilted. A slight breeze plays with strands of their hair.

– Francis'll cop it, won't ya, Francis. Then we c'n chuck it on the barbie.

– You don't wanna be shootin dingos, says Pete. I knew a blackfella once, the days when I drove a semi-trailer out of the Pilbara. 'E speared a dingo. Went down to finish im off and a whole bloody pack of dingos descended on im. They found 'is bones later.

There are murmurs of agreement.

– I met one down at the lease once, says someone else. 'E came straight towards me. I was shittin myself. 'Ad to make a run for a digger. Thought I was headin for heaven, ay.

Everyone has a dingo story. When the stories die down, an eeriness creeps in, the men aware of the shush of the wind in the tops of the trees, edgy now.

Suddenly Francis jumps to his feet. – Fuck!

– What is it?

– A fucken centipede, is what. I lost it, but it was there a second ago.

– Watch out for them toes, Billy, says Harri, nodding towards Billy's bare feet. The little pinky looks a bit like a female centipede from a distance. 'E might try 'n knock it up.

– Ave you iver seen a chook tackle a centipede? Sim asks Harri. They're spunky little fellas, the way they go for em.

There's a loud bang, and then a second one. From out of the fire something hot and wet shoots at their faces and chests. Flaming twigs catch on their T-shirts and hair. The men roll backwards, swatting at flames, hollering, feeling their faces with their fingers to discover where they've been hurt. They are horrified when their fingers come away red and warm and sticky. Is it their own flesh, or someone else's? As the yelling dies down, they look through the flickering flames and see the same red goo on everyone's cheeks.

Standing apart from the group, the powder monkey has his neck thrown back in silent, helpless laughter.

– I put em in the flames, he gasps, laughing too hard to breathe. It's fucken *beans*!

– Jesus!

– Two cans. You buncha suckers!

Billy's the quickest to his feet, throwing out an arm to try and grab at Francis's ankle but Francis has legged it already.

– Get the arsehole!

Three of them make chase. Billy runs after Francis at full pelt, able to dodge trees only at the last minute when they loom suddenly before him. It feels good to stretch his legs – the first time in years he's run this fast. The other two men aren't so fit.

– Can't run no more, I'll throw up.

– Bring im in, Saint!

He hadn't stopped to put his boots on, and he can feel every small stone under his feet. His soles have gone soft in these last few years. Christ, he'll probably end up stepping on a snake. He stops, his heart pounding in his chest, ears straining. He's lost the sound of the powder monkey's thuds.

– Francis?

He struggles to quieten his own breathing so that he can listen. All he can hear are the men back at camp swearing as they wipe hot baked beans from their hair and clothes.

He makes a tunnel with his hands. – FRANCIS YOU'RE A DEAD BASTARD!

Billy chuckles to himself. He is if they can find him. He hears the crack of a branch and turns to face it, thinks he spots a flash of colour and tears off again. Every now and again, a square of green or blue shows up ahead, constantly changing direction. Jesus, this bloke is really determined. He's still going faster than Billy. Billy speeds up, aware of a tightening in his calf muscles.

– Francis, for Chrissake, give me a fucken break!

He slows to a walk, scans the blackness for a glimmer of that stupid orange mullet – something he never thought he'd be happy to see.

Darkness pours in as if from a jug. Billy's T-shirt is sticky and he peels it off, letting the air get to his skin. He tucks it through a belt loop on his jeans.

The only sound is the swish of the wind in the trees. He hasn't got much choice but to go back, though it shames him to return empty-handed. He turns in a full circle to get his bearings, hunts for the flicker of the fire, but he can't even see that any more. If there hadn't been so much cloud, he'd have been able to work out what direction he was heading from the stars. He walks a few more paces, turns in a circle again.

– Harri?

A breeze traces the line of his jaw, teasing his teeth. He must have come further than he thought.

– HARRI!

There are trees here, denser vegetation than where they struck camp. He grabs hold of the low, sweeping branch of a ghost gum, stark white against the darkness, and hauls himself onto it. Balancing upright, he can see a cluster of orange lights pooled in the distance, the sky above them paler than elsewhere. Kalgoorlie, presumably. He scans around and eventually sees the fire, the flames blacking out occasionally as a figure walks in front. Relieved, he jumps down and picks up a jog, his head hanging, trying to watch where he steps. There's a cut on one sole which is stinging.

Ah, sod Francis. For the first time in months, years even, Billy feels a twinge of anger. Sod the piss ant for leading him on a wild-goose chase. He'll have had the last laugh now, too. By the time Billy gets back, all the food will have been eaten, beans and all. He wipes the sweat from his lip. It's strange being out in the bush like this at night; he's not used to it. The darkness at the bottom of the shaft at Lanfranki has a different quality: a closed-in, fetid dampness, somehow reassuring with the weight of the earth around you. Out here, the darkness is vertiginous. You could free-fall, like in those nightmares he used to have as a kid. Or maybe he's just drunk.

He speeds up, eager to be sitting down now with a shot of Bundy and a smoke. He shoulders his way through thickets of wattle that he doesn't remember seeing earlier, crosses what looks like a dry stream bed.

Billy Can!

He stops dead. Did he imagine it? He shakes his head, irritably, goes on. Directly in front, flames scratch at the blackness. He can make out five or six silhouetted men, leaning back on their haunches. They look like they've finished the food. Probably steadily drinking themselves into stupors now. He puts his hands around his mouth.

– He outran me, the short-arsed prick. Is he there?

No answer. A wiry bush scrapes his ankle. Long, rakish shadows are flung in his direction, one crossing his face. He can feel the vibrations of feet on the ground, as if they are milling around. A handful are coming towards him.

– Harri? Pete?

Something snaps beneath his foot. There's an answering echo of two sticks knocking together, steady as a bird trying to crack the shell of a snail: *chip-chip, chip-chip*. Clap sticks. He'd know the sound anywhere.

And then the voice of a man singing, twining in and around the clap sticks in a reedy, nasal chant.

Billy shudders. These are not his men. This is not his camp fire.

The figures walk slowly towards him. He can't make out their faces, not even when the flames leap up behind them. Occasional whoops and trills and cries are flung into the night: there must be a dozen or so people here. The singing gets louder, more insistent, straining between the same notes, over and over. The milling of feet has become a regular stamping.

The figures halt. Billy does the same.

– Reckon I got the wrong campfire, he calls out. I'm with the mining mob.

Billy Can, don't be an idiot. It's no good disowning us.

The voice is inside his head.

– Excuse me . . .?

Billy, cut the crap.

– Who are ya? he shouts, still refusing to believe it.

You know perfectly well, Billy Can.

– Where are ya from? Even as he pretends to himself, his palms are starting to sweat.

From out there, in the desert, Billy Can, same as ever. Where we've been since the beginning.

Suddenly panicked, Billy lurches backwards, stumbles and falls.

– What do you want from me? he gasps. His heart is pounding right up in his throat. He tries to gather his limbs around him, get himself back on his feet, but his legs are trembling wildly.

We've come to look after you, Billy Can. It's quite straightforward, really. There's a job we have to finish. No need to panic – we're on your side. We love you, if you remember.

– Jesus. Why do I feel so afraid?

Don't ask us. You never used to be such a wimp.

He brings his hands up to cover his face. – Fuck. I thought I'd lost youse!

There is a shushing sound, as if a dozen mouths have sucked in air. Billy shuts his eyes and clenches his fists, tells himself that it's just the wind he hears; some naturally occurring sound. That he's not going mad.

And then a voice comes sharp and clear.

Sometimes we have to punish those we love, Billy Can, in order to set them free.

He looks around, frantically.

– Punish? Why punish? What for?

Don't tell us you've forgotten, Billy Can! Surely you still see it in your dreams – the beautiful arc, the frightened eye, the smash of the windscreen . . . You still have the scars on your face.

Instinctively, Billy brings a hand to his cheek. A spasm of tension runs through him. In the darkness he can see the white of an eye, blinking.

We have come to redeem you, Billy. To set you free.

– Bollocks!

He jumps to his feet and starts to run – he doesn't care where, just away from these voices, away from the fire. He thrashes through the dense wattle, oblivious of the snagging branches. Suddenly his way is blocked by a shadowy figure stepping into his path. He pulls up short, hurls himself around in another direction. Again a figure bars his way.

We won't let you escape from us a second time.

– What are you trying to do to me? he screams, his voice rising hysterically.

There's a trickle of laughter.

You wanted guidance, didn't you? A clear path, you said. You wanted to be taught what was right and what was wrong. What it was all about.

Billy puts his hands over his ears and shakes his head, violently. *No.* He will not hear these voices. They do not belong to him.

You yearned for someone to take your hand – someone strong who could give you direction. You yearned for a world in which everything made sense – one in which people didn't shy away from speaking the truth. In which transgressions were punished and a person could be redeemed.

– Leave me alone!

Don't you want to be redeemed, Billy Can?

– I want to be left alone!

There is a pause before an answer comes back.

How can you say that to us, Billy Can? When we've loved you all this time?

The bodies close in. All of a sudden there's a blunt kick to his shin. His legs give way beneath him. His cheek thuds against the earth. For a moment he is aware only of blood pumping inside his flattened ear. Then he is lifted: strong hands grabbing the tops of his arms, fingers locked around ankles. His right cheek and right arm are squashed beneath him as he is rolled on one side. The recovery position, he thinks, with a shiver of cold amusement.

But then there is the sound of ripping fabric, a blanching as air meets his groin. His legs have been exposed right up to the hip. There's a babble of voices and he cowers from them, his whole body rigid with tension. Rough hands wind a strip of cloth around his head, trapping eyelashes carelessly. Something cool and gummy is slapped onto his exposed thigh by a rough palm.

– Don't hurt me, he says.

It's for your own good, Billy Can.

The muscle in his buttock has begun to tremble uncontrollably.

– *Please* –

The jerks shoot down his arms and legs.

It's time you realised, Billy Can, how important we are to you. You should've known that you wouldn't be able to live without us.

And then he feels what he knew all along he would feel. It starts with a sharp point grazing the skin high up on the side of his thigh. Jesus, *no*. The point steadies, holds still. The voices have gone quiet. Now is the time to free-fall, he tells himself. Now. *Now*. Fall through space, on and on, before they can do any damage.

There are several jabs and then the spearhead is pushed right through the skin, the full heft of a body behind it. Sweat pours off him. His heart beats so fast he's convinced it will stop. He opens his mouth in a silent, agonised yell, although in fact what he feels is a terrible burning sensation rather than real pain. Someone yanks the binding cloth aside and stuffs something between his teeth. He bites down, splintering wood. Through the gaps in the cloth he can see the barbs lining the shaft of the spear. A gush of warm blood swims over his thigh, mixing with his sweat and running into the crack of his buttocks. His thigh muscle is spasming violently. He wonders if he is shitting himself.

We're going right the way through, barbs and all! cry the voices. And when we've done that, we'll tend to that other little job, the one which was left half-finished . . .

Splinters of wood at the back of his throat make him choke. Perhaps

he will die out here in the bush. Bleed to death at the hands of these face-
less voices. If that's the case, there is nothing for it. He is at their mercy,
helpless as a newborn. The moment this occurs to him, a lightness swamps
him. Is it gratitude? Love? Joy? Fuck knows. But when he feels the sharp
point of the spear come through the first leg and press against the skin of
the second, lower leg, he finds himself almost welcoming it – thrilling at
the completion of his disfiguration. Barbs and all, they said! There is no
going back now, no going back to the boy he used to be. His muscles
relent. He becomes as soft as fudge. Every limb limp. He feels exonerated.
Ecstatic. Free.

the bush tucker tour

A long, empty stretch of bitumen slices through the red plain between
Ayers Rock and Katherine, low mulga scrub on either side, the occasional
white-limbed gum. On a scrag of verge a Hertz campervan has pulled over
and a man and a woman get out and stare up at a tree with an old tyre
hanging in one of its branches.

– This must be it, honey.

– I guess.

They scan the road in both directions. The bitumen bubbles at both
ends. The woman is dressed in a golfing hat, a baggy T-shirt, three-quarter-
length cotton trousers and ankle socks. Blotched yellow calves bulge in
the gap between socks and trousers. The man has a large, freckled head
with suckerless curls trailing out from his temples and a streak of white
sun-block running down his nose. As they stand there, the woman offers
the man a swig from a water bottle and he wipes the neck with his hand
before putting it to his lips.

They wait for half an hour. At one point, an opportunistic crow flies
overhead, comes back for a second look, then perches hopefully in a nearby
tree. When nothing else in the landscape changes, they retreat to the
shelter of their campervan and slip into a heat-stifled sleep.

Fifteen minutes later they're woken by a vigorous rapping on the
window. Blocking out the sun is the face of a black woman with a wide,

malleable nose. Her eyes are two slits in a pudding. Behind her is a much older man, a stick of a thing with his skin hanging off his chest in over-lapping waves and a hunted expression in his eyes. The man winds down the window.

– Emmeline, squawks the Aboriginal woman, jerking her thumb at herself. Old fella, Arthur.

Emmeline spits on the ground and waggles a finger in the direction of Arthur's crotch. Mournfully, the old man does up the zip of his trousers.

– Very nice to meet you, says the tourist, scrambling down from the van and holding out a well-padded hand. I'm Dexter J. Kramer and this is my wife, Nancy.

Dexter smiles broadly. Nancy, catching the old Aborigine staring at the sturdy cut of her leg, gives him a hands-off glare. Neither of them will look her in the eye. She takes this as a sign that they're up to no good.

– Keep a tight hold of your camera, she hisses to Dexter as they set off.

– I think they look authentic, dear, mutters Dexter. We're very excited about the bush tucker tour, he adds loudly. Aren't we Nancy? Lead on!

The Aboriginal couple set an unhurried pace. There is nothing much to see around here but scrubby bushes and endless termite mounds. The sky is its usual seamless blue, just a few claw scratches of cloud. No different to Texas, really. They pass some white-trunked gum trees – the sort which look to Nancy as if they had been skinned alive, although in truth she hardly notices them today, so intent is she on scrutinising their guides for signs of ill intent.

– Look! He's got a knife on his belt.

Dexter, who has been staring at the way Emmeline's breasts roll in separate directions as she walks, puts on a baseball cap fitted with an anti-fly veil.

– I'm sure it's –

– Don't tell me *that's* an authentic Aborigine tool, interrupts Nancy, whose mind is already spooling images of the two of them being tied to a tree while the couple run off with their daypacks.

– Relax, Nancy. I'm sure they're good sorts, really. Remember that nice Aborigine at Ayers Rock who practically saved my life?

Nancy did. He had tapped her gruffly on the arm in that rude way the Abos did, and she had been about to brush him off when she realised that he was holding out a bottle of water. Red-faced and on the verge of passing out, Dexter had accepted the water gratefully and Nancy had stuffed a ten-dollar bill in the young man's shirt pocket, which he seemed mightily pleased about. Afterwards she regretted giving him quite so much; it had probably corrupted him.

It had been the highlight of their trip, Ayers Rock. They'd decided to climb it, even though the sign said the local Aborigines would prefer them not to. They agreed it would have been such a terrible waste of money to have come all this way and stay at the bottom. Besides, Dexter needed all the exercise he could get.

The effort had definitely been worth it: the view from the top was breathtaking. You could even see the curvature of the earth. This had given Nancy the heebie-jeebies, and she had made her way down for the most part on her buns. But at least they did better than those thirty-four tourists before them whose hearts had conked out on the way up. Dexter had read somewhere that the local Aborigines grieved for these unfit tourists as if they were members of their own mob, which struck Nancy as somewhat disingenuous, considering they didn't want them there in the first place.

Emmeline and Arthur are waiting for them by a small tree with dark, fissured bark. The old man rests his hand on the trunk, his own skin so weathered and lined itself it could have sprouted from the same tree.

– Dis beefwood tree. Blackfellas burn im. Mix with bacca.

Dexter and Nancy look at him blankly. They have a hard time understanding this pidgin English the Abos speak. Emmeline mutters something. Arthur snaps at her, shaking his head: absolutely not. She barks back. He shakes his head even more vehemently than before. She continues to raise her voice until the old man gives in, turns sheepishly to Nancy and Dexter and sticks out a surprisingly long tongue with a coppery brown gutter running down its length. Causing the bleed of colour is a little mound of well-masticated chewing tobacco.

– We get the picture, thank you, says Nancy, turning her face away. Good heavens. It was enough to put you off your lunch. Dexter wipes the corners of his eyes with his handkerchief.

– Don't laugh, Dexter. You'll only encourage them.

A few paces further on the burly Aboriginal woman comes to a halt at another tree, and waits for them to catch up.

– Dis shitwood, she says.

Dexter and Nancy catch one another's eye.

– Big fire, im stink proper bad. Blackfella make im coolamon. Winnow im seeds and carry baby.

They nod. Nancy tries to think of a question, more to show she's understood than anything else, but can't for the life of her think of one. Meanwhile the old man is marching purposefully towards a third tree.

– Dis spearwood. Blackfella make –

– Yeah, yeah, we get the picture, says Dexter, taking off his daypack and wiping his heat-raddled face. You make your spears out of this one to kill your kangaroos with. Sure thing. Now, what about witchetty grubs? We wanna see one of those.

The old woman's face lights up. – You wan eat witchetty grub?

– We'd like to *see* one, corrects Nancy.

– Where that *ilykuwarra*?

Enlivened, the woman waddles over to a clump of bushes, gets down on her hands and knees and starts hacking at the ground with a stick. It looks to Nancy as if the earth has recently been disturbed already. After no more than thirty seconds, she plunges in a finger, winkles around, and emerges with a large, white, lifeless maggot draped across her palm.

Her eyes are wide with disappointment as she brings it over to show them. Both Nancy and Dexter back off.

– Im dead!

– No! enjoins the old man, coming over to inspect the witchetty grub, his up-till-now opaque features contorting themselves into theatrical expressions of shock.

– Im proper dead.

– Anyone would think it was someone they knew, mutters Nancy.

– We bury im, Emmeline says, and Arthur nods in eager agreement.

– Until the next tourist comes along, mutters Nancy.

Dexter lets out a frustrated sigh. His feet have swelled up inside his leather walking boots and he's got a stitch in his side from walking too soon after breakfast. They've been going for forty-five minutes and so far haven't discovered anything worthwhile.

– What about fire? he asks. Can you guys make fire?

Nancy leans against a tree, feeling faint.

– Doan touch dat tree, missus, says Emmeline sharply.

– I'm not doing it any harm, Nancy retorts. I suppose you're going to tell me only Aborigines are allowed to lean on trees.

She glares at Emmeline defiantly, until something sharp stabs her wrist. She looks down and screams. Enormous green ants are running up her arm and disappearing beneath her shirt sleeve.

– Dex! Dex! They're attacking my armpit!

Dexter, struggling not to laugh, unloops the camera from across his wife's shoulder but manages to get it tangled up with her daypack. Nancy slaps frantically at herself.

– Get them off me, Dexter!

– I'm trying, Nance, I'm trying. You'll have to take your shirt off.

– Not in front of *them*!

Dexter raises two tufts of bleached eyebrows at the Aborigines, but they stay exactly where they are, looking on expressionlessly. Eventually he manages to strip Nancy down to her bra.

– Tenacious little critters, aren't they? Put up quite a fight! Ach! I think they're moving on to me!

When the final ant has seen the underside of Dexter's boot, the Aboriginal couple resume walking.

– What about fire? calls out Dexter, reluctant to take another step unless there's guaranteed pay-back. Let's just do fire, and then we'll head back to the car.

– We find berries now.

Dexter looks around him. Nothing looks lively enough to sprout berries for a ten-kilometre radius.

– We don't want to see any berries. Just start a fire, and then we'll go back.

– Berries part of tour.

– Dammit, we're not interested in berries! Who's paying for this, anyway?

The old couple confer animatedly for a while and then, abruptly, start walking back towards the road. Nancy scratches miserably under her arm. Emmeline snaps off a spray of dried-out gum leaves.

– You start fire traditional way? Dexter catches up with her, eager to break the tension and hoping that his imitation of pidgin English will win them round.

The large woman gives a nod.

– Great. Can't wait.

They are almost back at the campervan when the old man taps Dexter on the arm and jabs a finger at his breast pocket.

– Huh? You want my keys?

The old man nods. Dexter shrugs, hands them over and watches Arthur plod over to the campervan. The sun beats down on the back of their necks. Dexter suspects he has just done something extremely foolish. Nancy suspects so too, but she's exhausted and miserable and hasn't the strength to reprimand him. In any case, she's more than half resigned to a terrible disaster in one form or other and part of her just wants to get it over with. She glances around for something to sit on, but after the escapade with the ants she doesn't trust putting any part of her body in contact with the earth other than her feet.

The old man leaves the engine of the campervan running as he gets out and flips the lid of the petrol cap.

– Open up, Arthur says, nodding towards the bonnet.

Dexter does as he's told. Arthur mutters something to Emmeline. It's her turn to refuse now, and she does so admantly. Arthur repeats himself more forcefully; she shakes her head again. This time he shouts at her, and with a great show of reluctance, which includes a resentful glare at Dexter and Nancy, Emmeline hands over an old cotton hanky with a flower embroidered in one corner. The old man twists it and dips one end into the petrol tank. Meanwhile, Emmeline hoists her large body into the driving seat and revs the accelerator while the old man holds the hanky against the positive and negative leads coming out of the battery.

It catches instantly. Holding the little spool of flame at arm's length, Arthur goes over to where Emmeline has left her spray of leaves on the middle of the blacktop and drops it on top, nudging the twigs with his foot. He fans the flames with his hand and then, as they start to leap into his face, stamps them down with his feet.

For the first time, Arthur's face breaks into a wide, toothless smile.
– Dat fire blackfella way! he says.

Meanwhile, Emmeline is holding out an expectant palm.

– Finish Coldiver Bush Tucker Tour, she says. Twenny dollar for im 'n twenny dollar for me. An little bit tip.

a secret from the world

Billy looks out from beneath a lattice of twigs and small branches that have been laid across his abject body. He has become a secret from the world – and even to himself.

For the first few days he asked questions. Where were they taking him? Why didn't they let him go? What had they done to him? He was weak and could barely manage more than a whisper. They never gave him any answers. He thought perhaps they didn't understand him; that they spoke a different language. Or perhaps he wasn't making any sound. The fainter he became to them, the more unsure he was of his ability to make sense of himself. After a while he stopped talking completely.

They are travelling cross-country. The vehicle, a ute with an open tray on which he lies, lists and rights itself in a way that makes him continually sleepy. The smells of sun-dried earth and scorched grass waft over his face. At times there are corrugations which set the tray juddering, his own body and the lattice of branches caught up in the movement too. For a moment he is back down the shaft, joined like an extra piece of steel to the airleg. He surrenders to this battery, just as he's always surrendered to it, even allowing his teeth to clatter together. Deep in his muscles there is an acceptance that these assaults will lay him to waste one day.

During the day he sees patches of blue between the weave of the branches. Sometimes he follows the disjointed progress of a bird. Sometimes the sun flashes through a gap and he's forced to close his eyes until either the ute or the sun shifts position. At night they remove the lattice and cover him with a blanket, although it doesn't stop him shivering from the cold. Stars blink on and off. The scent of sandalwood smoke clings to the blanket. When his shivering becomes uncontrollable they wrap his limbs up tightly with more blankets, as if in swaddling, and then he relaxes at last, infused with a deep security.

All he knows of them at first are their feet, which he can see from beneath the lattice, lining the edge of the tray. They are crusty and archless, these feet, with thick yellow nails that look more like the talons on a hawk. He has only a vague impression of their legs. Above that, he has a sense that their bodies disappear into thin air.

Every so often, a callused hand yanks the blanket away from his chin and presses the neck of a bottle to his lips. Once he felt the dry graze of a beard on his cheek. The water is acrid, tinged with a chemical sweetness, as if the bottle had originally been used for orange squash. Another time a can is cracked open, and a warm delicious stickiness melts into his mouth and trickles around his neck. His tongue tingles with carbonated fizz. He searches for a pair of eyes to lock onto, grateful as a feeding infant, and just once he finds them – old, rheumy eyes, a yellowish curdling in the whites, a faint blue patina clouding the pupil.

Occasionally, one of them raps angrily on the top of the cabin, shouts something sharp and the ute comes to an abrupt standstill. They jump over the edge and there's a hiss of peeing against the wheels. Three times a day they reach beneath his blanket and grab hold of his inflamed penis, clutching it as if it were a mouse that might get away. He winces as they try to angle it towards the neck of a bottle. He does his best to relax. Usually they have to wait some time, but they don't seem to mind about this. When it comes, the urine drains into the plastic bottle with a deep bell of a note, and when they carry it away, Billy feels strangely proud of himself.

He has no sense of time, or of how many days have passed. There are moments when he wakes, grapples for the memory of who he is, what has happened, why he has been buried alive. The first thing to return is the insistent, rhythmic throbbing of his thighs and penis. But his memory offers him nothing he wants to dwell on, and he relinquishes his grip on consciousness without regret.

Sometimes, when the ute is motionless, flames ripple in the darkness. He sees the whites of their eyes, watching him. Once, he even receives a cheeky wink. He becomes wreathed in smoke, can barely breathe for it. Perhaps, he thinks without any real fear, they have set fire to him. And then he slips away again, swims like a fish in the depths of his mind where no one can reach him. He finds himself back in the house up north. There is pre-recorded laughter from the living room. He slips between the rooms like a ghost, observing, unseen. His father reads a paper at the kitchen table. His mother lies with her feet up on the sofa, watching telly. He has the feeling neither has moved or spoken since he left.

Once he's woken by whistles and hoots and he peers out from his blankets to see a shadowy mingling of bodies in the darkness. Greetings are exchanged. Figures with different smells and different eyes come and get a glimpse of him. Another mob; another language he doesn't understand. He shuts his eyes, dives back down to his mute, underwater world. A woman walks towards him down the hallway. Billy? Billy, is that you? The face is Janelle's. Behind her are three smiling boys. He stoops to their level and holds out his arms to embrace them. But now the woman in his arms is his mother. He can smell the cheap Lily of the Valley perfume she used to wear. Billy? What are you doing? She is older now. Her lips are a slash of orange. Where her teeth should be are a line of jagged termite mounds, crumbling to dust. Who'd have thought it – my son, a digger! She laughs long and hard as she extricates herself from his arms. Don't look at me like that, Billy. I niver did like lookin in them eyes.

Only once does he catch a glimpse of Maisie. She's hiding behind the door of his bedroom. He knows she's there and he creeps in, wanting to surprise her. She clambers out the window, giggling. Come on, Wallamba! Follow me! He goes after her, but in the yard he finds his way blocked by fishing rods and sheets on the line, an overturned camping table – Stan's debris an unnegotiable battlefield. Billy shouts for her to wait but the obstacles keep crashing into him.

Someone cups his head in his hands, tenderly, the touch of a priest. Water spills around his mouth and he slurps at it, eager for what he can get. He is given slices of bread dipped in sickly-sweet condensed milk out of a red-labelled can. He doesn't want to slip away again. He'll cling on now, keep his eyes open. Let the world take him back.

The next morning they lift him out of the ute. Heavy objects drag at his waist. There's a gentle shove on his back. He starts walking, stiffly, unsure how much weight his legs can take. Behind him he hears the drone of the engine receding.

Around him is open bush. It is hot and cloudless. As he walks, his shadow gets shorter and shorter until it's bobbing at his feet like an obedient dog. Tied to his belt hooks are plastic water bottles: they rub painfully against his thighs as he walks. He opens one and drinks half in one go, then pours the rest over his head.

He finds the shell of an overturned car, a fragile young wattle growing through the space where the windscreen used to be, and crawls inside. He sleeps through the worst of the day's heat with his feet sticking out the window. He doesn't emerge until dawn the following day.

They have also hung packets of meat from his belt hooks. Peeling back a leaf bound with twine, he finds still-pink meat oozing blood. He recognises the taste of bush turkey. It is tough and chewy. He scrapes the bone clean with his teeth, and continues to suck on it for the rest of the day.

He sees nothing but a camel wobbling in the heat mirage on long, knobbled legs.

– Hey, Billy shouts, his throat cracking from thirst and disuse, but the camel shows no sign of noticing him.

On the third day he emerges over the brow of a hill to see roos yo-yo from the scrub before him, freshly disturbed, their bounds out of sync. Billy waves his arms.

– Hey! Hey!

They are greys – twenty or thirty of them.

– Hey! Wait for me!

He presses his legs together and tries to bound after them but his muscles won't obey and he collapses to his knees. He carries on watching the roos, smiling at the simple grace of their tails, the sleekness of their flexing backs. He smiles with all of his face.

At dusk he sees a flock of white corellas sitting like bits of torn sheet in the branches of a tree, stark cut-outs against the slate blue sky. The sun has laid off its squabble with him for the day, although not before burning the back of his neck red-raw. Quietness seeps into his pores. He thuds down a gentle slope and sees that it's covered with a purplish haze: Patterson's Curse – every kid knows that. The sight is beautiful, over-whelmingly so, and Billy stands there staring stupidly, not knowing what to do with so much beauty, how to contain it, how to make it a part of him. He walks over it, criss-crossing back and forth, til the light fails completely and his shadow becomes indistinguishable from the purple of the flowers. When he can love it no more he crumples into the flowers and sleeps as he falls.

The next morning he wakes with a swollen tongue. The water bottles are empty. He has been thinking of them as ballast, and now that the water is gone he feels in danger of drifting away. The bush turkey is also finished; by the time he ate the last piece it was beginning to turn.

Even in his delirium Billy knows he must find water. He stumbles down the slope, his ripped jeans flapping like cowboy chaps. At the bottom of the hill two parallel streams glisten sleekly in the sun. He can hardly believe his luck. He lopes with an unsteady gallop, not daring to take his eyes from them in case they dry up before he gets there. He doesn't want to risk blinking. His empty bottles rattle together like muted cow bells. Small birds fly squeaking from the Patterson's Curse. Below him the water flows so fast that for a moment he wonders if he is running across a steep incline, although he cannot feel whether the gradient is falling to the left or the right.

At the first stream he tucks his long hair carefully behind his ears so as not to dirty the water. He falls to his knees, jarringly. Oh, for the bliss of that first soaking! His sticks out his swollen tongue and lowers his face to the glistening, bubbling surface. He can hear its singing hiss.

Immediately he jerks back in pain. His lip and the tip of his nose have been seared. This water is liquid mercury! Tears stream down his face as he rips one of the empty bottles off his belt and clamps it tight to the flow. Nothing happens. Harder, Billy, press it harder. Any minute now the water will stream over, he thinks, pour over his hands, a delicious cooling sluice. *Any second now*. He can't understand why there's no rising scale as it fills the bottle. He has no choice but to wait, however long it takes. There is water here – he can hear it. After a while he lies down between the two streams, holding a bottle out to each. He'll wait for however long it takes.

He hears voices.

– *Bloody hell. You don't half stink.*

The voice is different, unfamiliar.

No, no, he tells the voice. You don't understand. The stream –

– *I s'pose you'll be hungry, eh?.*

He is flat on his back in the ute again, but this time there is no lattice over his face. A rhythm rocks his limbs. *Ker-chunk ker-chunk ker-chunk.* A soft shaft of light warms the lids of his eyes as he sways from side to side.

– Here, ham and pickle alright?

He opens his eyes. A man in a uniform is holding out a sandwich. Billy takes it. It's dry as oats in his mouth but he still can't get it down fast enough. Big pieces of fatty ham that he doesn't have the strength to chew. He chokes on the half-masticated food mounting up. The next moment the man has pulled him upright, and acid vomit is tearing like a stick at the back of his throat. The uniformed man is supporting him under his arms. Billy watches the vomit fly in loosely held strings away from him, warm air scuffing the back of his head. And then he realises where he is: he has his head out of the window of a train.

He needs to flee. As soon as the guard leaves him alone to fetch water he lurches down between the carriages in the opposite direction. Flat-baked, rust-red landscape streaks past. Pale faces stare at him. He wants to merge into this crowd, sit anonymously in a corner, look out of the window, wait for their arrival at the Alice and disembark like any other passenger, as if he'd come all the way from Adelaide or Port Augusta. As if he was there for a reason. The pickle is tart on his tongue. People recoil as he approaches, nudge one another, fall silent. He swings open the door of another carriage. More voices in this one. Loud voices.

– We liked Adelaide very much. So clean and tidy! We can't recommend it enough.

– Isn't it rather hot?

He sees an empty seat and collapses into it, his temple hitting the rounded, red velvet headrest. He nestles in, tucks his arms around his waist.

– Well, it is a little, but there are plenty of cafés. We're used to it, coming from Texas. We couldn't get over how clean it was, could we, Dexter?

– Very impressive.

– Tell them about that scrap with the Abos in the Kimberley, Dexter. They tried to drive off with our campervan!

– Well, they didn't exactly –

– Tell them about Ayers Rock. You've done Ayers Rock, of course. No? Oh, you missed out. It was the highlight of our trip, wasn't it, Dexter? Of course, Dexter nearly had a heart-attack. There are places you're not supposed to go in, sacred caves and all that, but we had a peek anyway. People go dewy-eyed about the natives, but Dexter says it's the Romantic ideal of the noble savage lingering on. He says life was tough and brutal and that's the way they are still. They don't know anything else. We should feel sorry for them, really.

Billy opens his mouth. His tongue is sour. He wonders if he has recently been sick.

– They had meaning, he says.

– What was that, dear? Oh, excuse me, you can't sit there, that's my husband's seat. Dexter? Dexter! Quick, I told you to keep an eye on our seats. Look what's happened now.

– Oi, young man! Get up!

– Excuse me, kid.

– Be quiet over there, will ya? We're trying to watch the film.

– Yes, well we'd like to too, only a rather unsavoury character has just helped himself to my husband's seat. Dexter, why don't you *do* something instead of just *standing* there.

– It's *Casablanca*, Nancy!

– I don't care what film it is! Go and get the guard.

– I'm going to pull the alarm bell.

– Will you be *quiet* down there!

Billy opens his eyes. A man has poked him in the chest – a sharp, unfriendly prod. He seems to have found it firmer than he'd expected. He seems taken aback by Billy's eyes as well, and steps away – at least one step, maybe two.

– Ah! He thinks I'm angry with him! jokes the man, nervously. He has an American accent. – Angry for stopping our train.

The American stands before him in baggy stubbies and knee-high socks. A video camera hangs over his shoulder.

– I am Dexter J. Kramer. This is my wife, Nancy. Pleased to make your acquaintance. What were you doing walking down the railway track? This is the middle of the outback! You might have got yourself killed!

– Get out of my husband's seat.

People are twisting around from their seats to stare at him. They are a sweaty mob, their T-shirts sticking around their middles. Hair crumpled from sleep.

– You don't need to be afraid of me, kid. I'm just a joker. Dexter the big fat joker!

Some people twitter nervously at this, though Billy senses they don't want to collude with the American tourist – at least not yet, not until they know which way this is going to go. The man is stretching out a fat hand crawling with gingery hairs. His English is nasal, dry – has nothing of the easy sway and openness of an Australian. He seems overly eager to prove he isn't scared.

– Let's try again, shall we? I'm Dexter J. Kramer. This is my wife, Nancy. We're pleased to make your acquaintance. Perhaps you'd be kind enough to tell us what you were doing walking down the railway track in the middle of the outback? We might easily have run you down.

Perhaps it had been a mistake to leave the guard's van after all.

– Get out of my husband's seat this instant!

Billy opens his mouth. What he wants – *all* he wants – is somewhere to sit. Why is this such an impossible thing to ask for? He feels the expectancy in the air, the thrill of danger, even amongst those who are pretending not to be listening. The American's sun-bleached eyebrows jut out from the rest of his face.

What? Billy wonders, his anger brimming over. Is it a show of gratitude they're after?

The first fist finds the gap between upper and lower teeth. The American staggers but does not fall. A woman screams. There is blood, pieces of broken teeth. A row of fingernails digs into Billy's arm. He flings the woman off, turns back to the American. Billy has the feeling that this man is responsible for all the trouble he has ever experienced, that he should knock him down before he does any harm to anyone else. The next punch splits the side of a nostril. The third rams into an ear. If he doesn't render this man useless, he will take Billy apart, cut him up into bite-sized pieces and carry him home in that rucksack. Blood

streams down the American's face and he falls back, his large scalp
scraping the wire baggage rack overhead. More pain in Billy's arm – a
set of teeth this time!

– Hey, what dja think yer doing? he cries, throwing the woman off.

He hurls himself on the man's chest. There's a muffled cry and he has
the feeling the two of them are crushing someone else beneath them on
the seat. But he doesn't stop. A river has broken its banks. Billy grabs the
man by the collar of his shirt and hurls him to the floor. Everything is slippery with blood. Billy aches to be left alone, to be allowed to return to his
life. The quicker he can get this done, the better. He kicks hard at the
man's crotch. He kicks again and again. He will be the man he wants to
be. Someone has clambered on his back, is forcing him down under their
weight. Billy's legs crumble all too easily beneath him, nothing but pillars
of sand, the pain blasting off like fireworks in his thighs.

Half-smothered beneath bodies, he hears a voice coming from high in
the corner of the carriage:

– *I think this is the beginning of a beautiful friendship*, it says.

Good, says Billy. Me too.

i hope this finds you

One night, after the children have gone to sleep, Janelle pulls a chair
up to the old wooden writing desk in the living room and lowers the lid.
The hinges complain beneath the weight of her elbows until she remembers to pull out the supporting shaft underneath.

She loves this desk. There are so many drawers and compartments to
discover. She keeps all sorts of things from her childhood in here – pencils
and pens, tubes of glitter, a sheet of gold stick-on stars. She finds a writing
pad and opens it to the first clean page. A blue cat with a letter in its
mouth struts across the top right-hand corner.

She writes his name, makes a circle of the dot above the i. A careful
comma which ends up as big as all the letters. *Dear Billy* . . .

She leans back in her chair, puts the pen in her mouth. Around her
the house is quiet, sighing with the deep breaths of sleep. It's almost

impossible to rouse the boys once they've gone out. You can sit on the edge of the bed and talk to them, stroke their hair, and they might move, but they hardly ever wake up.

She leans forward.

i hope this finds you well. im not sure where you are. We are fine – me, Tommy, Athol and Clyde that is.

She stops, puts the pen in her mouth again. It's not the letter she imagined she would write, but once you start, all the other letters you've ever written in your life have a way of creeping in. Across the street is the irregular outline of roofs against the paler sky. No squares of light in any windows. It's Saturday night, everyone out on the town. She feels as if she's the only person sitting by herself for miles around.

The boys keep asking when your coming round Tommy especially. He did a brilliant drawing of you in your orange overalls at school. The other day he points to that photo of Joe by my bed and says wheres Billy? See he gets you muddled up.

Janelle puts her pen in her mouth. This is more like the letter she'd imagined, but even now she has the urge to retract every sentence once it's finished, once it's too late. She wonders if she will send it. Where she will send it.

Your shift boss Harri came to see me the other day. He brought all your stuff from your caravan. Hes a nice man Harri. he says me and the boys can come and stay with him and his wife Laura at their property in the Alice some time. i was rapt. he says she's spot on, his wife Laura, that she and me will be great mates. i like the way he says that, spot on. i wonder why we didnt ever visit them in the Alice before, you and me. why didn't you think of it Billy? Anyway, you know where we are if you want us. And your stuff. We arent moving to Esperance just yet although that is still the long term plan. Your loving

– she scribbles out loving, then realises she can't leave it like that, and writes over the top –

your very own Ellie XXXX (that's kisses, one from each of us, not the beer.)

this is my band

– That yours?

Jimmi looks up. A little boy, stark naked, is pedalling his bike in circles around the mattress.

– 'Syours if you want it, says Jimmi. He leans back against the wall of his house.

The boy nods and rides off, his buttocks lifting from the seat while he fast-pumps, then sitting back down to free-wheel. He swerves away from a heap of garbage just in time, then weaves through a row of rusted oil drums. When he gets to the last house he lets the bicycle fall, wheels still spinning as he runs inside.

Jimmi would've given the mattress to Emmeline and Arthur if they hadn't disappeared a few weeks ago, when Sydney Coldiver left town. Nobody knows where they've gone. Leaving it out on the edge of the road seemed the next best thing to do. He knew it'd either be demolished by termites or dingoes or crows, or carted off by someone within a day or two.

He surveys his vegetable garden. The bare soil is too cracked and dense to reason with the blade of a spade, but still there is evidence of life – steely, determined life. Coarse, yellow stalks climb up the fence, reaching out with dry tendrils. Clusters of still-green tomatoes, melons and pumpkins squat in the shade of their own wizened leaves. The occasional toughened bean blinks through the foliage. The bough of a mango tree hangs over the garden, heavy with enough breakfasts to last him two whole months. Beneath the bough lie the rotting remains of wasp-eaten fallers, halfway to compost.

There's a shout from down the road. Jimmi looks up to see the naked boy emerging from his house with two other kids in tow. Enough hands to carry a stained old mattress away. He goes back inside, pleased that he won't have to look at it any more. In the main room, a circular woven rug in gold and brown and cream, stuck with little shards of spinifex, now lies on the concrete floor, covering the turkey blood stain. His chair with its woven seat, a little more unravelled than before, serves as a stand for a bulky old TV. Where the mattress used to be, a once-vibrant but now faded hammock cuts a generous curve through the air, the ropes disappearing through opposite windows and tied to sturdy mangoes either side.

He's about to throw himself into the hammock when a noise startles him.

Dring-drriiing!

He stares at the bright red telephone.

– Yeh?

He scratches at the seat of his brown trousers.

– Yeh. Yeh. Now's alright.

He puts the receiver down. As he straightens up he notices an old jam jar filled with water standing on the window sill. A flower with an orangey-pink trumpet lolls against its lip. After a moment's hesitation, he takes it out and tucks it, stalk still dripping, behind his ear.

The first to arrive is Shane, carrying his guitar awkwardly by its neck. It's about the same size as the boy himself, and similarly tatty, little chips knocked out of the curves, just like the cuts and grazes on the boy's own body. But once it's wired up, the machine has a surprising amount of life, and Shane can persuade it to part with some excoriating chords.

– I can play pretty, too, if you want. He wipes the heel of his hand across the strings. – Man, I c'n even make you cry.

One dirty foot tapping, this scrawny adolescent has talent, Jimmi has decided – the sort of talent that someone should've spotted in himself once, years ago. He's going to nurture it, develop it; someone has to, after all. When he closes his eyes and listens to Shane play, he can almost hear the spirit of the full-grown man in there, and he wants to see that man out.

Judd arrives five minutes later with arms laden: tambourines, a triangle, various sizes of drum. This brother makes up for his lack of obvious ability with a flair for innovation. He proudly displays a hoard of stolen utensils from the kitchen cupboards at school – rubber spatula, wooden chopsticks, rolling pin.

– Quiet! yells Jimmi, when Shane joins him in experimenting with this pile of clobber. Quit the racket, both of youse!

There's a cough behind him. He turns around and immediately does a double-take. A woman stands framed in the doorway, dressed in a plain white dress with delicate straps over her smooth shoulders. In her nose is a tiny, glittering stud. Jimmi opens his mouth but finds nothing to say as Estha glides serenely between them, taking her place behind the microphone with a knowing smile.

Jimmy forces himself to snap to. – G'day, Estha. Good ter see ya.

Standing back, he surveys this motley crew he has brought together with his jet black eyes. He's glad he shaved today. He even washed his hair a few days ago: the springy mop is fluffed with life.

– I'm boss, he says. We gotta get that straight. You play what I say, OK?

Shane and Judd eye one another, shiftily.

– That depends how good your songs are, boss, teases Estha.

The boys titter, but Jimmi silences them with his glare.

– This is my band. Youse either in it or not. No half measures.

He looks at them one by one until he's given a nod by each.

– OK, boss.

– Alright. Good stuff. No worries.

He closes his eyes and brings his palms together. It takes a few moments to recover the atmosphere, the way it made him feel. But once he does it's like stepping onto a ready-made raft in a moving current. He opens his mouth and, unaccompanied at first, lets out his thin, tenor voice.

------

the only one who steps out into the rain

Billy sits on top of the newly made bed in clothes that have been found for him: wide grey trousers, far too big around the waist, a faded blue shirt with the cuffs rolled up. Everything is held in and up on his gaunt, tall body with a soft brown belt, the end of which sticks out stupidly, no loop for it to go through. They probably belonged to that poor bastard who croaked in his first week, Billy has decided.

Cecily has brought him another plate of chips, still apparently believing that this is all he likes to eat.

– They all say you'll be back in the blink of an eye.

– Some faith in me they have.

He picks at the chips one by one. Cecily eats some herself.

– Got a visitor downstairs, says Cecily.

Billy carries on eating in silence.

– A woman. Cecily gazes absently towards the man in the next bed, propped up against his pillows, trying to pretend he's not listening. She gets up and pulls the curtain crisply between the two beds, as she so often does. – Says she's ya mother.

Billy has a chip halfway to his mouth. He returns it to the plate.

– There's a turn-up for the books.

Cecily can't help shooting him a quick look of triumph. – Seems ter want ter see ya.

– Meddling bitch.

– You shouldn't talk about yer mother like that!

– Like fuck I shouldn't.

– You should be ashamed of yerself, Billy.

Both of them have lost their appetites now. Billy knows Cecily's got a personal investment in this: she wants to hand him into the care of another woman, someone who will look after him as she has done, so that her work will not have been wasted. He sits there, puffing through his nose, angrily. After a while he goes back to eating, stuffing the chips in without tasting them.

She helps him put some shoes on, easing the reluctant feet into their unfamiliar cages. She presses the soft fabric over the toes in the way that shoe-fitters in Perth did when he was small. They're about two sizes too big.

– Mebbe you'll grow into em.

– *Mebbe*.

He says it sharply, mimicking her staccato way of speaking, appealing to her eyes with his own. She meets his gaze then looks quickly away. At first she seems hurt, but soon he catches her struggling to hide a smile.

Billy laughs: his turn to enjoy a triumph now.

He takes the lift down to the ground floor, passing along the corridor on his crutches and nodding at one or two of the staff he has got to know over the past weeks. Some of them make a fuss about his civvies. You look like you've walked out of a bank, they say. All I need is a bag of swag over me shoulder, he replies. They walk on, marvelling what a good job they've done. He would never have joked with them like that when he first came in.

She's standing in the corner of the canteen with her back to him, pushing coins into a vending machine. She has on a fitted cream skirt and a turquoise top, the ridge of her bra strap showing through the thin fabric. The coins slide down with a chunk. When nothing rolls out, she slams her palm against the front of the machine.

– Bloody bugger.

– Can I have a Violet Crumble instead?

– You'll get whatever comes out, Miss Pretty. *If* anything comes out.

A little girl with brown skin and a startling mass of gold, corkscrew curls slides off a chair nearby, her dress riding up around her hips. Under one arm she clutches a knitted croc. Billy stares at her. She has the prominent brow, tobacco-brown eyes lost in shadow beneath. She and Crystal turn their heads at the same moment.

– Well, look at you, says Crystal. You've grown a body on ya.

Billy feels giddy. Whatever animosity had been bubbling in him a moment ago is vanishing as swiftly as water pouring through a sluice. He cannot get enough of the face of this little girl.

– What are those? the girl asks, staring at Billy's crutches.

Billy lifts one up. – Extra legs.

– This bloody machine's eaten my money, says Crystal, flatly.

– What dja need em for? asks the girl.

– This. Billy gets down on his knees and slides one of the crutches under the vending machine. He comes away with a large safety pin twisted into a hook. Within a few seconds, he has persuaded the vending machine to part with three cans of Coke and a Violet Crumble, free of charge.

– That's right, you set her a bad example. Crystal puts her hand on the dazzling head of hair. – Entcha gunna thank im, Beth?

– She's rilly pretty, says Billy.

– What's wrong with your real legs, though?

– You caught her on a good day, says Crystal. Usually she won't get out of her jarmies, willya, Miss B. She even wears jarmies to school.

– You'd fit right in around here, says Billy.

Crystal fidgets with her nails, her eyes flitting round the room. – Quite a surprise. Seein ya.

– Yeh.

– I got a call from some bloke called Harri.

– Ah, didja. Billy nods, smiling.

– Says 'e only just tracked you down imself. Lucky 'e did, says Crystal. Could've been anywhere in the world for all I knew.

Billy hunches into his crutches, not knowing what to say.

– Well. C'n a woman smoke in here?

He leads them to a table. His hands are shaking slightly. Crystal pulls out a chair for Beth. She climbs onto it, knees first, then twists around to sit. Within seconds she slips off again.

– She'll be alright. Likes ter go and introduce herself ter everyone else in the bloody room. Anyway. There's somethin bad to tell ya, Billy. It's Stan.

Billy looks up.

– He's dead, Billy. I blame meself, so does Stevo. We shoulda seen it coming, but it's no use thinking that now.

Billy looks dumbly at her pack of Horizon 50s. Crystal pushes the pack towards him.

– It was a bloody mess. Beth was the one to find im, poor kid. Hung imself from a tree.

Their eyes meet through the flame of Billy's lighter.

– I'm sorry, Billy. It's an awful thing ter hev ter tell ya.

Billy pulls his cigarette away.

– I'd hev told you sooner, only I didn't know how ter reach ya. I should've left years ago, I suppose. Might've saved im if I did. Some great gift to mankind I must've thought I was, indispensable. But Stevo disappeared soon after I got pregnant with Beth and, well, I needed im. I got that one wrong, didn't I?

– When did it happen?

– Few weeks ago.

Billy stares at the table. – I reckon I'm to blame too.

They both look at where Crystal is making shapes out of spilled sugar granules with a finger.

– Everyone's got to be responsible for themselves in the end, dontcha think? says Crystal quietly.

Billy nods at the table.

Beth, careering up to the table, surprises them both by slamming an empty jam jar down between them.

– That woman gave it to me, she says loudly. For grasshoppers. For Lizzy.

Crystal manages a weary smile. – That'd be Lizzy the lizard.

– Oh, right, says Billy.

– 'E chomps through a dozen bloody grasshoppers a day. We got im in a biscuit tin, in the car.

– We need to go and catch some, says Beth.

She is beautiful, this child, with her slow way of blinking, the luminous framework of her startling hair. When she looks back at Billy, her eyes are empty of everything but this need for grasshoppers. Go on, he says to himself. You know about children now.

– I know a place.

– Billy's got bad legs, interrupts Crystal. You'll hev ter get yer own grasshoppers. What we're doing cartin around a lizard in a tin beats me, anyway.

– I love Lizzy.

– Yeah, well, if you rilly loved him, you'd let im out. He'd be a lot happier then.

She gives a brief, awkward glance at Billy.

– There'll be some in the paddock behind the car park, says Billy. I've heard em out there, chirpin away.

Billy's heart is thudding. His legs feel drained of strength. He looks at Crystal's hands. Her fingers draped over the cigarette still look young – pale and slim, the nails cut straight across.

– It's good you've got a kid, says Billy, turning to her suddenly. Help you through it. Kids are what matters, where everything starts.

Crystal looks him in the eye.

– Yep. She's good news, ay.

They hold each other's gaze, then look at Beth, fiddling with the lid of the jam jar.

– So, me and Miss B are movin to Sydney, Crystal says, injecting an artificial brightness in her voice. I got a job at David Jones selling cosmetics, believe it or not. I always wanted ter go back ter the city.

– That sounds good, says Billy.

– And Miss B will go to a decent school, none of this School of the Air crap like what you had. She looks momentarily confused. – Oh, I brought something for ya.

She retrieves a plastic bag from the floor, twisted around at its neck. It lands with noisy clunks on the table.

– No prizes for gissin what's in there. I thought you wouldn't want me to leave em behind. Hope there wasn't anything else you wanted. We cleared out pretty good.

Billy looks at the bag and allows his smile to hitch up. – Thanks.

– So, what are you gunna do now? Go back to the mines?

Billy shakes his head. – They won't take me back. Wouldn't want to if they could.

– What, not even when you're better? I heard it's good money.

– Not for a bloke with dicky legs.

Crystal grinds her cigarette out in the ashtray. – So will ya get work here in Alice?

– Maybe.

– As good a place as any, I spose, she says, without enthusiasm. Beth, do ya need to use the dunny before we go?

Beth is looking at Billy intently, squirming, her body angled uncomfortably in the chair.

– I played with your stones.

She says it as if it were a confession. Billy meets her gaze.

– Mum said I could.

– That's alright.

– I liked the smooth ones best, she says. The ones that Stevo made. Stan used ter like the rough ones.

Crystal folds her still-smoking stub over in the glass ashtray. – Played with them for hours, she did, she says quietly.

Billy looks at the bag, the outlines of the individual stones just showing through.

– You c'n keep them if you want, he says.

Beth shakes her blonde ringlets. – Stevo told me to give them to ya. He said I'd find my own in Sydney.

– That'll be interesting, mutters Crystal.

Billy smiles. He takes the bag and puts it by his feet.

– Were you Mr B when you were little, like I'm Miss B? Beth asks.

Billy catches Crystal's eye but she looks away, her eyes flecked with guilt. Billy finds himself laughing.

– No, but it's never too late to start. Mr B – I like it.

Crystal manages a small smile too. Then she looks down and checks her watch.

– We better git a wriggle on. Aiming to make Erldunda before dark. Sorry we can't stay longer. I didn't know whether you'd still be here or if you'd even –

– That's OK.

Crystal gazes at her empty hands, as if searching for ideas.

– We'd be rapt if you'd come and see us in Sydney, wouldn't we, Miss B? she says, her face lighting up. Maybe you could come with Stevo, one time. Or not. I dunno.

Billy nods. – Yeh, I'd like ter come.

– Jiss make sure you bring some grasshoppers with ya, ay.

At the top of the hospital steps he puts the bag of stones down and tucks one crutch under an arm. He takes Cecily's shoulder and presses his lips into her plump cheek. It gives like a cushion. He grins again, liking the fact that her last sight of him is as he is supposed to look, more or less – clean-shaven and upright, at least. A socialised creature.

– How did it go with your mother?

– Alright. My dad is dead.

Cecily looks at her feet. – Sorry bout that, she mumbles.

– He wasn't happy.

Cecily looks out at the road, gives a nod.

– Are you ready for this? she says after a while.

– I feel ready.

– Don't come back now.

– Thanks.

– The women out there won't let you back, I reckon. Not when they discover what you got tucked between your legs!

She gives him one of her smirks.

– You're a real man now, Billy. Here.

She presses something small and pliable into his chest. He turns it over. James's notebook.

– Aw, yeh.

– Dr Porter has been trying to get you sectioned. He thinks you're a schizophrenic.

– Yeh, I know.

– You're the closest he's come to a decent case study for his end-of-year presentation.

Billy flicks through the notebook, almost every page dense with pencil jottings.

– Does 'e know I've been discharged?

Cecily looks at her watch. – You haven't. You've got an appraisal with Ann in half an hour. Better get out of here quick chop.

– And what about Dexter J. Kramer?

– You ain't worth suing without the hospital behind you. Oh, this is for you, too.

She loops a plastic supermarket bag over his wrist.

– Two oranges, a hospital toothbrush guaranteed to make your gums bleed or you git your money back, and your medication. You gotta finish the antibiotics. And register with a doctor straight away. If the legs don't heal up completely, the infection will come back worse. Don't be a silly bugger about it.

– Are ya gunna get into trouble for this, Cecily?

– It's the sorta thing they'd expect you ter do, walk out.

He smiles. – I owe you.

She wipes the back of her hand across her mouth. – That's bull. You only owe yourself.

Billy looks up at the sky. The light has dimmed in the last few minutes: strange clouds are moving quickly overhead. He turns his attention to the steps, tackling them one at a time, sideways on. Cecily watches him go, concentrating on his behalf. At the bottom he's brushed by a man in a white coat, hurrying in the opposite direction, and for a second Cecily worries that it'll knock the confidence out of him. Billy hesitates a while, then takes a step back under cover of the hospital roof, his shoulders hunching. His head seems disproportionately small now that his hair has been cropped short. She sees him look up and looks up too and realises that it has started to rain: a few big, heavy drops. Within ten seconds it's a downpour and people are starting to hurry towards the steps, yelling in amazement as they hold bags and folded newspapers over their heads. Huddles of people converge on the bottom step beneath the overhang of the roof, sharing exclamations – a sudden bond. It hasn't rained here in over a year.

Cecily watches Billy to see how he will cope with this unexpected event. She knows what he wants – what all of them want; to somehow follow one of these people into the streets of the Alice and let them lead him into a new life. To have the decisions made for him. It wouldn't have to be much of a life; in fact it would be better if it wasn't.

– You're not considered a local until you've seen the Todd flood three times, she'd said to him the day before. That means you gotta hang around for about ten years.

He had taken this in, smiling, as if he were fully intent on following whatever rules were necessary in order to belong. He seemed to want to belong, but you never could tell completely. She watches him round his shoulders again, tighten his grip on the crutches. He looks at the people milling around him, cowering under the hospital roof. There are discharged patients with their families waiting for taxis, nurses wanting to get home at the end of their shifts. But no one wants to cross the unprotected forecourt where the rain is streaming down in long, shining threads – they'd be drenched to the bone within seconds. They lean their heads together, discussing how long they think it will be before this outburst eases off.

She hears the sound of the crutches and turns back. Of them all, he is the only one who steps out into the rain.

it moves on

Outside the roadhouse, a sickly yellow streetlamp flickers briefly, then goes out. Moments later it springs on again. Goes out, springs on, goes out. For a minute or two it disco-lights the pale new boards that Stevo's nailed up across the roadhouse windows.

On the servo forecourt next door, a marble-twisted eye opens – Yakka, registering the alteration in the constituents of the night, even in her sleep. She sticks her nose in the air and sniffs. There is no wind tonight, but she can sense one approaching.

Nearby, Stevo lies on the sofa cushions with his arms flung wide as if in anticipation of a passionate embrace, belly bursting between singlet and boxers like an overripe tomato. An upturned rubber thong, worn to shreds, lies where he last kicked it. It was too stifling to sleep indoors tonight, so here he is on the forecourt for anyone passing to see. He gives a complicated snore and the envelopes of Yakka's ears flick up.

The streetlamp goes out again, and this time it stays out for good. The darkness of the surrounding bush bites down on the tail end of the town. Yakka's nostrils twitch. A warm wind suddenly ruffles the hairs along her back like the return-stroke of a hand. She tries to catch the wind in her teeth, to suck it up her nose, but the wind is too quick and gets away.

Above, something glimmers like a slick of spilled cream in a sky that is a little darker than before: the Milky Way, shuffling its outer edges. Yakka looks up and sees a cosmic reflection of the zig-zag markings on her own muzzle. With a little whine of contentment, she resettles her nose on her paws, lets her ears fold over, and closes her eyes again.

The wind gusts over the galvanised roof of Stevo's house and drops down the other side. It takes a quick spin around the paddock. A rattle and a rustle in the gum trees, and then it moves on.

epilogue

the voices

The spirit child stops running and wipes her nose on the back of her hand. She tips her head to one side. For a minute there she thought she heard someone whistling.

Directly ahead there is a stand of snappy gums with clusters of delicate, pale green leaves. She could do with some shade and a comfortable place to sit, so she runs over and hauls herself onto one of the lower branches – a perfect bough that looms in a pinkish curve against the blue. Leaning her head back and swinging one foot, she looks around her. The red sandstone plain with its horseshoes of spinifex and termite mounds goes on for as far as she can see.

She jerks upright. There it is again. It sounds like 'Waltzing Mathilda'. It's very faint; very far away. Fully alert now, she listens with all her attention.

Who's there?

The whistling fades away. Then, from another direction completely, comes the soft, lilting voice of a little girl, singing. It's a nursery rhyme, although the spirit child can't make out the words. She follows it through one verse and a jangly chorus. It breaks off suddenly.

Please don't stop, the spirit child begs.

There's a small silence, and then the song starts up again: a second monotonous verse. The spirit child draws her knees up to her chest and closes her eyes. The broken light plays on her face. It might be an irritating song and totally out of tune but there's something soothing about it.

Sing, she urges quietly. Sing.

Suddenly there's a burst of warbling soprano from behind her right ear, so loud that it nearly knocks her off her perch. The spirit child leaps to her feet and turns around but sees nothing except the empty spinifex plain. She looks the other way. Nothing. In the distance, the nursery rhyme girl has arrived at the chorus again – upping the volume this time, which sends her even more off-key. The spirit child sits down and is about to shut her eyes when a deep, thunderous baritone bubbles up from below, making the leaves tremble over her head.

– *Don Giovaaaaani!!!*

The spirit child curls her toes over the branch and stands up.

Sing! she cries. *Sing!*

Even as she's getting her balance she hears new voices: a hearty, country singer accompanied by a guitar to her left – *We're the boys from the bush and we're back in town* – and a responding bellow from her right: *Oh, what a terrible place is a pub with no beer!* Suddenly she doesn't know where to turn. She can hear voices in every direction, a whole discordant gaggle of them coming from all over the continent. They clash and trill and screech and trumpet, competing to drown one another out – but it doesn't matter because it's mesmeric, all this singing, it shows that people can hear her, and she can hear them. The spirit child imagines them singing as they run down the street in the rain, leaping puddles, grasping folded-up newspapers over their heads. She imagines them singing as they tramp through dripping ferns in the rainforest, a chorus of burping frogs all around. *Sometimes, all I need is the air that I breathe and to love you!* She imagines people singing into the soaring, resonant heights of the eucalyptus forests, startling koalas from their sleep. She imagines them singing in mid-air as they fly over ragged sandstone mountains in a blustering-engined Cessna, the passenger door ripped off and a sharp-eyed cattle dog barking at their side. *It's still the same old story, a fight for love and glory* . . . She imagines them singing in the shower, working up a good lather under their armpits, soap streaming down their chests and legs, pausing for a moment – because it was as if they had sensed someone listening just now, someone outside the bathroom door – and they call out, Molly? or Frank? Is that you? Dja need to come and use the loo? But they know that Frank or Molly is in the kitchen frying eggs for breakfast and sliding them onto a plate, and so they start up again. *Jiss one cornetto!* they holler, tonsils quivering, belting out with wild abandon these songs which are half-drowned in the jet of water thrumming against the shower door, but which are making their way into the ether nevertheless. Waderloo! *Do-de-do do-de-do, Waderloo!* they go, abruptly switching songs whenever they don't know the words – *It's such a perfect day* . . . – and wondering why they don't sing more often when it makes them feel as good as this – because it massages your heart, opens up your ribcage, makes the oxygen thrill in your veins. *O mia diletta!*

The spirit child claps a hand over her mouth. She can't remember ever hearing such a dreadful racket in her life. She jumps down from the snappy gum branch and runs across the sun-baked earth. Something catches her eye on the ground and she stops and picks it up.

This for me?

She grips the shiny pink ribbon between her front teeth, pulls her untamed hair back roughly and ties the ribbon in a bow, tugging the ends hard to make it stay.

Then she waves her arms about like a conductor.

Sing! Sing! shē shouts, and the voices get louder and louder – so loud that she has to clamp her hands over her ears.

acknowledgements

I would like to thank London Arts for helping to fund the writing of this book, and the MacDowell Colony for providing a cabin in the woods at a critical moment in its development.

I am indebted to the one-and-only Rossco Clarke, who hired me as his assistant sparky and so began a fateful journey; Colin Russ and Peter Lacy for taking me barra fishing and being so gracious in the face of my incessant questioning; Heather Millar for being my friend and bringing me to Australia in the first place; Lara Ivanovic for persuading me, rightly, that two poms let loose in the outback have more fun than one; Peter and Judy Dring and family for their ever-welcoming hospitality and help with all things Western Australian; Malcolm Douglas for introducing me to his kangaroos; Dr Rachel Elderkin and Dr Simon Harries for advice on medical matters; and Rob and Cath Brooks for the crash course on nickel mining. Thank you to Clare Alexander and Catherine Blyth for unstinting support and editorial brilliance; Ethan Nosowsky, Ella Berthoud, Carl Thomas, Brendan Charles and Charmaine Yabsley for their expert reading, encouragement and love; and, once again, my parents David and Doreen Elderkin, for keeping faith.

P.S.

Ideas,
interviews
& features...

About the author

2 Profile

4 Life at a Glance

About the book

6 The Bigger Picture

Read on

10 Have You Read?

11 If You Loved This, You'll Also Like...

Profile

'WRITING STORIES is something I've felt compelled to do ever since I can remember,' says Susan Elderkin. 'At the age of six I taught myself to do joined-up handwriting so that I could get my stories down more quickly. God knows why I thought the world needed them so urgently.'

Brought up in Surrey with an older brother and sister by her architect father and mother, a concert pianist turned piano teacher, hers was in fact a musical childhood first and foremost. She was an accomplished pianist and flautist until she was 18, when she realized that being a musician wasn't where her heart lay and promptly stopped playing. Meanwhile, she carried on churning out stories. When she was ten she wrote a detective novel called 'The Last Smuggler' – 'a blatant Enid Blyton rip-off' – that brought her to the attention of her headmaster. 'He called me in and said I had a peculiar way of spelling "peculiar", but that I shouldn't let that stand in my way because I had what it took to be a writer.' It was several years, she says, before she realized that 'peculiar' didn't have a 'q' in it.

She went on to read English at Cambridge, spending her time reading rather than writing, and it was only when she went to live in Los Angeles, aged 23, that she began taking her writing seriously again – in between sunbathing sessions on Venice Beach. 'That was when I went to Joshua Tree National Park for the first time and got totally hooked on the desert. I lay spread-eagled on the top of a granite boulder and had one of those epiphanies when your perception of the world shifts and you know nothing is going to be the same again. I had fallen in love, I suppose. I decided right then that I would come back one day and write a novel out in the desert.'

With the stories she had written that summer she gained a place (and that year's Curtis Brown scholarship) on the University of East Anglia's creative writing MA course where she started a story about an overweight man practising yoga in the desert. Encouraged by her fellow writers to turn it into a novel, she swiftly wrote two chapters and applied for a Wingate Scholarship to buy her time to finish it. 'With the money I got straight back on a plane to LA, although I didn't have a clue what I was going to do when I got there. A friend and I did a Thelma-and-Louise trip around Arizona in an open-topped Chevy and I decided that the Sonora Desert, just south of Tucson, was the right place for the book.' A series of serendipitous meetings resulted in her being lent a car and a house out there, and she stayed for several months. 'I went hiking every day, discovering all the plants and animals – and the local cowboys,' she says. 'I became fascinated by the sort of people you find in remote places. In Arizona they're like the cacti – often loners, with their own brand of prickles and spines. It seemed to me that if you got to grips with the landscape, you could start to understand the people.'

When she got back she became a freelance journalist, contributing interviews to various magazines. This proved invaluable experience. 'It taught me to be less precious about getting words down, and that was a great thing to take over into fiction. You've got to explore when you're writing, and it's only ▶

❢ You've got to explore when you're writing, and it's only by getting on with something that you work out what it's about and how to write it. ❢

3

LIFE
at a glance

Author photo © Delia Noel

BORN

Sussex, 1968.

EDUCATED

Local comprehensive
in Dorking;
Downing College,
Cambridge;
MA at the University
of East Anglia.

CAREER

A bit of almost everything
from waitressing to work-
ing as an ice-cream seller at
Chessington Zoo and
teaching English in a
Slovakian shoe factory. She
became a freelance jour-
nalist in 1994 and teaches
creative writing in the UK
and abroad.

MARRIED

No

PUBLISHED

*Sunset Over Chocolate
Mountains* (2000)
The Voices (2003)

◄ by getting on with something that you work out what it's about and how to write it.'

Her first novel, *Sunset Over Chocolate Mountains*, brilliantly combined her desert research with experiences from her time teaching English in a Slovakian shoe factory after she left Cambridge. 'I was teaching thirty male computer technicians to read their manuals,' she recalls. 'The lessons were hilarious because I couldn't understand the manuals any better than they could. They would take me on tours round the factory, which was like something out of a fairytale with its red-and-white striped chimney and row upon row of sewing machines and really dated shoes.' Not in the note-keeping habit in those days, Elderkin had to rely on her memory. 'In some ways it was good not to have brought back too much information as you can get straitjacketed by facts. All you really need is what's right for the story.'

The novel was a critical success, and she moved on to her second, *The Voices*, set in another remote place – this time Western Australia. 'I steeped myself in Australiana to write it. It was a bit like doing a PhD on the country – I had to learn its geography, politics, history, biology, and a whole new language. But it wasn't arduous because I loved it – the rust-red earth, the musky eucalypts ... It totally got under my skin.'

Now working on her third novel, Elderkin says she is resisting setting this one in a far-flung corner of the world. 'I felt it would be good for me to concentrate on other aspects of writing, rather than place. Besides, I've got to break this desert fixation sooner or later. It's very antisocial.' Having said that, if one of her characters suddenly decides to jump on a plane to the Sahara, she says she's not going to stand in their way. 'I read somewhere that an author shouldn't judge their characters. That means you have to go along with them, whether you like what they're doing or not.' ∎

LIFE *at a glance*
(continued)

AWARDS

A Betty Trask Award (2000); named by Orange Futures as one of the twenty women writers to watch out for in the twenty-first century (2001); selected as one of *Granta*'s best young British novelists of the decade (2003); *The Voices* shortlisted for the Ondaatje prize (2004).

❛ I felt it would be good for me to concentrate on other aspects of writing, rather than place. Besides, I've got to break this desert fixation sooner or later. It's very antisocial. ❜

The Bigger Picture

I am a desert junkie. So it wasn't surprising that I should find myself in Australia. What was surprising, perhaps, was that I should find myself in a pub in Derby, on the edge of the Kimberley, trying to get myself hired as an assistant to an electrician.

The electrician's name was Rossco, and he was known locally as one of the few people bold enough – or crazy enough – to drive up the notoriously treacherous Gibb River Road in the wet season 'jiss for the sport'. Much of the Kimberley is semi-tropical with a sweltering dry season and a very wet wet season, when the rivers flood and entire communities can be cut off for up to four months at a time. Wild and craggy, there are deep gorges fed by plunging waterfalls, edged by pandanus palms and home to lurking crocodiles. There is also acre upon acre of nothing but iron-barks and cattle and, lapping tantalizingly to the south, the expanse of the Great Sandy Desert. What had drawn me to the area was that, even by Australian standards, it is remote and I suspected that I would find the sort of people I liked to write about here – people in touch with the land, and of the land.

Rossco had a government contract to service air-conditioning units in far-flung Aboriginal schools in the Kimberley, and every few months he made a round trip of these communities, dropping in on his mates' cattle stations along the way. Some were accessible by 4WD; others required a small plane to get to. As chance would have it, he was due to set off on one of these trips the very next morning. I was determined to go with him.

'Don't suppose you need an assistant?' I asked him.

Rossco took a slow draught of his beer then looked me up and down. 'You a sparky?'

'No, but I can change a plug,' I said.

He gave a little grunt and turned back to his beer.

'And I can read a map.'

This was clearly an even more derisory skill in an area with so few roads. He snorted half his beer back into his glass. Then something seemed to occur to him. He wiped his lips and twisted round on his stool.

'Tell ya what,' he said. 'I'll hire ya. On one condition.'

'What?'

'I'll supply the swags, the food, the petrol and do the driving. But you've gotta buy all the beer.'

We shook hands on what was in fact a more equitable arrangement than I realized at the time, and he handed me his business card. 'Serendipity Electrical Services', it read. I reckoned I was on the right track.

Setting a novel in a country other than the one in which you live is always going to be a challenge. Writing a novel involving Aborigines brings with it extra issues – for a white person, it is considered more or less taboo. But in the course of reading about Australian Aborigines, I had come across something that particularly intrigued me – the art of 'love magic', when a woman sings up the man she wants to marry and makes him love her for ever. I wanted to find out more.

In the event, what I found in the Kimberley was more personal and more ▶

> ❝ Writing a novel involving Aborigines brings with it extra issues – for a white person, it is considered more or less taboo. ❞

◀ relevant. I met Davey, an Aboriginal stock-man with ten black toenails and no front teeth, who drove a bull buggy like it was a horse. I sat round a campfire with Daisy, who insisted on sleeping on the roof of her van because she believed the dingos howling in the distance to be the ghosts of murdered people. I saw the sky after rain, a strip of clear white on the horizon, a woolly grey blanket above, and then saw Daisy notice it too. I waded into a river in my clothes while Roy, who never once looked me in the eye, kept watch for salties, revolver at the ready. I drove in the billowing dust of a ute spilling over with gangly-limbed men coming back from the grog run, cartons of beer stacked high. I shared a tyre for a seat in the back of another ute with Jake, drunk and mad as a cut snake, who threw anything you gave him, and a few things you didn't, over the edge. I heard the words of a song and they stuck in my mind: 'And the spirits will take care/Of the place we once called home.' I left the Kimberley with-out finding anyone to tell me more about love magic.

But it was right that way. Once I was there, I understood that it wasn't my place to ask.

Novels have a way of surprising the person who writes them. You start off thinking it's going to be about one thing, and halfway through – or even only a page in – the novel sticks out a teachery finger and goes, *not that way, but this!* As a white person, I was never going to understand Aboriginal culture, but what I did get a sense of, like many others before me, was a landscape imbued with an intense spirituality, where every tree, every

❛ As a white person, I was never going to understand Aboriginal culture, but what I did get a sense of was a landscape imbued with an intense spirituality ❜

rock, every creature bristles with something ancient and infinitely larger than yourself. And along with this feeling comes another – how one culture, believing itself to be spiritually depleted, yearns for the spiritual riches of another, older culture, and attempts to appropriate it. It didn't take me long to realize that my book would itself be a metaphor for this act of appropriation.

While on the road with Rossco I didn't change a single plug, but I talked to a lot of people, heard a lot of stories, and drank quite a lot of beer (although not as much as Rossco). However far you travel, though, you inevitably come back to yourself. The stories you tell can only ever be the ones that were inside you all along.

Susan Elderkin

The names of the Aboriginal people have been changed. Rossco is not related to the Rossco in the book. ∎

> ❝ The stories you tell can only ever be the ones that were inside you all along. ❞

Have You Read?
Sunset Over Chocolate Mountains

After the death of his mother, Theobald Moon escapes England and buys an acre of land in the Arizona desert. Gradually he adjusts to his new life, planting a cactus garden around his mobile home, discovering new-age philosophies, indulging his sweet tooth and befriending Jersey, a neighbouring cowboy. His simple existence is disturbed by the arrival of an ice-cream van and its occupants – Eva, a Slovakian shoemaker, and her lover Tibor, a concocter of weird and wonderful ice-cream flavours – who have also come to make their fortune in the Land of the Free. The novel weaves between the freezing forests of Slovakia, the commanding and hazardous desert, and ahead in time to when Moon is living there with a young daughter, Josephine. As Josephine grows up and is forced to start school, their happiness and stability come under threat as she discovers the outside world, teenage rebellion, and a desire to clear up the mystery of her origins.

Elderkin's first novel is a magical story about the yearning for love and belonging. The evocation of the desert and its colourful cast of characters is imaginatively underlined by the intertwining structure, which builds with page-turning intensity to its grimly chilling climax. Praised for 'its confident prose style, well-developed appreciation of the absurd and Lawrentian moments in the desert' (*Saturday Independent*), *Sunset Over Chocolate Mountains* won a Betty Trask Award and was published in nine countries. ■

If you loved this,
you'll also like…

BOOKS

Cleave
Nicky Gemmell

The Songlines
Bruce Chatwin

The Sound of One Hand Clapping
Richard Flanagan

Cloudstreet
Tim Winton

Dirt Music
Tim Winton

English Passengers
Matthew Kneale

The Ballad of the Sad Café
Carson McCullers

The Bone People
Keri Hulme

The Drowner
Robert Drewe

Plainsong
Kent Haruf

FILMS

Rabbit-Proof Fence
(Phillip Noyce, 2002)

The Last Wave
(Peter Weir, 1976)

Beneath Clouds
(Ivan Sen, 2002)

Australian Rules
(Paul Goldman, 2002)

Black and White
(Craig Lahiff, 2002)

Walkabout
(Nicolas Roeg, 1971)

The Chant of Jimmie Blacksmith
(Fred Schepisi, 1978)

Dead Heart
(Nick Parsons, 1997)

The Tracker
(Rolf de Heer, 2002)

Where the Green Ants Dream
(Werner Herzog, 1984)

For further information, visit the author's
website: www.susanelderkin.com